FALLING FOR HER

FALLING FOR HER

MONICA MURPHY

"Boyfriend" - Selena Gomez
"Boys Ain't Shit" - SAYGRACE, Tate McRae, Audrey Mika
"Wish I Was Better" - Kina, yaeow
"Autopilot" - Tiffany Day
"not ur friend" - Jeremy Zucker
"Can We Kiss Forever?" - Kina, Adriana Proenza
"Almost In Love" - Olivia O'Brien

Find the rest of the Spotify playlist here:
https://bit.ly/FFHplaylist

She was beautifully complicated and terrifyingly simple, in a world that had no idea how to love her.

— T.M.T

CHAPTER 1

JAKE

"How about that one?"

We all snicker when we see who Diego's discreetly pointing at as we walk past her in the hallway. Some freshman who looks about ten, with big blue eyes and a mouth full of metal. She's cute enough, but way too young.

"I don't think so," I tell my friends as we stride toward the quad.

It's lunchtime. Our senior year. We're able to drive off campus now, but not today. Coach wants us to watch game film of the team we're playing tomorrow night. So we have about fifteen minutes to grab food before we all meet in the team room to study our opponents. Learn their weak spots, their strengths. See if they're better defensively or offensively.

When I say Coach, I'm talking about my dad. I just try to keep that shit separate. It's easier that way.

"Check her out," says Diego—one of my best friends—nudging me in the shoulder and now not-so-discreetly pointing at a group of girls sitting at a nearby picnic table.

"Which one?" Again, they're young. Maybe sophomores? I

don't really recognize any of them. If they're a couple of years younger than me and not friends with my sister Ava, who's a junior, or on the football team, I don't bother getting to know them.

That makes me sound like an asshole, but I don't have the time. I have my circle of friends. I even have my circle of acquaintances. This year, my last year in high school, I don't need to add to either group. I'm perfectly content with what I have.

"Any of them." Diego slaps me on the back, a giant grin on his face. "You need to find someone, bro. This single, I-don't-bother-with-any-girl business is getting old."

I don't bother with any girls anymore because when I do, they tend to take my heart and rip it to shreds. It's ridiculous, but when I fall, I tend to fall hard.

Sophomore year I got my heart broken twice, once by Cami Lockhart. We got back together the beginning of junior year only for her to cheat on me—and I found out via Snapchat.

That sucked.

I've never bothered with a girl again. Fuck 'em. I'd rather focus on football and my friends and school, exactly in that order.

"Too young," I tell Diego, and Caleb, my other best friend, bursts out laughing.

"Oh come on. She's cute. I'd bet she's down," he says with a smirk.

Caleb is an actual asshole. He hooks up with an endless stream of girls, yet most of them don't complain. It's like they're proud to be a Caleb fan girl.

"Find him a senior then," Diego says, stopping in the direct center of the crowded quad. He settles his hands on his hips and turns in a slow circle, scanning the area with a narrowed gaze. Diego has a girl and they're supposedly madly in love. I mean, good for him. They seem totally into each other—for the most part. They've been together for over a year, and Jocelyn treats him like a god, while she's his princess, as he calls her. I'm pretty sure they've talked about getting married, which is just…insane if you ask me.

"Her."

We all swivel our heads to see Tony—our quietest friend—inclining his head toward a table to the left of where we're standing.

There's a girl sitting there, her back to us. Alone. She's wearing a black T-shirt, her reddish-blonde hair spilling down her back in loose waves. Her elbow's propped on the table and she's resting her cheek on her fist, an open book in front of her. Like she's reading. For fun.

What the hell?

"No way," Diego says with a dismissive wave of his hand. "Jake's not into smart girls."

I'm immediately offended. "Who says?"

"You, with the choices you've made in the past," Diego points out.

He's got me there. Cami wasn't that smart. None of the girls I've dated were. Not really.

"I like her hair," Tony says, his tone, his entire demeanor impassive, like we're talking about the weather. "She's cute."

"You should go for her then," Caleb suggests to Tony.

"Nah. Not my type." Tony's gaze meets mine and he tilts his head, like he's giving me permission to talk to her.

Huh.

"How do you know she's a smart girl?" I study her, taking in her narrow shoulders, the elegant slope of her back. She brushes her hair back from her face, tucking the strands behind her ear and offering me a glimpse of her profile. She's pretty in an understated way, I guess. Upturned nose. Pale skin. Freckles.

I don't recognize her at all.

"Because she's reading a book, dumbass." Caleb sounds enormously pissed off, though I know he's not. That's just how he always sounds. "If you don't ask her to wear your jersey, I think I'll ask her instead."

Yes, this is what we're doing on a Thursday afternoon during lunch. Trying to find a girl for me to ask to wear my jersey on game day. It's a big deal at our high school, and so far during my reign as the varsity team's quarterback, I've only had one girl ever wear my jersey, and for only one time. It was Cami Lockhart, right at the beginning of our junior year, when I thought there was a possible chance we could work shit out and be a couple again.

But then someone sent me her private story off Snapchat —a video of her making out with motherfucking Eli Bennett, the quarterback for our rival school's team, and I was done. Finished.

For some reason, this year my boys want to see me make a claim. Find a girl. They tell me I'm too grumpy. That maybe if I'm getting some on the regular, that'll mellow me out. Some of them even complain I'm too focused, which I don't get. Why wouldn't they want me focused?

Focused wins games. I've had that drilled into my head over the years by my dad.

"No way," I tell Caleb when he acts like he's going to approach the mystery girl sitting at the table. "I'll do it."

I don't know why I'm bothering with this. I don't know her, but I'm guessing she knows me. Most girls would probably be flattered if I asked, but I'm not that sure if she's into football, or if she even goes to the games. But it would be cool to see her wear my number around school all day.

Maybe I could make it a thing. Give it to a different girl every week. They'd start fighting for their chance. It could turn into a contest. Maybe it would go viral...

"Go ask her." Diego gives me a shove in the girl's direction, his hand right in the center of my back. "Before you chicken out."

Okay, that shit's annoying. And it's just the incentive I need to make it happen. Glancing over my shoulder, I glare at my three best friends, but all they do is make clucking noises at me in return like they're a bunch of chickens.

Assholes.

Slowly I approach the table, wondering what I should say first. I don't have a problem talking to girls. I never really have. I almost wonder if this is because I grew up in a household full of women. Don't get me wrong, Dad is a strong personality and is a big influence on me, but he wasn't around much when I was little. He was busy working all the time.

Growing up, I was always with Mom, my older sister Autumn and my younger sister Ava. Our little brother Beck didn't come along until years later, and by then I was resigned with the idea that I'd never even have a brother.

So I was constantly surrounded by girls. Autumn and Ava used to fight like cats and dogs. Now that Autumn's gone, away at college in Santa Barbara, we don't see her that much. Ava is happier with Autumn gone, I think. Having an older sister trying to boss you around all the time gets old.

I know I got tired of Autumn's bullshit. Now, I miss her. Not that I'd ever tell her that.

Deciding I need to approach this mystery girl straight on, I walk around the table, keeping a wide berth so she doesn't get suspicious or think I'm a stalker. And once I'm facing the table, I take a good, long look at her.

She's vaguely familiar, so I'm assuming she's a senior like me, or maybe a junior. Our school is small, so most of the time I feel like I know everyone, but I can't place her. I don't remember her name. Her hair is this burnished, reddish-gold color and her eyes are big and blue. Her features delicate—except for her mouth. Full, bee-stung lips that fill my head with dirty images.

Every one of them involves my dick.

Not that I'm actually interested in this girl. I don't even know her. But as far as my first choice to wear my jersey this week, it's not a bad one.

Not a bad one at all.

One of my friends, I'm not sure who, makes a bok-bok noise and I send them all a menacing look before I march right up the table and clear my throat. "Hey."

The girl lifts her head, sky-blue eyes meeting mine, her expression open. Friendly.

Until she keeps looking at me, her gaze narrowing, that open, friendly expression disappearing within seconds. Almost as if she realized who she's looking at and doesn't like what she sees.

Damn.

When she still hasn't said anything, I decide to keep talking. "What's your name?"

Her eyebrows shoot up. "You don't know my name?"

I know this sounds weird, but I like the sound of her voice. A lot. "Should I?"

"I know yours." She sniffs, shutting the book she was reading. "Jacob Callahan."

Ah, see? She knows me. She'll totally agree to wear my jersey. "You have the advantage then."

"Because you still don't remember my name?"

I shrug helplessly and flash her a smile that's hopefully equal parts bashful yet charming. "Guilty."

She rolls her eyes, resting her arms on top of the table. "Did you have a question or something?"

Her tone is short. Dismissive. This girl is totally trying to get rid of me. "Yeah, as a matter of fact, I do have a question for you."

"I'm waiting on pins and needles," she says, her voice going up a notch, those blue eyes of hers extra wide.

They're pretty, I'll give her that. *She's* pretty. There's a sprinkling of freckles across the bridge of her nose and she has very white teeth.

"I was wondering if you wanted…" I let my voice drift and I glance down at my shoes, kicking at the base of the picnic bench. I'm trying to up the anticipation a notch. Going for the golly, gee bashful vibe. Girls seem to like it.

"Wanted what?"

Huh. Guess she's not one for anticipation.

"If you wanted to wear my jersey tomorrow." I lift my head, my gaze meeting hers straight on, and I see the surprise in her eyes. I've shocked her with my request.

Come on, I can see why. I'm me and she's…whoever she is.

She studies me for a while, and now it's my turn to wait with anticipation. Her full lips part, like she's about to say something, but instead, she looks away from me, grabs her things and starts shoving them into her backpack.

As if she's about to leave.

When she shoots me an irritated glare, slides off the picnic bench and walks away without another word, I chase her, surprised by how quick she is. My friends are laughing, I can hear them as I follow after this chick—still don't know her name—but I can't worry about them right now.

Even though they're total assholes for laughing at me.

"Hey!" I call out, but it's like my voice only spurs her on. She's practically in a full jog as she heads toward Adams Hall, and I wonder if her plan is to duck into a classroom and hide from me.

Putting a little speed behind my step, I catch up with her

easily, hooking my fingers around her upper arm and stopping her escape. She turns to face me, the look on her face so full of disgust I immediately release her and take a step back.

"Why are you chasing me?" she asks breathlessly. Her cheeks are pink, and she's practically panting. I get the sense that maybe she doesn't exercise much? I mean, I'm not even winded.

"You never answered my question."

She lifts her chin. Blows out an exaggerated breath, like what I'm asking is too damn much. After enduring the last five minutes with this chick, I don't even want her to wear my jersey now. She's making way too big a deal about this.

But for some weird reason, I have to know what her answer is.

"My name is Hannah," she finally says, and it all hits me at once. I do know her. Barely. Hannah Walsh. Senior. Moves in a completely different crowd. As in, she doesn't really move with *any* crowd. I've never had a class with her ever, because she takes all the advanced courses. My friends were right.

She's a smart girl.

"Right. Hannah." I nod and smile. "I know you."

She smiles in return, though it doesn't quite reach her sky-blue eyes. "Uh huh. Sure you do."

"I do. You're friends with…" My voice drifts. I don't know who she's friends with. I can see their faces, but at the moment, I can't recall their names.

"Please." She reaches out, settling her hand on my forearm, and it's like a spark of electricity between us the moment our skin makes contact. She snatches her hand away like I burned her. "Stop trying so hard."

I almost want to laugh. This girl is telling *me* to stop trying so hard? Does she even know who she's dealing with? The power I wield at this school? I'm the most popular guy in the senior class—maybe in all the classes. This is my year to shine. My year to reign.

And this Hannah nobody is telling me to stop *trying* so hard?

Get the fuck out of here.

Can't back out now, though. I'm fully committed.

"So what do you say, Hannah? Are you in? Do you want to wear my jersey tomorrow?" Not like I want her to anymore. She's been rude from the moment I started talking to her.

"Gee, I sure appreciate the offer, but…" She scowls at me, her lush lips pursed. "No."

CHAPTER 2

HANNAH

Jocks suck.

No, really. Like I'm supposed to be *honored* the king of the high school, Mr. Quarterback himself, has asked me to wear his precious jersey on game day? I can only imagine me walking around campus with his number plastered on my chest and back, like I'm his piece of property.

Nope, I don't think so.

Besides, he doesn't like me. He doesn't even know I exist. This must be a trick. A set up of some sort. Are Jake and all of his jock friends asking the least popular senior girls to wear their jerseys so they can somehow mock us tomorrow?

If that's the case, what a bunch of assholes.

"Did you really just turn me down?" Jake Callahan both sounds and appears mystified. I'm sure no girl at this school has ever refused him before.

Hmm. Maybe I deserve a medal.

"Yes, I did." Swear to God, my fingers still tingle from where I touched him. He must give off some sort of magnetic field that's irresistible to most humans. I can't deny that he's attractive, because yes.

Yes, he definitely is.

With the dark hair and the blue eyes, the granite jaw and the sharp cheekbones. Plus, he's *so* freaking tall. Those broad shoulders and lean hips and long legs. He's a god among us mortals, and I'm sure we're supposed to bow at his feet and do what he requests, no questions asked.

Well, screw that. I trust no one. I certainly don't trust some pretty jock who was dared by his friends to ask me to wear his jersey.

Please. I'm not that dumb.

"You'll regret this," he says, like some sort of threat. The arrogance on his face is obvious. He's offended.

And I can't help myself.

I start laughing.

Jake frowns. Glances over his shoulder, and I can only assume his friends are drawing near. He better watch out. I'm sure he doesn't want them to see he's getting turned down by a loser like me. "What the hell is so funny?" he asks, his voice like a hiss.

"You," I say, my laughter eventually calming down. "Believing I should automatically say yes to your request. Telling me I'll *regret* turning you down." I throw up some quotation marks with my fingers around the word regret. "Do you think I'm some sort of joke?"

His frown deepens. "I never said you were a joke."

"Please. I heard you and your friends talking about me." Somewhat. This is more like pure speculation on my part. For once, I was alone at lunch. My best friends went to a club meeting I had zero interest in attending. I don't mind being alone, especially when I'm halfway through a YA fantasy book I'm completely obsessed with.

"Spying on our conversation?" he asks, both eyebrows shooting up.

I scoff, glaring at him. I was reading said fantasy book when I heard Jake and his jock friends stop just behind me. My ears strained to hear exactly what they were saying, but I only caught snippets of their conversation. Pretty sure they practically dared Jake to ask me. Again, probably some kind of set up where I'm humiliated in front of the entire school a la Stephen King's *Carrie* and nope, I'm not going to down that road. I've seen all three versions of the movie and read the book. Pig's blood is not going to get poured on my head.

"God only knows what you had planned for me tomorrow," I tell him, crossing my arms in the ultimate stay-away-from-me pose.

"Um, I was going to give you my jersey in the morning," he says slowly, like I'm having trouble understanding him. "Clearly you don't want to wear it."

"Clearly." I raise a single brow, my one facial expression talent. I practiced this move in front of a mirror for months until I finally nailed it.

"Sorry I asked." His tone is snotty. Defensive.

"I'm sorry you asked too." I sound pretty snotty and defensive myself. Cautiously, I back away from him as he takes a step forward. "Aren't we done with this conversation?"

I see his pack of friends making their way toward us, giant smiles on their asshole faces. See? Jocks suck. They're coming over here to watch us and mock me.

I need to get out of here.

"You have issues," he says. I suppose for lack of any other reason that I said no.

"I do," I agree with him. "One in particular. You."

And with that, I turn and walk away.

Scratch that. I *run* away.

My heart is racing as I head for the library. Where did I come up with the balls to say something like that to Jake Callahan in the first place? So unlike me. Completely unlike me, really. I'm the quiet girl who remains in the background and tries her best to say nothing to anyone beyond her friends and teachers. I'm sure that's why he didn't recognize me at first. We've gone to school together since he moved here right before we started the seventh grade, but we've never spoken a word to each other before until today.

Like, why should he know who I am? We don't run in the same social circles. I pretty much keep to myself, and I definitely stay out of other people's business. I don't have many friends.

And I like it that way.

Only one more year, and I'm out of here. My grades are stellar—my overall grade point average is 4.5, which means as long as things remain the same, I'll graduate as a valedictorian. I'm also the poor girl with a sob story, and I've been working hard on the essay I need to submit along with my college applications since the end of junior year. I'm hoping I can get into any college I want.

I hope.

I pray.

And I'm not even a religious person.

Tugging hard on the heavy door, I enter the library, thankful for the cool rush of air coming from the vents directly above me. It's quiet. I can hear the hum of the computers, the low murmurs of conversation from a nearby table where three people are sitting. I don't recognize them and can only assume they're underclassmen. Besides them, there aren't any other students in here.

Typical.

I wave at Sonya the librarian as I walk past her desk. She's eating a sandwich and scrolling on her phone, looking like everyone else at this school during lunch. She's young, in her mid-twenties, and I love her pink hair that's cut into a sleek bob.

Not that I could ever pull something off like that. I don't want to draw anyone's attention.

I go to the very back of the room and settle in at my favorite table, pulling out the book I was reading earlier and opening it to the page where I left off. I'm hungry, but I already ate what I packed for lunch during fourth period and my stomach is growling. I don't have any money to buy something at the snack shack, so I'm screwed. I aimlessly dig through my backpack, hoping I can find an old forgotten granola bar or a bag of fruit snacks, or maybe even some change, but there's nothing.

"Hey."

Startled, I glance up to find Marty Torres smiling down at me. He's one of my best friends. He's really tall and super skinny and his Adam's apple is huge, which I know makes him self-conscious, but I don't even really notice it anymore. He's a senior like me, and we became close since during our sophomore year, when we literally had every single class together.

Thank God we like each other, or it could've been awkward.

"Hi," I say to him with a tiny smile as he sits in the chair across from me.

"I thought we were going to meet in the quad after I got out of the meeting." His tone is vaguely accusatory. He suffers from social anxiety and the last place he ever wants to be is in the quad at lunch. He's trying to get over his anxiety by easing into situations that make him uncomfortable, and like the shit friend I can sometimes be, I completely forgot.

"Where's Sophie?" They went to that club meeting together, or so I thought.

"Oh, she said she had to talk to someone. I don't know who." He shrugs, and I can tell he's disappointed that Sophie seemingly ditched him.

A sigh escapes me. I didn't realize he was alone. "I'm so sorry. I was on the run from a jock." I reach across the table and rest my hand on Marty's arm. Notice how I feel absolutely nothing when I touch him.

Annoying.

Marty frowns. "What are you talking about?"

I launch into my story, not leaving out a single detail. Marty's big brown eyes get wider and wider when I repeat our conversation. How Jake reacted. How I ran out on him.

"You actually said that to him," Marty says when I finish, his voice deadly serious. "You turned down Jake Callahan and laughed at him when he told you you'll regret this."

"Yes," I say with a nod and a little laugh. "I did. I mean come on, Marty. I'll *regret this?* Who does he think he is? The mafia?"

"Probably. One of his best friends is Tony Sorrento, and that name alone sounds like someone who knows how to put out a mob hit," Marty says, making me laugh again. "Plus, Jake's dad is, like, a fucking bazillionaire. I'm sure Drew Callahan can buy and sell all of us."

"I'm sure he could," I agree.

Marty slowly shakes his head as he watches me. His mop of dark curls tumbles into his eyes and he shoves them off his forehead with an impatient grunt. "What if Jake and his jock crew do something to you to actually make you regret your choice?"

"Please. I'm not that important." I wave a hand, ignoring the unease that slides icy fingers down my spine. "What can they do to me?"

"Make your life an absolute living nightmare." Marty

leans across the table, his voice shifting lower. "They're dicks, Hannah. They'll make fun of you in class."

"I don't have any classes with them." Thank God.

"And they'll write mean shit on your locker," Marty adds.

"I never use my locker. Everything I need is in here." I pat my backpack like it's my trusty old friend.

"They'll spread rumors about you on social media." I start to counter his words yet again, but he cuts me off. "I've seen it happen before. They zero in on a vulnerable target and make that person's life a living hell. Usually it's a girl."

"What a bunch of misogynistic dicks," I mutter.

"And their leader is usually Diego," Marty finishes, his voice full of disgust. Diego is Marty's cousin, and they've never gotten along, even when they were little kids. Diego is the athlete and Marty is the brains, and Marty's told me that at family functions they barely tolerate each other.

"Do you really think Jake will say something rude about me, when I'm the one who turned him down in the first place?" I ask incredulously. "If he tries to spread rumors or whatever, I'll let everyone know what I said. His friends heard me."

"They'll back Jake no matter what. It'll be your word against theirs." Marty makes a face. "They can mess up your school year with a few choice words. I told you what they did to me in middle school."

He's right. He did tell me, and I vaguely remember it. Diego told all of his friends that Marty was gay in the sixth grade—Marty hadn't come out yet—and they made his life absolute hell. Until Marty's overprotective warrior mother marched into the principal's office and demanded the school do something about it. His mother even went to Diego's mother—they're sisters—and told her she'd beat her ass—direct quote—if she didn't tell her shitty son to stop being mean to his cousin. Family comes first, Lisa Torres has always said.

I wish I had a mother like Marty's. Someone who'll rush in and defend her child no matter what. Not that my mom is a bad mother, it's just…she's always so busy with work, or her boyfriend. She doesn't seem to have much time for me.

But anyway.

What sucks is that during middle school, Diego got all of his friends to go along with him and make fun of Marty. They would pants him in the locker room during P.E., which was the ultimate in embarrassment for a boy who's accused of being gay and is, you know, actually gay. And whatever other horrors twelve-year-old bullies can come up with, they dished it out with glee, making Marty retreat into himself even more, and that breaks my heart. They kept it so under wraps, I didn't even know it was going on. By the seventh grade, Diego was done with Marty, and they all left him alone.

Diego finally apologized to him. He made a big deal about it when we were in the eighth grade and said sorry to Marty during lunch one spring day. Marty accepted the apology reluctantly—he'd been prepped by his mother to expect it so he had the advantage, and Diego acted like that absolved him from all wrong doing. I thought the apology was bogus.

Too little, too late, if you ask me.

Diego is an asshole. I don't know how his girlfriend Jocelyn stays with him. She's actually a really sweet, smart girl. Not smart enough to get rid of her jerk boyfriend, though.

"It won't be that bad," I tell Marty, my voice soft, my heart hurting for him. He's just watching out for me, and I appreciate that.

He shoots me a skeptical glance, but otherwise says nothing.

Not everyone is out to get us. Yes, I'm pretty sure Jake Callahan and his friends don't give two craps about me and were hoping to, oh I don't know, put me through some sort of weird and humiliating ritual for their first game of the season. I'm sure he's already forgotten about me. I'd bet he's already found another victim.

I'm just glad it wasn't me.

* * *

MY LAST CLASS of the day is my favorite so far—I'm the teacher's assistant for Art 1. The class is full of mostly freshmen, a handful of sophomores and juniors, and only a couple of seniors who kept forgetting to get their fine art requirement out of the way until their last year of school. We all have to take at least one fine art class in order to graduate, and most of us get it over with our freshman year. This means nobody really knows me in this class, which is just the way I like it.

I love Mrs. Sanborne, my art teacher. I'm in Honors Art 4, the highest art class my small high school has to offer, and there are only eleven of us in the entire class. Mrs. Sanborne and I have clicked since my freshman year, so when she asked me to be her TA for Art 1, I jumped at the chance.

It's the one class where I didn't feel enormous pressure to perform. One less class where I have to study and stay on top of things or else I could get behind. As the teacher's assistant, I clean and organize all the paints, brushes, canvas—whatever Sanborne needs me to do, I do it. I don't really talk to anyone but the teacher, and no one pays any attention to me anyway. I can do my own thing and organize to my heart's content.

I'm in the back of the room, digging around in the cabinets that line the entire wall and looking for leftover tubes of paint when I hear Mrs. Sandborne talking to someone. A male someone.

A male someone with a familiar voice. And I'm not talking about Marty either.

Crawling out of the cabinet, I rise to my feet, brushing my hair out of my face before I wipe the dust off my clothes. The teacher is only a few feet away, her back to me as she tilts her head and talks to the very tall, very male student in front of her.

"No, Mr. Callahan, I can't fit you into my other art classes," Mrs. Sanborne says, sounding irritated. "Art 1 is the only class you qualify for."

"But the team conditioning class is this period," he says. "I can't miss it."

Oh crap. It's Jake Callahan.

I turn away from them, not wanting him to see me. But I don't move.

I want to hear what he has to say.

"Don't they offer a conditioning class before school as well?" Mrs. Sanborne asks. "For situations just like this?"

Our small school can't always accommodate everyone's schedule. Usually for football gods, they do. But I guess Jake can't get out of his fine arts requirement. He shouldn't have waited so long.

"Or can't you take Theater 1?" Mrs. Sanborne asks before he can respond. "It shouldn't interfere with your conditioning class."

"They only offer it second period, which would make me have to change my entire schedule. Plus, that class is full of freshmen," he mutters, like that's the worst thing in the world.

I almost start laughing. I actually have to clap my hand over my mouth to stifle it.

"This is my only Art 1 class scheduled this year," Mrs.

Sanborne says, crossing her arms. "You can either take this, or theater. It's your choice. I'm not budging, Mr. Callahan. Not even for you."

I wonder if Jake's made other teachers "budge" for him before. I'm sure administration has stepped in a time or two. I bet his dad has a lot of power here as well, but would he actually do that? I've heard his dad, former NFL quarterback Drew Callahan, is pretty laidback. He has the respect of everyone at this school, teachers, admin and students alike. The year Asher Davis was quarterback, they won league and district championships, but lost in the final battle for state. Last year, they won league, but not district. I heard Jake was devastated and is determined to win everything this year, no matter what.

How do I know this? Uh, social media. School rallies. In fact, we have one scheduled tomorrow, between fourth and fifth period.

"Whatever," Jake mutters before he strides out of the classroom, his long legs taking him far in a short amount of time.

Impressive.

Ugh. Not impressive! Forget that guy! He wanted to make fun of you and you're standing here in a daze, secretly admiring him.

Mrs. Sanborne turns to face me, shaking her head. "It's not my fault he waited until he was a senior to meet his fine art requirement."

"That's what I was thinking," I say with a little laugh.

"Certain people in this world believe they can get whatever they want, and they don't have to put in the hard work," Sanborne continues. "And you are definitely not one of them, Hannah. I've never seen someone work so hard, and I've been here almost twelve years."

I smile, basking in her compliment. I do work hard. Harder than most.

Definitely harder than Jacob Callahan.

CHAPTER 3

JAKE

"Go, go, go, go, *go!*" Dad shouts from the sideline, his hands cupped around his mouth, his words all for me. The ball is in my hands, I'm ready to throw it, when out of nowhere, someone tackles me, taking me straight to the ground, my head knocking inside my helmet.

Fuck.

"Better watch out." Caleb, the very one who took me down, smacks the back of my helmet before he stands, offering his hand to me. "I don't even think you saw me."

I take his hand, muttering a thank-you under my breath. He's right. I didn't. Caleb is one of our best defensive ends. This is why I'm so damn glad he's on our team. Our coaches decided to do a best of the best game for practice today, pitting the first-string offense against the first-string defense, and the game is kicking my ass. It doesn't help that it's ninety-five degrees in the shade. Didn't we move to the mountains for a reason? Like cooler weather?

"Come on, Callahan! You can do this!" someone yells, and I realize it's Diego.

Thank God for friends. Though we give each other

endless shit, when it comes down to it, they have my back. Even when I'm full of doubt.

Am I ready for tomorrow night, our first game of the season? I thought so.

But now I'm not so sure.

We run through a few more plays, and I finally get the ball to my tight end—Tony—and he runs it into the end zone with ease. But there's no encouraging words or even slaps on the back when the game is through. Everyone's stressed. You can feel it in the air, see it shimmering along with the heat.

I'm not helping matters. I'm tense as hell. We all are. Tomorrow's game shouldn't be a difficult one; it's not even a league game. They're a semi-local team we've been playing against for years, and nine times out of ten, we win. We have home field advantage, which always helps. The crowds, the cheer team, the band—hell, everyone will be cheering us on, even the community, and I should revel in it. It's my last year and I should feel on top of the world.

But I don't. Shit is getting to me and the season has barely started.

The defensive coach blows his whistle and tells us practice is over. I jog along with everyone else toward the locker room, my gaze locked on my dad, who's clutching a clipboard and no doubt going over the play sheet.

"Jake, a minute?" he says as I pass by, not even bothering to glance up.

He must have telepathy, I swear.

I stop before him, running a hand over my sweaty head, clutching my helmet in my other hand. "What's up, Coach?"

Dad looked up, his gaze meeting mine. "What the hell, Jake? You let Caleb sneak up on you and he was literally growling like a maniac the entire time he made his approach. You didn't hear him?"

No, I didn't. And I feel like a dumbass for it, thank you very much. "I was too focused on throwing the ball, I guess."

"Son, there's nothing wrong with being focused. But you have to be focused on *every single thing.* Every little aspect when you're in the moment. A simple move could turn into brilliance, or it could turn into disaster." Dad tilts his head, contemplating me. "What I witnessed a few minutes ago could've been a disaster."

"I never dropped the ball."

"Thank God for that." He reaches out, tapping the edge of his clipboard against my chest. "Watch yourself."

I nod, my jaw growing tight. Can't the old man ever give me a compliment?

Lately, that would be a no.

"You going straight home?" he asks.

I nod again.

"I'll be here for another hour at least, probably longer. I'm staying for Beck's practice." My little brother is in youth football and he's a defensive lineman. The little fucker could probably take me down if he was determined enough. "See ya later."

Dismissed, I make my way to the locker room, keeping my head down as I enter. Pretty much everyone is near buck-ass naked, and I'm not in the mood to see a bunch of swinging dicks or hear their bragging mouths.

When am I ever in the mood for that?

Never.

"Bro, what happened to you?" Diego asks as I stop in front of my locker and turn the combination with a few quick flicks of my fingers.

"What do you mean?" I open the door and tug my gym bag forward, unzipping it. I know exactly what Diego means.

"Caleb got you good. It was like you were in a different zone."

"I was. I was trying to throw the goddamn ball. I didn't even hear him."

Diego remains silent for a moment, watching as I pull my clothes out of my bag, toeing off my cleats at the same time. I'm tempted to pass on the shower and wait until I'm home, so I tear off my practice gear and start changing into my regular clothes. I'll smell terrible, but I want out of here. I'm over this.

"You get off on watching me strip or what?" I ask Diego when he still hasn't said anything.

He slowly shakes his head. "You're a grumpy fucker. I'm kinda sad that boring chick turned you down at lunch. Maybe she could've eased your pain."

"Fuck that chick," I say vehemently, tugging my shorts on. Hannah or whatever her name is. She laughed at me. She looked at me like I was a joke. She should consider herself lucky that I even spoke to her.

God, I sound like a complete asshole, even in my own thoughts.

"That's what I was hoping you'd do," Diego says with a chuckle. "Seriously, though. Since school started, you're walking around campus looking ready to murder someone. You need a sweet little pussy in your life to ease your stress, and I'm not talking about a cat."

Caleb joins us at the tail end of Diego's comment, and they both start laughing like they just heard the funniest joke of their lives. I glare at both of them, annoyed with myself more than anything.

I'm sure everyone thinks I'm acting like a sensitive baby lately. And I probably am. Doesn't help that I feel like I'm carrying the entire world on my shoulders.

More like I feel like the success of the varsity football team depends on me and my abilities, which is pointless. I know I'm not the entire team. I need all of these guys in order to do well, but there's so much pressure on the quarterback. And it doesn't just come from my dad.

It comes from everyone. The entire freaking town.

"By the way, I did a little investigation into your little kitty cat, Jake," Caleb says, wearing a shit-eating grin as he rubs his hands together. "I've gone to school with her since we were in kindergarten, and honestly? I kind of forgot she existed."

"She was pretty mean to our boy earlier," Diego adds, his gaze sliding to mine. "Like, she laughed at you and shit."

No kidding.

"When we were little, she was always quiet. Kept to herself mostly. Pretty sure she's the same way in high school, since I forgot all about her," Caleb continues as I finish getting dressed. I don't care about Hannah Whatever Her Last Name Is. She turned me down so forget her.

"Pretty sure she hangs out with my cousin." Diego rolls his eyes and Caleb starts laughing. "God knows how she tolerates him."

I remain silent, letting them talk, letting the stress of the day ease out of me. I wouldn't mind sitting in our hot tub when I get home. Though Mom will nag my ass into eating dinner first *as a family*—her favorite guilt trip. And shit, I gotta drive my little sister home too. Ava is a junior, cheer practice ends the same time football practice does, and she is an absolute pain in my ass.

Well, some of the time. We actually get along decently. Mom says when we get older, we'll be extra close since we're also so close in age.

Whatever, Mom. I think she just *hopes* we'll be close.

"You want to go grab something to eat?" Diego asks me when I pull my gym bag out of my locker and slam the metal door shut.

"I gotta take Ava home," I say, thankful for the excuse. I'm not in the mood to shoot the shit and listen to them talk about how I need to get laid.

"You can bring your sister." Caleb wags his eyebrows at me and I shove at his shoulder, sending him stumbling a few steps back.

"You're not allowed to even *look* at my sister." My sister is a no-friend zone. I don't want any of my friends near her. Not a one.

We're giving each other crap as we leave the locker room, and my spirits are lifting. Maybe I need to stop taking things so seriously. Life just keeps sending me roadblocks lately, and I don't understand why. Like that art class I have to take—that's scheduled during my conditioning class. I could take the one before school starts, but man, that sucks. It means I have to be at school even earlier than usual, and I hate that.

That art class is gonna mess everything up. The story of my freaking life, swear to God.

I'm headed toward my truck, Diego and Caleb walking on either side of me, when a blast from my not so distant past magically appears in front of us, stopping our progression.

"Jake. Hi." Cami Lockhart in the flesh, smiling at me like I'm the best thing she's ever seen. She's wearing really short shorts and a sports bra. That's it. Her tanned, toned body is pretty much on full display and I can practically envision my friends' tongues rolling out of their mouths like they're cartoon characters. "Can we talk?"

Why in the hell does my ex-girlfriend want to talk to me? Though I shouldn't be surprised. This is the game we play. We break up to get back together. It happened our sophomore and junior years, so here she is, probably trying to make it happen again for us this year.

And every time, like a sucker, I've fallen for it.

"Sure." I send Caleb and Diego a look, and they start

walking, calling out their goodbyes to Cami and totally forgetting about me. I turn to face her. "What's up?"

"You have a good practice?" She tilts her head to the side, her ponytail sliding down her neck and well past her tits. She has thick brown hair, light blue eyes, curves in all the right places, and she's the varsity cheer captain. She is the cliché yin to my yang. Quarterback and cheer team captain, forever together with heart eyes.

Ava, who just joined the cheer team this year, hates her guts, and doesn't hold back around me when she complains about her either. I think Ava doesn't want me to forget how badly this girl has messed with my head.

But when Cami's standing in front of me barely wearing any clothes and looking at me like she wants me to touch her in all of her forbidden places, I sort of forget.

"It went okay," I tell Cami, blinking at her when she reaches out and skims her fingers down the front of my chest, her expression…hungry. She's acting a lot more forward than usual. "How was your practice?"

She rolls her eyes. "Some of the girls on the team are such idiots. I don't know how they made it."

That's one thing I remember about Cami: she thinks everyone else is subpar. "I'm guessing with practice they'll get better."

"You sound like your sister." I assume Cami doesn't like Ava either. Feeling's mutual. "So hey. I was wondering…are you going to Tony's tomorrow?"

Tony is the quietest guy on our team. He's my quietest friend, period. But he knows how to throw a party. And he throws one at his house by the lake every Friday night after a home game. His parents are divorced, and his mom got the house, along with a large cash settlement. She's gone pretty much every weekend, making it easy for Tony to throw his infamous bashes. "Yeah, I'm going."

"I'll be there too." Her smile turns shy and she glances down at the ground. "Maybe we could hang out. At the party."

This girl is not shy. She's loud, and she goes after what she wants. And when she realizes she doesn't want it after all, she dumps it. Fast. I know this from experience. "I'm not sure."

She lifts her head, eyes blazing. "What do you mean, you're not sure?"

"Cam, if you're trying to get back together with me, I have to be real with you. I don't know if it's a good idea."

"Oh, you're always so negative." She waves a hand, as if dismissing my worries. "We make a *great* couple."

No, we really don't. There's always a lot of fighting involved. We get on each other's nerves. Even the sex isn't that great, though honestly, we started fucking our sophomore year and I had no idea what I was doing. Three pumps max and I was done. Hell, she'd barely touch my dick and I was close to coming. I had zero control. My skills have improved greatly since then.

Though it's been a while since I've had sex. Since I've even wanted to have sex. There's no one here at this school who interests me.

This is why maybe getting back together with Cami isn't such a bad idea. We have history. We understand each other. And maybe we could improve on our past sexual encounters.

Is it really a good idea, though? She's also controlling. She blabs to all her friends every single detail about our relationship. She doesn't understand the meaning of the word private.

The worst thing of all? Pretty much my entire family doesn't like her.

"We've tried this before—" I start, but she cuts me off.

"I'm different now." She smiles prettily, her hand resting

on my chest again, her fingers curling into the fabric of my T-shirt and giving it a slight tug. "I've changed. I know what I want. And what I want is…you."

I think about what my friends have said. How I need to relax and get laid. I bet Cami would be down. She always was before.

"You want to wear my jersey tomorrow?" Shit. The words fall out of me before I give myself time to reconsider the offer.

Her entire face lights up. "I would love to," she breathes.

Guess this is going to happen. "I'll bring it to you in the morning."

She takes a step closer and rises up on her toes, brushing her mouth against my cheek. "You'll win tomorrow. I just know it," she purrs close to my ear.

I watch her walk away, hips swinging, my gaze zeroed in on her ass, noting how her butt cheeks are practically hanging out of her shorts. Cami and I, we would look good together. Everyone wants the cliché, and we could deliver. Maybe we could make this work again.

And then again, maybe not.

CHAPTER 4

HANNAH

It's Friday after school and we're at Pete's Place, a local restaurant not too far from the high school, gorging ourselves on fries and chicken strips. We also bought an order of fried zucchini because eating them makes us feel like we're making better choices, considering it's a vegetable. A fried vegetable, but whatever.

I'm sitting at a table with Marty and my other best friend, Sophie, who I feel like I've known my entire life, considering we've gone to school together since preschool. The three of us used to joke and call ourselves the misfits, but I'm starting to believe we truly are exactly that.

A group of misfits. Our social circle exists of exactly the three of us. That's it. Sounds boring, but we always have a good time so…it's fine.

Most of the time.

"We're going to the game tonight, right?" Sophie asks as she shoves another fry into her mouth. She's scrolling through her phone, her golden blonde hair falling into her face. Sophie is really tall, almost six feet, and with long, graceful limbs. She's a dancer and competes with the local studio's team every year, and it mostly consumes her life. Having a snack at Pete's goes against everything she's been taught, so I'm sure she'll be hard on herself and practically fast over the weekend.

Me? I just keep gorging myself on the delicious fried food and not bother exercising whatsoever. I don't think I've overexerted myself since my P.E. class my sophomore year.

"Um…" I send a look to Marty, who's furiously shaking his head, his eyes wide, his expression horrified. "No. Why would we do that? We never go to the football games."

Sophie lets loose an exaggerated sigh, glaring at both of us. "Didn't we make a pact at the end of last year that we were going to participate more? Go to all the games? Have fun at the rallies? Go to the dances? Maybe even snag an invite to a party out by the lake? It's our senior year, guys. Our last chance to have some fun before shit gets real and we have to grow up."

"I'm beyond ready to grow up and leave this town," Marty mutters, and I nod my agreement, though I don't really mean it.

Growing up terrifies me. The idea of going to college both excites and scares me. I don't know how I'm going to make it on my own. Which means I probably won't and I'll live with my mother for the rest of my life, the two of us versus the world.

God, just thinking like that makes me terribly depressed.

"You are both absolutely no fun." Sophie points at us with an extra-long fry before she eats it. "Guess I'll go to the game by myself then," she says after she swallows.

"You won't go by yourself," Marty says. "You can hardly come to school by yourself."

"That's not true," Sophie says. She used to be more on the shy side, though recently she's come out of her shell. She used to freeze up and never talk around anyone, especially in middle school.

Funny how she's never has a problem performing on the stage though.

"Listen, I want to go to the game." Sophie gives a little shrug. "I'm sure I can convince some of the girls from the dance studio to come with me. They always go."

"You're going to hang out with a bunch of sophomores then?" Marty rolls his eyes. "Boring."

The majority of the girls on Sophie's dance team are younger than us. "At least they'll want to go with me, unlike my best friends who are totally ditching me to do…what exactly? Spend Friday night at home watching Netflix?"

"There's a new series I wouldn't mind starting," I say weakly, clamming up when Sophie shoots me a pointed look.

"You of all people should go," Sophie says, staring at me. "Then you can witness if Jake Callahan plays a perfect game or falls on his beautiful face."

I hate that she called his face beautiful because she is so right. He's annoyingly attractive. And I don't want to talk about him. Yet here I go, talking about him. "Did you see Cami Lockhart wearing his jersey today?"

It kind of hurt, witnessing her strutting around campus with the number four emblazoned on her chest. Though why am I hurt? He asked me first, so I suppose that should make me feel better. She was his *second* choice.

At least that's what I was thinking around third period after I saw her in the hall, trying to make myself feel better.

By lunch, I witnessed Cami hanging all over Jake in the quad. She had her arms wrapped around his neck, like they were together. A couple. I vaguely remember them being together our sophomore year for a while, and if you really think about it, they make sense. They should be a couple. He's the star quarterback, she's the cheer captain. He's attractive, she's attractive. He probably has a black soul. And she definitely has a black soul.

Right after lunch, there was a rally, and while I tried my best to feel enthusiastic and full of spirit, it was tough. The entire football team was on the floor in the middle of the gym, Jake standing front and center and waving at everyone when they announced his name, an arrogant smile on his face. He got the biggest applause out of all of them and I couldn't help but notice Cami bouncing up and down as she stood with the rest of the cheer team on the sidelines, screaming out Jake's name.

God, it was so annoying.

"I hate Cami Lockhart," Marty says, glancing over his shoulder as if to make sure no one is nearby before he continues. "That bitch made my life a living hell freshman year."

Lots of people have made Marty's life a living hell at some point during his middle and high school career. Why are people so cruel?

"She's in our world religions class," Sophie says, nodding toward me. "And I'm not quite sure how she got in there. She's kind of an idiot."

I have to agree—Cami is a complete idiot. She asks the most ridiculous questions in class, ones I assume everyone knows the answer to already. I'm not sure how she got in our honors class that has dual enrollment—we're getting college credit for taking the class—but there she was the first day of school, her expression assured, like she belonged there.

"I thought she's been in remedial classes her entire high school life." Sophie says laughingly and I send her a look, feeling guilty about what I thought only a moment ago. She goes quiet immediately, though Marty's still laughing, and I guess I can't blame him.

Cami definitely sucks. And she's a bitch, we all know this.

But should it really make us feel better to make fun of someone else? She clearly has some sort of learning disability. Or she's just plain dumb and doesn't pay attention. But we shouldn't lift ourselves up by tearing down others.

I sound just like my mom when she used to talk to me about that sort of stuff after someone made fun of me, but it's true.

"Forget Cami. Just—go to the game with me, you guys, okay? It'll be fun." Sophie smiles. "Please?"

"It's so expensive to get into the game," I say in protest. It's a weak protest, but still.

Sophie rolls her eyes. "It's a dollar to get in with an ASB card."

Oh. I have an ASB card. I also have a dollar. Somewhere. But I can't forget the only reason I'm able to eat this meal is because Sophie and Marty covered the cost for me. I'm that broke. Plus, you order two chicken-and-fries baskets and it can feed four people. We didn't need to order the fried zucchini, but Marty had a craving, as he called it.

"You'll give me a ride?" I ask Sophie.

She nods. "Definitely. I'll even give you a ride." She smiles over at Marty, who ducks his head.

"I really don't want to go," he practically moans. "My tía will be there cheering on my asshole cousin, and it could turn into a whole thing. I bet my other cousins will be there too. And then they'll make me join them when they go down to the field to talk to Diego after the game…I don't want to deal."

He seriously dislikes his cousin. And I don't have a doubt that everything he just described would totally happen. His family is hardcore. Meaning, they all get together for every little thing. Marty's birthday? They all show up in force— upwards of fifty people in his parents' tiny house at a time.

Diego's playing football? I'm sure they all show up en masse for that as well.

Not that I'd know. I can't remember the last time I went to a football game. Maybe the beginning of our sophomore year?

"So it's me and you then?" Sophie asks, quietly letting Marty off the hook. We aren't out to torture him.

"Sure," I say quickly, trying not to second-guess myself.

"Yay!" Sophie actually claps her hands and bounces in her seat. I'm actually shocked by her behavior. She's so animated, like she's sincerely excited about going to a game and a party. If this happened our junior year, she would've come up with every excuse possible not to go. "Okay, this is going to be fun. We'll go back to my house and get ready and then we'll go to the game."

"Wait a minute—get ready?" I glance down at myself before I return my gaze to my friend. "I can't just wear this?"

A grimace flits across Sophie's face for the briefest moment before it's replaced by a sunny smile. "Um, no. Let's get dressed up!"

"I don't have anything to dress up in. Besides, it's a football game." I'm wearing a pale lavender T-shirt and a pair of jeans. The shirt has paint smudges on it because I made a bit of a mess today in art class. Oh, and I'm wearing my favorite —and only—pair of Birkenstocks, which are kind of ratty looking. And if I'm being honest with myself, they're a little smelly.

Okay, they're a lot smelly. But I can't afford to get another pair and I love them so much, especially when I wear them with a cute pair of socks.

"You can raid my closet," Sophie offers.

I start to laugh. "You're way taller than me."

"And I have things that are too short that you are more than welcome to try on." Sophie has an answer for everything. I kind of hate it. But I love her too much to let it bother me. "Are you sure you don't want to go, Marty?"

"And witness my family lose their minds over the faux amazingness that is Diego? I don't think so." Marty shakes his head. "Though I'm sure you two will have a great time."

I wish I felt as positive as Marty sounds.

* * *

We show up to the game right when "The Star-Spangled Banner" starts. Instead of paying and walking inside, we have to wait until the national anthem is finished. We stand in front of the table where we buy our tickets, our hands over our hearts, the ladies who are working the ticket table doing the same thing. It's serious business, and I notice how solemn everyone is. Respectful.

It makes me feel like I'm about to witness something really important.

The second the anthem is over, the entire crowd whoops and yells, and the ladies take our money before stamping the back of our hands. A few members of the girls' basketball team are trying to sell us game programs, and Sophie, the kind soul that she is, buys one for two dollars.

"Why do you want that?" I ask her as we make our way to the stands.

"So we can look at the pictures of the football team and see which guy is the hottest. Duh." Sophie rolls her eyes and laughs, and I can't help but laugh with her.

As we approach the stands, I can hear the band playing our school fight song. The cheer team is on the sideline, shaking their metallic blue poms to the beat as they do a simple dance. I spot Cami Lockhart in the front row, right in the middle. Her smile is big and perfect, straight out of a toothpaste commercial, and there's a temporary tattoo of a badger paw, our school mascot, on her cheek.

I look away and focus my attention on the bleachers before us. There's a variety of ages sitting in the stands. Older people. Parents. Little kids. Middle schoolers.

"Want to sit in the student section?" Sophie asks me.

It's packed tight with a variety of grades, and I realize quick we're going to have to sit near the bottom. "We won't be able to see the game."

"True." Sophie glances around, then points. "Let's go sit over there."

We sit up high and across the aisle from the student section, near the snack stand the football booster club runs. The scent of chili lingers in the air and my stomach grumbles, despite eating way too many fries and chicken strips earlier at Pete's. But the booster club is famous for their Frito boats, and I might have to convince Sophie to get one to split before the game is over.

We stopped by my house before we went to Sophie's, and I dropped off my backpack and grabbed a fresh pair of jeans and my wallet, which had a five-dollar bill in it, plus six quarters and other miscellaneous change. I gave the quarters to Sophie for our after-school snack at Pete's, though she tried to give them back to me. I couldn't take them. Even if it was only a dollar-fifty, I felt better giving her a little bit of money than none at all.

I don't like feeling like someone's charity case. Sophie's family has more money than mine, but they're not what I would call rich. Not even close.

"I'm glad we're sitting over here," Sophie says once we've settled in. "The student section is so crowded."

The band is directly in front of us, though down at the bottom of the bleachers, and it seems extra loud when they play. To the point that we're wincing and plugging our ears with our fingers. It's not that the band sounds awful, it's just that they're so…noisy. When they finish their song, Sophie and I send each other a look before we start cracking up.

It's nice, having a friend who understands you, even when you don't say anything at all.

The game starts, and I watch as our defense slams into the opposing team's offense. I try not to look for him, but my gaze wanders, tripping over every boy's jersey number printed in white on their backs until I find number four.

He's standing right next to his father, his helmet off, dangling from his fingers. He's actually taller than his dad, which is impressive, because Drew Callahan, former Super Bowl-winning quarterback, is a pretty big guy. It's still wild, to think that he's a coach for our little high school football team up in the mountains.

Not that I really care about football or anything like that. I mean, what do I know? I don't keep up with sports. It's been just my mom and me since my brother Joe graduated high school and went into the Navy six years ago. My father was never really a part of our lives. Mom has had a few boyfriends, but nothing too terribly serious until recently. And when she's not with Rick, she's busy working, trying to keep a roof over our head.

Sophie has the game program open in her lap and flips through the pages until she gets to the varsity football team photos. It's a two-page spread, with individual photos of each boy on the team, in order by number. Of course, my gaze lands on number four.

His expression is serious. He's squinting in the sun, his dark hair glinting in the light, his jaw like granite, his jersey stretched tight across his broad shoulders. It's unfair, how gorgeous he is.

"You know, you never did say much about what happened between you and Jake Callahan," Sophie muses.

Oops. She caught me staring.

I tear my gaze away from his photo and smile at my friend. "I think he was trying to set me up."

Sophie frowns. "What are you talking about?"

I explain everything that happened. How his friends were standing around. How they were making fun of Jake. How I figured they were making fun of me too.

"Was Tony there?" Sophie asks when I finish my story.

"Um, I think so?" Yeah, maybe he was. That guy is notoriously quiet. Most of the time he blends into the background. Kind of like me. And Sophie.

"He's actually really nice," Sophie says, her gaze going to the field. "He's in my environmental studies class. We sit at the same table."

"He's a jock," I remind her. "His friends are all assholes. Just like Jake."

"They're not *all* assholes," Sophie says, her cheeks turning the faintest pink. "I don't mind Tony."

"He's best friends with Diego. Just like Jake is." I send her a look when she turns to face me. "They're our mortal enemies."

"Diego is Marty's mortal enemy. Their problems go back to when they were in diapers and they hated each other even then." Sophie blows out an exasperated breath, her gaze focused on the field. "I know those guys have been mean to Marty in the past, but I like Tony. We're…friends."

I'm stunned silent. She actually wants to be friends with one of the jocks? I can't believe it.

"There's no denying Diego has hurt Marty over the years, but I'm not going to lump the entire football team together like that because they're all friends," Sophie explains when I still haven't said anything. "Until he proves me otherwise, I'm going to continue thinking Tony is a nice person."

"Okay," I say, drawing the word out. I'm sure she can feel my doubt.

"Tony told me about the party at his house tonight," she says, somewhat changing the subject.

"Right. You mentioned that earlier." I may not hang out with the popular crowd, but we always seem to know exactly what they're doing at all times. Gossip spreads fast in a small high school.

Tony Sorrento's family is loaded. I'm pretty sure his parents divorced a few years ago, and his mom got the massive house that sits right on the edge of the lake in the divorce. And from what I've heard around school, his mom is never around. She goes out of town pretty much every weekend, making it easy for Tony to host his notorious parties.

"He asked me if I was going, and I said—yes." She bites her lip, her expression wary as she studies me. "He also said I could bring a friend too, if I wanted."

Realization dawns and I lean away from her, my mouth falling open. "You did this on purpose! You brought me to your house, helped me pick out an outfit." I wave a hand at my favorite jeans and the cute top I'm wearing, courtesy of her closet. "You did my hair." She actually curled it, something I never make time for. "And you brought me here under false pretenses. You don't care about the game. You want to go to the after party so you can...what? Hang out with Tony Sorrento?"

Sophie frowns, her expression full of hurt. "I wasn't trying to trick you, Hannah. I just knew if I mentioned a party after the game, there's no way you'd agree to it. If you don't want to go, I can drop you off at your house before I head over to Tony's."

I'm flabbergasted by her casual suggestion. Is she for real right now? "You'd go to his house, to the party *alone?*"

She shrugs, but I see the uneasiness in her eyes. She's just putting on a brave front. "Sure. I'm not scared."

That is the craziest thing I've ever heard. Like, ever. Rumors fly after every one of Tony's parties. Alcohol and drugs are always present. People get naked in his hot tub, or they jump into the lake—of course, Tony's house has a dock and probably a couple of boats—without any clothes on. People get together, couples break up, and plenty of people end up staying the night. It sounds insane.

I've never been. I've never wanted to go, but…

No way can I let Sophie go to the party alone. No friend would allow that. Even if she did go by herself, she probably wouldn't talk to a single soul. Or worse, someone would roofie her drink or whatever and she'd end up passed out on a bed, where someone might take advantage of her.

She *needs* me.

Oh, and my imagination has a way of running completely wild.

"I'll go with you," I say after a few tense minutes. "You can't go alone, Soph. God knows what could happen."

"You're really going?" She turns to me, grabbing hold of my shoulders and pulling me in for a hug. She clutches me tight, rocking me from side to side. "Oh my God, I'm so glad! We're going to have the *best* time, I promise. It'll be fun. And if it's not, if either of us feels uncomfortable, then we'll leave."

She makes it sound so simple. All I can do is smile when she releases her hold on me. She beams throughout the first half of the game, despite the fact that we're losing. She keeps her gaze trained on Tony for the entirety of the first two quarters, and I can't help but wonder if someone has a little crush.

And if someone is going to end up getting crushed before the end of the night.

CHAPTER 5

JAKE

"You want something to drink?" Cami purrs, flashing those baby blues at me, her lips curved into a promising smile. She's been giving me *fuck me* vibes all night, ever since she ran onto the field after the game and tackle-hugged me when I was still in full gear, wrapping her bare leg around mine like she was making some sort of claim. Since the cheer team has to roll up and put away the mats they cheer on during the game, all of them, including my little sister, glared at Cami while she hung all over me.

Not that she gave a shit. She takes full advantage of her captain status, instead of living up to their expectations.

"I'm good," I tell her with a lazy smile, leaning back in the lounge chair I'm sprawled on in the backyard of Tony's house. The place is packed, crowds of people in the house and outside, and I'm still riding my game high, feeling good after our hard-fought win. I underestimated the opposing team—one of many mistakes tonight—and after the last three years of them being an easy win, they were a complete challenge.

In the end, we pulled it out of our asses. Tony caught the winning touchdown with twenty seconds still on the board. My dad was losing it on the sidelines, yelling and screaming at the top of his lungs, the people in the stands were cheering their heads off, and it felt amazing. I was on top of the world.

I still feel that way.

"Got any room for me?" she asks in this babyish voice I've never heard before, right before she settles her body next to mine without waiting for my answer. She drapes her arm across my stomach, her fingers toying with the hem of my T-shirt as she gazes up at me with adoring eyes.

A guy could get used to this. Even though I know what she's done to me in the past, I can forget all about it if she keeps this up.

"Make yourself comfortable," I say with a laugh, spreading my arms wide.

"You played really great tonight," she says, resting her head on my chest. No one's paying attention to us. It's like we're in our own little world, and while I enjoyed the adulation and congrats from everyone when I first showed up at Tony's, the quiet time with Cami is nice. Though I know the minute my friends spot me cuddled up with her, they're gonna give me shit. They already gave me a bunch earlier today when they saw her strutting around campus with my jersey on.

They think she'll mess with my head, just like she's done in the past. Deep down, I know they have a point, but…

I'm trying to stay positive.

"Thanks," I tell her, wrapping my arm around her shoulders. "You, ah, looked good in your uniform."

Cami laughs. "You don't pay attention to us when you're playing. I know you don't."

She's right. I don't. I can't really see them. The rest of the team and coaches block them from view when they stand on the sidelines.

"I can hear you, though." And she's the loudest one on the cheer team, swear to God. Her voice always rises above the rest. "Thought I heard you say my name once or twice."

"More like ten or fifteen times," she says teasingly. "I was scared you were going to lose."

"Gotta have more faith in me than that," I tell her, giving her a squeeze.

"Oh, I do." She lifts her head, her gaze meeting mine, and I'm tempted to lean down and kiss her.

"What the fuck are you two up to?"

The moment completely ruined, we both turn our heads to see Caleb standing at the end of the lounger, a devilish grin on his face. "Get lost," I say.

"Hell no. You've got some 'splainin' to do," he tells me, just before he cups his hands around his mouth and yells, "Diego! Get your ass over here."

With a big sigh, Cami detaches herself from my grip and scrambles to her feet, glaring at Caleb and Diego, who's now joined him. "I'm not going to sit here and listen to your friends insult me all night."

She's talking to me, but she's glaring at them.

I sit up. "I can't control them." Well, I could if I really wanted to. "I'm not their babysitter."

Maybe she needs a reminder of all the shitty things she's done to me over the years. I know Caleb and Diego will give her an earful. They can't stand her.

"I'm out," she says to me, sending me a meaningful look before she adds, "You know how to find me."

Diego and Caleb make *ooooh* noises as she walks away, and she gives them the finger, never once looking back. The girl has attitude, I'll give her that.

"You guys suck," I tell them good-naturedly once she's gone.

"Please. You don't need that ice queen slobbering all over you," Caleb says, shaking his head as he hands me a beer, which I take readily. "You've gone down this road before with her. Too many times."

"Yeah, and I'm willing to do it again if it'll get me some free ass," I say, pleased when they laugh. This is exactly what they want to hear me say, right? That I'm just looking to get laid?

It's sort of true, the looking to get laid part. Cami seems willing. I bet I could ask her to suck my dick in the guest bathroom right now and she'd be down. Maybe then I'd relax a little. And they'd all get off my jock and let me be.

"Free ass is great and all, but she'll give you more than that, and you know what we're talking about," Caleb says, his expression serious for once. "She's brought you nothing but heartbreak."

Like these guys care if my heart's broken or not. I crack open the can of beer and drain half of it in a couple of swallows. "Find me someone else then."

I don't mean it. I'm not interested in anyone else. Not really. Cami is easy. And I'm not meaning it in *that* way. More that we're familiar with each other. She's not a challenge. She knows what I'm about, and I know what she's about.

"We already tried and then you shot us down, remember? Speaking of that…" Diego glances around the backyard, and I realize even more people have showed up in the last few minutes. Pretty sure I see a group of guys from the opposing team standing in a circle nearby—what the hell—and I know for a fact their cheer team is here. They're wandering around Tony's house still in their uniforms, flirting with all the guys.

"Pretty sure I just saw the chick who turned you down cold yesterday."

"Wait a minute. She's here?" Caleb asks, just before he starts laughing. "Get the fuck out."

"Maybe she's looking for you," Diego says, pointing at me. "You should go find her. Chat her up. She's got dick-sucking lips—maybe she'll give you a blow job."

"Please. You guys are so full of shit," I mutter, finishing off the beer and crumpling the can in my fist before I let it drop on the grass. "Why would she come to Tony's? She doesn't hang out with us."

"Nah, I'm serious. She's actually here, with that tall girl who dances. Sophia?" Diego frowns.

"Sophie," I correct. I know of her. Super tall. Kind of awkward. Pretty blonde hair.

So not my type.

"Yeah, and the tall girl was talking to Tony. I just saw them together," Diego adds. "Ol' What's Her Name was tagging along like the good third wheel she is."

I love my friends, but sometimes they're total assholes. Which I guess works because sometimes I'm a total asshole too.

"Fuck that chick." I said exactly that the last time we talked about her. "She turned me down flat. She can go play with one of her loser friends."

It's the beer talking. I know it is. The last one I just drained is my third. No way can I drive home. And if I showed up with beer on my breath? Forget it. Dad will kill me. Hope Tony doesn't mind if I stay the night. That's our usual agreement, so I'm sure he won't care.

"She's one of those nobodies who hangs out with Marty, but I doubt he lets her play with him, if you know what I mean," Diego says just before he cracks up.

See? Total assholes. Diego doesn't like his cousin. Marty is completely harmless, and we've always gotten along. I wasn't a part of that middle school attack Diego led against Marty back in the day, and I'm glad for it. But Diego has complained before that his mom always compares him to Marty when it comes to grades—and Diego doesn't measure up. Marty is extremely smart. He'll go to a good college, and he'll end up with a respectable career someday that'll make his family proud.

The only thing Diego cares about is football, and I don't think it'll take him beyond college. His family knows this. It's like no matter what Diego does, it doesn't measure up to Marty's brain. And that has to be frustrating.

"I'm out of here." I struggle to get off the lounger, my body sore, but my mind is on Cami. I need to go find her, sneak her into a dark room, and have my way with her. I'm over this talking shit business with my friends.

I need to let off some steam.

They call after me as I walk away, making their usual annoying comments, but I ignore them, heading toward the house. Lots of people say my name when they spot me, and I smile and nod at all of them, like I'm a freaking politician. A few of them clap me on the back and say good job. Most of them give me a high five as I walk past.

It feels good, knowing I have everyone's respect. Makes me excited to play next week's game.

I spot Tony standing near the back door of his house, talking with Sophie and that Hannah chick on the patio. They don't even notice my approach and I decide to leave them be. No need to engage in conversation with a girl who hates me.

The moment I have that thought, her head turns, and her gaze locks with mine. I come to a stop, staring at her like an idiot. She looks…different tonight. Her hair is wavy, and it looks like she's got gloss or something on her full lips—her dick-sucking lips, as Diego called them—making them shiny. She looks…

Pretty.

The moment feels like an eternity, but we study each other probably for only ten seconds, tops. She looks away, returning her attention to her friend and mine, and the moment is broken. Gone.

Like it never happened.

Ignoring the weird twisting feeling inside of me, I enter the house, in search of Cami. And just like she said I would, I find her, holding court in Tony's family room sitting in a giant chair, surrounded by her friends sitting on the floor, most of them girls on the cheer team. My sister isn't with them.

In fact…is my sister even here? At Tony's? I whip out my phone and text her.

You're at home, right?

No response. Not even the gray bubble with the three dots appears.

I'm overprotective of Ava, even though she's a little social justice warrior. That's what Mom calls her and it fits. She's always advocating for the underdog. I don't want her anywhere near my friends, and they know it. They're all selfish assholes.

Most guys are.

"Jakey! There you are!" Cami yells, and I wince. *Jakey?* That sucks. "I knew you'd find me."

I watch her for a moment as she plays queen bee among her friends, smiling and preening and basically telling them how to feel as they gossip about other girls from our school. My older sister Autumn was one of the cheer captains her senior year, and she wasn't a bossy bitch like Cami. Yeah, Autumn had to get stern with them sometimes, she told me, but for the most part, she was fair. And she got along with the entire team.

She was just a bossy bitch to me and Ava at home.

My phone dings, and I check it to see a response from Ava.

I'm with my friends.

Which friends? I'm looking at the entire cheer team right now, minus you. I hit send.

My actual REAL friends. I'm at Ellie's house. Chill.

I shove my phone back into my pocket, deciding not to respond. Ellie is Ava's best friend, and I'm guessing my sister is probably spending the night. I don't have to stress about her being at this party, or my friends trying to get with her. Plus, I don't have to worry about her ratting me out to Mom and Dad for drinking.

Though I've got shit on Ava too, so we have an understanding, if you get what I mean.

"Cam," I call. When she glances up at me, I flick my chin at her. "Let's go."

She frowns, her expression full-on irritated. "Where?"

"Just come on." Do I have to spell it out for her?

She gets out of her chair—it looks like a damn throne, I swear—and picks her way through the girls that are crowded around her on the floor. She stops just in front of me, her expression one of pure innocence, blinking up at me with her long eyelashes. Did she get extensions or whatever they call them? They remind me of the little hairs that stick up on caterpillars. "You want to go back outside?"

I take her hand and drag her along with me, not bothering to answer her. Not that she'd listen to me. She's too busy currently bitching me out.

"By the way, if we're going to try to make this work, you have to talk to your friends, Jake. They treat me like absolute garbage, and I won't tolerate their insults. They talk about me like I'm not even there and they say the *worst* things," she says as we head up the stairs. "You don't stop them. You don't say anything. Whose side are you on, anyway?"

I release my grip on her hand and run up the stairs, waiting for her at the top as she slowly makes her way toward me. She's wearing a top with a low neck that shows off her tits, and denim shorts that are so short, the pockets are hanging out from the bottom. She looks good and she knows it.

Cami stops directly in front of me, crossing her arms and plumping up her chest even more. My gaze drops to her cleavage. "Did you even hear a word I said?"

"Yeah, yeah. You want me to talk to my friends. They insult you and they're jerks. What else is new?" I tilt my head toward the hall and start walking. "Let's go find a bedroom."

"Jake." She stomps after me, annoyed, and I sort of don't care. "All you want from me is sex."

I turn to face her. "Isn't that what you want from me?"

She blinks up at me. "Well. Yes. But I was hoping we could have something…more than that."

My mood deflates. "You want us to get back together."

"Not yet," she says quickly, and I'm guessing she can tell she's losing me. "I'm suggesting we should try hanging out together first. See what happens."

My friends are right. I shouldn't go down this road again with Cami. She'll act like she wants to get with me, toy with me for a while, we'll fuck around, I'll start having feelings for her yet again, and then she'll dump my ass.

If I let this happen, that'll be the third time. I'll end up looking like a complete asshole. My friends will tell me I asked for it.

And I won't be able to deny it.

"I don't know, Cam." I rub my hand along my jaw, contemplating her. She's cute as hell. Sweet when she wants to be, which is rare. I'm realizing the older she gets, the worse she behaves. She's mean as a snake to other girls, and I think she's secretly jealous of every single one of them. I remember her being insecure in the past.

Do I really want to hang out with a girl like that? I do have some standards.

"What do you mean, you don't know? I thought we were going to try this." Oh, she's furious now. "I wore your jersey today!"

"Just because you wore my jersey doesn't mean we're fully committed. Come on, you know that," I tell her.

She makes a pissed off sound and actually stomps her foot, like she's having a tantrum. "Fuck you, Jake Callahan. Fuck you for being such a tease!"

And with that, she hurries down the stairs, making so much noise you'd think it was a herd of cows running.

"What the fuck?" I say out loud, running both hands through my hair and tugging on the ends. Here I thought I'd get at least a blowjob out of the interlude, and instead I get a fight with an ex that feels all too familiar.

Maybe that's the punch of reality I need.

CHAPTER 6

HANNAH

"Okay." Sophie shuts off the car's engine and turns to look at me, her eyes wide and unblinking. "Here's the plan. We'll just walk in like we own the place. If we act scared or like we don't belong, we'll stick out. And that's the last thing we need."

We're going to stick out already because neither of us has been to one of Tony's parties ever in our lives, and the popular crowd will wonder what we're doing there.

But I'm not going to point that out to Sophie. She seems anxious enough.

It was all well and good during the game, when we were contemplating only the *idea* of the party. We giggled as we watched the cheer team perform their halftime routine. We yelled extra loud after the band finished performing, giving them the recognition so few in the stands ever do.

Now we're here, and I'm tempted to chicken out. I bet Sophie is too.

"There are a lot of people in that house," I point out, glancing around at all the cars surrounding us. "Are you going to be okay walking in there?"

She's working on her shyness, she's been telling me that since school started. But sometimes, she gets anxious. Heck, so do I. I'm not good in big crowds either, and that house is filled with people I know of, but don't actually know. Not really. A lot of them I've gone to school with since kindergarten, but we were never what I would call friends.

"I'll be fine." She exhales shakily and I get the sense she's telling herself that more than answering me. "We can either sit in my car for the next hour mentally preparing ourselves to walk inside that house, or we can actually…you know. Walk inside that house."

I hear a shrill scream in the near distance, followed by a male voice bellowing, "Fuck you, Mike! Stay away from her!"

My gaze meets Sophie's and I see the fear in her eyes. She looks ready to bolt. "Let's go inside," I tell her.

Her eyes widen as if she didn't expect me to make that suggestion. I bet she believed I'd say let's stay in the car. "Really?"

"Yes," I say with far more determination than I feel. "Really. Let's go."

We climb out of the car in tandem, meeting at the back of her mom's silver Honda. The air is cooler up here by the lake, which makes sense considering we're higher, elevation-wise. Shivering when the breeze hits, I rub my hands over my bare arms, trying to warm myself up. "No skinny dipping in the lake for me," I say dryly. "It's way too cold."

"You could always jump in the hot tub naked," Sophie suggests with a wry smile.

"Right. Only if you jump in the hot tub naked with me." I nudge her in the side as we make our way toward the front of the house.

"Guess we're both of out luck then," Sophie says with a grin, but it wavers a little and the smile eventually falls from her face. "Why did I think it was a good idea to go to this party again?"

"Because you have the tiniest crush on Tony Sorrento and you want to see him tonight," I remind her, though she hadn't necessarily admitted she has a crush on Tony. Yet.

Sophie parked pretty far from the house, only because the long, winding driveway had been lined with cars and we didn't have a choice. So many people are here, it's kind of mind blowing. The massive house looms in the distance, every window seemingly lit, loud music and the dull roar of conversation pouring from it.

"I don't have a crush on him," Sophie protests, but it's weak. "More like I just think he's…nice."

"Uh huh," I say with a snort.

"I'm sure you wouldn't mind seeing Jake Callahan," she teases.

I roll my eyes, annoyed that she keeps bringing him up. I've never thought about him once the entirety of high school until he approached me yesterday. Now I supposedly have a crush on him? Get real. "You're making a big deal out of nothing. He's too wrapped up in Cami."

"But he asked you to wear his jersey first," Sophie reminds me. Like I need the reminding.

"As some sort of weird dare made by his friends. He doesn't like me. He didn't even know my name." Not that I care.

Ugh. Okay, I do care just a little. Even though my brain tells me whatever Jake wanted from me wasn't going to be good, my heart still asked the question, *what if?*

What if he was actually interested?

What if he spent a few minutes with me, he'd be dazzled by my sparkling personality?

What if we became *the* couple of the senior class?

What if, what if, what if?

Clearly I'm living in a dream world, because he couldn't give a single crap about me.

We head up the stairs leading to the front door, all discussions of boys momentarily forgotten. The music is so loud it's deafening, though I swear I just heard the sound of broken glass beyond the front door. People are crowded in the backyard too. So many voices are drifting in the night air, the high-pitched sounds of girls giggling and the deep voices of boys talking. Plus, there's the unmistakable sound of water splashing.

Yep. Someone's probably already skinny-dipping in the lake or hot tub.

"Should I knock?" Sophie asks when we stop directly in front of the large, imposing door.

I shrug. "Would anyone hear it?"

"Good point." Sophie reaches for the handle and pushes the door open, and we walk inside the very crowded living room.

There are people everywhere, covering every square inch of the furniture inside the room. A girl sitting on a boy's lap waves at us, then squeals when he dips her upside down over his knees, leaving her hanging there for a second, her hair dragging on the carpeted floor.

Sophie and I send each other a look as we move on.

We enter the kitchen next, and there's a group of people sitting at a round table in a nook that faces the backyard. They're murmuring to each other as they pass a joint around, and I can't help but be surprised. I figured most everyone had switched to smoking weed with a vape—specifically a wax pen.

"Looks like everyone's outside," Sophie tells me as she hurriedly makes her way to the French door that leads to the backyard. Drugs scare her, so I'm sure the group at the table is quietly freaking her out. "Let's go see if Tony is out there."

I follow after her, wishing I'd brought a sweater as we step outside. Now that we're even closer to the lake—I can see it just beyond the line of trees—it's even cooler back here. I notice a lot of people are wearing sweaters or sweatshirts, making me jealous.

"Soph! You made it!"

We both turn to find Tony Sorrento approaching us, his lips curved into the faintest smile. He looks as Italian as his name sounds, with his thick, almost black hair, dark eyes and olive skin. He's actually really attractive, though always quiet, which made me think he didn't have much of a personality. This is the most animated I've ever seen him.

"Hey Tony," Sophie says shyly, her eyes going wide when he pulls her into a quick hug. I bet she didn't expect that.

"I'm glad you came," he says to Sophie, his gaze only for her.

Aw.

"Um, this is my friend, Hannah," Sophie says, turning toward me.

Tony nods. "I know Hannah. How's it going?"

"Hey," I offer weakly, feeling lame. I'm surprised he knows me, but he was there with Jake yesterday during the jersey incident. "Thanks for inviting us."

"Any time," he says, focusing on Sophie once more. "I didn't think you'd come."

"I didn't think I would either," she says truthfully. "Hannah convinced me we should go."

"Your house is really nice," I tell him, which is an understatement. His house and yard and everything about is impressive. Blatant wealth on display.

"Thanks. I can't take any credit. My mom got all kinds of money in the divorce settlement and she renovated this place a couple of years ago. Since I'm the youngest, I think she's waiting until I graduate before she sells it," Tony explains.

I'm pretty sure that's the most words I've ever heard Tony speak at once before.

Sophie starts talking about the yard and the lake, and I can't help but tune out after a few seconds. Their conversation flows easily, which doesn't always happen with Sophie, especially when she's getting to know someone. So she must feel pretty comfortable with Tony already, and I like that. I trust my friend's instincts.

And really? I just want her to be happy.

I let my gaze wander around the backyard, zeroing in on the back door that just slammed shut, and I lock eyes with of all people, Jake Callahan.

He stares back me, his expression stony, his jaw tight. He is so attractive, it annoys me. And why is he looking at me like that? Like he can't stop? He actually licks his lips and I'm horrified by the way my body seems to heat up at seeing his tongue.

What's wrong with me?

I look away from him, unable to take it anymore, and I try my best to focus my attention on what Tony is saying.

"...so yeah. This is where I live." He sounds vaguely nervous, which I find kind of endearing. "You want a tour of the house?" Tony asks us. Well. He asks *Sophie*. He turns to me at the last second as if trying to include me.

"Um, sure," Sophie says with a shy smile.

Hmmm. I get the sense Tony actually likes Sophie. How adorable.

"Let's go," Tony says to Sophie, and I hang back when they start for the door that leads through the kitchen.

"You two go on," I say when they both turn to look at me questioningly. "I'll stay out here."

Sophie frowns, her eyes filling with mild panic. "I can't leave you out here alone. Come with us."

"I'll be fine," I reassure her. "And look at me. I'm definitely not alone."

I am surrounded by all sorts of people, and there's a group of unfamiliar guys standing nearby in a circle, clad in green-and-white shirts. Pretty sure that's the team we played against tonight's colors. Why are they are?

"You sure you'll be okay?" Sophie asks.

"I'm fine," I say with a firm nod. "Go."

"It won't take long," Tony says, his attention on me. "We'll be back in a few minutes."

"Take your time," I tell him, and I mean it. I can find a chair to sit in and people watch. There are all sorts of things happening here tonight, and I usually hear the gossip second- or third-hand.

Tonight, I have a front-row seat.

Sophie and Tony disappear inside the house, and I find an empty chair not too far from the hot tub. There's a table next to me, covered in empty beer cans and water bottles, and I spot a water bottle that's still sealed. I grab it, crack the lid open and take a drink, my gaze scanning the yard. I spot Cami Lockhart. Alone.

Interesting.

She marches past me, not even giving me a second of her attention, which is fine. We were friends in elementary school. She even invited me to a few slumber parties when were around ten or eleven, but once we got older, she forgot all about me. I wasn't popular enough, I suppose.

I watch as she approaches a group of girls that includes a few members of the cheer team, and she speaks loudly enough that I can hear her. "Jake Callahan is a total asshole. God, I hate him."

"Oh my god, Cami, what did he do to you now? What happened?" one of them asks, and I can tell from the eagerness in her tone, she's dying for all the details.

Well, sister, so am I.

"I was trying to tell him how much he means to me, but all he wants is sex." The disappointment in Cami's voice rings clear, not that I can blame her. I mean, she's a total snake, but who wants to be used by a boy just for sex?

No one I know. Not even Cami.

"I wouldn't turn him down if all he wanted was sex from me," another girl says jokingly, making them all crack up.

"Hmm, typical slut behavior. I don't expect anything less from you," Cami says snidely.

Oh, and very loudly, making sure everyone can hear her, I'm sure.

I wrinkle my nose in disgust over Cami's remark. I hate slut shamers. The girl was just making a joke.

I think.

"Get over yourself," the other girl says, now sounding annoyed. "You don't rule over all of us, no matter how hard you try."

I lean in a little to my right, trying to hear what Cami says next. I can practically feel her anger radiating toward me, and I know whatever she's going to say, it'll be mean as hell. This could possibly turn into a big argument, and the details will be diluted by Monday morning, so it's kind of fun that I'll witness the entire thing in the moment.

"Hey."

I startle with a little yelp, practically dropping my water bottle when I hear the very deep, very male voice. Glancing up, I find one of those green-and-white-shirt -wearing guys standing directly in front of me, a friendly smile on his face. "Oh. Hey," I greet him.

He smiles, shoving his hands into the pocket of his jeans. "What's a pretty girl like you doing here sitting alone?"

At first, I look around because I don't think he's talking to me.

But he is. And is he actually…flirting with me? Huh. He's not bad looking. Golden-brown hair, golden-brown eyes, broad shoulders.

"I'm just waiting for my friend," I say, sitting up straighter.

Dang it, I didn't get to hear what Cami said. She just stormed away from her group of friends too, one of them calling after her, "Bye, bitch!"

The boy watches her go, his gaze lingering on her for a second before he returns his attention to me. "She looks pissed."

"She's always pissed," I tell him, making him laugh.

"Glad I didn't talk to her then," he says with an easy smile. "I'm James."

"Hannah," I say with a smile in return.

"Can I join you?" He nods toward the empty chair next to mine.

"Sure," I say dazedly, shocked that a boy would want to talk to me.

But I suppose if I don't put myself out there, then this sort of thing never happens. And since I never put myself out there, this never happens.

Until tonight.

"You friends with the guy who lives in this house?" James asks me.

"Sort of," I answer with a little shrug. "He's giving my friend a tour of his house right now."

"Uh huh. Rich fucker," James says, sounding a little annoyed.

The high school we played against tonight is from the next town over, and I know most of the population is lower to middle class. Pretty much the same as our town, with the exception of the rich people who live by the lake. Since I'm not one to hang out with the rich peeps, I suppose I could relate to his comment. But the people who live up here with their parents didn't choose to be rich, just like I didn't choose to be poor. Who am I to judge them?

"I guess his parents got divorced and his mom recently renovated the house," I tell James. Why, I don't know. I'm sure he doesn't care.

"Must be nice," James says, his tone snide.

I decide to change the subject. "I'm surprised you guys are here." He frowns at me, and I continue, "Showing your faces at this party after losing tonight."

"Were you at the game?"

I nod.

"Then you saw it was a pretty close one," James says. "Next year, we'll get them for sure."

"You're not a senior?"

He shakes his head. "I'm a junior."

"Oh." I blink at him, surprised by his answer. "I'm a senior."

"Really? I've always had a thing for older women," he says with a grin.

I laugh, but I'm kind of uncomfortable. I don't want to get with a boy who's younger than me. And I definitely don't want to get with a boy who goes to a different school.

"You want something to drink besides the water?" James asks, nodding toward the bottle in my hand.

"I'm good," I tell him, thinking of all the articles I've seen about guys drugging a girl's drink. The next thing she knows, she wakes up naked and alone in a bed.

Forget that.

"I'm gonna grab a beer. Be right back." He rises to his feet, winks at me, then saunters away.

I watch him go, sinking my teeth into my lower lip as I contemplate my current situation. It might be…fun to practice flirting with this guy tonight, considering there won't be any consequences if I'm a complete fail. I'll never have to see him again. And if it's a success, that's as far as I can take it. I don't really know him. I don't particularly want to know him that well, but what's the harm in casual conversation?

Glancing up, I see Jake standing across the yard, a beer clutched in his hand, his friends standing on either side of him, both of them talking up a storm. He's not listening to a word they're saying. No, his focus is one hundred percent on…

Me.

And I don't understand why.

CHAPTER 7

JAKE

*W*hat the hell is she doing at Tony's tonight? I don't get it. I don't notice this chick for pretty much the entirety of my high school life, and now she's all I can see for the past two days.

It's fucking annoying.

I watch as some jerk from the opposing team chats her up and she smiles at him, this bewildered expression on her face like she can't believe that dude is talking to her. He gets up, says something to her, and she shakes her head no before he walks away. She stares off into space, sinking her teeth into her plump lower lip before she glances around, her gaze falling on me.

I don't look away. It's like I can't. She's actually really pretty. And her mouth—it's all pouty and swollen-looking, the shiny stuff long gone. Her lips are this rosy red shade that's one-hundred percent natural. She looks like someone just kissed the hell out of her.

Wonder what it would be like if *I* was the one who kissed the hell out of her. What does she taste like? Would she be all timid and shy? Probably. If I took it slow and coaxed it out of her, would I eventually have her moaning in my arms?

"Jake, what the fuck?"

I blink myself back into focus and turn to frown at Diego, who's studying me as if I've lost my mind. "What?"

"We've been talking to you for like the last five minutes and you haven't said a damn word," Diego says, Caleb adding a "yeah" to second that opinion. "You drunk already or what?"

"I guess so." That must be it. It's the alcohol making me think like this. I'm nursing my fourth beer, feeling a little buzzy, but I'm not stumbling, out-of-my-mind drunk yet.

"I was trying to tell you that Cami is making eyes at your ass right now," Diego says with a grin.

I scowl at the ground, my shoulders going tense. "She already turned me down. I'm not about to chase after that again."

"Thank the lord above!" Caleb yells, staring up at the sky, his hands together as if he's praying. "Praise Jesus and all the saints! Jake is finally over the heartless bitch!"

"Shut up," I tell him, though I'm not that worried about Cami hearing. "You're making a spectacle of yourself."

"So were you, following after Cami like you actually thought she'd let you slip a hand beneath those iron-clad panties of hers," Diego says, shoving at my shoulder. I let him do it, not bothering saying anything in return. I suppose I deserve the abuse because clearly I lost my head when it comes to that girl.

"Where's Jocelyn?" I ask Diego, referring to his girlfriend.

He makes a face. "Volleyball tournament in Mammoth this weekend. Volleyball fucking sucks. It consumes her life."

"What, like football consumes yours?" Now it's my turn to give him a shove. "At least she's passionate about something that has nothing to do with you."

Diego's the type who wants his all of his girlfriend's attention, all the time. Me? I feel like I'm being smothered when a girl acts like that.

"I guess," he says morosely, shoving his hands in his pockets. "But without her around hanging all over me, I can look my fill at all the girls here tonight."

I ignore what he says, though Caleb offers him a high five. Diego…isn't the most loyal when it comes to his girl. Yeah, they're in love and they have all sorts of plans for the future, but when certain situations present themselves, Diego doesn't always do the right thing.

Sucks.

They start talking about all the girls, and I start to zone out. I glance over to where Hannah was sitting only a few minutes ago, but she's gone.

Huh.

"I'll be back," I tell them absently as I take off. My friends don't even hesitate in their conversation, they just keep rolling with the comments as I make my way toward the table where Hannah was sitting only moments ago.

The group of players from Mariposa Springs stare me down, and I smile at them, smug as fuck since we whooped their ass. "Who let you dumbasses in?" I ask.

"Someone invited our cheer team, so we thought we'd show up for protection," one of them says. Pretty sure he's their quarterback. He's a cocky-looking asshole with longish brown hair and mean, beady eyes.

"Don't worry, we've got a handle on your women," I tell them, crossing my arms and staring them down. I don't want them here. Hell, I don't want their cheer team here either, but it's a free country, and I'm guessing Tony or someone else from our team invited them, so now we have to deal.

I'll be having a talk with my team first thing at practice on Monday. We can't let the enemy into our realm. Next thing I know we'll have our biggest rival team hanging out here after we play them in a month for our homecoming game, and that's some straight-up bullshit. I hate every single one of those guys on their team, especially their quarterback. Eli Bennett is the one who fucked Cami behind my back when we were together and rubbed it in my face.

I seriously hate that guy.

"Fuck off, Callahan," the quarterback says, his upper lip curled into a sneer. "Go run home to Daddy. Maybe he can put you through some extra drills this weekend so you won't choke like you did tonight."

Anger rolls through me, and I drop my arms to my sides, curling my hands into fists. I refuse to get involved in a fight with these assholes tonight. Can't risk it.

Don't want to risk it.

Blowing out a harsh breath, I turn my back on them and start to walk away, coming to a dead stop when one of them speaks. "That's it. Go on. Run away like the pussy we all know you are."

My vision goes red. Without thought I turn and run toward them, my arm cocked and my fist making contact with the quarterback's nose. I hear the crunch more than I feel it, and the guy hits the ground like a rag doll, his legs crumpling beneath him.

And just like that, it's on. I hear Diego and Caleb coming to my defense, yelling at the top of their lungs. They go racing by me as their fists start flying. Girls are screaming and running, trying to get out of our way. Out of nowhere someone socks me right in the face, a rock-hard fist glancing off my jaw, and my head whips back, a murderous sound escaping me upon contact.

Now all I can see is black. I'm blindly punching. There's more screaming. The crash of furniture. Glass breaking. Girls crying. Swear to God I hear Cami yelling at me to stop it, and at one point, I feel something trickle down my face, on my lips. I wipe at it before glancing down at my fingers.

Blood.

Tony suddenly appears, and he is full-on enraged. Angrier than I've ever seen him. He's a big dude, and when he's like this, we all know he means business. His voice is deep and firm as he's bellowing at everyone.

"Knock this shit off!" He pushes himself into the center of the fight, breaking up two guys who are about to throw hands, bracing his palms on either of their chests to keep them from lunging toward each other.

"This is bullshit," he says, his voice even. Measured. Edged with a hint of rage as his gaze sweeps over the members of the Mariposa Springs team. They've all managed to cluster together, their chests rising and falling rapidly, just like ours. "Get the fuck out of here, and don't ever come back. I catch even a glimpse of one of you assholes on my property in the next five minutes, and I'm calling the cops."

The members of the other team take a few steps back, glowering at all of us. Some of them are bleeding. I see one guy who's gonna have a major shiner come tomorrow, and then of course, there's their quarterback, whose hand is cupped around his bleeding nose.

Seeing him gives me an immense rush of satisfaction. That's what he gets for calling me a pussy.

For the most part, though, they appear unruffled. When I glance around at my friends, they're similar. A few bruises and scratches, but otherwise, we're fine.

"Fuck you!" a couple of them roar at us before they walk out of the backyard together. No girls follow after them, and I realize their cheerleaders must've already taken off.

"Whose bright idea was it to invite those bozos and their freaking cheer team?" Tony asks once they're out of earshot. "Seriously, that was a huge mistake."

No one cops to it. Figures.

"Baby." I turn to find Cami running toward me, slamming into my body and making me grunt when she hugs me tight.

What the hell?

"You're hurt," she says when she glances up at me, her hand going to the side of my face where that dude punched me. I wince when she touches my jaw. "You're bleeding."

"I know." I shake her off me. "I gotta clean myself up."

If I come home tomorrow morning cut up and bruised and my parents see me? They'll freak out, and I don't want to hear it from them. I need to at least clean up the blood, bandage myself up. I can explain any bruises as part of the game, or I can make up some story about us roughhousing during the party.

"Want my help?" Cami asks in a simpering tone, batting her fake eyelashes at me.

"No," I practically snarl, causing her to back away from me with wide, fearful eyes. She is so over the top. I fucking can't with this chick right now.

"Bro, you okay?" Caleb asks as he approaches me, his brows pinched together in concern. There's not a mark on the guy, and I can't help but feel a little jealous. "What the hell did they say to you to turn you unglued like that?"

"I don't want to talk about it." I make my way toward the house, Caleb keeping pace. "You think Tony's pissed at me for starting it?"

"More like he's mad those jackoffs were here in the first place. He's not mad at you," Caleb reassures me as we enter the kitchen. Most of the girls went inside when the fight started, and they're all huddled in the kitchen, staring at us like we're savage beasts who've come for their blood next. Some of them bolt out of the room, like they can't even stand to look at us. "Go use one of the bathrooms upstairs," he says, pointing to the back stairwell. "I'll wait for you down here and drive your ass home."

"Nah, I'm staying the night. You probably should too," I protest as Caleb starts pushing me toward the staircase that leads to the second floor.

"Fine, whatever. Let's stay the night. Now go." He gives me a shove and I make my way up the stairs slowly, my entire body aching. The game brutalized me.

The fight did even more damage.

Mentally cursing myself and trying my best to ignore the throbbing in my jaw, I make my way down the dark hallway, opening doors in search of a bathroom. This house is a monstrosity. I don't know how Tony can stand living in it. My house is huge, but at least there are five of us currently filling it. Sometimes I feel like I can't escape them, though. Beck barges into my bedroom all the time unannounced, so much that I had to start locking the door at night.

But at least I have my family. With his mom gone all the time, Tony spends a lot of nights and weekends here alone.

I finally find a bathroom and flick on the light, stopping in front of the mirror to check out the damage. And fuck me, I look terrible. My lips are red with drying blood. There's a massive bruise forming along my jaw, and there's a cut across my cheekbone that looks kind of deep.

Damn. Whoever punched me got me good.

Twisting on the faucet, I let the water run until it's warm. There aren't any washcloths handy, so I grab one of Tony's mom's fancy hand towels and dunk it in the water, then press it to the cut on my face.

I let out a hiss the moment the cloth makes contact with the wound, immediately dropping the entire towel in the sink, getting it soaked.

"Fuck me," I mutter under my breath, grabbing another towel off the rack and running it under the water.

"Are you okay? Do you need help?" a sweet voice asks, and my lids fall shut in irritation. I do not want to deal with some girl who's going to lose her shit at the sight of blood. Taking a deep breath, I work my tense jaw—damn it, that hurts—before I slowly turn and open my eyes, fully expecting to find Cami there for some reason, desperate to nurse me back to health.

But it's not Cami.

It's Hannah.

She gasps when she sees my face, her eyes going wide. "What happened to you?"

Her reaction annoys me. *She* annoys me, and I don't understand why. "Where've you been? Didn't you see that fight break out in the backyard?"

Her mouth drops open. "There was a fight?"

Is she completely clueless? "Yeah." I turn toward the mirror once more, scrubbing the towel across my lips to get rid of the blood. It leaves a rusty stain on the pale pink towel, and I wonder if that will come out. "There was."

"Are you all right?" She takes a step into the bathroom, and when I glance in the mirror, I can see her standing right behind me, wide eyed and pale, looking as if she wished she were anywhere but here with me.

"Not particularly, no." I run water over the red stain on the towel, glad to see most of disappear. Then I press the damp towel to my face, directly over the wound, as gently as possible.

It hurts like a motherfucker.

"Hey." She touches me, her fingers on my arm, burning my skin. She immediately drops her hand. "Let me look at that cut."

"Why?" I ask warily, our gazes meeting in the reflection.

"I want to see how deep it is," she tells me, her voice soft. Like she's talking to a wild animal she's trying to tame.

"Move the towel." She hesitates, those big blue eyes meeting mine. "Please."

I turn to face her and slowly remove the towel from my face, but she's already shaking her head. "What's wrong?"

"Sit there."

She points at the toilet, and I can't help it—I laugh. "Seriously?"

She walks around me and slams the toilet lid down. "Seriously." She points at it again.

For some weird reason I do as she says, sitting down on the closed toilet, my legs spreading wide because I'm too tall for the thing. She steps right in between my legs, so close I can feel her body heat, smell her light floral scent, and then she's touching my cheek, gently prodding around the cut, making me wince.

"It's deep," she murmurs, and I swear I feel her breath waft across my face. It takes everything I've got to contain the shiver that wants to roll through me. "But I don't think you'll need stitches."

"Whatever you say, doc," I tell her, taking advantage of having her so close and drinking her in greedily. We're practically face to face only because I'm sitting, but not by much. This close, I can see the delicate spray of freckles across her pert nose. The stubborn jut of her chin. How blue her eyes are.

They're like the sky.

She reaches over and turns off the water and then grabs the discarded damp towel from the counter, bringing it to my face and softly wiping at the wound, her movements precise. Careful.

"Think they have a Band-Aid in this place?" she asks, her lips curved in the tiniest smile.

I stare at those plump pink lips, all my earlier thoughts of tasting her flooding me, and my skin grows warm. She's not even paying attention to me, too focused on cleaning the cut, her delicate brows furrowed, her eyes narrowed as she takes a step away from me and studies my face.

"You have a bruise on your jaw," she says.

No shit, I want to tell her, but I don't. "Hurts like a bitch."

"Who started it?" She trails her fingers along my jawline, and I grimace when she hits a sensitive spot.

I don't want to answer her. "Am I going to live?"

She contemplates me for a moment, and I'm sure she wants to ask who started it again, but I return her stare, hoping my face is like a blank wall.

"I suppose," she finally says, her hand dropping from my face, and she goes back to the sink, opening one drawer and searching through all the shit inside before moving on to the next. She plucks out a tube of antibacterial ointment and sets it on the counter, then crouches down to open the cabinets and pushes nearly half her body inside. I can hear her knocking over all kinds of stuff over before she finally drags herself out of the cabinet with a crumpled box clutched in her hand. "Found some."

"Great," I tell her with as little enthusiasm as possible.

But I gotta admit, there's something kind of sexy about a girl who's doing her damnedest to take care of me, no questions asked. She's not passing any judgement or acting scared. Hannah is being very straightforward. No nonsense.

Mom would probably like her.

I shake my head and immediately banish the thought.

She opens the box of Band-Aids and grabs a couple, then picks up the ointment and makes her way back to me, standing in between my legs once more. "Hold these," she demands, handing me the Band-Aids still in their wrappers.

I take them from her, our fingers brushing, and a jolt slams through me. She seems completely unaffected by me as she steps even closer, undoing the lid on the ointment and squirting the clear cream on her index finger before she reaches out and dabs some of it on the gash on my face.

A hiss escapes me, and without thought I reach out, my fingers locking around her wrist, keeping her from touching me further.

"It hurts?" she asks.

"Yeah," I rasp, marveling at how small, how delicate her wrist bones are. If I wanted, I suppose I could crush her.

Not that I want to.

"I'll be gentler. I promise," she says, her voice, her expression solemn.

Slowly I let go of her, and she goes about her task once more, her touch featherlight as she dabs at my face. My eyes are at tit level, and the shirt she's got on is low cut, offering me a glimpse of smooth pale skin and faint cleavage.

Just like that, my dick jerks and my head feels like it's going to explode.

I don't understand my reaction to her. She's not my type —I tend to stay in my social circle and she's definitely not a part of it. She was rude as fuck to me yesterday, yet now she's taking care of me like she's a nurse and I'm her patient. It's weird.

And confusing.

CHAPTER 8

HANNAH

I cannot believe I'm in a tiny bathroom at Tony Sorrento's house, tending to Jake Callahan's wounded face on a Friday night. He has a long gash on his cheek, a giant bruise forming on his jaw, and a glower in his intense blue eyes that tells me he is thoroughly pissed off.

I feel like a complete idiot, but seeing him like this, injured and with a hint of vulnerability, it's kind of hot.

The cut hurts him. Every time I touch it he winces and glares at me, like it's my fault he's in pain. I couldn't find any butterfly bandages, but I can make do with regular ones. I just need to use two or three so I can bring together his skin so hopefully the cut won't scar badly.

Yes, I'm a regular plastic surgeon, look at me.

"Okay," I tell him, trying to smile, but when he's watching me like that, like he wants to tear the room apart with his bare hands, he makes me nervous. "I'm going to use a couple of Band-Aids to hold your skin together."

He frowns. "What are you talking about?"

"You'll see," I say lightly, trying to act like this is no big deal. I grab one Band-Aid and tear off the wrapper, biting my lip when I see what's printed on it.

"What's wrong?"

I glance up to find him watching me, his blue eyes dark and turbulent. He has beautiful eyes. Such an unusual shade of blue, with a hint of green, though right now they remind me of an angry sea. The artist in me would love to paint him, which is laughable.

Like he'd ever let me.

Realizing he's waiting for my answer, I turn the Band-Aid so that it's facing him. "I hope you like Dora the Explorer."

He exhales loudly and shakes his head, his mouth going flat, as if he's completely disgusted. "Just put it on."

I do as he requests, tearing the strip that protects the sticky part off and then hold the Dora Band-Aid close to his cheek. "I don't want to hurt you, but I probably will."

"Do it," he says, his voice sharp, his gaze cutting. "Get it over with."

Taking a deep breath, I somehow put both hands on his face, the Band-Aid dangling off one finger as I try my best to bring his skin together. Doing so makes the wound ooze blood and I press my lips together, managing to get the Band-Aid on his face long-wise, going opposite the direction of the actual cut.

"I need to put on at least two more," I tell him as I unwrap another Dora Band-Aid.

"I'm going to look ridiculous," he mutters.

"At least it happened on a Friday night, right? You can go home and take the Dora bandages off tomorrow. By Monday, no one will know. It'll be our little secret," I tell him before I start in and do the same exact thing I did with the first Band-Aid.

He utters a curse word under his breath when I pinch the other end of the cut together. Then he mutters another one.

I ignore his complaining, one-hundred percent focused on applying the Band-Aids to his handsome face when I suddenly jerk, my elbow almost nailing him in the nose when he rests his big, warm hand on the outside of my thigh.

"Sorry." He drops his hand immediately. "Trying to brace myself."

His touch was like a brand. I can still feel where his fingers pressed against my flesh, burning me from the inside out. My mouth dry, I flick my head toward the counter. "Grip the granite."

He does as I say, his knuckles turning white when I push together the center of his wound before applying the last Band-Aid. I step away from him when I'm done. "Okay. You're good."

"Do I look stupid?"

"You look like you're five years old and really into Dora and Boots," I tell him truthfully.

He doesn't bother answering me. Or even smile, and I wonder if he ever really does. Why is he so angry? His life looks pretty decent from my vantage point. If I were him, I'd have no complaints.

But I'm not him. I have no idea what he deals with daily, nor do I know or understand his struggles. I'm sure he has them. We all do. Just because you have money and live in a big house and both your parents love you doesn't mean you don't have issues.

He definitely has some advantages, though.

I toss the Band-Aid wrappers in the tiny trash basket between the counter and the toilet, and then I wash my hands with warm water, the soap's strong floral scent filling the tiny space as I scrub and scrub. When I'm done, I use one of the bath towels and dry my hands before I turn to find Jake quietly watching me.

"Thank you," he says after a short stretch of silence. "For helping me."

I shrug, not wanting to make a big deal out of this. "I heard you cursing and had to come see what was wrong."

"You really didn't see the fight?"

I slowly shake my head. "I must've already been up here."

"With that guy?" He frowns and I'm startled by his accusatory tone, or that he even noticed.

Did he see me with James?

"What guy?" I ask carefully.

"The asshole from Mariposa Springs. The one who was sitting with you outside." His mouth thins and he looks away.

A thrill moves through me. He did notice. Why does he care?

"We all ended up in the house and Tony was showing us his game room upstairs. We heard yelling coming from the backyard, and Tony shot out of the room, but I didn't realize what was going on," I explain.

Jake's gaze meets mine once more, his eyes blazing. "What happened to that guy? Is he still here?"

I shake my head. "He followed after Tony once he got a text. My friend is still in the game room. Oh no." I was looking for the bathroom so I could pee, but I forgot all about that when I heard the cursing and found Jake standing in the tiny bathroom. I pull my phone out of my back pocket to see I have a text from Sophie asking where I am.

Helping someone out. BRB

She responds immediately. **I'm downstairs. Whenever you're ready, let's go.**

My heart sinks. I'm not ready yet.

I sort of never want this moment to stop.

But Jake is apparently ready for it to end. He rises to his full height, towering over me, and just like that, it's as if he's filling up the entire space, stealing all the oxygen from the room and I can barely breathe. I take a step back, bumping into the towel rack, and I grimace when it digs into my spine.

"Watch it." He leans toward me, slipping his hand behind me and blocking the rack. Without any effort he drags me forward, so close, I practically step on his feet. "You okay?"

"I'm fine." I gaze up at him, glad to see the glower on his face has eased somewhat. He doesn't look as savage as he did earlier, so that's a relief. "I suppose we're even now."

"You helped me a lot more than I did you," he says, slowly removing his hand.

I miss his touch, which is dumb.

So dumb.

"Hannah!" Sophie appears in the doorway, taking a step back when she spots Jake standing next to me. "*Oh.* Uh, what's going on?"

"She was helping me," he says sullenly, jerking his thumb in my direction before he makes his way toward the door. Sophie quickly steps aside, letting him pass. "See ya, Hannah," Jake calls over his shoulder.

And then he's gone.

Sophie pushes her way into the bathroom and shuts the door, grabbing hold of my hands and giving them a squeeze. "What in the hell was that all about?"

"I was helping him. Just like he said," I say mysteriously, pulling out of her grip so I can try to tidy up our mess. The counter is wet, and so are the towels we used to clean up his face. I mop the counters as best I can.

"With what? Oh my God, tell me you didn't just let him feel you up in this bathroom."

"What? No! Of course not. I don't even know him," I say.

"You don't have to know someone to let them feel you up," Sophie sing-songs.

"Are you listening to yourself right now? You sounds ridiculous," I tell her. I scoop up the wet towels and look around before deciding to drop them into the tub. I pull the shower curtain closed and turn to find my friend smirking at me. "What is your problem?"

"You're not giving me all the details."

"What happened with you and Tony?" I throw back at her, needing a diversion.

"Nothing." The disappointment on her face is clear and her shoulders slump. "He had to go downstairs and break up a fight. I guess they got into it with the guys from the Mariposa Springs team. Can you believe it?"

"That's why I had to help Jake. He got hit. He had a bad cut on his cheek," I explain.

"Is that why he had Dora the Explorer Band-Aids on his face?" She starts to giggle. "I didn't fail to notice that."

"They were the only Band-Aids I could find," I say with a shrug.

"And to think you were talking to one of those Mariposa guys. He seemed nice, too," Sophie says.

"James wasn't involved in that fight," I point out.

"Yeah, but all of his friends were, and don't forget, he zoomed out of the room right after Tony did." Sophie shakes her head, leaning against the counter. "Maybe I'm not cut out for this sort of thing. Football players. Wild, drunken parties. Fights."

"We're seniors, Soph. If we're not ready for this now, when will we be?" I ask.

"College?" She raises her brows, and we both start laughing.

I can't help but think about what Sophie said as we drive home. Maybe she's right. I'm not ready for this sort of thing. Wild parties. Gorgeous, moody boys. Mean girls. Beer and drugs and fights. I'll probably never be ready for this type of life. This was most likely my one chance.

It was fun while it lasted.

CHAPTER 9

JAKE

It's Saturday morning and I pretty much snuck into the house after spending the night at Tony's. I'm in the bathroom I share with my sister, slowly peeling one of the Dora Band-Aids off my face when Ava appears in the doorway.

Our gazes briefly meet in the reflection and her brows shoot up when she catches sight of my messed-up face. "What happened to you?"

I keep my gaze fixed on the mirror, wincing as I peel off the last bit of Dora and toss the bandage in the trash. "Got in a fight."

"Ah, I heard about that." She enters the bathroom like she has no boundaries—typical—and leans her hip against the counter, watching me with her arms crossed. "How does the other guy look?"

"Pretty sure I broke their quarterback's nose, though it wasn't the QB who hit me," I say as I start to take off the next bandage. We both stay quiet, Ava observing me with that all-knowing gaze of hers. She gets it from our mother.

"You're doing that all wrong," Ava finally says, sounding completely put out.

I glance in her direction. "What do you mean?"

She marches right up to me and grabs my shoulder, turning me so I'm facing her. Without warning she reaches up and rips the Band-Aid off my face with one quick flick of her wrist.

"Ow! Damn, that hurt," I growl at her.

Ava doesn't answer me. Instead, she tears off the last bandage just as fast, then tosses them both in the trash. "See? You're done."

"It still stings." I examine the cut in the mirror, pleased to see it doesn't look as ghastly as it did last night, before Hannah took care of me.

Uneasiness fills me at even thinking of her name. I dreamed about her. About us. In the bathroom, all alone, a candle flickering on the counter, her face in shadows. She was standing between my legs, but instead of taking care of the cut on my cheek, she bent her head and slowly pressed her mouth to mine. I pulled her in close, my arms wrapped tight around her waist, her lips parted and…

I woke up. Disoriented, hungover, uncomfortable having fallen asleep on one of Tony's couches in the family room. All sorts of people were still there, and after I took a piss and washed my hands, I was out of there.

"It's going to sting no matter what, and you'd still be trying to take that Band-Aid off if it was up to you." Ava shakes her head as she washes her hands. "I can't believe you guys got into it last night with that team. Does Dad know about this?"

I ignore her question. He probably doesn't know about it. Yet. "How did you hear about the fight?"

"Duh, it was all over everyone's stories. Snapchat. Instagram. Photos. Videos. The Mariposa Springs guys posted their own videos after it happened too, talking mad shit about all of you. Especially you." She meets my gaze in the mirror and turns off the sink. "There's even video of Cami running toward you and calling you *baby*."

She's trying to distract me from those assholes talking about me by mentioning Cami. And it's not going to work. I'm instantly pissed, though what can I do about it?

Nothing. Not like we can declare a turf fight and finish each other off like they did in *The Outsiders*. Yeah, I both read the book and watched the movie in the seventh grade and it's stuck with me ever since. The book was way better.

"Nothing happened between Cami and me," I tell my sister as she dries her hands. I've got some Neosporin out of one of the drawers and I'm applying it to the gash. The bruise on my jaw isn't as bad as I thought it might be, but I still look kind of rough.

Worse, I look like I got into a fight.

"Really?" Ava arches a brow. "From what I saw on the video, and the fact that she was wearing your jersey yesterday, I'd guess you two were back together."

"We're not together," I say, my voice flat as I screw the lid back on the Neosporin. "I wouldn't lie to you."

"Just…don't even think about having a casual thing with her, Jake. She's not good enough for you. She's not good for anyone," Ava says.

"Did she say anything about me before the game? When you guys were getting ready?" I ask.

"Please. If it has anything to do with you, she makes sure I never hear it. Unless it's something she wants me to take back to you." Ava rolls her eyes. "I hate her."

"Then why are you on the cheer team?"

"Because Mom and Autumn convinced me it would be *fun!*" Ava does a little jump and I crack a smile. "They lied."

"You could quit."

"No way. I'm not a quitter. Besides, Brandy would kill me." Brandy's the cheer coach and health aide at the school. "I like going to all the games. I actually enjoy practice and stunting. And it's fun, dancing during halftime, cheering you guys on from the sidelines. Makes for some great photo ops."

Right. Feels like that's all anyone cares about—the photo opportunities. I'm guilty of it too, but girls are way more into that stuff.

"If you hear Cami talking about me, let me know, okay?" I make my way out of the bathroom, pausing to give Ava a quick shoulder squeeze before I move past her. "Thanks for ripping off the Band-Aids."

"No problem," she calls after me as I head down the stairs.

Since I arrived home, I haven't left my room and it's almost noon. I'm sure Mom is dying to talk to me. She's also probably dying to make me breakfast. It's been a weekend ritual since we were little, and as we all became teenagers, we started coming downstairs later and later. I know it disappoints her, but hey, she still has Beck. He follows her everywhere she goes.

Walking into the kitchen, I spot Beck sitting at the counter, nibbling on a piece of bacon while Mom is standing in front of the stove, monitoring the progress of a giant pancake. "Good morning," she tosses over her shoulder.

"Morning." I'm glad she's not looking at me. Gives me more time to steel myself against her reaction.

Because there's definitely going to be a reaction.

"I heard you moving around up there, so I started making you breakfast. Though really I suppose I should've made you lunch," she teases.

"It's still before noon." Barely.

I reach out and ruffle Beck's hair, and he ducks away from my hand. "How many pieces of bacon have you had so far today?" I ask him.

"Seven," Beck says, his mouth full as he grins up at me.

"He's going to have high blood pressure by the time he's fifteen," I accuse Mom, grabbing a glass and pouring myself some orange juice.

"You sound like your father." She flips the pancake.

My heart sinks. Is he around? I don't want to face him either. He'll definitely figure out what I've been up to. "Where is he anyway?"

"Your father? He went for a run."

Relief floods at me as I settle onto the stool next to Beck. "Can I have two pancakes?" I'm starving.

"I'm gonna go outside!" Beck yells as he climbs off his stool.

"Don't go too far, mister. We have a game to get to!" Mom calls after him as he heads out the door. Beck plays for the youth football league, which means she and Dad will be gone most of the afternoon.

Good. I'll probably sleep the entire time they're gone.

"I'll start the next pancake for you now," Mom tells me as she plates the first pancake. She adds a couple of slices of bacon and turns to hand me my breakfast when her eyes go wide. "Jacob, what happened to you?"

You know it's serious when she calls me by my full name. "I'm fine. Got caught up in a little—roughhousing last night."

Mom's lips go tight as she sets the plate of food in front of me. I drop a slab of butter on top of the pancake, watching as it melts so I don't have to look at her. "Roughhousing, huh? Is that what you're calling it these days?"

I say nothing. Just grab my knife and spread the melting butter everywhere before I pick up the syrup and drizzle it all over my pancake. My stomach growls and I take a bite of bacon before I start cutting up the pancake.

"You're not going to say anything else?" Mom asks me.

"What else is there to say?" I glance up to find she's

glaring at me. I hate disappointing her. It's the worst thing ever, and I know she doesn't like to see me hurt. Imagining me getting into a fight. I've done it before. Sometimes, I have a temper, and when I act like this, she says I give her strong Uncle Owen vibes.

I love my Uncle Owen. He's a retired professional NFL player too, just like Dad. My father is more on the calm side, whereas my uncle can get excited over nothing and everything. When I was a kid, I wanted to be just like him.

I still sort of do.

"Let me look at you," she says quietly as she comes around the counter and stops directly in front of me.

Slowly I lift my head, my gaze meeting hers. Her green eyes are filled with worry as she lightly touches my jaw. "You got into a fight."

More silence. It's just easier than trying to explain myself.

"With who?"

"It doesn't matter." I shake my head.

"I hate that you don't talk to me anymore, Jacob. You used to." Mom pats my cheek, avoiding the cut, but her palm makes contact with the bruise and it hurts like hell. I wonder if she did that on purpose. I grit my teeth and keep quiet. "I also used to think trouble followed you, but now I feel like you create it."

There's no use in arguing with her, because she's probably right. I have a short fuse. I got into a fight in the fifth grade and was suspended, and I wonder sometimes if that was the reason we eventually left the Bay Area and moved up to the town we're in now, far from the city and the giant schools filled with problems.

Small schools are filled with problems too. I had to go to counseling in elementary school, and they even made me see a therapist once a week. My parents were concerned about my anger issues, and how I would sometimes lash out. Once we moved up here, though, I stopped going to therapists. I stopped getting in trouble too. Mostly.

I've got my emotions under control. I have for years now.

But what happened last night sent me over the edge. I don't like it when people make assumptions about me and my dad. I especially don't like it when assholes call me a pussy.

Yeah. That shit sucks.

Mom cleans up the kitchen as I finish my breakfast, both of us silent. I think about what she said, how I used to talk to her. We were close, Mom and me. At certain points in my life, I felt closer to her than I did to my dad. She's easy to talk to and she listens with no judgement, no expectations. Dad tries his best, but there are always expectations there, just beneath the surface. He expects me to do certain things and to behave a certain way, and after a while, that shit gets exhausting.

As I got older, though, I clammed up. Plus, it got awkward. How could I talk to Mom about my friends and what we do? What we say? How we like to party? All the girls who throw themselves at me? The few girls I've actually messed around with? Mom wasn't a huge fan of Cami. I think Mom saw right through her, and now it's even worse, what with the way Ava complains about Cami to Mom on an almost daily basis.

Yeah. It's best that I cut Cami off last night. This would've ended in disaster.

Again.

"I'm going to take a shower," Mom says when she's finished with the kitchen. "If you see your father, let him know we have to leave soon for Beck's game."

"Okay." I scrape the last of the pancake crumbs from my plate with my fork and eat them, then make my way to the sink so I can rinse the plate.

Mom follows after me, slipping her arm around my waist and giving me a one-sided hug. "Please be careful. It's your senior year. You want to enjoy it, not make everything worse."

Easier said than done.

* * *

I'm in my room when Dad knocks on the door then opens it, not bothering to wait for me to say come in. That's not his usual style.

He barges into my room and marches right up to the side of the bed where I'm sitting, his hand going underneath my chin so he can tip my face up and examine it with eyes that look almost exactly like mine.

His are full of anger, though. Anger mixed with concern.

"I saw the videos," he says through tight lips as he turns my head to the side. "I know you were the one who started it."

Some rat bastard on our team must've showed him. You can't trust anyone.

"They got you good," he says, chucking me under the chin and making my teeth snap together before he removes his hand from my face.

I grimace through the pain. "You should see their quarterback."

"Is that the one you hit?"

I nod. "Broke his nose."

It was confirmed on social media late last night. Not that the other QB is going to do anything about it.

"Sorry, can't offer you the praise you're looking for." Dad rests his hands on his hips, scanning my mess of a room. "You need to clean this up."

"Will do."

"And you need to stop the fighting. This doesn't need to be a new trend for the season." He sends me a measured look. "Your mother is worried about you."

I hate worrying her, I really do, but I had the situation under control last night. I still do. Not that I can tell Dad that. "Tell her not to worry."

"Give her nothing to worry about and she won't." He kicks at an empty Nike shoebox, sending it skittering across the floor. "You're not going anywhere the rest of the weekend. You hear me?"

I nod once, my gaze going back to my phone. Not like I had any plans anyway.

"I feel like an asshat telling you that, I hope you know. You're too old for this shit, Jake. You're a freaking senior. You're going to be an adult soon." I'm sure my parents find that prospect terrifying. Well guess what? Sometimes, so do I. "I shouldn't have to remind you to clean up your room."

"I'll take care of it."

He lets out an exasperated breath and I'm hit with guilt. Sometimes I think I'm a disappointment to my parents. Autumn is the overachiever of the family, the dutiful oldest child. Ava is the activist, the one who wants to take care of others and always do what's right. Beck is the adorable baby who can do no wrong in anyone's eyes. All he's gotta do is smile and say something cute and everyone in the house goes *aww!* Myself included.

Me? I'm the dumb jock who'll only get into a good college because of my football skills and the fact that my father is retired NFL. That's it. No other reason.

Maybe those assholes from Mariposa are right. Maybe I wouldn't make it if it weren't for my father.

Grabbing my phone, I open Instagram and hit the search button, typing in the letters:

H

A

N

N

A

H

Of course, she pops right up in the list of other Hannah's that I might know. Her user name is hannahwalsh2626.

And of course, she's got a private account.

Frowning, I squint at her profile pic, trying to figure out what it is. Definitely not a photo of her. Feeling like a dumbass, I take a screenshot and zoom in to see it's some painting of a couple of birds on a tree branch. Their heads are bent close together, as if they're kissing, and I wonder if she painted it.

I wish her account wasn't private. I want to see more photos. I want to look at her and not have to worry about someone else watching me.

We only have a few mutual friends, most of them people I don't really know. My thumb hovers over the blue follow bar. If I hit it, she'll get a notification that I want to add her. Would she add me back?

Shit, I feel like an insecure middle schooler right now. Fuck this.

I toss the phone onto my bed and it lands with a plop facedown. No way can I follow her. She might misinterpret the meaning behind it, when it's really just curiosity that's making me want to do this. I just want to look at her photos. See what she does, what she likes, who she hangs out with.

And then I'll forget all about her.

Yeah. That's it.

HANNAH

"Mom, do you want me to make you dinner?" I call from where I'm sitting at the tiny table in our so-called dining room. Really it's just an extension of the kitchen. I'm on my laptop doing homework on a Saturday night—I know, so pitiful—and Mom is getting ready to leave for work.

"I already had a sandwich," she answers from her bedroom. I can hear her muttering under her breath, and I glance at the clock on my laptop screen. She's going to be late if she doesn't leave soon.

Mom magically appears in the kitchen, going to the refrigerator and pulling out the bag she uses for her lunch. Though really, is it called lunch when your break is at three in the morning? I'm not sure.

She works at the front desk of one of the local hotels, and she's on the graveyard shift. She hates the hours, but it's the only job she can find that pays so well considering her limited experience. She'd been a restaurant server for years before that, and she was tired of always being on her feet, dealing with rude customers and getting awful tips.

Mom misses those tips now, but she appreciates the quietness of her job and the fact that she can sit through most of her shift. I worry about her, though. Dangerous people are out in the middle of the night, but she reassures me that it's pretty safe there. No one comes in unless they're looking for a room, and there's a security guard who patrols the parking lot.

"You already made your lunch?" I ask.

She nods. "I did. And I need to leave or else I'm going to be late. You okay with being alone?"

I am never okay with being alone, but I can't tell her that. She'd quit her job on the spot tonight and that absolutely cannot happen.

"I'll be fine," I tell her with what is hopefully a reassuring smile. "I'm thinking about looking for a part-time job this week."

"No." Mom grabs her black purse that's hanging on a hook near the front door and slips the strap over her shoulder. "You have to concentrate on school."

"It's really no big deal. I don't have any extracurricular activities after school. I can work weekends." I'm in leadership this year, but I don't hold a position. I'm more of a grunt. I actually make most of the posters and banners we put up around school, and I love seeing my work all over campus.

"But then you'll miss football games and whatever else is going on. Isn't homecoming happening soon?"

"Not for a while. In like, a month." I sigh, knowing I'm going to lose this argument tonight. "You should probably get going before you're late."

"Bye! Love you!" She's out the door, and just like that, I'm all alone.

I hate Saturday nights.

I force myself to focus on the essay I need to write for AP

English, but after struggling for almost an hour, I realize the words just won't come. I slam the laptop shut and wander into the kitchen, poking through the cabinets, trying to figure out what I want to eat, even though it's already pretty late, past nine. I come across a sealed pack of generic saltine crackers and the last Cup Noodles in the package.

Score.

A pitiful dinner for one, I muse as I fill the container with water and pop the Cup Noodles in the microwave before I grab a glass and pour myself some orange juice. Another fun Saturday night. I could find something to watch on Netflix— Sophie lets me sign in to her family's account—and start a series or movie while I eat. Then continue watching while wrapped up in my favorite blankets on my bed and my cat Maxine sits curled at my feet.

A far cry from what I was doing last night, that's for sure.

Sophie and I texted earlier, talking about Friday night's events, especially when we saw the videos circulating that people caught of the fight. Jake definitely started it, popping the Mariposa quarterback right in the face. Pretty sure he broke his nose.

The video that bothered me the most was of Cami running up to Jake, calling him baby while she hugged him tight, her cheek resting against his chest. I saw the aggravated expression on his face when she did that, and he pushed her off of him fairly quickly, but still.

It stuck with me. Those two are this close to being together—again—and I can't compete with someone like Cami Lockhart. They were together before. They've probably done all sorts of things together, while I've done absolutely nothing.

Please. Why am I even thinking like this? Because I had a moment in a bathroom with Jake? He was just glad I was there to help him bandage up his wound. That's it.

But I remember the way he looked at me, his gaze guarded when I approached him while he was sitting on the toilet—so romantic, ha. Those long legs of his spread wide as I stood between them. He grabbed my wrist. He touched my thigh. Every time he put his hands on me the air grew thick with tension and I didn't know what to do, what to say. Or how to act.

Maybe it was all in my head. Most likely it was one-sided. I don't like his type anyway. Aggressive jock with a chip on his shoulder, ready to throw down on someone at a moment's notice. Volatile people scare me. My mom's last boyfriend was like that. He always yelled at her, finding fault with everything she did. His constant mental abuse messed her up and she stayed single for a long time after they split. I think his abusive words hurt far more than any punches he could've given her. Bruises fade.

Insults linger.

The microwave beeps and I take the extra-hot cup out carefully, dumping the contents in a bowl and giving myself a steam facial. I grab a fork and the crackers and return to my seat at the table, tearing into the package before I start scrolling through my viewing possibilities for the evening.

A notification sounds on my phone and I pick it up, then immediately drop it with a clatter when I see what the notification says.

Jake Callahan has requested to follow you.

What in the world?

I pick up my phone and send a text to Sophie. **Did Jake Callahan just try to follow you on IG?**

She responds quickly. **Nooooo. Why? Did he follow you?**

Yeah.

OMG maybe he LIKES YOU.

My heart is racing as I respond to her.

No way. He's probably already back together with Cami.

So why is he sending you follow requests when he's supposed to be with Cami? is Sophie's response.

Good question.

Did you already accept it? she asks.

I'm about to respond when I get a FaceTime call from her.

"Don't accept it yet," is the first thing she says.

"Hello to you too," I say just before I shove crackers in my mouth.

"Let him wait. Make it seem like you're super busy. It's a Saturday night. For all he knows, you're out on a date."

"Great idea. As you can see, I'm very, very busy." I flip the camera and give her a scan of my current situation. Sitting at the table with my closed laptop and my exciting dinner. I flip the camera back to my face. "I was trying to write my English essay, but I got stuck."

"I was born stuck," Sophie laments. "I'm so jealous he followed you! I wish Tony would do that."

"He hasn't?"

"No." Sophie shakes her head. I'm so glad she's owning up to her crush. "I'm starting to think he doesn't like me like that."

"He probably does," I tell her, wanting to be encouraging. "Maybe he's just…taking his time."

"Please. He's already moved on." She mock pouts. "It's okay. We'll focus on you and Jake Callahan now."

"There's no me and Jake Callahan now. Or ever. You're projecting your crush idealizations onto me and a guy when we don't even like each other."

"I saw the way you two were looking at each other in that bathroom last night." She raises her eyebrows. "Sparks were flying!"

"Ugh. They were not. I have to go. My ramen is getting cold." She starts to protest, but I end the call. She won't be mad at me for cutting her off either. We do that to each other constantly.

I take my time eating my noodles and crackers. Scroll through Instagram and watch everyone's stories. I watch stories on Snapchat too, until I'm done eating and I've rinsed out my bowl and my glass. I grab my old laptop and head to my bedroom, contemplating taking a shower before I accept Jake's follow request until I finally think, *screw it.*

Going back into IG, I accept his request, send him a follow in return and then leave my phone on the charger by my bed while I go take a quick shower. And I make them quick because I'm all alone almost every evening and what if someone broke into our apartment and hid in my room?

These are thoughts that keep me up at night when my mom is at work. So silly, but I can't help it. We don't live in the best part of town, though it could be worse. Our apartment complex is close to the high school, and I can walk home, which is nice. Most days, I prefer to stay late in the library after school and do my homework. By the time I leave, everyone's gone for the day or they're still at practice. My walk home is quiet, and I don't have to deal with other students driving by and honking or making snide remarks as they drive by.

People can really suck sometimes.

I also make my shower quick tonight because I want to see if Jake already accepted my follow request. By the time I'm back in my bedroom fifteen minutes later with wet hair and my body covered in my favorite Bath and Body Works lotion, I'm a jittery mess.

Checking my notifications, I see I have one.

Jake Callahan accepted your request.

Without hesitation I open Instagram and look at his

profile. They're mostly photos of him playing football. One of last year's team together. A photo of his entire family surrounding his older sister after her graduation ceremony a couple years ago. Another photo of the football team our sophomore year, when they moved Jake up to varsity for playoffs.

How I remember this, I don't know.

The photos actually go way back. There's one of him and his siblings when they're all much younger, along with their mother. She's so beautiful. Long blonde hair and big green eyes, a serene smile on her face as she's surrounded by her four equally beautiful children.

I wonder what that's like, to have such a big family. Both parents who love each other and a giant house, knowing you're well taken care of and fed and you can buy whatever you want, whenever you want it.

I can't imagine a life like that.

Sighing, I set my phone down and sit on the bed with my legs crossed, braiding my hair as I start watching some teen movie about a girl with supernatural powers who hates the world. Sounds fun. Not too scary. I can't watch anything scary when I'm home at night alone. That'll ramp up my anxiety to the point that I could end up at Sophie's house begging to spend the night, and I never like to impose.

Maxine jumps on the bed just as I finish braiding my hair, and I tug my blankets over me, smiling when my cat settles onto my lap. She's ten and a round ball of tabby-and-white fluff. I adore her, and she adores me too. I pet her behind her ears, the soothing sound of her purrs lulling me as I settle deeply into my pillows and watch the movie.

A Snapchat notification pulls me out of my sleepy trance and I check the time: 10:02 p.m. Still a little early for me to consider going to sleep, especially on a Saturday. I glance at my Snapchat notification and my eyes go wide when I see what it says.

Jake Callahan has added you!

What in the world is going on? Why is he following me on all of my social media?

I don't get it.

I open Snapchat and click through until I'm looking at his profile, which doesn't say much—none of them do. I decide to add him back then set the phone back onto my tiny bedside table, my heart pounding. He's checking out my social media. He probably looked at my IG photos, which are mostly boring. Maybe even a little embarrassing, because all they do is showcase how much of my life is dull, especially compared to his.

Another Snapchat notification comes through, and with trembling fingers I pick up my phone to find he's sent me a snap.

I open it to see it's a selfie. He took it with the flash on, and it's a side view of his face. The Dora Band-Aids are gone, and actually, the cut doesn't look as severe as it did the last time I saw it. Plus, the bruise on his jaw isn't that terrible either.

The snap says: **It's not so bad.**

Biting my lower lip, I take a selfie, but make sure it's only from my eyes up. My eyes are my favorite feature. And since I plucked my eyebrows earlier today when I was bored, cleaning them up a little bit, they look pretty good too.

The cut looks a lot better. Dora must've helped.

I send the snap before I second-guess myself.

The movie is still playing and I'm trying to concentrate, but it's hard. My head is filled with way too many questions, every one of them having to do with Jake Callahan. Why is he snapping me? Why is he sending me photos of his damaged yet attractive face? God, if he's some sort of creeper who's looking for topless shots or nudes while bored on a Saturday night, he's barking up the wrong tree.

He snaps me back almost immediately, and I open it with still-trembling fingers, blinking at the new photo he sent me. It's similar to mine, just from the eyes up, and his are *so* beautiful. A glittery blue that almost looks fake, with hints of swirling green. Dark brows furrowed, equally dark hair flopping over his forehead with a little bit of curl.

A sigh escapes me. If I could screen shot this and he'd never know, I'd stare at it for hours. Days.

But Snapchat sends notifications when you screenshot anything, so I'm screwed.

The snap says: **It was Boots.**

Smiling, I press my fingers against my lips, tugging on my lower one with my thumb and index finger while I still stare at his photo for a little bit more. Finally, I take a photo of myself, rolling my eyes and I caught myself mid eyeroll, which is perfect. I type out my response.

Right. Boots made alllll the difference.

I send it and eagerly await his response.

Again he replies, and I open it to find it's half his face now, his nose showing, one eyebrow arched.

I always preferred Swiper.

You would, I snap back and then hit send.

What is my life?

CHAPTER 11

JAKE

What the hell am I doing? Snapchatting with Hannah on a Saturday night, holed up in my bedroom like some sort of loser. Diego and Caleb both hit me up earlier, asking if I wanted to hang out, but I passed. Hanging out is code for finding some alcohol, smoking some weed—something I really don't do—and since Diego's girlfriend is still out of town, they're probably with some girls.

No thanks.

Beck's spending the night at a friend's house. Ava went over to her best friend's house too. I'm the only loser at home, and my parents are currently downstairs watching a movie, cuddled up together on the couch.

Blech.

This is why I'm in my room. Bored out of my mind. Snapchatting with a girl I'm not supposed to like.

She sends me another snap and I don't even hesitate in opening it. I've played those games before. Haven't we all? The girl we like sends us a snap and we wait ten minutes before we open it.

Pathetic.

It's another selfie, and she's starting to show more of her face, which I can appreciate. Her hair is damp and pulled into two tight braids, which is a cute look for her. Her cheeks are rosy and dotted with freckles. Her blue eyes are extra bright, and I stare at her for a while, drinking her in.

She's pretty. She intrigues me.

I have no fucking clue why.

I'm glad your face is healing is what she said to me.

Deciding fuck it, I take a full-on selfie this time, my lips quirked into a bogus smile, though no teeth are showing. Not much in the mood for smiling. I'm still mad over my earlier conversation with Dad. Mad at myself for losing control and hitting that smug fucker at the party last night.

But if I hadn't hit him, I wouldn't have ended up in a bathroom being taken care of by Hannah, so maybe it's a positive, that the fight happened? Is it actually a positive that I had my encounter with Hannah?

I don't know.

Thank you for helping me last night.

She takes our conversation to text, and I wonder if that's because she's uncomfortable with sending me a selfie. **You're welcome. I really am glad you're doing better.**

Thanks.

I contemplate what to say next. I should leave it at this. We've said what's necessary and we don't need to keep talking.

Yet I want to keep talking.

What are you doing? I hit send.

Watching a movie.

Another snap text from Hannah follows the first one.

What are you doing?

Hanging out in my room.

Alone? she asks. **Forget I asked that. It's none of my business.**

A chuckle escapes me and I can't help but smile. **Yeah, I'm alone.**

I thought the great and mighty Jake Callahan never spent his Saturday nights alone.

I decide to be truthful with her. **I usually don't.**

So why are you alone tonight?

I'm mad at myself for the fight. For the way I played that game. And for Cami.

Damn. I'm being really honest with her right now.

You can't change the past.

That's all she says. She doesn't ask any questions, doesn't get all nosy and demand to know what's up with Cami, nothing.

I like that.

Contemplating what to say, I finally type **You're right.**

We talk a little more—I ask her about the movie she's watching. She asks me if I have any homework. The conversation starts to fizzle out and I decide to end it by saying good night.

Good night, she says in return with a sleepy emoji.

See you Monday, I add.

Right. Monday.

* * *

AND THEN IT is Monday and I'm walking down the hall before first period, heading for my locker. I'm tempted to turn away when I see who's waiting there for me, but I may as well get this over with, so I approach my locker with a frown, thankful my friends aren't around to witness this.

"What do you want?" I ask as she moves out of the way so I can turn the door lock.

"Nice to see you too," Cami says snottily. "I wanted to talk to you."

"There's nothing we have to talk about." I tug on the locker handle and it opens with ease. I shove a couple of books inside just as Cami thrusts my jersey toward me, practically nailing me in the face with it.

"I wanted to return this to you."

"Thanks." I take it from her and shove it in my locker.

"My mom washed it already."

"Great." I slam the locker door shut and turn to face her. "I'm surprised you didn't keep it. So you could try to wear it again on Friday."

Her mouth pops open. "Why do you always have be such a dick?"

Good question. Cami brings out my dickish qualities, I guess. "Listen. We had a fun thing a long time ago, and then it fell apart. It's never been a good idea for us to keep trying, yet we keep doing it. We have to quit each other." I pause. "I mean it."

"Okay, whatever you say." She turns and walks away just as the first period bell rings. I watch her retreat, testing myself, checking out her ass, the swing of her hips, but I feel nothing.

Only relief.

Turning, I head toward first period, nodding at people as we pass each other by, my gaze searching. I have no idea what Hannah's schedule is like. I've never noticed her in the halls before. I could've been passing her every day for the last three years, but I couldn't tell you if that actually happened.

I feel like a complete asshole.

I'm about to walk into class when I spot goldish-red hair glinting in the sun. I pause in the doorway, watching as Hannah walks by with her friend Sophie, both of them talking animatedly. They don't notice me, and I'm glad. It allows me to look my fill.

She's wearing a black T-shirt and faded jeans that mold to

her legs and ass. Her hair is pulled into a high ponytail and it swings as she walks. She's not my type. Not at all. I've been a superficial asshole throughout high school who only dates girls that are part of my crowd. The popular crowd.

But I think about how Hannah treated me Friday night. What she said to me Saturday. And I want…

I want to know more.

"Bro, you're blocking the door." Caleb shoves me out of the way, stopping when he sees my face. "Hey, you don't look so busted up after all."

I touch the bruise on my jaw. "Gee, thanks."

"Did you see Womack?" He's the QB for Mariposa Springs. "He looks fucking terrible. His nose is as a big as a tomato. Red as one too."

We both laugh as we head for our desks. I have zero regrets for punching that asshole in the face. He deserved it. And considering it's Monday and he's remained quiet, I figure I'm not getting in trouble over that fight either.

"Eli Bennett posted on his story that he hoped you were coming for him next," Caleb says as we settle into our seats.

"What? Are you serious?" That little fucker.

"Yeah, I think he actually wants to fight you." Caleb shakes his head. "I can almost guarantee we're going to get into a full-blown war with those assholes when we play them at homecoming."

"Bring it," I say, mentally telling myself to calm down. Dad will probably kill me if I start a fight with our number-one rival team. He worked with them last summer at a training camp we all went to. Even Mom, Ava and Beck came with us, and our family stayed at a cabin by this huge lake. It's a Christian camp normally, but they let other organizations rent it out early on in the summer, and my dad led a week-long camp and bonding session for both us and two other teams. Including our rivals.

I thought it was a big bunch of bullshit having to deal with them, but whatever.

Distracted by what Caleb told me, I go through the rest of my morning classes with anger simmering in my gut. I'm also mentally prepping the inspirational speech I want to give my teammates when the coaches aren't around. That usually happens when we first slip into the locker rooms immediately after practice and the coaches are still out on the field cleaning up.

We're gonna fuck the Mustangs up. They won't even know what hit them. Every game leading to that one will just be a practice run.

By lunch, I'm a glowering asshole, but what else is new? I sit with my friends while they talk. Caleb is loud as hell as usual. Diego is going to get in trouble if he keeps shoving his tongue down his girlfriend's throat for everyone to see. Tony is quiet—that's not new—and I can't stop myself from looking around, trying to spot Hannah.

"If you're looking for Cami, she went off campus with her friends. I saw them all pile into a car," Tony says mildly as he takes a sip from his Coke can.

I make a face. "I'm over her."

"Thank God," he says dryly. "Who you looking for then?"

"No one," I say too quickly, just when I spot her.

She's sitting at a table on the far edge of the quad, again with Sophie, along with Marty, Diego's cousin. The wind has picked up, sending little wisps of hair flying all around her face and she keeps batting them away, laughing.

I wish I could hear the sound of her laugh.

Everyone else at my table ignores me, eventually even Tony, and I prefer it. They think I'm pissed about Cami and the fight and the upcoming games, and that's perfect. Let them believe that.

It's partially true, but that's not the reason I want to be left alone.

By seventh period, I feel like I'm going to explode. I enter the art classroom and settle in at my table, glad there's at least one other senior and a few juniors in this class so I'm not completely surrounded by obnoxious freshmen. I make small talk with the other people sitting at my table, mostly me asking questions about our upcoming project and when it's due, when Hannah enters the room.

And purposely avoids my table.

Huh.

I watch as she goes the long way around the room to end up at Mrs. Sanborne's desk. I'm still sort of pissed at that woman for not helping out my situation, but I assume she's stuck. Kinda like I'm stuck.

But maybe it won't be so bad, being stuck in this class with Hannah.

The bell rings and Mrs. Sanborne rises to her feet, clapping her hands together. "Okay guys, we're going to work on pencil drawings this week. I'm going to teach you some new techniques and I want you to apply them to what you plan on drawing. Hannah is going to hand out sketchpads to everyone. You all have pencils, yes?"

A couple of hands shoot up saying that no, they don't have pencils, and I dig one out of my backpack, anticipating Hannah coming around with the sketchpads. She goes to every single table, running to the back counter where the pads are stacked in between, until finally she's at mine, which she saved for last. She hands me my sketchpad last too, keeping her gaze averted as she says, "Here you go."

"Hey Hannah." I take it from her, making sure my fingers brush against hers.

She snatches her hand away like I burned her, her big blue eyes meeting mine. She looks scared. "Hi."

"Thanks." I hold up the sketchpad.

"You're welcome." She runs away.

"Damn, bro, first you push Cami off you and now you're scaring away that loser? Are you wearing girl repellant or something?"

I glance up to see a guy sitting across from me with an amused look on his face. His name is Rob Schaffer.

He's a complete dick.

"Don't call her a loser," I say through clenched teeth.

Rob holds his hands up in front of him. "Whoa whoa, my friend. Calm down. No need to get hostile."

I hate it when people tell me to calm down. It actually makes me feel less calm. "No need for you to call Hannah a loser," I say. "And I'm definitely not your friend. So you can fuck off."

The silence at our table is tense and Rob glares at me for a moment, fuming. I glare right back, like I don't have a care in the world.

"I don't need this shit. I don't care if you're the star quarterback or not. No need to act like such an asshole." Rob raises his hand and Mrs. Sanborne runs over to our table, a harried expression on her face. "I don't want to sit next to him." He points at me.

Mrs. Sanborne glances in my direction before returning her attention to Rob. "Why not? What's the problem?"

"He called me a motherfucker and said he's going to beat my ass if I don't shut up," Rob says, lying through his teeth.

My lips part. Is he serious right now? "That's not true. I didn't say any of that," I tell the teacher.

But the look she sends me says she doesn't believe me. Figures. "Mr. Callahan, do you need to go see Mrs. Adney?"

"No," I retort. No way do I need to talk to the vice principal. I mean, I like her. She's always been cool to me, even when I've gotten into a little trouble. But with this particular situation, I'm completely innocent. Rob is making shit up.

"I refuse to sit next to him." Rob shakes his head, his expression downright fearful as he pushes his chair out, creating more distance between us. "I don't want him at our table."

The other people at the table murmur their support for Rob.

What the actual fuck?

"Jake. Come with me." Sanborne waves a hand, and I grab my backpack and sketchpad, sending one last long look at Rob before following her to a small table that's in the back of the room, slammed up against the wall. "Do you mind sitting here?" she asks with a wince.

"What, am I under quarantine?" This is all sorts of fucked up.

"This is the table my TA uses to work on projects for me on occasion. She's quiet and mostly keeps to herself. I'm sure you two will get along just fine. Right?" Sanborne sends me a pointed look.

"Absolutely." This couldn't have worked out better if I tried.

I settle into the chair that faces the front of the classroom and drop my backpack on the floor by my feet, then flip open the sketchpad to a blank page. I'm listening to the teacher discuss the various techniques for drawing faces with pencil, but my attention span is shot to hell when Hannah approaches the table, coming to a full stop when she sees me.

"What are you doing here?" she asks.

"Sanborne put me here," I answer with a little shrug.

"Why aren't you at your table?" She glances over her shoulder before returning her attention to me.

"Because Rob said I called him a motherfucker and threatened to beat his ass," I mutter with disgust.

Her eyes go wide. "Oh my God. Did you really do that?"

"Hell no," I whisper.

"Are you two okay back there?" Sanborne asks.

Everyone swivels around to look at us, and I see Hannah's cheeks go red with embarrassment. "We're fine," she answers weakly.

"Ohhh-kay," Sanborne says, her voice full of doubt.

I just glare at everyone until they turn back around and face Sanborne once more. With the exception of Rob, who smirks in my direction, looking mighty pleased with himself before he returns his attention to our teacher.

I wish I *could* beat his ass. He'd deserve it.

Hannah settles into the chair closest to mine, a sketchpad in her hands. She flips through it, and I can see page after page of drawings, some of them so realistic I want to tell her to stop so I can really check them out, but I keep quiet. I'm not about to bring attention to myself again. I don't want to get kicked out of the class.

I freaking need this class.

By the time Sanborne is done talking and telling all of us to try our hand at drawing, I feel like I'm about to burst with my need to talk to Hannah. "You mad at me?"

Her head bent, she's concentrating on the movements of her pencil across the paper. "What?" she asks distractedly.

"Hannah." She glances up at me when I say her name, those pretty blue eyes extra wide. "Are you mad at me?"

She frowns. "Why do you think I'm mad at you?"

"Oh, I don't know. Maybe it's the way you've avoided me since class started," I tell her. "I was the last person you gave a sketchpad to."

"Maybe I saved the best for last?" she says weakly.

I don't smile. I don't say a word. This usually works for me.

But Hannah's quiet too. And stubborn. I can tell by the jut of her chin. The way she studies me, her expression blank.

Damn. She's good.

"Are you only going to talk to me on Snap, but not at school?" I ask, my voice low.

She blinks rapidly, like she can't believe what I just said. "*No.*"

"That's what it seems like."

A sigh escapes her and she drops her head, refocusing on the sketchpad. "I don't know how to talk to you."

"Huh?"

"In person." She looks up, then immediately looks away. "I'm an idiot."

A smile starts to curl my lips and I immediately tell myself to stop. "You're not an idiot."

"I'm sorry if I hurt your feelings," she murmurs morosely.

"You're forgiven."

She lifts her head when I say that, her plump lips turned upward, and I'm hit with a sudden flash of wanting to kiss her.

Yeah. No. Not going to happen.

"Great, thanks so much," she returns, then gestures toward my blank sketchpad. "You better get started. She's going to want to check out your technique."

"I've got the best technique in this school, don't you know?" I can't help but say, and Hannah's cheeks turn pink again.

She's really cute when she blushes.

"Don't be a perv," she says, grabbing my discarded pencil and pointing it toward me. "Start drawing."

"Do I have to?" I slide my fingers onto hers, my thumb curling around hers before I pluck the pencil from her grip.

"Y-yes. You do." Her voice is shaky, and I wonder if my touch affected her.

I hope it did. All I have to do is look at her and she affects me.

Whatever's happening between us is confusing as hell.

"I didn't listen to a word the teacher said," I tell Hannah, and she scoots her chair closer to mine, launching into the same lecture Sanborne did, almost word for word.

I listen to the rhythm of Hannah's speech, the excited way she speaks. She loves art, I can tell, and she genuinely wants to help me. I stare at her mouth, the way it moves, how her front teeth protrude the slightest bit, giving her this sexy overbite. I'm fucking entranced, caught up in her spell and when she finishes lecturing me with the faintest smile on her face, all I can do is smile in return.

"Oh. So you do smile," she says softly.

I turn it into a frown. "No I don't."

She laughs, and I soak up the sound.

It's just a pretty as I thought it would be.

CHAPTER 12

HANNAH

I cannot believe Jake Callahan is sitting at my table. I can't believe he's flirting with me either. I must be imagining it. At one point I'm fairly positive I'm dreaming. Crap, I even pinch myself on the inside of my wrist, so hard I whimper a little, to see if this is all real.

Yep. It sure is.

The way he touched me when he took the pencil, it was almost—dirty. Like my entire body erupted in tingles when his fingers brushed against mine, those tingles settling between my legs. And no boy has ever made me feel like that. Ever.

All over a freaking *pencil*.

And that smile. He wiped his face clean of it when I called him out, but it was there for the briefest moment, and oh God, he was heartbreakingly gorgeous. He has perfectly straight teeth. Nice lips. He could be a model. Like, he is the most beautiful boy I have ever seen in my whole life.

No way is he interested in me. He's just toying with me. Maybe he likes having fangirls.

If you would've asked me a few days ago if I was a Jake

Callahan fangirl, I would've said no, now I want to sign up and have an official fan club card and everything.

This is what he does to me.

"You should probably get to work," I suggest to him when he still hasn't drawn anything on his paper.

"Okay." He starts sketching and I watch him for a moment, but I can't figure out what he's drawing, so I focus on my own sketch. Sanborne is wandering around the class, stopping at tables and checking out everyone's work, and I assume she doesn't need my help.

So I stay with Jake. Secretly drawing him. I'm not that good with faces, but I need to practice, and what better subject to practice with? Sophie is over me sketching her and so is Marty. I've sketched my mom a couple of times, but she always gets embarrassed.

"What are you drawing?" Jake asks after we're quiet for a few minutes.

I bite my lower lip for a moment before I admit, "You." I dare to look up at him to find he appears extremely pleased with my answer.

And that's not a look Jake Callahan wears normally.

"Can I see?"

"Absolutely not." I shift my sketchpad away from him. "Besides, I'm not even close to being done."

"I want to see it when you're finished," he says.

I ignore his request. "What are you drawing?" I ask him, bracing myself for his answer.

"Rob." He doesn't look at me as scratches his pencil across the paper, his brows furrowed in concentration. "I'm going to make him look like the ugliest monster you've ever seen."

I press my fingers to my mouth to contain my laughter. It's not nice, what Jake is doing. But it wasn't nice what Rob did to him either, so I can't really blame Jake for his actions.

When Mrs. Sanborne stops by our table, I start talking

before she does. "Is there anything you need me to do?" I don't want her thinking I'm slacking off. She told me earlier that she didn't have anything for me to do today, so that's why I'm sketching with the rest of the class.

"Keeping Mr. Callahan occupied is what I need most from you right now," she says pleasantly as she glances over Jake's shoulder. "Interesting start you have there."

"Thanks," he says, never lifting his head to acknowledge her. "I'm glad you like it."

"Uh, what is it?"

Again, I press my lips together to keep from laughing.

"You'll see," he says mysteriously.

Mrs. Sanborne sends me a pointed look before she moves on.

"Have you ever sketched anything before?" I ask once she's gone.

"When we were younger, yeah. But it was just school stuff," he answers, still focused on the sketchpad. "I was never any good at it."

"I think everyone can draw if they at least know the basics," I tell him.

"Says the girl who is an actual artist," he adds.

I stare at him, wondering how he knows I'm an artist, and if he can feel me looking at him.

"I checked out your IG," he eventually says, still drawing. Still concentrating. "Figured most of the work you shared was your own."

Oh, right. "It was," I say softly, both panicked and touched that he so thoroughly examined my Instagram photos. Though I assumed he had. That's exactly what I did to him. I shrug, trying to play off any talent I might have. "I'm okay."

"You're better than okay." He lifts his head, his intense blue gaze meeting mine. "You're actually really good."

My face heats and now I'm the one who can't look at him. "Thank you."

"Is that what you're going to study in college?" I glance up to find he's still watching me. "Art?"

"Oh, no. That's not practical. What can I do with an art degree?" Absolutely nothing. Mom and I already talked about this. I need to study something worthy of my time. I've considered being a nurse. Mom really wants me to be a doctor, but the thought of being in school for that long…no. Can't do it.

I don't know what to do. And I hate that I'm expected to have my future all figured out before I graduate high school. I'm not even eighteen yet. How am I supposed to know what I want my lifelong career to be? Some people have their lives all figured out, but I'm definitely not one of them.

"I'm sure there's lots you can do," Jake says. "Have your own art gallery?"

"Impossible," I tell him, shaking my head.

He leans in closer to me, so close I can smell him. Pine and something else I can't quite put my finger on. "Anything's possible if you want it bad enough."

It's easy for him to say those sorts of things. He doesn't know what it's like, to have no money. And while I know if I work hard for something, I could succeed, I don't have the advantages that he has. Never having to worry about money would make my life choices that much easier.

"I suppose," I say, instead of giving him an info dump of my concerns and worries. He doesn't care. And besides, I don't trust him. Worse, I don't trust the way I feel when I'm around him.

He makes me yearn, and that feeling is completely foreign to me.

Time goes by way too fast and then the final bell is ringing. School's over. Sophie has dance class and I know she's already running to the parking lot so she can hop in her car and leave. Marty is in cross-country, so now he's always busy after school.

No more after school stops at Pete's anymore.

Me? I'm on my own, hiding out in the library.

I slowly put away my stuff in my backpack, and I get the sense Jake is maybe…waiting for me? Weird. "Don't you have to go to practice?" I ask.

He shrugs his backpack over his shoulder. "Don't have to be there for another twenty minutes."

"Oh." I slow my movements, gesturing toward Mrs. Sanborne. "I need to talk to her before I go."

His expression blanks, like he just slipped a mask over his face. "Got it," he bites out. "See ya."

He leaves before I can say another word.

Hurriedly I shove the rest of my things in my backpack, annoyed by his reaction. Why did he just bail on me? Why was he waiting for me in the first place? I didn't want to go with him anyway, if that was his plan. He'd probably try to walk me out to the parking lot, and I don't have a car. I'd feel like a complete loner if I told him I was going to the library, and he'd most likely take pity on me.

I don't want his pity. I don't want his attention at all, if I'm being real. He's a distraction I don't need.

Sure you don't.

Ignoring the taunting voice in my head, I exit the classroom, only to find Jake leaning against the wall.

Like he was waiting for me.

"I thought you had to talk to the teacher." His words are like an accusation.

"I thought you had practice," I toss back at him as I start walking. The art room is all by itself on campus, and there's no one really around us at the moment, though I can see everyone walking just down the hill from where we're standing. Our campus is sprawling, almost one hundred acres, and it can be easy to find a spot where no one else is nearby.

But there are always eyes watching. And ears listening. Something I need to remember.

He falls into step beside me, like he wants to continue our argument. "You lied to me."

I come to a stop, as does he. "What do you want from me?"

He's frowning. "What do you mean?"

"I mean, what are you doing, Jake? You've never even looked twice at me for the last three years, then out of nowhere, you ask me to wear your jersey." I stare at him, narrowing my eyes. "Why did you ask me?"

Sniffing, he looks away, his jaw going tight. "It doesn't matter."

"Oh, but it does." It so does.

"Why did you help me after the fight?" he throws back at me.

"Because you were hurt."

"That's the only reason?" He raises his brows, crossing his arms so that his biceps bulge. He's muscular without being too bulky, and I wonder what it would feel like, having those strong arms wrapped around me. Protecting me. "Most girls want to get close to me for all kinds of reasons."

This boy infuriates me. "Well, I'm not most girls."

I sound like every girl in a sappy rom-com movie, swear to God.

"No, you are most definitely not," he says, scanning me from the top of my head to the tips of my toes.

The tingles are back, sweeping over me like his gaze, and I'm instantly annoyed at my reaction. Who does he think he is? God's gift to teenage girls? I don't think so.

Okay, maybe I think so, but I'm too mad at him right now to really believe it.

"If you think I've got some raging crush on you, you're wrong." I turn on my heel and start walking, heading for the library.

He follows after me, like he's a glutton for punishment. "I don't know if I believe you."

"You're the one who added me on Instagram first," I remind him from over my shoulder, which is such a stupid thing to say.

"You're the one who kept talking to me."

I whirl on him, glaring. "You're the one who talked to me first!"

"You could've left me on read."

"You could've left *me* on read," I retort.

This conversation is ridiculous. There are no other words for it. We're fighting over who spoke to who first? Really?

"Jake!"

We both turn to see a couple of his teammates watching us down the hill, in front of Adams hall, confusion written all over their faces. I'm sure they're boggled by us talking. Arguing. Whatever you want to call it.

"What?" Jake calls out to them.

"Practice is gonna start soon," one of them says.

"I know that," he answers irritably.

"We're waiting for you." This is from Caleb, who's sneering at me like I'm a pubic hair he found in his sandwich. I send him a dirty look and he holds my stare until I'm the one who looks away first. Diego stands next to him, and he's glaring at me too. The only reason he doesn't like me is because I'm such good friends with Marty. We've barely spoken five words to each other in all the years we've been in school together. "Let's go."

Jake glances over at me, not saying a word, and I lift my chin, glaring at him in return. This goes on for what feels like an eternity, but probably only lasts all of a minute, before he turns and jogs toward where his friends are waiting for him. The moment he gets close, it's like they draw him into their circle, surrounding him, absorbing him, Caleb's gaze meeting mine once more before he dismisses me with a single shake of his head. It's a reminder that Jake belongs with them.

Not me. Never me.

I never believed it in the first place, but their message is loud and clear.

I'm not good enough for Jake Callahan.

CHAPTER 13

JAKE

*P*ractice is a nightmare. The coaches make us condition harder than usual for a Monday after a game, and for whatever reason, I feel out of shape. Out of breath. Before I even get a chance to put my helmet on, someone's tackling me. A little shit from the JV team knocks me to the ground face first, making the bruise on my jaw throb with pain. I jump to my feet with my fists curled, ready to beat his scrawny ass, but Dad comes running over and somehow ends up between us before I can do any real damage.

He pulls me away. Gives me a lecture. Threatens to suspend me from the upcoming game, which secretly scares the shit out of me. No way can I miss a game. Not right now.

But still, that kid got lucky. He appeared ready to shit his pants. He also apologized profusely over and over, until I finally told him to shut the fuck up, which he did.

Still don't know how he knocked me to the ground, but whatever.

Can't worry about it.

Once practice was over, I was too tired to give my

planned speech, so I trash canned the idea. A few of the guys were talking about the fight Friday night while we were getting changed in the locker room, and how Eli Bennett is basically asking for us to fuck him up by constantly taunting us—me—on social media.

I agree, but don't chime in. What's the point?

"We play them in little over a month," Diego says as he shoves his T-shirt over his head. "Until then, every team is just a practice run until we can do them in."

I had the same exact thought.

"The Mustangs don't stand a chance," Caleb crows just before he starts doing this weird dance move, circling his hand above his head like he's about to throw a lasso. "Giddy up, purple ponies, and get the fuck outta here!"

Our rival team's colors are purple and gold. For fun, we call them the purple ponies instead of mustangs, which is their mascot. The year Ash Davis was our quarterback—he's also my older sister's boyfriend—he brought a My Little Pony (purple) pinata to the team dinner and we beat that thing to shreds.

It was so satisfying.

Even more satisfying? We beat them out on the field the next night. Didn't even allow them a chance to score.

"Maybe we should get through all the upcoming games first before we start shit talking the Mustangs," I tell them, and both of my friends turn to gape at me.

"What the hell, Jake? Eli is threatening your ass daily on his Snapchat stories and you don't care?" Diego asks incredulously. "Remember what he did to you with Cami?"

How can I forget? It's burned in my brain forever. But here's the deal: I'm not with Cami anymore. I don't care about her. So I don't care anymore that she fucked Eli behind my back either.

"Water under the bridge," I say, grabbing my practice duffel out of the locker before I slam the door shut.

Caleb reaches out, trying to rest his hand across my forehead. "You sick, dude? Got a fever?"

I slap his hand away. "Don't touch me."

"It's the girl. It's all her fault," Diego says, his voice low. He's frowning. In fact, he looks really pissed off.

"What girl? The redhead? The one who turned him down?" Caleb asks, pointing at me. "Like he gives a shit about Hannah."

The anger rises and I want to tell him to shut up, but I clamp my lips together to keep from saying something I might regret.

"Why were you with her after school, bro?" Clearly, Diego doesn't approve. Which makes no damn sense.

"She's the TA in my art class," I tell him. "We were leaving at the same time."

"Uh huh." Diego sounds like he doesn't believe me, which I find infuriating. I turn on him, wishing he'd just come right out and say what's bothering him.

"Aren't you the one who told me I needed to chill? And that I also needed to get laid?" I ask Diego.

He scoffs. "Not with that chick. Like she'd let you touch her. She might let you feel her up, but that's about it. She's got *virgin* written in pink neon lights across her forehead."

Huh. Never really thought about it, but I don't doubt that Hannah's a virgin. Honestly, that's kind of hot. I could teach her a thing or two...

"Nothing wrong with having a virgin every once in a while," Caleb says, a giant grin on his face. "Plenty of virgins will let you do all sorts of dirty, nasty things to them while they save themselves for Jesus."

"You're an idiot," I tell him, shaking my head with disgust.

"What? It's true! Remember Samantha Groves?" When

both Diego and I nod, he continues, "Before she moved last year, she let me do all *kinds* of stuff to her. I stuck my dick in pretty much every hole she's got, with the exception of her pussy. She kept that thing locked up tight."

I really don't want to hear him brag about how he took poor Samantha Groves' virginity in every which way but the one they think counts.

"So you stuck your dick in her ear? Her nose?" Diego asks, his expression one-hundred percent serious.

Caleb bursts out laughing. "I bet she would've let me if I asked."

"Samantha doesn't matter. What matters is this Hannah chick and how she's all wrong for Jake," Diego says, turning his attention onto me. "You should leave her alone."

"Why?" I stand up straighter, staring down at Diego. I've got a good two inches on him. Maybe even three. "What's it matter to you?"

"She's not your type. She wouldn't fit in with our group," Diego explains, though it's not much of an explanation, if you ask me. "She's a loser. I don't like her."

"Oh, and since *you* don't like her, I'm supposed to fall in line and do whatever you say? I don't think so." I grab my bag and start to leave the locker room, irritation making me walk faster. Don't know who died and made Diego our overlord, but he can go suck a bag of dicks for all I care.

They both call my name but I ignore them, and they don't bother chasing after me either, which is a relief. I'm sick and tired of everyone's shit today. Even Hannah's. That fight we got into right after school was pointless. But she *did* lie to me. Why? It was like she didn't want to talk to me once class was over, and really?

That kind of hurt.

Shoving my weenie-ass thoughts into the darkest corner of my brain, I make my way toward the parking lot, jump into my truck and fire it up. I pull out of the lot before I catch a glimpse of any of my friends, desperate to escape. I don't want to talk to any of them. Practice sucked. I'm sure my dad has a few choice words for me. He's probably pissed over the interaction I had with that lameass freshman.

I'm disappointing everyone right now, even myself.

And I don't like it.

Driving down the road away from the school, I catch a figure walking along the left side of the road, reddish-gold ponytail swinging, and I slow down a little.

It's Hannah. I know it is.

Since the streets are pretty much abandoned, I hit the brakes until I'm crawling, keeping pace with her as she continues to walk. I realize she has ear buds in, her gaze is focused straight ahead, and I'm tempted to honk, but I'd probably scare the shit out of her, so I don't. I just…wait.

Wait for her to notice me.

And she does. Eventually she turns her head to the right to find me driving along beside her, and her eyes go wide before she glances over her shoulder. I'm sure other cars are making their approach from the school parking lot. I'd bet at least one of them is being driven by a friend and teammate, but at this moment I don't care.

I roll my window down. "You still mad at me?"

She nods, staring straight ahead.

"Want a ride?"

"No," she says, still not looking at me.

"I'll follow beside you until you let me drive you home." Why am I doing this? Why do I torture myself with her?

Because you like her, you dumb fuck. The fact that Diego says you shouldn't just makes you want her that much more.

The realization hits me like a punch to the face.

"I live right up the street." She gestures ahead of herself.

"Come eat with me then," I suggest. I had zero plans on

grabbing food before I head home. I know Mom and Dad planned on barbecuing steaks tonight, and right now, that sounds fucking delicious. I'm starving.

But if I have to eat a burrito from Taco Bell in order to spend more time with Hannah, I'll make the sacrifice.

"No thank you," she says crisply, her sexy-as-fuck mouth forming into a pout.

Yeah. That's my favorite thing about her. That mouth. It's the stuff of fantasies. Specifically one of me imagining those lips wrapped tight around my dick and swallowing it whole.

"Come on, Hannah. Let me buy you Starbucks at least." I'm stubborn, but so is she. I kind of like it, sick bastard that I am.

She stops. I hit the brakes hard, my tires squealing. "Starbucks?"

"Yeah." I nod.

Watching me closely, she murmurs, "This changes nothing. I'm still mad at you."

Her stubbornness is a total turn on. I tilt my head to the side. "Get in."

Hannah dashes across the road, a car honking at her as it passes by in the opposite direction, and she climbs into my truck, slamming the door hard. She settles her fine ass into the passenger seat, glancing around the interior with wide eyes. "This is really nice."'

"It's brand new." My parents gave it to me at the beginning of the summer.

"It smells good."

"Like me?" I ask, teasing her.

Seriously, I'm teasing her. Who the hell am I?

"No, like new car smell." She smiles serenely and I gun the engine like the show-off teenage guy I am.

The truck jerks forward, Hannah's head knocking back against the seat as I tear off down the street. I turn the corner way too fast, my tires squealing even louder this time before I press hard on the gas and punch through the green light. It turns yellow in the middle of the intersection and I swear I hear a little scream escape from her mouth.

I'm a rude motherfucker for doing this to her, but sometimes it's kind of fun to drive like a total ass through town.

As long as there aren't any cops around.

Within minutes we're pulling into the Starbucks parking lot and we have a decision to make. "Drive thru or go inside?"

"Drive thru please," Hannah says primly, folding her hands in her lap.

Guess she doesn't want to get caught with me either.

"What do you want?"

"Um, hold on…" She grabs her backpack from the floorboard and starts digging around in the small front pocket, pulling out two crumpled dollar bills. "Pretty sure I have enough for a tall…"

I rest my hand on her arm, halting her search. "Whatever you want, whatever size you want, get it. My treat."

Her skin is soft. Electricity seems to flow from my fingertips into her skin and the air grows heavy between us.

She lifts her head, those beautiful blue eyes meeting mine. I could stare at her for hours, right here in the Starbucks drive thru line. She makes me want to forget everything and just focus on her.

"I don't want to be your charity case," she says defensively.

I make a noise. "I'm buying you a coffee and that makes you my charity case? Come on, Hannah. I'm doing this because I'm trying to earn your forgiveness."

She licks her lips and holy shit, my dick actually twitches beneath my shorts. More fantasies hit me. Every one of them having to do with her mouth on whatever part of my body she'd like to explore first.

"I'll pay next time," she says, her voice low. "I'm trying to find a job."

I don't think Hannah's family has much money. I wonder if that has anything to do with Diego's dislike for her. What, so she's poor? Ash Davis came from fucking nothing and he was one of the best quarterbacks we've ever had at this school. He's kicking ass at Fresno State and plenty of NFL coaches are currently eyeing him.

Money doesn't matter. Hell, Diego's family is not what I would consider wealthy. Not that I care. He's being a complete hypocrite.

I push all thoughts of my friends out of my mind and instead, focus on the girl sitting next to me.

"No problem," I tell her, not wanting her to get all worked up over an overpriced coffee. "Tell me your order."

"Um." She dips her head, a smile teasing the corner of her lips. "I want a venti iced caramel macchiato, low fat milk, upside down, with extra caramel."

"Low fat, extra caramel, that makes sense." I'm teasing her again. She lifts her head, brows wrinkled in confusion, but I'm sure I don't look as scowly as usual so her expression visibly relaxes.

"What are you getting?" she asks, but I don't answer. It's my turn to pull up to the screen and tell the barista our order. I rattle off the specifics of Hannah's drink, getting them all right, and then I request a venti ice water.

"No coffee for you?" Hannah asks after I roll up the window.

"Nah." I don't need to drink it all the time like most of the girls I know do.

"Then why'd you offer to bring me here?" she asks softly.

"I wanted to get you into my truck," I tell her honestly.

"Oh, so you're like a pervert who offers the little kids candy to get them into your creepy van," she says, her voice light, her lips still curved upward.

"Yeah. That's it. That's me. I'm a complete perv who'll abduct you with promises of venti macchiatos with extra caramel." I'm so close to smiling, it almost happens. But then the car behind us honks and I realize I need to drive forward. So I do.

"My friends were dicks to you earlier," I tell Hannah once we've come to a stop.

"You were kind of a dick to me too," she says as she drops her backpack onto the floorboard.

This girl doesn't hold back. At all. "Yeah. Uh. Sorry about that." I'm not one to apologize, because most of the time I'm not sorry for my actions. Oh, I punched you in the nose and broke it? Not sorry. I called you an asshole because you are in fact, a total asshole? Yeah, not gonna apologize for that either.

But I feel bad for what my friends did to Hannah. It was rude. And she's right.

I was rude to her too.

"They don't like me," she says, her voice very matter of fact.

"They just don't know you," I start, but I go silent when she sends me a pointed look.

"I don't think they want to know me, and that's fine. I don't want to know them either." She laces her fingers together, wringing them like she's all stressed out. "They think I'm a joke."

"No, they don't." I think of how Diego called her a loser, and it makes me angry on her behalf.

Of course, just last week I thought the same thing. Offended that she didn't want to wear my jersey, which is lame.

"They dared you to ask me to wear your jersey. Like some sort of prank or whatever." Her solemn expression is unwavering when she turns it on me. "I'm a joke to them."

I give her all of my attention, letting the words come out of me without hesitation. "You're not a joke to me."

The car ahead of us drives away and I pull up to the drive thru window, holding out a twenty before the barista can give me the total. It's some chick who graduated last year, and when she sees my face, she goes into instant flirt mode. "Jake, hiiiiii! How are you?"

"Good." I nod, wishing she'd stop looking at me and make my change.

"How's football?"

"It's all right." I shrug.

She stares at me, the twenty still clutched in her hand, her glossed lips curled into an inviting smile. "You're looking good."

Her tone is suggestive, her expression inviting as she studies me.

"My change, please?" I nod toward my cash pinched between her fingers.

"Oh! Right. Sorry." She taps a few buttons on the register and the drawer opens. I can feel Hannah watching me, boring holes into my back, and I'm sure she's not happy about the flirtation.

Should I tell her it happens a lot? And how none of those girls matter to me whatsoever?

Hannah probably wouldn't believe me.

The barista—I can't remember her name—hands me my change and then grabs the cup of ice water from the counter, offering it to me. "Here you go. Your macchiato will be done in a minute."

I hope it's less than a minute. I don't think I can take much more of this one-sided conversation.

But thankfully the windows slide shut, cutting off the girl and the noise from within the Starbucks, and I breathe a sigh of relief.

"You know Meghan?" Hannah asks.

Ah. Right. That's her name. "Not really," I admit.

"She acted like she knew you."

"They all act that way," I tell Hannah, taking a sip of my water before I offer it to her. "Thirsty?"

"I'll wait."

Damn. I was hoping to see her wrap those sexy lips around my straw.

The windows slide back open and I turn to see Meghan holding the venti drink toward me. I take it from her. "Thanks," I say as I hand it to Hannah.

"You're welcome! You should call me sometime. I'll add you on Snap!" Meghan slams the windows shut before I can say anything else.

"Jesus," I mutter under my breath as I pull out of the drive thru and turn my truck into a parking spot not too far from the building. "How's your drink?"

Hannah takes a sip and I watch, entranced. Seriously, what the fuck is wrong with me that this girl has me so wrapped up in her? It's bizarre. "It's delicious. Do you think she spit in it?"

I bark out a sharp laugh, the sound rusty. "I hope not."

"She said you should call her sometime and I'm sitting in the truck right next to you." Hannah shakes her head, still sipping on her drink.

I'm still staring at her too. "Actually...I don't think she noticed you."

Her mouth drops open. I think I offended her. "Why? Because she was too hypnotized by your good looks?"

"You think I'm good looking?" I grab onto what she said, desperate to change the subject.

She says nothing. Just raises her brows.

I shrug. "I do have that effect on girls."

"Egotistical much?"

Leaning back in my seat, I kick my legs out, stretching my torso. "Just being real."

Hannah's gaze sweeps over me, and I know she's checking me out. I'm kind of sweaty from practice and I need a shower more than anything, but she doesn't seem to mind. "I don't know if I find your arrogance healthy or off putting."

"I feel the same way about your bluntness," I toss back at her.

"You think I'm blunt?"

"You have no problem telling me what you really feel."

"Huh." She chews on the end of her straw, then takes yet another sip of her macchiato. "This is really good, by the way. The extra caramel makes it perfect."

"Glad you're enjoying it."

"Thank you."

"You're welcome."

"Even though you basically kidnapped me."

"You were perfectly willing once I said the magic word," I remind her. I wonder what she would do if I told her I wanted to kidnap her for real. Like, just for a few hours. Maybe take her up to the lake. Go for a little hike. Find a secluded spot surrounded by pine trees where we can talk and I can stare at her mouth for a while without having to worry if we're surrounded by other people. Just me and her. Maybe I'd even kiss that mouth.

Bet she'd tell me to go to hell if I tried.

CHAPTER 14

HANNAH

I check the time on the truck's dashboard. It's almost six. I stayed at the library way longer than usual, only because I was doing research on a history project and I was on a roll. I didn't want to stop myself and lose the momentum, so I stayed until the librarian had to kick me out.

Of course Jake saw me walking home. And of course he somehow convinced me to get into his truck and bought me my favorite coffee from Starbucks.

I don't understand what's happening between us, but I'm mentally preparing myself not to get my hopes up. Just savoring each tiny moment as they come my way and stashing them deep in my memory banks so I can pull them back out and marvel over the fact that for a short time in my life, Jake Callahan seemed to be interested in me.

Weird.

"I should head back home," I tell him, sucking the last of my macchiato from the cup. "I need to make dinner."

"You can cook?"

I shrug. "Sort of. I'm not that great, but I like to do it for my mom before she goes to work."

"Where does she work?"

"At the Gateway Inn. She manages the front desk."

Jake's frowning. He's adorable when he frowns. He's adorable when he smiles, though that doesn't happen often. He's adorable when he's just sitting there staring off into space. Though I'm sure not many people would use that particular word to describe him. He has a bit of a reputation around school.

As a total asshole.

"The hotel at the end of town? Is that what you're talking about?" When I nod, he continues, "What time does she go to work?"

"Nine o'clock."

"At night?" He sounds horrified.

I nod again. "She works the graveyard shift."

"So your dad's home."

Slowly I shake my head, not necessarily wanting to reveal these tiny details of my life, but… "I haven't seen my dad since I was little. I don't really remember him."

"You've got a big brother at home, right? Or a sister?"

"I have an older brother, but he's in the Navy."

"You're telling me you're at home alone then? All night long?"

"Um, yeah?" Oh, from that dark expression on his face, he really looks like he doesn't approve of my situation.

"Where do you live?"

Here's where my shame washes over me, but I'm already in it this far. "Take me home and I'll show you."

Jake starts the truck and pulls out of the parking lot, and I give him directions. We go back the way we came, until we're on the corner of the intersection where it felt like he nearly tipped the truck over, he was going so fast. My apartment complex sits on that very corner, across the street from the elementary school.

"I live right there." I point at my building as we wait in the left turn lane for the light to switch to green.

His jaw goes tight. His lips thin. The light is green and he turns onto the street sharply, pulling into my parking lot and hitting the brakes hard. "This place isn't safe," he says as he glances around, his upper lip curling.

"I've lived here the past six years and nothing has happened," I tell him as I grab my backpack and sling it over my shoulder.

"I don't like it."

"Let my mom know your thoughts. She'll tell you to mind your own business." I sound defensive because I'm feeling defensive. And embarrassed. I know we don't live in the best place and we don't have the greatest neighbors. The police have been called out here a few times, but usually for nothing major. Domestic disturbances. One time an old guy got thrown in jail for drunk in public. That sort of thing.

Jake says nothing as I reach for the handle and open the door. "Thank you for the ride," I tell him. "And for the coffee."

"Don't be mad at me," he says, and I pause, turning to face him. "I'm just—this place doesn't look the greatest, and it makes me worry. About you."

"I'm a big girl, Jake. I can handle myself." I hop out of the truck before I say something dumb like *thanks for caring*. Shutting the passenger side door, I then head for the apartment building. I walk up the stairs, glancing over my shoulder to see he's still waiting for me. Watching me as I unlock the door and step inside.

Only then, does he pull out of the lot, driving away in a squeal of tires and revving engine.

Making me feel...

Safe.

* * *

It's past nine-thirty and I'm sitting at our kitchen table, still working on the history project that won't die when there's a sharp knock on our front door.

I go completely still, glancing around the mostly dark apartment. There's a dim lamp on the end table next to the couch. Maxine is curled up on a blanket on the couch, and she lifts her head at the sound of the knock as well, then ducks back down and closes her eyes.

Must be nice, to be a cat with no major worries.

Maybe if I'm really quiet, they'll go away. Someone probably has the wrong address. Or it's our neighbor. She's a nice lady, but she drinks a lot and sometimes she gets so drunk, she comes over to our place so she can cry over her problems with Mom. My mother is always sympathetic to other people's plights. She's very soft hearted.

Sometimes I think I'm too soft hearted. Just like her.

My phone dings with a Snapchat notification, and it's so loud I jump in my seat. Heart racing, I see it's a message from…

Jake.

I'm at your front door.

Wait, what?

I slide the chair back and rise to my feet, glancing down at myself. I took a shower earlier and I'm wearing a pair of shorts I used to wear for P.E. when I had to take it and a T-shirt with One Direction on the front. Someone left it behind in one of the hotel rooms a few years ago, the tags still on it, and Mom gave it to me. I've always had a minor crush on Harry Styles, so of course I kept it. I have no makeup on and my hair is still wet. I must look—

"Hannah. Open up," Jake says from outside.

I rush toward the door and turn the deadbolt, then undo the chain before I open the door. "What are you doing here?"

Jaw tight, eyes dark, I can only describe his expression as determined. "Let me in."

I could tell him to go. He has no business being at my home this late at night. But having him this close, my entire body goes haywire. It's like I can't resist him.

"Come in, but give me a minute," I tell him before I take off for my bedroom.

My heart hammering in my throat, I close my bedroom door and lean against it, trying to calm down. Jake Callahan is in my apartment. On a Monday night. Why?

Why, why, why?

Hurriedly, I clean up the clothes I've left discarded on my bedroom floor, tossing everything into the hamper I keep in my tiny closet. My bed is unmade but it's not like he's going to see it. In fact, I should keep the door closed and then he'll never see it.

Good idea. Best idea ever.

I grab a scrunchie and pull my hair into messy bun, then pluck a hoodie that's draped across the foot of my bed, sniff it to make sure it's clean before I yank it on. It's still kind of warm—it's late August, and while the nights are sometimes cool, it's not necessarily cool enough for a hoodie yet. But this will have to do. I don't have a bra on and I don't feel like digging one up either. A hoodie will hide that fact.

Hopefully.

I exit my bedroom to find the front door is closed and locked. Jake is sitting on the couch, Maxine in his lap as he rubs her behind her ears with those long fingers of his. Her eyes are closed and she's leaning into his hand, like she's never felt anything better in her life, and I'm actually envious of my cat.

Girl, I feel you. I want what you're getting.

"Maxine likes you," I say, and he glances up, his gaze meeting mine before he returns his attention to my cat.

"Maxine is pretty sweet," he says. "She's cute."

At those words, she resettles herself in his lap, curling into a ball and closing her eyes as if she's down for the night.

Traitor.

"Why are you here?" I ask him.

"I couldn't stop thinking about you," he admits, his voice low.

My heart stops.

"All alone at night with no one else around," he continues, scratching my cat beneath her chin. "I was worried about you."

"My mom has worked this shift for the past year and a half." And slowly but surely, I've gotten used to it. Mostly. "I appreciate your concern, but really, I'm okay."

He doesn't respond to me. Just keeps scratching my cat and sending her straight into heaven until he finally asks, "You got anything to drink?"

With a sigh I go into the kitchen and check the fridge. "I have some orange juice. Or milk. Or water."

"I'll take some orange juice. Please."

Ah, he's using his manners. Usually he just demands stuff.

I pour him a glass of orange juice and set it on the end table closest to where he's sitting. That way I don't have to touch him.

The last thing I need to do tonight is touch him.

"Thanks." He reaches over and grabs the glass, somehow not irritating Maxine when he shifts, and I'm impressed. He drains the glass halfway before setting it on the table once more. "You should sit down."

I do as he says, choosing to sit on the loveseat instead of

on the couch next to him. "Isn't it kind of late for you to be out?"

Oh my gosh, I sound like a mom.

"It's not even ten," he says with a shrug.

"Where do your parents think you are?"

"At a friend's house. It's the truth, right?" He arches a brow, spreading one arm along the back of the couch. He's wearing a white T-shirt that sets off his tanned skin and black joggers. He looks just as casual as I do, which is only a tiny bit reassuring, because while I'm casual bordering on plain, he's casual bordering on absolutely gorgeous, and life just isn't fair sometimes, ya know?

"Is that what we are?" I ask. "Friends?"

"I don't know what I'd call us," he says, and I appreciate his honesty. "But I couldn't sit at home knowing you were here all by yourself."

His words soften me and I can't help but sigh. "Look, I appreciate you wanting to—protect me, but I've got this. I live here. I'm not scared. I've got a phone and I know how to call 9-1-1. I have protective neighbors." She's a drunk neighbor most of the time, but yes, she's somewhat protective. "This is my home, and I feel safe."

"Do you have a car?"

I blink at him. "What?"

"A car." He makes a motion with his hands like he's turning a steering wheel, the jerk. "Do you have one?"

"My mom drives it to work."

His expression turns irritated. "Do you have your license?"

"Yes, but we only have the one car, and she had to use it to get to her job," I explain, repeating myself.

"So if something were to happen to you, you'd be stuck here. You couldn't drive away," he points out, his voice flat, his gaze stormy.

"Well…yeah."

He grimaces, running a hand through his hair. "I hate that."

"What are you going to do, give me a car?" I ask incredulously.

His expression tells me he's actually considering it, which is just insane. "It's not a bad idea…"

"Absolutely not." I rise to my feet and march over to him, grabbing my cat off his lap so I can go deposit her on my bed. It's distracting, watching Maxine sitting all cozy on Jake's lap, fully accepting him. Like he belongs here with us. And what he's saying is completely ridiculous.

He's completely ridiculous.

Once I've dumped Maxine on my bed, I come back out into the living room to see Jake hasn't moved from his spot on the couch. He's drained the last of the orange juice from his glass, and now he's got the television remote clutched in his hand as he turns on the TV.

"You can't stay," I tell him.

He ignores me. "Want to watch something?"

"Jake." I stop so I'm standing directly in front of him, my hands resting on my hips. I'm mad. And the tiniest bit thrilled that he's so…protective of me. My brother Joe is six years older than me, and he left for the military right after he graduated high school. We're not close. We never have been. Mom always makes sure I'm doing all right, but she's also distracted by work and her own problems, and she sort of just lets me…fend for myself most of the time.

No one really pays attention to me or asks if I'm okay. Oh, my friends do, but they're wrapped up in their own lives. Sophie is always busy with dance—she practically lives at the studio. Marty acts like he's hanging on by a thread a lot of the time.

And here's Jake. We barely know each other, yet he's

already watching out for me. So concerned over my wellbeing, he's compelled to come over to my house late at night to make sure I'm safe.

"Hannah," he answers, his tone similar to mine. Exasperated. Irritated.

"You have to leave."

"Oh, come on. Let me stay for a little while." He pauses, sending me an imploring look. "It'll make me feel better."

I stay put, hands still resting on my hips, lips tight as I contemplate him. He lifts the remote, trying to change the channel, but of course nothing happens.

"You're in my way," he says dryly.

I step to the side with the most annoyed sigh I can muster, and settle my butt back on the loveseat.

If he's going to stay, I can't sit with him on the couch. No way.

"What are you doing all the way over there?" he asks, like he can read my mind and knows why I'm not sitting by him.

"Nope. I'm not budging." I cross my arms and focus on the TV.

I swear I hear him chuckle as he starts changing the channels, rapid-fire.

"How are we supposed to figure out what we want to watch if you can't keep it on one channel for longer than three seconds?" I ask irritably.

"Have any suggestions?"

"Why don't you let *me* have the remote?"

"If you want it, come and get it." It's a taunt.

And a dare.

Heaving myself out of the loveseat, I cross the room to pluck the remote out of his hand. But he has quicker reflexes than me. He grabs hold of my wrist, and before I know what's happening, I somehow end up in his lap.

His. Lap.

I'm sitting sideways, my legs dangling over one side, and I twist my upper body so I'm facing him. He watches me with a smug smile curving his lips, and I'm breathless from being so close to him.

Close to him? More like I'm on top of him.

His thighs are hard beneath my butt. He smells clean and fresh, like he just got out of the shower, and I can even smell the faint scent of fabric softener emanating from his T-shirt. He's incredibly warm and despite the volume of the TV, I swear I can hear him breathing.

It sounds the littlest bit accelerated.

"Here you go," he says, gently placing the remote in my hand. I try to climb off his lap, but he circles his arm around my waist, keeping me in place. "Where you going?"

I keep my head bent, my entire body starting to tremble. "I don't understand exactly what you're doing by coming here, Jake. But if you think I'm going to let you use me as your side piece you can mess around with under the cover of darkness, it's not going to happen. I hate to break it to you, but I'm not a sure thing."

His arm loosens around my waist, but he keeps it there, still holding me. The TV is so loud—some reality show is currently on and I think people are staying somewhere out in the desert and they're completely naked? I'm not sure.

"Just…sit with me, okay? I'm lonely on this big couch all by myself, especially since you took Maxine away from me," he tells me, his mouth right at my temple.

I don't know what to do, or what to say. I sit on his lap for a moment, trying to calm my racing heart until finally, I slowly nod. He lets go of me and I stand, then settle onto the couch next to him, but not too close.

"You want to watch *Naked and Afraid*?" he asks.

"This is an actual show?" I'm kind of horrified.

"It's crazy. My dad loves it. He's addicted."

We start watching it and soon I'm completely wrapped up in the story of these two strangers who are both survivalists, trying to make it in the jungle for twenty-one days, completely naked. All the right body parts are blurred out, though we're given plenty of glimpses of their bare butts. It's kind of weird. Yet I can't stop watching it.

When there's a commercial break, Jake gets up and uses the bathroom. I take the opportunity to check my phone, tempted to send Sophie a text letting her know who's at my house but…

I set the phone down. This is my secret.

Our secret.

Jake comes out of the bathroom a few minutes later and grabs the blanket that's in a pile at the opposite end of the couch. "Want to share it?"

I watch him warily as he settles that long body of his back on the couch, shaking out the blanket and draping it over himself. He pats the spot next to him. "Come on."

Scooting closer, I grab the edge of the blanket and slip beneath it. Now we're so close I can feel his warmth again, and it's like a drug. I want to get closer. Curl my body into his side. Feel his arm slip around me. Rest my head on his shoulder. I want to hear his heartbeat. I want to press my face against his chest and inhale him. Get high off him.

I want. I want. I want.

But I need to remember…

He's not mine to have.

CHAPTER 15

JAKE

She falls asleep just when the second episode of *Naked and Afraid* ends. I can tell by the shift in her breathing. Turning carefully, I study her, wondering what I should do next. I don't want to wake her up, which means I can't leave because I can't lock the deadbolt behind me.

I could pick her up and carry her to her bedroom…

I'm still not sure why I'm here, or why I care so much. I'm drawn to her. I like how strong-willed she is. She doesn't hold back. She states her mind and doesn't care whether she's offended me or not.

The girls I've been with in the past would do whatever I wanted them to, no questions asked. Cami was a bit of a struggle, but only because she wanted me to follow *her* rules. I don't like being told what to do.

Clearly, neither does Hannah.

Slowly I rise from the couch and make my way to the back of the apartment. There's a short hallway, a closed door on the left and a closed door on the right, with the bathroom directly in front of me. Pretty sure I saw her go right when she took her cat back to her bedroom so I reach for the doorknob and turn it, entering the room.

I flick on the light. It's definitely her bedroom. And it's kind of a mess. There's a dresser to my left and the top of it is covered with a variety of jewelry and hair ties, a lanyard with her school ID and a key lying on top of the pile. The bed is small, a fluffy pink comforter tossed back, revealing pale pink sheets. She has a bunch of blankets at the foot of the bed and Maxine is sitting on top of the pile, completely blissed out.

Lucky cat.

Turning off the bedroom light, I walk back out into the living room, heading straight for the couch. Without hesitation I scoop Hannah into my arms. She's light. Doesn't weigh much. I curve my arm behind her neck to stabilize her head and I walk slowly, carefully back to her bedroom, but it's no use.

She blinks her eyes open, confusion written all over her pretty face. "What are you doing?"

"Sshh, go back to sleep," I tell her, not answering her question.

I gently set her on the bed and she sits up, the bun on top of her head flopping to the right, strands of hair curling around her face. "I fell asleep."

"Yeah." She seems a little freaked out, so I create some distance between us by heading for the door.

"You carried me back to my room?"

I lean against the doorjamb and slip my hands into my sweat pockets, watching her. She can draw that conclusion herself; I don't need to answer her.

"Why are you being so nice to me?" She sounds completely confused.

"I'm not that nice," I tell her, my mind going wild with all the things I'd love to do to her. Not a one of them could be considered nice either.

"You must be, if I let you into my apartment."

"Maybe you need a lecture about not letting bad people walk through your front door," I say.

She somehow ends up on her hands and knees as she crawls to the edge of the bed and starts petting her cat. Sounds like a euphemism for something else, but she is literally petting her cat Maxine, propping her head on the pile of blankets and stretching her body out along the end of the mattress. Her exposed legs are long and pale and smooth. Those shorts she's wearing ride up and I'm hoping for a glimpse of her ass, but I probably won't get that lucky.

What the hell am I doing here again?

"I don't think you're a bad person, Jacob Callahan," she murmurs to her cat, though she's really talking to me. "I just think you want everyone to believe you are."

There's no reason for me to reply. She can go ahead and keep believing that.

But it's not true.

"I'm gonna go crash on the couch," I tell her, jerking my thumb toward the living room just before I start to leave.

"Wait a minute!" She practically falls off the bed, and I turn, reaching out so I can help her, but she bats my hands away. "You can't stay here overnight. My mom will be home around six-fifteen!"

"I'll just say for a couple more hours," I start, but Hannah shakes her head, her mouth set in a firm line.

"Absolutely not."

"You're kicking me out."

"Yes!" She starts for the front door and I follow after her, not getting too close so I can keep an eye on those legs. "Your time is up."

"What a shame. I was hoping I could test out that couch."

"It's not very comfortable."

"Are you saying you would let me sleep in your bed?"

She stops mid-stride and slowly turns around, those big blue eyes gazing up at me. "Um. No."

I tilt my head to the side, pressing my lips together. "You really mean that?"

"Don't start working your—sexual magic on me. I barely know you," she retorts.

I can't help it—I start to laugh. "You think I have sexual magic?"

"You're so annoying." She marches to the door, turns the deadbolt, undoes the chain and then throws open the door. "You should go."

My laughter dies as I make my way to the door, pausing right in front of her. "This has been fun."

"Whatever."

"Might come by again tomorrow."

Her mouth drops open for a moment, but she closes it just as quick. "Um, that really won't be necessary."

Unable to stop myself, I tap the tip of her nose with my index finger. "You don't get to make that decision, Banana."

Now she's frowning. "That's completely unoriginal, you know. Calling me Hannah Banana."

"I just called you Banana."

She reaches behind me and pushes me as hard as she can, so I have no choice but to walk out of her apartment. "See you at school," she calls out.

Before I can say anything, the door is slammed shut, and I hear her turning the lock into place. I whistle as I walk down the steps, my heart light for the first time in…

A while.

* * *

We keep up the same pattern for over a week, me and Hannah. I see her throughout the day at school, but we never speak to each other. We make eye contact when we pass each other in the halls between classes. Or I'll catch her watching me during lunch in the quad.

Sometimes, she'll catch *me* watching her at lunch.

Only during seventh period art class do we get a chance to talk, though it's usually not for long. Sanborne keeps her busy most of the time, which always leaves me wanting more. I let Hannah go her way when class is over, and I head to the locker room to change, though I'd be willing to spend those extra few minutes before I have to actually report to practice talking to her.

She doesn't seem to want that. She doesn't seem to want anything from me. Truthfully, I don't think she wants to be seen with me on campus, which is the craziest thing ever. Every single girl I've been in a relationship with, or even just talked to casually, that's the first thing they do—show off that we're together.

But deep down I know my friends will most likely give me endless shit if they spot me talking to her, so I kind of have to agree. It's better if we keep things on the down low. It's an unspoken agreement we have.

Each night I show up at her apartment around nine-thirty, and we watch TV together. She forced me to watch some reality dating show that was somehow awful yet completely addicting all at once. Last night we watched a movie on Netflix I could barely pay attention to. I'd rather stare at her, talk to her. Watch her mouth move as she speaks. It sounds insane, but her lips are mesmerizing. Lately, I think about kissing them all the time. I want to get closer to her at her house, but she keeps her distance. She'll share the blanket with me, but she never sits too close. She definitely doesn't try to do anything to me, with me. It's like there's a wall between us.

I'm determined to break that fucking wall down.

We had an away game last week that was over two hours away from home, and no one came but a few parents and a handful of students. We easily beat the opposing team. A part of me wanted to see Hannah in the stands, but Mom was there, cheering me on, cheering Ava on too. Oh, and Beck was there, of course, screaming his head off and at one point, he was even standing on the sidelines with Dad.

It's Thursday again, practice went well, and I'm feeling good. It's another away game tomorrow, versus a team that's had a terrible record against ours for years, so I don't believe they'll be that much of a challenge. I'm trying my damnedest not to let my teammates—*friends*—get in my head when they talk a bunch of crap, and so far it's working. My archrival Eli Bennett is making Snapchat stories and mentioning my name pretty much every single night, challenging me to this and that and whatever else, but I ignore him.

He's all talk and little action. I refuse to bow down to his antics. He's a major showoff and wants everyone in on our rivalry.

Ridiculous.

Every Thursday night we have a team dinner put together by our booster club and sponsored by a local restaurant in town. This week's menu features Mexican food, and everyone on the team is heaping their plate with rice, bean, enchiladas and burritos. Everything smells delicious, and by the time I'm seated at the table and ready to consume my plate in record time, Caleb and Diego sit down on either side of me, their expressions serious.

This ought to be fun.

"You need to tell us what's up with you," Caleb starts.

I'm too busy shoving a burrito in my mouth to come up with an answer at first. "What are you talking about?" I ask after I swallow.

"Why are you suddenly in such a good mood all the time?" Caleb appears completely baffled.

"I am not." Am I? I scoop up some rice and eat. Hopefully they made enough so we can all have seconds.

"You are," Diego says, his voice like steel. As if he's annoyed. They should be glad I'm in a good mood. Doesn't that make their lives easier? "The past week you've been acting cheerful and whistling and shit."

"Really?" Whistling? I don't whistle.

"We have one question for you," Diego continues, Caleb nodding in agreement.

"What's that?" I ask, my mouth full.

Diego glances around before he lowers his voice and says, "Who are you fucking on the low?"

I gape at both of them, swallowing down the now-dry rice. "No one," I croak.

"Bullshit," Caleb says, pointing at me. "You've got some side ho who's giving it to you good, and you're not telling us about her."

"That's not true." I mean, it sort of is true, but I can't call Hannah my side ho. She doesn't even let me *touch* her.

I'm hoping that'll change later tonight.

"We tell you to go out and find someone and you do, but you won't let us know who she is." Caleb is actually whining. He sounds like a baby. "That's not fair, man."

"Is it Cami?" Diego asks, his expression stony. "Come on, tell us. You're back together, aren't you."

I actually snort. "It is most definitely not Cami. We haven't said a word to each other since the day she gave me my jersey back."

"It sucks that you're holding out on us and keeping secrets," Caleb says, and he actually sounds sad. "I thought we were friends."

"Oh fuck off, both of you." Tony suddenly appears, and he sits across from us at the table. "I can hear you guys giving our boy here shit all the way from the food line."

"No way, really?" Diego appears panicked, which is pointless. No one from our team cares what we say about our so-called love lives. Well, there are probably a few gossips, but I'm not too worried. I haven't said anything incriminating.

"Haven't you noticed he's been in an extra-good mood lately?" Caleb asks Tony.

I start eating again, though my appetite has waned. I'm in a good mood? I haven't really noticed. I've been so focused on catching moments with Hannah, I guess I haven't had time to sit around and get pissed about the usual stuff.

So yeah. My mood adjustment probably has everything to do with her. Not that I can tell them that.

"Why does his good mood have to depend on the attention of another?" Tony asks the other dumbasses at our table. "Maybe he's feeling better about…everything. We've been in school a couple of weeks and it's pretty stress free. The team has really come together. We're seniors. Life is good."

"Yeah, what Tony said," I mumble before I take a drink of water.

"Whatever you say, Dr. Sorrento," Caleb tells him before he and Diego start cracking up.

These two jackasses can be so annoying sometimes.

"Let's talk about something else," Tony suggests. "Like how Eli Bennett can't keep his damn mouth shut about our upcoming game."

"I refuse to send a response video, no matter how many times he challenges me," I immediately say. "We don't even play them for another month."

"I agree. Silence is still a response," Tony muses. "I say the week leading up to the game is when you should post a video about Eli."

And that's more than three weeks away. "I don't want to do it at all." I mean, it might be fun to talk shit on that asshole. We've hated each other since the day we met, when we went to middle school together. We played on the same youth team, which was a major disaster. We both play the same position. We're both pretty damn good. We're both super competitive.

We drove our coaches crazy.

"Aw, come on. We gotta rub it in his face a little. This is his senior year too. The fucking Mustangs haven't won a game against us yet," Diego says with a grin. "And I can't wait to call them a giant bunch of pussies after we beat their asses yet again."

"Eli is the king of trash talking, that's all. He knows how to get under our skin. Specifically *your* skin." Tony points at me. "I think you remaining quiet is twisting him up. He's probably getting in his own head now and it's fucking with his mental state."

"Probably," I say absently. I despise that fucker, and I really don't want to think about him unless I absolutely have to.

"They haven't won a game yet this season," Caleb says, but that's not a big deal. We've only played two games, with our next one tomorrow.

I'd rather focus on that game. I can't worry about the future. I've got stuff I need to take care of now—tonight. I have a test in Spanish tomorrow that I haven't studied for at all. I wonder if Hannah would help me. I bet she's good at Spanish.

She's pretty damn smart.

Everyone makes small talk and I offer up the occasional

response, but for the most part, I remain quiet. I go back into the food line for seconds, chatting up all the booster club volunteers who are helping serve the team tonight. I listen respectively when Dad talks, offering up an inspirational speech that gets both the JV and varsity teams fired up. I roar along with them, but my heart isn't completely in it. Not that I don't care about this game, I'm just not that worried about it.

All I can think about is when can I leave so I can rush home, take a shower, and then head to Hannah's apartment.

By the time the dinner is mostly finished and people are leaving, Dad approaches me with a concerned look on his face.

"You okay?" He rests a hand on my shoulder and gives it a squeeze. "We haven't talked much lately. Just brief conversations at practice or in the morning before you leave for school. And at night you're never around. You're always over at your friend's house."

"I'm good," I tell him with a quick nod, keeping it short. Not wanting to dwell on the words *friend's house.* He might start asking questions I don't want to answer. "Just trying to stay focused for tomorrow."

"Don't worry about that game. Save your energy. We'll most likely blow them out," he says as we exit the building. The team dinner is always held at the huge church across the street from the high school. Quite a few booster club families are members.

"You're telling me not to worry?" I'm surprised. He usually doesn't say stuff like that. He always wants us to, and I quote, *stay on our toes.* "That's a first."

"I'm more worried about the last half of the season— we're somehow scheduled against all the big players at the end. And it starts with our homecoming game." The one against the Mustangs. "I hear Eli Bennett is coming for us."

"When is he not coming for us?" My voice is full of disgust.

"I've heard about his videos calling out the team—calling out *you*. I even saw one this afternoon." He slowly shakes his head. "I thought that kid was better than this."

"What do you mean?"

"All the shit talk and threats will get him nowhere. I worked with him and his team over the summer. They have tremendous potential."

"Oh, I remember." I still have a problem with how Dad trained them at that summer camp.

Dad shoots me an irritated look. "Hey, it's not like I handed them our playbook and asked them to make copies to study."

"It doesn't matter, Dad. You helped them at the football camp and gave them some tips. All your tips should be saved for *us*." I jab a thumb at my chest. I probably sound selfish as hell, but it's true. Why would he help them?

They're the fucking enemy.

"We still beat them in that seven on seven game, right?" Dad smiles but I just scowl at him in return. "Lighten up, Jake. You're going to give yourself premature wrinkles."

"You sound just like Mom," I mutter as we both start heading toward our cars in the parking lot.

"I should, I hang out with her enough. Speaking of that, you seeing anyone lately?" he asks, his voice casual. Almost deceptively so.

"No," I lie.

"Hmm."

"What, are Diego and Caleb talking to you about me?" I clamp my lips shut. I say anything else and I'll give myself away.

"No, not at all. I just figured with you never around at

home lately, that maybe some cute girl has caught your eye," Dad says.

He sounds ridiculous—like such a dad. Cute girl who's caught my eye? Please.

I mean, it's true, but I'm not going to let him know that. Talking about relationship stuff with your parents can sometimes be really embarrassing. Like this very moment. I'm not in a relationship, not even close. Hannah and I are just friends. That's it. I'm still not sure if I want to take it further, though I can't deny that I'm attracted to her.

The entire situation is confusing.

"Nope. I've been focusing on football. That's it," I say breezily. "Or I've just been hanging out with my friends. It's my last year in high school and I'm trying to soak it all up before it's over."

"Good idea." Dad claps me on the back. "You headed home?"

I nod. "I'm going back out, though, after I take a shower."

He studies me for a while, his gaze narrowed, and I watch him back. Our features are so similar, it's almost scary. I know exactly what I'm going to look like when I get older, so it's almost like staring in a mirror of the future. And I'm sure he's dying to ask me questions, but he's always been the dad who says *until you give me a reason to* not *trust you, I trust you.*

Well, there was the nose breaking incident. He's still pissed at me for that.

"Where you going?" he finally asks.

"Tony's." The lies fall from my lips easily. "I might stay the night."

"His mom is gone?"

"As usual. He doesn't like being in that house all alone." That's not a lie.

"Poor kid. It's like his parents can't be bothered." Another clap on the back from Dad. "See you when we get home."

"I'll follow you," I tell him, relieved he's not asking me anymore questions.

I hate having to lie, but I feel like I have no other choice. Telling the truth will only lead to more questions.

And I'm not in the mood to answer them.

CHAPTER 16

JAKE

I show up at her place a little later than usual, just before ten. I almost backed out. By the time I got home after the team dinner and took a shower, I was exhausted and ready to collapse. My bed tempted me.

But seeing Hannah tonight tempted me even more.

I texted her before I left the house, letting her know I was running late and she responded with a simple okay. I think of the *okays* Cami would text me in the past. Or worse, the *fines*. They always had hidden meaning. She didn't like to be kept waiting. She wanted to be my top priority, and I tried my best to make her feel that way, but what I gave her was never enough.

She enjoyed the status of being with me, but part of that status is me working my ass off on the football team. Endless practices. Conditioning. Gym time. Camps. And when I couldn't spend time with her in the way she wanted, she got pissed.

Hannah is nothing like that, though I suppose we haven't spent a lot of time together yet, so she could prove me wrong. But for now, she lets me just…be me. It's like the popular part of me doesn't matter to her. She doesn't demand we walk together in the hallways at school. Doesn't want to take photos with me so she can post them on her social media later. She's chill. Quiet. Funny. Stubborn. Opinionated.

I like pretty much everything about her. In fact, I'm pretty damn eager to see her.

Within twenty minutes of leaving my house, I'm pulling into the parking lot of her apartment complex. It's small. There's not a lot of apartments here, but it's pretty shabby-looking. Rundown. There are old cars parked in the lot with spiderwebs growing beneath them. Some of the lights are out. The paint is faded and peeling on the buildings, and as I walk along the cracked sidewalk that leads toward her stair-well, I can hear yelling coming from the unit beneath Hannah's.

Good times.

Running up the stairs to her second floor apartment, I knock on the door three times, which has sort of become my signature. She answers the door within seconds, a little smile curling those sexy lips of hers. "Hi."

She looks good. Her hair is perfectly straight and hanging far past her shoulders, and her expression is warm. Inviting. Like she's happy to see me.

"Hey." I smile in return and her smile grows as she opens the door wider for me.

"Come in."

That's another thing I've noticed, I think as I enter her tiny apartment and she shuts and locks the door behind me: I smile more when I'm around Hannah. All that unnecessary anger that seems to build within me dissipates the moment I see her. It's as if her mere presence eases my stress.

"Sorry I was running late," I tell her as I watch her head

into the kitchen and go to the refrigerator. "We had our team dinner tonight and that always sets me back some."

"That's okay. Are you guys ready for tomorrow's game?" she asks from the kitchen.

I watch as she pulls two glasses out of the cabinet and fills them both with ice before pouring orange juice into them. I prefer ice in my OJ and it turns out she does too.

"As ready as we can be. Our varsity team beats them pretty much every year, so I'm not too stressed." She walks back into the living room and hands me my glass. "Thanks." I take a sip, contemplating if I should say it and I decide fuck it. I'm gonna. "Are you going to the game tomorrow?"

Last week's game was far. I don't blame her for not going. This one is an away game too, and it's a drive, but I'm hoping she can make it.

Hannah wrinkles her nose as she sets her glass on the end table. "I'm not sure yet."

Disappointment fills me and I shove it aside. "Cool." I nod, acting like it's no big deal. Deep down, I really want her there.

But I'll look like too much of a needy bastard if I tell her that.

"You want to watch a movie?" she asks. I can tell she wants to change the subject.

"Sure."

We settle in on the couch together, as is our routine. I study her as she sits on the other end of the couch, taking in what she's wearing. Black leggings that make her legs look long and a white V-neck T-shirt. Her hair seems extra shiny, and there's not a lick of makeup on her face. Just those big blue eyes and the cute freckles and the gorgeous mouth that makes me want to kiss it.

Clearly I'm sexually frustrated. This girl gives off confusing vibes. She seems into me, she'll flirt with me, yet she won't sit close to me, like I might have cooties or whatever. Is she afraid of me? I've never given her reason to be, beyond being kind of an ass to her during our initial interactions. That night when she cleaned up my face after the fight, she didn't act scared at all. More like she didn't back down from me despite my shitty behavior, and I liked that.

I liked it a lot.

"You always sit so far away," I tell her after she starts the movie.

She sets the remote on the coffee table before she angles her head in my direction. "You're kind of a couch hog."

I raise my brows. "You serious right now?"

Biting her lower lip, she nods. "Yep."

God, she's killing me what with the way her teeth are sinking into her lush lip. I want to bite it. Taste it.

Taste her.

"You're so tall and, uh…big." Her cheeks turn pink as she continues talking. "You take up a lot of room."

"So you're saying I'm too tall and *big?*" I ask.

She nods, her cheeks now turning from pink to red. "How tall are you anyway?"

"Six-three." I pause. "And a half."

"That's really tall."

"Taller than my dad." A real point of pride for me, something I can brag about when people compare me to him.

That's about all I've got so far.

"How tall are you?" I ask when she hasn't said anything. The movie might be playing, but the volume is turned down low and we're not paying any attention. Sometimes I think we use it for background noise. Half the time I'm distracted by her presence. I can't concentrate. It's only getting worse.

Tonight I'm at about a level negative five. Meaning I can't concentrate on anything for shit. With the exception of her.

"I'm around five-six."

"So not a complete shrimp."

She smiles. Shakes her head. "No. In elementary school I was always one of the tallest girls in class, if not the tallest kid overall. Even taller than the boys. I hated it. Found it embarrassing."

"What happened?"

"Oh, I just stopped growing. I was considered a tall girl up until the fifth grade. By the sixth, all those other tall girls got taller and I remained the same." She shrugs before grabbing the blanket that's lying on the couch in between us and pulling it over her.

"Hey, that's my blanket." I tug on the other end, pulling it halfway off her. She stops it from leaving her completely with a tight grip.

"Your blanket? Um, do you live here?" Her tone is teasing yet with a hint of nervousness.

"No, but that's the blanket I use every night when you refuse to sit close to me." I watch her, hoping she can get a read on what I'm trying to tell her: that I want us to sit close.

"We've shared it before," she points out.

"At first. Now it's just mine." I give it another tug, but her grip is firm. "You going to share?"

"I guess so." She's not letting go of the blanket yet, though, so we'll see.

"You'll have to sit closer to me then." I flick my head, indicating I want her next to me.

Her teeth sink into her lower lip again, and it takes everything I've got to hold back the groan that wants to escape. Just looking at her tonight has my dick twitching. I feel like a walking, talking hormone right now.

Without a word she relinquishes her hold on the blanket and scoots closer, until she's sitting right next to me. Close enough I can smell her—a light floral scent clings to her skin and hair. Close enough I can touch her—I readjust the blanket over both of our laps, so it's covering us from the waist down. I keep my hands to myself.

For now.

We're sitting side by side, our arms brushing as we both face the TV. I only last maybe twenty seconds tops before I angle my head just right so I can look at her. She keeps her gaze firmly on the screen, but she won't stop moving. Her lashes lower the slightest bit, and they keep fluttering, as if she's looking around. As if she wants to glance over at me. Her mouth doesn't stop moving either. She purses her lips. Parts them. Smashes them together again. Her tongue sneaks out, wetting her upper lip, and fuck me, I'm getting hard beneath my gym shorts.

Get your shit together, bro.

"Why don't you ever do your hair in braids?"

She glances over at me, her eyes wide. "What do you mean?"

"When we first started talking, that one night. You had your hair in braids." Reaching out, I play with the ends of her hair. "It was cute."

"I usually only put my hair in braids after I get out of the shower."

Her words cause me to immediately think of her naked.

"And sometimes I'll sleep with them in, and then when my hair is dry in the morning and I undo the braids, it's all wavy," she further explains.

"My sisters used to do that."

"Yeah? I think most girls do."

I touch her hair again, running my fingers through the ends. She's not what I would call a full-blown redhead. There's varying shades of red and brown and even a few streaks of blonde in her hair. It's a bunch of colors all at once, and I realize as I keep combing my fingers through the silky soft strands, she's gone very, very still.

My fingers barely brush her neck and I see goose bumps form. She's so still, I'm not one-hundred percent sure she's even breathing.

"I have a secret," I tell her, my voice low.

Her gaze shifts to mine, but otherwise she remains locked in place. Almost like she's afraid to move and I'll stop touching her. "What is it?"

Very gently, I tug on the ends of her hair. "I can braid hair."

Her delicate brows wrinkle. I'm sure my revelation wasn't what she expected. "Really?"

Nodding, I release my hold on her hair. The disappointment on her face is obvious. "Scoot up and I'll show you."

She presses her lips together before she does what I ask her, pushing forward so she's sitting on the edge of the couch cushion. "Like this?" She glances over her shoulder, our gazes meeting.

The tension between us grows, and I'm suddenly consumed with the need to kiss her. I wonder if she can feel it.

Nodding, I reach out and rest my hands on her hips, gently angling her body to make it easier for me to braid her hair. I wish I could keep touching her like this, but I need to be patient.

"Shift back just a little," I tell her, and Hannah moves, her curvy ass coming closer, knocking against the outside of my thigh. "Okay, that's good."

I sit up and gather her hair in my fist. It's thick and smooth, and I tug on it a little to test her. She doesn't react at all, just allows me to pull, and when I let it go, her hair falls against her shoulders, fanning out. "You have pretty hair," I tell her as I separate it into three parts and start braiding.

It's been a while since I've done this, but yep, it's my secret talent. No one beyond my family knows I can braid hair. I don't even think Dad is aware of it. Mom was always braiding Autumn and Ava's hair when they were little, and I learned from watching her. Sometimes, I'd braid one of my sister's hair, usually Ava's. She didn't like sitting still for Mom, always complained and cried that Mom pulled her hair too tight and hurt her.

But Ava never complained or cried when I braided her hair. She'd sit there calmly for me every single time.

Kind of like Hannah is right now. She remains quiet, her ass against my thigh, her scent wafting toward me. She smells so fucking good. Having her this close, feeling how warm she is...I'm having to use as much restraint as possible so I don't attack her. I notice the tighter I pull on her braid, the more her head tips back, a little gasp escaping her when my fingers brush against her nape.

I do it again, just because I can.

When I finally finish, I ask her, "Do you have a hair tie?" She slips one off her wrist and hands it to me without a word, and I twist the black hair tie around the end of her braid. "There you go."

She immediately reaches back, touching the plaits of her braid lightly, testing it. "Wow, you *can* braid."

The surprise in her voice makes me chuckle. "Did you ever doubt me?"

"Maybe a little." She flashes me a quick smile over her shoulder before she faces forward once more, her head dipping forward. "Um, don't be mad but...could you maybe take the braid out?"

"You want me to undo all my hard work?" I try to sound put out, but it's hard. I don't mind having my hands on her hair again.

Actually, I'm dying to touch her again.

"It's just...I straightened my hair earlier, before you got here. And a braid will ruin that completely."

Girls and their hair. Guess I'll have to use this to my advantage then.

"Come closer," I tell her, my voice husky, my pulse starting to kick up at just the thought of what I'm about to do.

She scoots backward, her butt now firmly pressed against my thigh, and I reach for her hair, slowly taking out the tie before I set it on the cushion next to me. Then with all the patience I can muster, I carefully unwind her braid, my fingers sliding into the twisted pieces and undoing them. She tilts her head back a little, as if she's liking it, and I know she is.

So am I.

This is fuckin' crazy. I shouldn't be getting off while taking apart her braid, but I am. I'm enjoying this more than I've enjoyed anything else in a long ass time. Right when I finish, she tilts her head to the side, exposing her long, pale neck, and I have to hold myself back from pressing my mouth there, right at the base, where her pulse throbs.

Once the braid is completely undone, I push her hair to the side and skim the back of my fingers along her nape, making her shiver. I draw my thumb around the base of her neck, up the column of her throat. I say nothing, and neither does she, but I can hear her breathing.

I hear me breathing too.

When she finally turns her head to the side, our gazes meet, hers full of confusion and lust.

I'm not confused. Not one bit. I know what I want.

And I'm going after it tonight.

CHAPTER 17

HANNAH

I don't understand what's happening between us.

Okay, scratch that. I get what's happening, but it's unfolding in such an…unusual way. I should've figured that we would've ended up like this, considering how he's come over to my house every night for the past couple of weeks, completely unsupervised. Just the two of us, alone. With only Maxine the cat watching us, keeping our secret.

Every night that he's here, the tension between us rises. I thought I could withstand it by staying away from him, but clearly, that didn't work. I wanted to be closer to him, and he knew it. And when he offered to braid my hair, I'd been so shocked, I readily agreed, figuring he'd do a crap job of it.

He didn't. Surprisingly enough, he's actually a decent braider, and the way he combed his fingers through my hair felt downright decadent. His fingers barely touching my neck are nearly my undoing. And when he traces the side of my throat, his touch featherlight, I turn to the side, my gaze meeting his, unsure of what to do next.

My lips are so dry I lick them, and Jake's gaze becomes hooded the moment he spots my tongue. I didn't even mean for that to happen. He just—his closeness makes me so nervous. I've kissed a few guys before, but nothing major. Nothing all-consuming and passionate like I read in my favorite books.

With Jake, I have the feeling it could be like that. Passionate. All-consuming. Scary in the best possible way.

His hand curls around the back of my neck, bringing me toward him, and I go willingly, my eyes fluttering shut when I feel his mouth press lightly against my jaw. He takes a deep breath, as if he's inhaling my scent, and everything inside of me turns to liquid. My lips are literally tingling, I want him to kiss me so bad.

So, so bad.

He shifts away from me, I can tell, and when I open my eyes I find him watching me, his lips parted, his gaze dark. "You're fucking with my head," he whispers.

I frown. His words, his tone, sounds…negative. "I'm—sorry?"

Slowly he shakes his head, his lips quirking into this closed-mouth side smile that's adorable. "It's not a bad thing. I mean, so far it hasn't been."

"Good to know," I say jokingly, then immediately regret it. Treating a serious moment with humor probably isn't the right thing to do.

His gaze never strays from mine as he murmurs, "You're all I think about."

Oh. I want to respond, but I can't come up with the right words, so I remain silent.

"I wake up in the morning and you're on my mind. I fall asleep thinking of you. I dream about you. It's like I can't stop." He cups the side of my face with his large hand, holding me still, and I stare up at him, willing him to say more. "You're not my type."

Well. That sentence was like a dump of ice-cold water.

I start to jerk out of his hold, but he tightens his grip ever so subtly, not letting me leave. "That's a good thing, Hannah. You're the complete opposite of any girl I've ever gone out with, and I like it. I like you."

I try to say something, but it comes out gargled and nonsensical, and I have to clear my throat before I can start over again. "I-I like you too."

His fingers gently slide down my face, his thumb streaking across my lips as he leans in. I'm lightheaded with anticipation, waiting, waiting, waiting...

Oh God.

His mouth is on my mouth. Soft. Warm. Lingering. He breaks the kiss, his lips hovering above mine for a moment that stretches on for so long, I'm afraid he's going to stop. But then they return. Firmer this time. Warmer. Damp. I kiss him back, sinking my mouth into his, parting my lips when I feel the teasing swipe of his tongue.

He's holding my face, cupping my cheeks in that ultra-romantic move I see in movies and TV shows and read about in books. Our mouths part with every pass of our lips, and then his tongue circles mine languidly, making my entire body tingle. We kiss and kiss, our bodies shifting, desperate to get closer, the old couch groaning with the movement. I cling to him like he's a lifeline, and he pulls me with him, until I'm falling onto his lap, his arm banded around my waist and holding me as close as possible.

"Your mouth drives me crazy," he murmurs against my lips minutes later, when our jaws are tired and our breathing is accelerated, like we just ran a marathon.

"What are you talking about?" He says things that are confusing. Or stuff that I downright don't believe. Like, how can my mouth drive him crazy?

"Your lips." His hand slips between us, fingers skimming over my bottom lip. "Fuck, they're so sexy."

Normally I would die if a boy said something like that to me. It would've taken everything inside of me not to burst out laughing, and I would've saved that little tidbit to report to Sophie first thing tomorrow, so we could laugh about it together.

But I'm not laughing. Not now. The way he's looking at me, how ragged his voice is. His forehead is pressed against mine and his index finger is tracing my lips, making me feel all tingly inside. I dart my tongue out to lick the tip of his finger as a sort of test, and oh my God, I think I just passed because then he's kissing me, devouring me.

Somehow I end up lying on the couch with Jake above me, our lower bodies crushed together, our mouths fused as he continues kissing me like he depends on it. Depends on me. I can feel him, can feel how hard he is, and I stare up at him when he lifts away from me, his chest heaving as he pushes his hair away from his forehead.

"I planned on taking it slow," he admits, his expression sheepish.

I start to giggle. I can't help it. "This is so not taking it slow," I tell him.

He smiles. Bends down to kiss me again, and I can tell it was supposed to be a quick little peck.

But I'm feeling bold. I wrap my hand around the back of his neck and keep him from moving away from my mouth. I part my lips beneath his, slide my tongue against his, and a rumbly groan comes from low in his chest as we instantly deepen the kiss. I'm being forward, and I'm never forward, but there's something about being with Jake like this, entwined with him on my couch late on a Thursday night, that has me feeling incredibly brave.

Maybe it's the way he's responding to me. Or the weight of his erection between my legs, which is as thrilling as it's also terrifying.

I'm completely new to this sort of thing. Totally out of my element. No guy has gone beyond first base with me, if we're keeping count, but I'm willing to take this further with Jake.

Definitely to second base. Maybe even third.

We keep this up for I don't know how long. Our mouths locked and our hands wandering everywhere we can reach. Our lower bodies grinding against each other in this natural rhythm as his erection strains against the front of his shorts. I both want to touch him there, and then again I don't. I'm completely inexperienced. I don't know exactly how he'd want me to touch him or where. So rather than make a fool of myself, I keep my hands above his hips, too scared to go below the waistline.

At one point, something lands on my head, pulling my hair, and I yelp in surprise, causing Jake to spring away from me. Turns out it's my cat, glaring at both of us before she hops off the couch with an indignant meow and trots off into the kitchen. I sit up, tugging my shirt down, running a hand through my thoroughly messed-up hair. All that worry about leaving the braid in my hair was for nothing.

I'm a wreck, thanks to Jake's wandering, amazing hands.

"I'll be right back," Jake mutters before he heads for the bathroom, shutting the door with a quiet click.

I sit in the middle of the couch, taking deep, cleansing breaths, wondering how I got here.

And how we're going to move forward.

I didn't want to push for any interaction at school because first, I was protecting myself, and second, I didn't think he wanted his friends to know about us. Not that I think he's ashamed of me or anything, because really, I didn't want them to know either. I don't trust them. Specifically Diego. He acts like he has a grudge against me.

It's unsettling, how much he seems to dislike me.

Jake remains in the bathroom for so long I decide to

follow Maxine into the kitchen, where she's sitting in front of her food dish, having a snack. I grab a bottle of water out of the refrigerator for myself and for Jake and carry them both back to the couch, settling in just when he exits the bathroom.

I watch him walk toward me, marveling at how easygoing he appears. I'm all wound up and a bundle of nerves while he seems completely unaffected. I try not to let my gaze drop to the front of his shorts, instead keeping my eyes on his.

He sits next to me on the couch, and I offer him the bottle of water without a word. He takes it, cracks the lid off and drinks from it for a long time before he twists the cap back on and then sets it on the floor at his feet. "I should probably go," he murmurs.

I'm suddenly fascinated with the way his mouth moves when he talks, I suppose because it just spent an inordinate amount of time on mine, kissing me senseless. His lips are swollen and damp, and I wish he would kiss me again. "What time is it?"

"Almost one."

My jaw drops open. "Seriously?" I squeak.

"Yeah." He smiles. Touches my cheek. "Seriously." Leaning in, he brushes my mouth with his. "I'll see you tomorrow at school?"

"Sure," I say breathlessly just before he kisses me again. "Won't you leave early for the away game?"

He frowns, his dark brows furrowed. "You're right. Guess I won't get to see you in art then."

I wait for him to ask me to wear his jersey. I've been waiting for it since he's been coming over, but so far, he hasn't mentioned it since our actual first encounter. Maybe he's afraid I'll turn him down again?

Maybe he doesn't want people to know we're sort of together after all?

I hate that last thought. And really, we're not together. Not like that.

Not yet.

"You'll try to go to the game tomorrow night?" he asks as he stands, stretching his arms above his head. I watch with dry-mouthed fascination as his T-shirt rides up, offering me a glimpse of his flat, perfect abs. I didn't dare stick my hand beneath his shirt when we were kissing earlier.

That was a dumb move.

"I'll try," I tell him as we walk toward the front door, though I doubt it'll actually happen. I don't have a car, and I don't think I have anyone to go with.

He kisses me before he leaves, and once he's gone, I slump against the door, a goofy smile on my face as I watch Maxine saunter toward the couch. My life is forever changed because of that kissing session on the couch.

I wonder if Jake feels the same way.

CHAPTER 18

JAKE

"We're fucking *killing* them." Diego raises his hand, and I slap it halfheartedly, then return my focus to the field. It's Friday night, we're more than halfway through the third quarter and we're leading the board 31-7. Nerves still eat at my gut, though I'm somewhat relieved by that score. It's a solid lead.

Away games always leave me unsettled. We've played this team every year since I was a freshman, but we're still visitors, uncomfortable on someone else's field. They just so happened to beat us both my freshman and sophomore year when I was on the JV team, though our varsity team has beat them for the past three years, so to come in and clean them up on their home turf feels pretty good.

But we're not out of the weeds yet. You can never get too confident, even when we're this deep into the game.

Yet another thing I learned that from my dad.

"Show some more enthusiasm, man. We're winning." Diego gives my shoulder a shake and I back out of his grip, shooting a glare at him. He steps away from me, holding his hands up like the police are holding a gun on him. "What's your problem?"

"Nothing." Not like I'm going to tell him anything. Diego wouldn't understand. He doesn't think like me. Feel like me.

And right now, despite the lead, despite the fact that we're most likely going to win this game, I feel...

Disappointed.

Let down.

"Whatever your problem is, I guess I can't complain. You've been a savage out there on the field tonight. That last spiral to me—damn, bro! It felt so easy, how it fell right into my hands," he continues, a giant shit-eating grin on his face.

We've been playing well this game, Diego and I. Normally I feel more connected to Tony. We have a rhythm together, and wherever I throw, he's usually right there waiting for me with open hands, ready to catch it.

Like Diego said, though, we're the ones on fire tonight, which is good. I like to change it up every once in a while, though it's not always by choice. I'm sure the opposing team watched our game tape, and they saw the relationship Tony and I have on the field. We threw them for a loop tonight, and it's working.

"Look, I'll show more enthusiasm when I see the final score on the board with us winning," I tell Diego, who makes a dismissive noise at my answer.

"Can't you be in a good mood for once in your life? Jesus." Diego stalks off, shaking his head, and I remain quiet, letting him go.

I can't tell him the real reason I'm so fucking grumpy.

Glancing over my shoulder, I check the stands yet again. The cheer team is right there, practically in front of my face, shaking their poms and their asses to some cheer about moving the ball and scoring six. They do a twirl, their skirts flaring, and

I spot Ava, her ponytail swishing as she spins. Luckily, Cami doesn't see me and I can't really see her either, since she's in the front row center spot for the crowd to watch her.

She wants all eyes on her, always.

I don't care about the cheer team, though. I'm looking for Hannah. Right before I left her apartment last night, I asked if she was coming to the game and she said she'd try, though her wary expression told me otherwise.

That should've been my first clue.

I didn't see her all day today at school, not that I figured I would, but I kept looking. Didn't even pass her in the halls this morning. At lunch, instead of hanging out in the quad, we were in the team room, reviewing our opposing team's game tape, watching for mistakes, searching for weaknesses. After lunch, both the JV and varsity teams gathered up our stuff, boarded the buses and took the hour-long drive to where we're at now. When we arrived, we ate an early dinner, warmed up and watched the JV game.

It feels like we've been here for days.

The joke's on me, because I assumed I'd eventually find Hannah in the bleachers tonight. Not like a lot of people from our school come to away games, especially when they're far. There's a decent amount of students from my school sitting together, but it's the usual crowd who come to games. Parents and family members, and the leadership kids who are full of spirit and rah-rah at every fucking school event we've got. Hannah is one of them; I know she's in the leadership class.

But I don't see her.

The disappointment that she didn't come tonight is like a punch in the gut. I'm upset. Even...hurt, which I know is ridiculous, but I can't help it. Like she can't come to one freakin' away game to watch me? I'm sure she's friends with all the leadership people. They're all here. Why didn't she ask one of them to take her to the game? Why didn't she come with her tall friend Sophie? I know she has a car.

"Fuck," I mutter under my breath, wishing I could kick something. Or better…

Punch something.

"What crawled up your ass and died?"

I glance to my right to see Tony standing there, his helmet off, his still-damp-with-sweat dark hair ruffling with the breeze. He's watching me with that calm, stoic expression he's always wearing, and I wonder what it's like, to always be so damn rational all the time. His parents are fucking idiots, I'm pretty sure he has more money than my family does—and that's saying a lot—and he's alone pretty much twenty-four-seven, yet he seems like he's got his shit together.

Me? I feel like a raging mess. Especially lately. And I come from a well-adjusted family with both parents always home and no real problems.

"Nothing," I tell him, turning my head so I don't have to look at him. I keep my gaze focused on the game, my chest feeling tight as I watch our defense work their hardest to keep the other team from scoring. It's a struggle, I can see it in their faces, their tense body language, and I'm pretty sure I just heard Caleb cuss someone out on the field.

"Bullshit," Tony says pleasantly. "You're wound up tight, and your hand is literally clenched into a fist."

Glancing down, I see he's right. I slowly relax my fingers, shaking them out. I need to get over myself.

"Are you pissed at me or what?" Tony asks.

I whip my head in his direction. "Why would I be pissed at you?"

He shrugs. "I'm not playing my best. I've had a few fuck ups out there. Missed a few throws."

"It's all good," I tell him, being one-hundred percent truthful. "Diego's coming through tonight."

"Thank God," Tony mutters, shaking his head. "Can't wait to hear what Coach has to say about my game play afterwards."

"We can't all be superstars all the time," I remind him. "Let Diego enjoy his moment of glory."

"And yours," Tony adds.

I say nothing. When we win, I get plenty of glory. But when we lose, it's all my fault.

At least, that's what it feels like.

"What's going on with you and that Hannah chick?" Tony asks out of nowhere.

"Nothing." I refuse to look over at the bleachers anymore. She's not here. She didn't come to watch me. I need to get over it.

"That's too bad," he says.

I wait for him to continue, but he remains quiet. One of our coaches calls a timeout and our defense team makes its way toward the sidelines. Still, Tony says nothing. I finally can't take it any longer.

"Why would you say that?"

"I think I like her friend," he says.

"Which friend?" I know who he means, but I guess I want to hear him admit it.

"The blonde. Sophie."

I glance over to find he's already looking at me. "Really? I've never seen you guys together at school."

"That's because you're not paying attention. Besides, we don't talk much at school." Tony shrugs.

"When do you talk to her?"

"At night, after she finishes her dance classes. Usually on Snapchat, though I Facetimed her last night." He says this so casually, like it's no big deal that he talks to her. That he wants to spend time with her.

Sophie is like Hannah—not part of our crowd. She's not

what anyone would call a loser either. At least, I don't think they would, though Diego has called Hannah a loser before, the asshole.

No one picked on Sophie that I ever saw, though I wasn't really paying attention either. She's just…there. Shy and quiet, she never really says much. When we first moved to this town and I started the seventh grade, I remember her being really tall and super skinny. She was taller than me. Taller than most of us guys. A couple of us caught up with her eventually, including myself and Tony.

She's nice enough. Not what I would consider hot, but she's sort of cute, if you like skinny blondes. Which apparently, Tony does. At least he's around six feet, so she won't tower over him.

"Did she come to the game?" I know I would've spotted her if she had, but maybe I'm blind to anyone else but Hannah.

"She couldn't make it. She had a special dance practice scheduled tonight. They're learning choreography for their upcoming competition season," Tony says, using words I've never heard him say before in my life.

I'm tempted to spill. To confess I've been talking to Hannah for the past couple of weeks. Hanging out at her apartment. That I finally kissed her last night and now I want more. How I'm disappointed by her not showing up at the game tonight. Tony would listen. He'd understand, not like our other friends.

Maybe Tony could talk me off the ledge, tell me I'm being an asshole—because I'm pretty sure I'm being one. My chest grows tight once again, the words ready to burst from me, but Diego reappears in front of us, a giant smile on his face.

"They're gonna hold them from scoring. I just fucking know it. Watch, all they're gonna get is a field goal." He holds up his hand for a high-five, and Tony gives him one, smacking his palm extra hard. "We need to celebrate tonight!"

Typical Diego. Always looking for a reason to party.

Our defense runs back out on the field, and within a few seconds, Diego's prediction comes true. Our defensive line holds them off, they kick for a field goal and get it, and now the score is 31-10. It's our turn to get back out on the field and play.

I need to keep my head in the game, and not on Hannah. Losing my train of thought isn't worth losing tonight. Gotta keep my focus on what's important: football.

Not girls.

CHAPTER 19

JAKE

"You want another one?"

Glancing up, I see Caleb has a beer can in his hand, holding it out toward me with an expectant expression on his face. Once I nod my answer, he tosses it and I catch the beer with one hand, cracking it open before I take a couple of swallows.

"Thanks," I tell him, then immediately belch.

Shit. This is my fourth beer. Or maybe my fifth? I don't normally get shit faced after an away game. I'm usually too tired, too completely over it and ready to collapse in bed, but tonight, I'm feeling down over not seeing Hannah. Which makes me the biggest pussy in all the fuckin' land.

We're at Diego's house. Somehow he convinced his overbearing mother to let him have a little get-together after we came home from the game, as long as we keep it outside. They have a decent-sized backyard, plenty of room to roam and lots of outdoor furniture for all of us to sit on.

It was supposed to be just for the team at first—Diego's mom frowns on him having any other girl over to the house besides Jocelyn—but once his parents' light went out in their bedroom, the girls started trickling in.

Not one of them is Jocelyn.

"Where's your girl?" Tony asks Diego, who's approaching our circle of chairs. It's me, Caleb, Tony and one of the juniors on the team, Wyatt, sitting together, talking. Drinking. Drinking way too much.

Diego makes a dismissive noise. "Staying the night with her volleyball team coach. They have a tournament tomorrow and they're leaving first thing in the morning."

"So you invite other girls to come over instead?" Tony's brows shoot up.

"It's the cheer team, come on. Big deal." Diego sends Tony a scathing look before he abandons us.

"He doesn't like to be called out on his shit," I tell Tony. Especially when he's acting like a cocky asshole tonight because of his excellent gameplay earlier. I don't mind the arrogance so much.

It's the shitty attitude toward us I don't like.

"Too bad. He's a shit boyfriend. We should tell Jocelyn," Tony says with disgust, shaking his head.

"Pretty sure Jocelyn already knows." This is coming from Caleb, who's the closest with Diego out of all of us.

I've heard the rumors. Witnessed Jocelyn break up with Diego only to get back together with him the very next day. She's willing to go all the way with him. Meaning, she won't give up on him despite everything he does. She lets him get away with all sorts of shit and tolerates his bad behavior.

"That sucks," Tony says before draining the last of the beer from his can and tossing it on the ground. "This beer sucks too."

"Best we could find at the last minute," Caleb says.

Diego has an older brother who'll get us alcohol when we ask. He just doesn't like being asked last minute, which is what happened tonight. I'm sure they got into an argument over it and now we're suffering with cheap ass beer.

"Hey, Callahan." This is from Wyatt. I turn to look at him. "You still fucking around with Cami?"

"Hell no," I say immediately, my stomach turning at just hearing her name. "We've been done for a while."

"Looks like Diego's pretty interested in her," Wyatt observes, his gaze locked on a spot across the yard.

I glance over my shoulder to see Diego and Cami standing close to each other by the fence, appearing deep in conversation, their expressions serious. I wonder what they could be talking about.

I also wonder if Diego really is interested in Cami. That's kind of fucked up. Goes completely against bro code. And the fact that he has a steady girlfriend who adores his lame ass.

"Don't be starting no shit, Wyatt. They're just friends," Caleb says, sounding irritated. "Those two...they have a love-hate relationship."

"There's a thin line..." Tony's voice drifts, and I send him a questioning look. He shrugs. "Between love and hate, dumbass."

We all start laughing, even though it's not that funny. I suppose it's because Tony is about the only person I'd let call me a dumbass to my face. Not even Diego or Caleb can get away with that shit.

"Why isn't your sister here?" Wyatt asks, and before I can answer, Caleb speaks for me.

"Jake doesn't allow Ava to show up to these parties," he says with a giant grin.

"That's not true," I mutter, though it sort of is. When she got on the cheer team, I gave her plenty of advice on whose house she should avoid when there's a party, and which guys on the team she should avoid too. I gave her all that info when she first started high school. Pretty much everyone at school knows to keep the hell away from my sister.

"Please." Caleb tosses his empty beer can at me, and I bat it away before it makes contact. "You encourage her to stay away from us."

"Because you're all pigs." I can't imagine any of my friends getting with my sister. They're all just…no. I know too many details, especially with Caleb. He's a complete manwhore and proud of it.

"She's cute," Wyatt says, seemingly unaware that I have strict rules about the football team and Ava. I don't like to hear any of them say that sort of thing about her, no matter how innocent it sounds.

"She's hot as fuck," Caleb adds, earning a dirty look from me. He knows better. But he's also drunk, and he's trying to antagonize me.

"Ava is off limits," I tell them firmly as I scan each of their faces, saving Wyatt for last. "You two are in the same grade, right?"

Wyatt nods, but he looks scared. Good. "We have a couple of classes together. She's cool."

He leaves it at that, and thankfully the conversation about my sister is over.

Deciding I need to walk around and talk to other people versus just sit slumped in a chair and mope over Hannah, I get up and try to mingle. It's pretty quiet. There's not a lot of yelling or carrying on like at Tony's parties after a home game. This feels more like a hook-up night. Everyone's pairing off and finding dark corners to get cozy in, or they're just leaving outright. I've had too much to drink so I can't leave, unless someone drives me home. Maybe Tony. I've only seen him drink one beer, but I haven't been keeping close tabs on him either, so I don't know.

I find Cami and Diego still talking over by the fence, and I approach them like I've got nothing to lose, which I don't. They take a few steps apart when they catch sight of me, and I'm surprised Cami doesn't run away. Nope, instead she remains where she's at, her arms crossed, still wearing her uniform like every other cheerleader here.

Sometimes I wonder if they wear them to catch our attention. See if we're interested in what they've got on beneath the short skirt.

"What's up, Callahan?" Diego says, his voice easy as he holds his hand out for a bro handshake.

I slap my palm in his and we perform some complicated handshake that has Cami rolling her eyes. "What are you two talking about?" I ask.

"Jocelyn," Diego says easily, slipping his hands in his front pockets. I'm immediately suspicious. "Getting some relationship advice from Cam here."

I want to laugh. Bet she gives really shitty advice. "Things okay?"

There's absolutely no reason for him to get "advice" from Cami. I call bullshit. But I have no idea what Diego's doing, so I just play along.

"Not really," Diego says with a sigh and a sad shake of his head. "But we'll work it out. Eventually. We always do."

I glance over at Cami, who's grimacing. "What's going on with you?" she asks me when she catches me looking.

Shrugging, I glance around at anything and everything but her. "None of your damn business."

"You're such a dick," she mutters.

"He's got the hots for some redhead, you know," Diego says, smiling when I send him a murderous glare. "That one loser you used to be friends with in elementary school, Cam. Remember when she came to your swim party the summer after sixth grade?" They both start laughing and the sound infuriates me. "What's her name again?"

He knows exactly what her name is.

"Hannah Walsh? Oh God." Cami starts laughing even harder and it sounds…nasty. Mean. "Really, Jake, why are you interested in her? She's so—*beneath* us."

Love how Cami includes herself, as if she's some high-and-mighty princess.

"You two need to shut the hell up," I tell them, my voice tense, my entire body vibrating with anger. "You don't even know her."

Not like I do.

"See, that's the problem. We *do* know her. I've gone to school with her since, like, kindergarten," Diego says, and Cami nods her agreement. "She was a little loser when she was five, and she's a big ol loser now. I have no idea what you see in her."

"She must put out," Cami adds with a sneer. "I bet she spreads her legs for Mr. Popular real fast."

"Nah." Diego slowly shakes his head, and I take a step closer to him, anger making my blood run hot. His dark eyes glitter as he stares at me, and he knows I'm mad. He can see it. He knows me well enough.

But the fucker doesn't give a shit. It's like he wants to get me riled up.

"It's that mouth," he says, his voice low. "All pouty and full. I called them dick-sucking lips a few days ago."

Cami makes a gagging noise.

"That's what Jake likes about her. I bet he's asking her to open wide every night with that pretty little mouth and making her choke on his fat cock," Diego says, his voice soft.

I clench my hands into fists, ready to pummel his face. Fuck this guy. Why is he goading me like this? He's supposed to be my friend.

"Why isn't she here then, huh? Where's your little girlfriend, Jakey?" Cami asks in that simpering baby voice she puts on. She thinks it's sexy, but it's annoying as hell. "What, is she not good enough for you to invite over?"

"Both of you need to shut the fuck up," I say between clenched teeth. I don't put my hands on women. And I really don't like getting in physical fights with my friends. It's messed up.

But Diego is tempting me to shut him up with my fist.

"He's embarrassed," Diego says, flashing a quick smile in Cami's direction. "Deep down, he knows she's not good enough to hang out with us. She's nothing but trash. It's cool, though. I get it. We all like to slum it every once in a while."

I see red, and it happens without thought. My right arm swings, my fist making full contact with Diego's smug face, directly into his shit-talking mouth, and he falls to the ground, causing Cami to jump backward as she screams at the top of her lungs.

"What the *fuck*, man?" Diego roars, hopping to his feet and charging me. I tumble onto the grass, Diego on top of me, his hands pummeling my ribcage, my stomach. He gets one good punch right by my eye, making my head knock back, and for a second I see stars. I can guarantee I'll get a black eye from that one. Cami is still screaming, yelling our names and begging us to stop as we roll around together on the ground.

After much struggling, I finally gain the upper hand, rising onto my knees, Diego's torso lodged between them as he lays sprawled on the ground. His expression is murderous, though he's smiling, bleeding from the cut in the corner of his mouth. His teeth are red and he turns to the side, spitting pink onto the ground. My stomach roils.

Guilt hits me, mixed with anger. Why is he letting a girl get between us? Why does it matter to him that I'm interested in Hannah?

"Go ahead," he taunts, lifting his chin, giving me the

perfect spot to aim for. "Hit me. Hit me, motherfucker. Go ahead and do it. You know you want to."

Why is he talking to me like that? Why does he want me to hit him?

It doesn't make any sense.

My arm is cocked back, I'm ready to punch him dead in the face again, but someone grabs hold of my arm, pulling me off of Diego with one hard tug.

"What are you doing? What the *fuck* are you doing?" It's Tony. He's in my face, his fingers curled into the front of my shirt as he jerks me around, trying to jerk some sense into me, I guess. His eyes are wide, they're staring straight into mine, and he looks furious. Downright horrified.

Shaking my head, I try to speak, but nothing comes out. My ribs feel like they're on fire. My head is spinning and I'm seeing two Tonys, not just one. "Oh shit."

I pull myself out of my friend's hold just in time to run over to a nearby flowerbed and puke my guts out. I clutch my stomach, my ribs aching as I retch over Diego's mama's marigolds. All that's coming up is foam and beer, and I can hear some of the girls squealing when they see me vomiting. Caleb is trying to take care of Diego, I can hear him repeatedly telling Diego to calm the fuck down, and Tony's standing next to me, offering me a paper towel he found somewhere.

The sound of a slamming door puts everyone on high alert, and that's my cue to get the hell out.

"What in the world? Are you *fighting* right now? Why all the screaming?" Diego's mom comes charging out of the house, clad in only a long, pink cotton nightgown and matching pink slippers, appearing ready to throw down. "Get out! Get the hell out of my yard! Diego, where did these girls come from, hmm?"

I wipe my mouth with the paper towel and let Tony and

Wyatt escort my ass out of there, their steps so quick, they're practically dragging me. I let them, not bothering to look for Diego or Cami.

I've got nothing left to say to them.

My head is still spinning, and my mouth tastes like absolute ass. They help me into Tony's BMW—thank God I didn't drive my truck over here, it's still at the school—and then Wyatt is climbing into the backseat and we're taking off, pulling out of the Garcia driveway with a roar of the engine.

"You good?" I ask him as he turns onto the street. I know I saw him with a beer earlier.

Tony nods, his expression grim. "That little fight sobered me the fuck up."

I say nothing else, just sit there in misery.

We remain quiet as Tony drives through town, his focus on the road before him as he keeps the speed just under the posted limit. I've got my arms wrapped around my ribs as I stare morosely out the window, trying to take deep breaths, but it hurts. It actually hurts to breathe. And my right eye is fucking throbbing right now.

Damn it, I was just healing over the last fight I got into, and now I'm injured all over again. I'm going to be a scarred-up mess by the end of the school year.

"You want some gum?" Wyatt leans over the center console with a stick of gum in his hand, holding it toward him. I take it from him with a low groan, undo the wrapper and pop it into my mouth, thankful for the rush of mint that coats my tongue.

"Thanks," I tell him, glancing over at Tony whose face is so tight, it looks like it might shatter. "You pissed?"

"Fuck yeah I am. What the hell happened that made you punch Diego, man? What did he say? Is he fucking Cami? Is that what he told you?"

I blink at him, startled by what he said. "What do you mean? Are they fucking?"

"I don't know. You tell me."

"I didn't ask him about that."

"Then why did you hit him?"

"Because." I look out the window once more. "He was shit talking Hannah."

"Ahhh."

"Don't 'ahhh' me. You gonna start shit talking her next?"

"No, you idiot. I want to go out with her best friend," he says, sounding annoyed.

"Who's this Hannah chick's best friend?" Wyatt asks from the backseat.

"Shut up, Wyatt," Tony and I both say at the same time.

"Whatever," Wyatt mumbles, throwing himself against the back seat. "I'm always the last to know what's going on."

"Tell us exactly what happened," Tony says to me, his voice somewhat calm. "What led up to you sucker punching one of your best friends?"

I explain everything. I start with Diego's attitude at the game tonight. Giving me shit for being in a sour mood. Acting like he's the king of the team because he scored so many touchdowns—thanks to my throws. Normally I prefer sharing the spotlight. It takes some of that harsh light off of me.

But I don't particularly like sharing it with an arrogant ass, even if that arrogant ass is my friend.

It's hard to tell Tony and Wyatt what Diego said about Hannah. I try not to go into too many details, but damn. If I don't, then they won't understand why I got so mad in the first place.

"Explain why that made you so pissed," Wyatt says when I'm finished. "You into this Hannah chick or what? You two together? Fuckin' around? Is Diego right? Are you making her choke on your dick or what?"

I'm half tempted to unleash my anger on Wyatt, but I restrain myself. He's lost in this story, and he's drunk. I like Wyatt. He's a transfer kid. He started here the beginning of his freshman year, coming from out of state, and it's hard to find your place among such a clique-y group who've gone to school together since the beginning of time.

I should know. I was that transfer kid once myself.

"You don't have to explain yourself," Tony says to me, sending a meaningful look to Wyatt in the rearview mirror. "I get it. *We* get it."

Wyatt continues mumbling in the back seat, clearly put out, but we ignore him.

"I like her," I admit to Tony. "And Diego's been against it since the start."

"Why does it even matter? That's what I don't get."

"I don't either," I mutter, reaching into the pocket of my jeans—ow, that hurts my ribs like a mother—looking for my phone.

But it's not there. I reach into my back pockets, staring at Tony's center console, but the phone isn't in either of those places either.

Shit.

"I think I lost my phone," I say.

Tony sends me a quick glance. "At Diego's?"

I nod miserably. "Yeah."

Fuck.

CHAPTER 20

HANNAH

*I*t's Saturday night and this weekend has absolutely sucked. The only bright spot being that my mom was home, since she didn't have to work, and we were able to get some things done around the apartment. That kept me busy. Things we'd been putting off for a while, like deep-cleaning both of our closets and the bathroom. Trashing lots of useless stuff and bagging up old clothes we didn't want anymore, so Mom can drop the bags off at the local thrift shop later. Cleaning was the distraction I needed, since I haven't heard from Jake at all since Thursday night. No texts. No snaps. No DMs.

Nothing.

I wanted to go to the game so bad, but I had no one to go with. I couldn't take the car and I didn't feel confident enough to ask the few people I talk to in leadership if they'd give me a ride. Plus, Sophie had a special dance rehearsal class Friday night, and Marty refuses to go to any and all football games thanks to his awful cousin.

So I stayed home instead, sad and miserable, locked away in my room with Maxine as my only company. Mom went out to dinner with her boyfriend, Rick. They invited me to go with them, but I turned them down. They didn't need me tagging along like a third wheel.

God, that is the story of my life, I swear.

Since I still don't have his phone number—lame—I sent Jake a DM on Instagram late Friday afternoon wishing him good luck with the game, but I never heard back from him. I don't even think he opened it.

Saturday evening Rick came over and he and Mom watched movies on Netflix, just like I did with Jake all last week. It made me miss him so badly, and I sat in my room with the cat, reliving Thursday night with Jake in my head. How he touched me. His mouth on mine. The words he said…

My phone dings with a notification and I see it's from Jake on Instagram.

My heart rate speeding up, I quickly tap the notification and it takes me to IG. I open my DMs and click on the one from Jake.

Too bad you weren't there.

That's all it says.

I bite my lower lip, wondering how I can respond. From that simple sentence, I can't tell his tone. Is he mad? Indifferent? Casual? I don't know.

God, I hate feeling unsure.

Deciding I need to answer him, I send him a response. **I'm really sorry I missed the game. Glad to hear you won, though!**

I don't hear from Jake for five minutes. Ten. Fifteen. I want to say something. I want to ask him what's wrong, but I restrain myself.

Finally nearly thirty minutes later, he responds. **I don't think this is going to work.**

My heart bottoms out. What does he mean, it's not going

to work? What's not going to work? Us? This conversation? Us?

He has to mean us.

All sorts of questions run through my head, but I can't ask him any. Not like this. Not over Instagram DM. How lame. And I don't want to look desperate. I probably already do. With shaking fingers, I send him a reply. **What do you mean?**

More waiting. Almost an hour ticks by. I'm crying. Not full-blown sobbing, but the tears won't stop sliding down my face and I keep wiping them away with the hem of my shirt. I don't know how he can go from practically mauling me on my couch Thursday night to telling me this isn't going to work by Saturday. It makes no sense.

He doesn't make any sense.

When he finally does respond, a gasp escapes me when I see it.

A photo of him and Cami. Kissing. It looks like she's sitting in his lap, and her arm is slung across his shoulders. Their lips are smashed together, their eyes closed. The image is a little fuzzy. Out of focus. His hand is cupping the side of her face, just like he kissed me a few nights ago, and revulsion fills me, making it hard to swallow.

Another message comes through.

Leave us alone.

And that's it. That's all I get.

I bury my face in my pillow and sob, hating how confused I feel. I'm PMSing too, which doesn't help my emotional state. I'm fragile as it is. Having Jake telling me it's over and sending me a photo of him and Cami together feels like a stab directly in the heart.

What makes it worse is I can't talk to Sophie. She let me know Saturday morning that her dad surprised the family with a quick trip to San Francisco so they can see *Hamilton* live, and while I'm thrilled for her and can't wait to hear all about it Monday morning, I wish I could FaceTime her right now. Sophie always knows how to make me feel better. She lets me get my rage out and encourages it. She'd call Jake a few choice words, we'd bash Cami and what a train wreck she is, and while it wouldn't solve all my problems, it would lighten my heavy thoughts.

Instead, I'm stuck with all those heavy thoughts, trying my best to focus on *Jane the Virgin* on Netflix. I love this show and I've already run through the entire series once, but it's like comfort when I'm feeling down.

And right now, I'm feeling really, really down.

MONDAY MORNING I come to school extra early so I can hide out in the library, head bent over a book like I'm studying as if my life depended on it. The words blur the longer I stare at them, and I try my best not to react every time the door opens. Yet I glance up each time someone enters the building, disappointment hitting me when it's not one of my friends.

Or Jake.

Ha. Please. Like he hangs out in the library. He probably forgets this building even exists. And why would I even want to see him? I'm angry at the callous way he treated me. Who the hell does that? Dumps a girl via Instagram DM with a few choice words and a photo of him and his ex? Like, that's just the rudest thing ever.

Did I get dumped because I didn't have sex with him Thursday night? Is that all he wanted from me? I mean, yeah, things got a little carried away, and I was perfectly willing to let them get even more carried away, but he was the one who ended it first. I thought he was being a gentleman.

Maybe he just wasn't feeling it between us.

Sighing, I rub my hand across my eyes, willing them to focus. I'm so tired. I didn't get much sleep last night, thanks to me worrying about showing up at school today. Plus, I'm confused. So confused by the way he treated me. All this hot-and-cold bullshit is too much.

I don't get it. I don't know what happened. The more I think about it, the more it seems that maybe that night actually didn't happen at all.

Finally Sophie enters the library, her eyes wide as she scans the tables. I assume she's looking for me.

When she spots me, she practically runs over to my table, collapsing into the chair across from mine and tossing her backpack on the table with a loud clatter. "Oh my God, I have so much to tell you."

I try to keep my expression neutral. I don't have the heart to tell her I don't care about *Hamilton*. Not this morning. "I can't wait to hear about the play," I say instead, like a glutton for punishment.

She waves a hand as if she's dismissing what I just said. "Forget the play. It was great. I'll tell you about it later. First, I need to let you know that I talked to Tony last night, after we got home."

Oh. Great. I don't want to hear her go on and on about Tony and how much she likes him while my potential relationship just crashed and burned. She'll make me feel like even more of an epic fail.

"Did he ask you out or something?" I ask warily.

"No, he told me everything that happened Friday night after the game, though he swore me to secrecy." She glances around as if making sure no one's listening to us before she lowers her tone. "He said I could tell *you* everything, though."

My heart pangs and I force a smile on my face. "What is it? What happened?"

"Well, I guess once they all got back to school after the game, a bunch of them went over to Diego's house and hung out in his backyard. They started drinking a lot, and Diego and Jake were talking, and it started looking a little intense, you know?" When I nod, she continues, "And then out of nowhere—Jake punched Diego."

I feel like my eyes are about to bug out of my head. "What? Are you serious?"

"Shh, keep your voice down," Sophie scolds me, looking around one more time, I'm sure she's checking to make sure no one heard me.

"Sorry, sorry." I clear my throat and try to compose myself. "Why did they get into a fight? Did Tony say?"

"Oh yeah, and you're not going to believe it." Sophie hesitates and I squirm in my seat, the anticipation nearly killing me. If this has anything to do with Cami, I'll be pissed. "It was over you."

"*What?*" Okay, I yelled that response, but she can't blame me. Hello, what she just admitted shocked the crap out of me.

Sophie sends me a stern look but doesn't call me out. "It's true."

"But why are they fighting about me?" I rest my hand against my chest, aware of the thundering of my heart beneath my palm. "I don't understand why."

"Hold on, let me explain what I know." She leans across the table, her voice even lower than before. "I guess Diego and Cami were saying—not nice things about you, and it made Jake angry. Tony didn't share all the details, because I'm sure he didn't want you to know exactly what was said, but he told me it was bad. Jake got so mad, he punched Diego right in the mouth, and then they were rolling around on the ground together, throwing punches at each other in a total free for all.

Tony said it was crazy. He had to break up the fight or it was going to get worse."

"That sounds terrible," I breathe, my mind racing, filled with all sorts of confusing thoughts. "But it doesn't make any sense, Jake running to my defense."

Sophie frowns. "Why not?"

I tell her about the messages I received from Jake Saturday night. How he sent me a photo of him and Cami. I even pull out my phone and bring up the messages so she can look at the photo. I barely glance at it as I hand my phone to my friend.

Seeing him kiss Cami makes my heart feel like it wants to shrivel up and die.

Sophie studies the image for a long time, pursing her lips before she finally looks up at me. "This photo is old."

I frown. "What do you mean?"

"Look at Cami's hair. It's a lot shorter. She wears her hair longer now." Sophie hands me back my phone and I re-examine the image.

Sophie is right. Cami's hair is definitely shorter in the picture.

"And she doesn't have all her precious golden highlights," Sophie adds, sounding the faintest bit annoyed. We're not big fans of Cami, even before this all went down.

"And they just…generally look younger. I'd guess that photo was taken a few years ago, back when they were together. Probably sophomore year." Sophie wiggles her fingers, indicating she wants my phone back, and I hand it to her. She looks over the photo once more. "Yeah. It's definitely old. Why would he send you an old photo of him and his ex?"

"I don't know? Because he's an asshole?" I shrug.

"He gets into a fight with one of his best friends over you Friday night, and then sends you these weird messages

Saturday." Sophie sets the phone down in the middle of the table. "You're right. This makes no sense. It almost makes me wonder…"

"Wonder what?" I ask.

"If someone else had his phone and sent you those messages," she says cryptically.

"Like who? How could they get a hold of his phone? Come on." I shake my head. "You're being kind of ridiculous."

"This entire situation is ridiculous!" Sophie's eyes are actually sparkling. She seems pretty hyped up. "And it's kind of exciting, if you ask me. Jake Callahan fought his best friend over you! That's like something out of a movie."

"Yeah, well I don't want to get caught up in the middle of their argument." That's the absolute last thing I want. "No thanks."

"You have to admit it's kind of romantic."

"If you think violence is romantic," I say with a sniff.

"Oh come on, you're being no fun. This is just so—over the top, I guess." She taps her finger against her lips. "I'm going to get to the bottom of this."

I'm ready to tell her not to bother when Marty suddenly appears at our table with a little wave. Once he's settled into the chair next to mine, Sophie fills Marty in on what she found out from Tony Sorrento about the Friday night fight. His expression goes from alarmed to full-on bursting glee when she mentions Jake punching Diego square in the face.

"Your crush is my new freaking hero," Marty says to me as he starts to laugh.

"It's not funny," I tell him. When he sends me an incredulous look, I forge on. "I'm serious! I don't like that they're fighting over me. It's totally unnecessary."

Then I tell Marty about my DM conversation with Jake on Saturday night, and he immediately demands to see the photo.

"It's old, right? Don't you think?" Sophie asks as Marty stares at my phone screen.

"Definitely." He sends me and Sophie a knowing look as he hands back the phone. "Did you see her eyebrows? Those are definitely from sophomore year."

"What are you talking about—*oh*." Cami's eyebrows are thick and heavily penciled in. They look terrible. Way too big for her face. She kept up that trend only for a few months. "How could I forget she used to do that?"

Sophie swipes the phone out of my hand and starts giggling. "Oh, those eyebrows are so bad," she says. "But I'm not going to say a word because that girl has caused me nothing but heartache, especially in middle school. She'll get her karma in the end."

"What did she do to you in middle school?" Marty asks. When we both send him a surprised look, he winces. "I was so wrapped up in my own drama, I don't remember anyone else's."

"Well, we all remember what she did to Hannah," Sophie starts.

Right. My first kiss was memorable, only because it was so awful. Sixth grade, the first boy-girl party I went to was at Cami's house. It was a swim party at the beginning of summer, and there were so many of us there. Everyone eventually got bored with swimming and playing in the pool, and we started playing spin the bottle.

I didn't want to play because I was too scared of that bottle landing on me, but I did it anyway. I didn't want to face the wrath of Cami. Our friendship by that time was waning, and I wasn't ready to give up on it. When it was finally my turn to spin, it landed on Rob Schaffer, the one who lied and told Mrs. Sanborne that Jake threatened him.

He's always been a jerk, even back then. He didn't want me

to kiss him, and I didn't want to kiss him either. He actually tried to run away from me and they all chased after him, then held him down in a chair while everyone chanted *kiss him, kiss him.*

They pretty much made me do it. And it was one of the most embarrassing moments of my life.

"Of course we do," Marty says, sending me a sympathetic look. "The Rob Schaffer kissing incident?"

I roll my eyes. "Please don't mention it."

"You don't remember her calling me a giraffe?" Sophie asks Marty.

"I thought Caleb started that," Marty says.

"Oh, he participated, but it was all Cami's idea at first," Sophie says irritably. "She put him up to it. He called me a giraffe pretty much the entirety of seventh grade." She starts to laugh. "It sounds so silly now, but back then I was mortified on a daily basis. Especially because I thought Caleb was so cute."

"We all thought Caleb was cute," I remind her.

"He still is," Marty says, and we all start laughing.

The five-minute warning bell rings and we gather our stuff, making our way to our first period classes. Nerves eat at me as I say goodbye to my friends, though I don't know why. I never see Jake around campus this early in the day.

But of course, my gaze finds him standing near a row of lockers, and my heart stutters. He's a head taller than pretty much everyone else filling the hallway, and I can't tear my eyes off of him, though I know I should. He has a black eye. The bruise is dark and circles almost his entire eye, and it looks terrible. Painful.

My heart breaks for him, that he got hurt.

Then I think of him sending me those messages and I'm upset all over again.

Thankfully, he's not paying attention to me as I approach.

He's too focused on whoever is standing in front of him, talking animatedly.

Air seems to freeze in my throat when I realize who it is.

Cami Lockhart.

I quickly look away from Jake and keep my head down, passing by him and Cami as fast as possible. Cami always talks so loudly that I can hear pretty much every word she says to him as I walk by.

"I have no idea what you're talking about." Her voice is firm, even filled with a little irritation. "And quit trying to make this into something that it's not."

My heart sinks and I pause for a moment, gaping at both of them like I can't help myself. What are they talking about? She was at that party Friday night. Of course she was. Did she try to start something up again with Jake? And did he fall for her yet again? I thought he was smarter than that, but…

Maybe not.

If they're together, then why would he defend me by trying to take out Diego?

Cami glances over in my direction and when she spots me, she frowns. "What the hell are you looking at?" she snaps.

I blink at her, frozen in place for a second too long. Just enough time for Jake to notice me standing there gawking at them. His gaze meets mine for the briefest moment, turbulent blue eyes full of surprise and concern, and we both stand there, gaping at each other.

When he doesn't move, doesn't even bother to say a single word, my heart feels like it just cracked wide open.

"N-nothing," I tell her before I practically run away from them, biting the inside of my lip hard so I won't cry. I refuse to cry in front of them, in front of anyone. I'm not much of a crier anyway, but seeing the two of them together, hearing their conversation, remembering his rude messages…

It's pushing me to my absolute limit.

I tell myself I can't look back. No way will I look at him again, and I definitely don't want Cami to catch me spying on her, but it's like I have no control over myself.

Glancing over my shoulder, I see Jake is staring at me, pain in his gaze. Confusion. He starts walking away from Cami, heading straight toward me. But Cami stops him, her hand on his arm, her tone sharp as she keeps talking. I can hear her high-pitched voice, but I can't make out what she's saying.

And I definitely don't want to know what she's saying either.

* * *

I MOVE through the rest of the morning in a fog. I sit in the quad at the beginning of lunch listening to Sophie talk about her trip to San Francisco, and how great the play was. Marty and I nod our agreement, and all I want to do is ask her if she's found anything else out about the fight and the photo and whatever happened to Jake's phone.

Right at the moment there's a lull in the conversation, Tony shows up at our table, his gaze going to me first. "You okay?" he asks gently, his brown eyes kind.

I blink up at him. "I'm fine. Thank you for asking."

"Oh." He hesitates. "I just figured Sophie told you what happened Friday."

"I did," Sophie says, smiling up at Tony like he hung the moon and the stars. "You want to join us?"

"I was sort of hoping I could take you to lunch." He glances over at me and Marty while we stare at him. "Unless you want to stay here and hang out with your friends."

"No." Sophie pops up, grabbing her stuff. "Let's go to lunch. You guys don't mind, right?"

She doesn't give us a chance to answer her. They're gone in an instant, and Marty and I are left behind in a semi state of shock.

"Did that really just happen?" Marty asks me once they disappear from the quad.

Nodding, I grab my plastic bag of spicy chili-lime chips from Trader Joe's and start munching.

"Do you think he's up to something?" Marty asks after a few minutes of silence. When I send him a questioning look, he continues. "Tony. Do you think he's setting our girl up for some major fail?"

"No way." I shake my head, thinking of the concern in his voice when he asked if I was okay. For some weird reason, I trust him, even though I don't know him that well. "Tony may hang out with those guys, but he's the calmest one of the bunch."

"The quiet ones are usually the ones you should watch out for the most," Marty observes, both of us casting our gazes toward the opposite side of the quad, where the popular people hang out.

I don't see Jake among them, which is a complete relief. But I also don't see Cami either, which worries me. What if they're together? People get caught messing around in the parking lot at school all the time. Considering we're seniors, we can leave campus for lunch. Maybe Jake and Cami snuck away to somewhere private so they can do…

Whatever.

The thought fills me with humiliation. Hurt.

A little bit of anger.

"We'll just have to watch out for her," I tell Marty. "If he hurts her, we'll take him down."

Marty's eyes go extra wide. "*Take him down?* Come on, Hannah, we don't have that capability."

"We do if he hurts our friend. I know I could," I say vehemently, casting my gaze toward the popular group one more time. Caleb is sitting next to Diego and his girlfriend Jocelyn, who appears to be yelling at Diego. He stares straight ahead, his lower lip still swollen and cut from the punch Jake must've delivered. Stone faced, with his arms crossed while her lips move a mile a minute. "What's up with your cousin? Why is Jocelyn yelling at him?"

I figured she'd be giving him all sorts of good treatment after he got beat up by Jake.

"My tía called last night to tell my mom they got into a huge screaming match in their front yard Sunday afternoon." Marty makes a tsking noise. "Looks like there's trouble in paradise."

"I thought those two were madly in love and were getting engaged after graduation." I've heard Jocelyn go on and on about her and Diego marrying once they were done with high school. Sounds a bit early if you ask me, but I figured she just knew what she wanted.

"Jocelyn says that stuff because she's trying her best to nail her boy down for good. She knows what he's up to, she just doesn't want to admit it." When I send Marty a confused look, he rolls his eyes. "Are you telling me you've never heard the rumors?"

"What rumors?"

He makes an exasperated noise. Sometimes I think I irritate him when I don't know what's going on, but I don't keep up with the school gossip like he does. "Diego is like the biggest cheater in the senior class, if not the entire school. So many chicks have bounced on his dick over the years, I'm surprised it's not permanently chafed."

There's an image I can never get out of my head. "Does Jocelyn know?"

"Yes, definitely. She's not as clueless as you." Marty smirks.

"Gee, thanks," I say sarcastically as I settle my gaze on Jocelyn yet again. She's pretty, and she always acts so confident. She's smart and friendly and everyone seems to love her. Yet Diego cheats on her again and again.

Why does she let him get away with it?

"I just thought everyone knew what a dog my cousin is. He's terrible. He doesn't deserve Jocelyn. That's why he'll most likely marry her," Marty says, shaking his head. "What other woman would tolerate his bullshit and still walk around with a smile on her face?"

It makes me sad just thinking about it. It also makes me realize that maybe I'm better off being rid of Jake now, before I get in too deep.

What if he's just like his friend? What if they're all like Diego, meaning Tony might cheat too? Girls always seem to chase the jocks, some more than others. Caleb is kind of goofy, but he makes girls laugh, he's flirty and he's cute, though sometimes he's rude. I remember the way he stared at me that time Jake and I left art together, and how they pulled Jake away from me.

Diego also flirts with everyone, but he has a mean streak. I've witnessed it lately myself, what with the way he glares at me like I'm dog doo stuck on the bottom of his shoe.

They all can have a mean streak. Even Jake.

So what the hell am I doing right now? Mourning over the loss of a *jerk?*

I must be crazy.

"She should break up with him," I say.

"Oh, she does. They break up all the damn time. I guess shit got bad when she heard about that party Friday night." When I send him a questioning look, he shrugs. "I didn't know about the fight. I just heard about the aftermath between Jocelyn and Diego. She found out he had girls at his house that night when she wasn't there. That's a big no-no.

My tía found out and lost her shit, then kicked everybody out. Party over." He makes a cutting gesture across his neck.

Dang. This party sounds like a complete disaster.

"So they broke up?" I ask.

"Sort of. They argued for all the neighborhood to see, which embarrasses my tía. I'm sure Diego begged Jocelyn to forgive him, and like every other time, she fell for his sob story. I don't even know what he says to her to convince her anymore." Marty sighs. "When I'm forced to go to family functions, most of the time he brings Jocelyn too, and we always talk. She's a sweetheart."

Marty keeps chatting about the popular group and how terrible they are, but my mind starts to drift. I can't help but wonder where Jake is. Where Cami is too. I'm sure they're together. How did that even happen? He told me he regretted even giving her another try, and now here they are, hanging out? Supposedly a couple yet again?

I don't get it.

By the time lunch is over, I'm in a full-blown funk. When I walk into my world religions class, I see Cami is already sitting at her desk, typing away on her phone, a little smile curling her perfectly glossed lips. She's not talking to anyone, but that's no surprise considering none of her friends are in this class.

Thank God I don't sit near her. She's in the back of the class while I sit closer to the front, and I edge around the last row of desks that are the farthest away from her, hoping she doesn't look up and see me.

I'm settled in my seat, breathing a sigh of relief that I wasn't spotted by the evil queen bee when Sophie plops into the desk next to mine. "Hey." She glances over her shoulder before she continues, "Um, I saw something when Tony and I came back from having lunch."

"What did you see?" I ask warily.

Sophie winces. "Jake was out in the parking lot with… Cami."

My stomach twists at her answer. "Seriously?"

She nods. "It's not like they were wrapped around each other like a pretzel or anything. He actually looked pretty mad."

"Doesn't he always look pretty mad?" I press my lips together and turn away from Sophie, trying to calm my chaotic thoughts. Were my suspicions correct? Did he go off campus with Cami? Did they mess around? I don't want to believe it, especially after what I did with Jake, but…

Stranger things have happened.

"I gotta go." I lurch out of my desk, leaving my backpack behind as I escape the classroom. I hear Sophie call my name, but I don't respond.

I swear to God I also hear Cami laugh and ask "What's her problem?" to no one in particular. I'm sure.

God, I hate her.

Running in the opposite direction of everyone else down the hallway, I barge into the girls' bathroom, grateful no one is inside. I lock myself away in a stall and press my forehead against the cool metal wall, closing my eyes, desperate to calm my ragged breathing. The late bell rings, but I don't even care, which is completely unlike me. All I can do is try to swallow past the gigantic lump in my throat, fighting the tears that want to spring to my eyes.

Keep it together, keep it together. He's not worth it.

He's not. I know he's not. I don't understand why Jake came to my apartment for weeks. Why he acted like he cared, as if he wanted to *protect* me. Why he kissed me and touched me and said he couldn't stop thinking about me. All of my teen romance dreams were coming true…

And now he's crapped all over them.

I cry a little because I can't help it. I let the tears fall, grabbing a wad of toilet paper and wiping at my face, mentally cursing myself for being so weak. My crying session lasts all of a minute, maybe two, and after I wipe my tear-stained face and blow my nose one more time, I slowly exit the stall. Walk over to the sink and splash cool water all over my blotchy face. Glare at my reflection in the mirror because, thanks to my pale complexion, it's super obvious I've just been crying.

Ugh. There's no denying my bloodshot eyes and flushed cheeks. I'm just going to have to deal with it.

Exiting the bathroom, I slowly make my way back to the classroom, thankful for the empty hallway. I quietly open the door and slip inside, and thankfully Mrs. Madsen doesn't hesitate in her lecture, though she does shoot a soft smile in my direction as I settle into my seat. I can feel Sophie looking at me too, all of her unspoken questions filling the air between us, but I don't dare meet her gaze.

I might start crying again.

Grabbing a pen and my notebook from my backpack, I flip the notebook open so I can take notes. It's the longest fifty-minute class period of my life, and by the time it's over, I'm exhausted.

Trying to keep my shit together is hard.

"Are you okay?" Sophie asks after the bell rings. She's gathering up her things, shoving everything in her backpack, and I'm doing the same.

Shrugging, I keep my gaze downward. "Not really. Can we talk about it later?"

"Sure. No problem. You're not..." Her voice drifts and I swing my backpack onto my shoulder, staring straight ahead. "You're not mad at me for spending time with Tony at lunch, are you? And that I told you I saw Jake and Cami together? I just thought you should know, after everything that happened over the weekend."

"No, of course I'm not mad at you!" I furiously shake my

head, glancing over at her to see she looks downright miserable. "This entire situation is so confusing. I don't know what to think, or how to feel."

"Maybe you should try to talk to Jake?" Sophie suggests.

I want to laugh. "Please. I don't think he's interested."

"He got in a fight with Diego over you," she reminds me, and now I do laugh.

"I don't see him trying to talk to me, so I don't know how much I believe that's the reason." I shake my head. "I'll call you later?"

"Don't forget I have dance after school," she says. When does she not? "And I'm getting together with Tony after that, but later tonight, maybe we can Facetime?"

"Yeah, okay." I nod, offering her a weak smile.

Once we part ways, it's like my feet are made of lead. Art 1 is next. My last class of the day is the one Jake Callahan is in.

I don't want to go, but I can't bail on Mrs. Sanborne. She might need me to…I don't know. Clean brushes? She has a bunch of old ones that appear permanently covered with thick globs of dried-up, crusty paint. It's a project she always talks about having me work on, but we never end up doing.

Hmm. That's not a bad idea actually. I could stay at the back of the classroom the entire time, where the giant sink is. It would keep me occupied and then I won't have to deal with Jake at all.

Perfect.

Fueled by my plan, I practically run the rest of the way to the art room, completely aware of my surroundings, my head swiveling to the left, to the right, back to the left…

No sightings of Jake so far.

Entering the classroom, I head straight for Mrs. Sanborne's desk where she's currently sitting, scrolling through her phone.

"Oh hey, Hannah. I was just looking over the new colored pencil project I found on Pinterest over the weekend. I've been so bored with my lesson plans lately—I'm trying to change it up." She smiles at me. "You want to check the project out? Maybe you could help me with it today."

Dread fills me. I don't want to help her with anything that has me dealing with the students. Not today. Maybe not ever. "But I thought you wanted me to clean all the paint brushes."

She frowns. "Really?"

"Yes." I nod, my expression serious. "You mentioned that to me on Friday."

Everyone knows Mrs. Sanborne can be a little flighty and forgetful sometimes. Some people have used that little fact in their favor, though I never have before.

Until today.

"Huh. I don't remember that. Though you have a better memory than I do. You all do." She sets her phone down. "Go ahead and get started on that today, but wrap it up quickly if you can. I'll have them finish up their pencil sketches, and we'll start on the colored pencil project tomorrow."

"Okay. Sounds good." I give her a brief smile before I make my way to the back of the classroom.

Most of the freshmen are inside the room already, and they seem extra loud today. Mondays are hard sometimes, especially at the beginning of school. I notice Jake is nowhere in sight, and neither is Rob, the only other senior in the Art 1 class.

I can't worry about when Jake finally arrives. Or if he even appears at all. Wouldn't that be great, if he didn't show up? Maybe he changed his schedule and decided to take Theater 1 after all. He'd rather deal with a bunch of freshmen overacting on a stage than have to see me in art every day.

That's what I'm hoping he'll do, at least.

But I couldn't be that lucky. As if he radiates some sort of magnetic force field—I've always secretly believed this—I can actually feel his presence once he enters the room. I hear Rob as well. In fact, I think they're actually speaking to each other, and as slyly as I can, I turn my head to watch them.

They're at the table, the one Jake was banished from originally, and Rob is demanding he go.

"I'm not moving," Jake says, his expression blank, that black eye he's sporting making him look extra mean.

And if I'm being honest with myself, it also makes him look kind of hot.

Yes, I know. I'm pitiful.

Jake's not looking at anyone. It's as if he's staring off into space. Numb. Unfeeling. Rather accurate words to describe him, if you ask me. I need to remember that. He doesn't care.

"I don't want you here, asshole," Rob mutters, glaring at him. "Mrs. Sanborne! Can you *please* tell Jake to sit somewhere else?"

Mrs. Sanborne approaches their table with a scowl on her usually smiling face, hands resting on her ample hips. "Rob, it seems to me you're the one who's being unreasonable this afternoon. I say you give Jake another chance." She tilts her head, her eyes going wide when she takes in Jake's black eye. "Goodness, what happened to you, Mr. Callahan?"

Rob glares at Jake. Jake glares at no one. He doesn't respond to Mrs. Sanborne either, and I hear her sigh with frustration. I watch it all unfold with wide eyes and my mouth hanging open, gawking at them like an idiot.

"Hannah."

Mrs. Sanborne snaps my name and my cheeks, my entire body goes hot. I meet her gaze, my breaths coming fast, almost like I'm panting, and I can feel the moment when Jake's eyes alight on me.

I'd give anything to disappear. Just vanish. Poof.

Gone.

CHAPTER 21

JAKE

Seeing Hannah's pained expression as she watches me, *fuck*. It actually…

Hurts.

A bunch of emotions hits me all at once. Concern. Need. Anger—not toward her, but the situation that started all of this in the first place. That fight.

I haven't talked to Diego since. We have classes together and he found other places to sit. So did Caleb, though he sent me a sympathetic look every time, as if it hurt him to take sides.

What the fuck ever.

Hannah's eyes are bloodshot and her pretty face is so damn pale, her cheeks splotchy. Has she been crying? Is she upset? She looks like she is. And I'm sure I'm the cause of it. I want to talk to her.

I should've talked to her at lunch, but I was dealing with a bunch of bullshit and I had to get my phone. My parents were so pissed I lost it—it's not the first one I've lost or cracked or completely destroyed over the years. And I didn't tell them the whole truth about the fight with Diego. How could I? They were mad enough about the phone. Besides, Dad is bound to find out by Monday's practice anyway, so I was only prolonging it.

After I confessed that I lost my phone Saturday afternoon, Dad immediately went on the Find My Phone app and pinged it—turns out my phone was sitting in Cami's fucking house.

How the hell did Cami end up with it?

Mom was furious. She figured I was with Cami Friday night, and while that was sort of the truth, it wasn't in the way Mom thought.

Yeah. I'm not on Mom's good side right now, that's for sure.

I couldn't message Hannah all weekend because my psycho ex had my phone, which she denied. I got Tony to text her and ask her to return it, but she played innocent. Claimed she didn't have it.

The little liar.

I had my team conditioning class before school, and while I wanted to talk to Hannah, I didn't really have the time. Plus, I was on a mission. The moment I found Cami near my locker, I confronted her. She insisted she had no idea what I was talking about, arguing with me the entire time, and when I spotted Hannah in the hall after the first bell rang, I wanted to go to her. Fucking terrible timing. The hurt expression on Hannah's face when she saw us together said it all.

She thought we were *together*-together. And that is so not the case.

At lunch, I immediately had Caleb on my ass, asking me how I was going to fix this. He wanted me to apologize to Diego and both of us forget the fight ever happened.

Yeah. I don't think so.

And then…I had to deal with Cami. I basically chased

after her, all the way to her car, her denying she had the phone the whole way. After a lot of hushed accusations and her full-blown screaming at me in the middle of the parking lot, catching the eye of our vice principal Mrs. Adney, who was patrolling the lot as she does, I finally got my phone back. Cami had it on her the entire fucking time.

I knew she did. I love it when I'm right but…I hate it when it comes to this kind of stupid shit.

Now seeing Hannah look so small, so hurt, and knowing it's all my fault, I'm consumed with worry. And guilt.

Lots and lots of guilt.

Without thought I push my chair back, my body tense, poised. Ready to leap to my feet and go to her.

"Yes, Mrs. Sanborne?" Hannah rubs her lips together and my stomach dips. Her lips are fucking everything.

I remember the teacher said her name, and I can feel Rob's eyes on me. Hot and full of hatred. Right back at you, motherfucker.

"Want to get started on cleaning those brushes?" Mrs. Sanborne says brightly, sending both Rob and me a measured look before she heads back toward her desk.

"Yes. Of course." Hannah glances over at us one last time, before she scurries away.

Rob scoffs. "She's pitiful."

"So are you," I mutter under my breath.

The two freshmen girls sitting at our table, the ones who were so hopeful and excited at the prospect of the only seniors in class joining them, are watching us with giant eyes and fear written all over their young faces. They both have braces, and they look so damn young. They're downright identical, with their blonde hair and big eyes, wearing similar clothing. I figure they gotta be friends.

Bet they wish they were back in middle school right about now.

"Fuck off, Callahan. You think you're so high and mighty, Mr. QB. King jock of the school. It's a bunch of horseshit." He waves a hand at me. "Looks like someone already knocked you off your pedestal. I say good for Diego. At least he got a punch in."

His words are infuriating, and I'd love to give Rob a taste of my fist, just like I did to Diego.

But that would be falling into Rob's trap, and I'm not doing it. I don't need the trouble. I also don't understand his problem with me. The last three years of high school, we've never had one encounter. I wouldn't call us friends, but we've had a few classes together. There was never any hostility.

There's plenty of it now, though. And most of it is one-sided.

"What the hell did I ever do to you?" I ask him, genuinely perplexed.

"You exist," he says, his words crisp, his gaze narrowed as he glares at me. "Isn't that enough?"

One of the freshmen girls titters nervously, sealing her mouth shut when I glare at her. I'm sure my black eye and beat-up face scares the crap out of her and her little friend. Her lips are puffy, most likely from the braces, her eyes wide and unblinking, and I sort of feel sorry for her right now.

But only a little bit.

Mrs. Sanborne gives us a quick lecture on using colored pencils, going on about blending and shading and a bunch of other stuff I don't bother listening to. I'm grateful the chair I chose faces the back of the room, so I can watch Hannah.

She's standing at the sink with her back to me, the water running constantly in the stainless sink, her shoulders hunched as she becomes Sanborne's slave for the period and cleans brushes. What a sucky job. I'd tell Sanborne to fuck off if she gave me that task, but I get the feeling Hannah actually enjoys it. She loves art. She told me Sanborne is her favorite teacher and she's taken an art class all four years of high school. Maybe she doesn't mind being Sanborne's little helper.

I should be working on my new sketch, but I can't concentrate. Instead, I watch Hannah. And the more I watch her, the worse I feel. My disappointment in her not showing up at Friday's game is completely forgotten. Why was I so upset about that anyway? Why didn't I bother getting her phone number? What the fuck is wrong with me?

I think of the shitty things Diego said about her, and what Cami said too. I don't understand why they feel the need to pick on someone for no real reason. They're bullies.

Hell, I've been accused of being a bully myself. I thought and said some shitty things when Hannah first turned me down after I asked her to wear my jersey. I lashed out. Yet she still helped me that night after I got in the fight. I didn't deserve her help.

I don't deserve her, period.

"Jake." Mrs. Sanborne's gentle voice washes over me, and I glance up to find her standing right next to the table. "You should get to work."

Reaching out, I grab a pencil from the box in the center of our table, not really caring what color it is, and start drawing. What the hell I'm creating, I don't know, but it's good enough for the teacher to keep walking, and I exhale a quiet breath of relief when she's gone. Abandoning the drawing as quickly as I started it, I glance up, my gaze snagging on Hannah yet again.

She turns to face me, clutching a bundle of wet brushes in her hands, her shirt damp and clinging in all the right places. I sit up a little, taking notice. She has great tits. And those lips. I remember what they feel like, plush and damp and so damn soft. And how she tasted. Sweet and warm—

"Jesus. Shut your mouth or a puddle of drool is going to end up on the table," Rob tells me, his voice full of disgust.

Snapping my jaw shut, I glance over at him. "Who the fuck do you think you are, telling me what to do?"

"You're pathetic." Rob slowly shakes his head, grimacing. "Slobbering over that nobody." He waves a hand in Hannah's direction. "Then walking around with Cami all day. But one of your *very* best friends is banging her behind your back. Please tell me you're not that clueless."

Unease washes over me at his words. "What the hell are you talking about?" I pound my fist on the table, making the freshmen jump and squeal. Unfortunately, that catches Sanborne's attention, and she marches over to our table, pointing at both Rob and me.

"Callahan. Go to the vice principal's office. *Now*," she demands, jerking her thumb over her shoulder toward the door.

I jump to my feet. "What about him?" I point at Rob.

"Oh, he's going too, but I'm staggering your visits." Rob opens his mouth to protest, but Sanborne silences him with a look.

Damn. Guess she can be pretty stern when she wants to be.

"Leave. Go," she tells me, making a shooing gesture with her arms. "I don't want to see you back here until tomorrow. And hopefully with an adjusted attitude."

I grab my backpack and exit the room fast, not once looking back. Rob laughs and Sanborne yells at him yet again, which is reassuring. At least she's not taking sides.

The main office sits on a hill just above the art building, and I pause, staring up at it. I contemplate not going at all. Just jumping in my truck and taking off until practice starts. I could avoid seeing Diego in the locker room if I did that. I'd just show up on the field, already dressed and ready to go.

But Sanborne would have my ass and so would Adney, the vice principal. And then Dad and the rest of my coaches would be furious. Shit, if Adney were really mad, she could suspend me from the team for weeks on end. No way can I let them down like that.

I decide to face my punishment and get it over with.

When I enter the front office, Kelli Stafford, the secretary, smiles at me. She's blonde and bubbly, and once upon a time, she was a cheerleader at our high school too. We have lots of second- and even third-generation families and students that work and are enrolled here. It's like people never leave this place.

"Jacob Callahan, what are you doing in here?" Ms. Stafford wags a finger at me, but she's smiling and there's an extra sparkle in her eyes. She's always liked me. Maybe I fuel some long-ago teen fantasy she had, I don't know.

"Hey, Ms. Stafford." I lean against the tall counter that surrounds her desk, standing near the door that leads back to Adney's office. "How are you?"

"Better than you, I think. I just took Mrs. Sanborne's call. Go have a seat. Mrs. Adney will see you when she's finished." She points at the row of empty seats beneath the glass case that's filled with old high school memorabilia and awards. "And please, don't call me Ms. Stafford. It's Kelli."

"Right. Kelli." I send her a flirtatious smile and settle into the chair closest to her desk. May as well flirt with her and make her afternoon, right?

She laughs, appearing ready to say something but the phone rings and she immediately answers it. Another student walks in, complaining that they don't feel so good, and off they go to the health aide's office. More phone calls. The janitors radio in on the walkie-talkie sitting on Kelli's desk. The communication never stops, and I sort of feel bad for ol' Kelli. This place is busy. Busier than I thought.

Long minutes pass and I'm scrolling through my phone, dealing with Cami asking me what's wrong and why I'm in the office. How does news travel that fast? I ignore her texts, though she keeps sending them, and I'm sort of relieved when Mrs. Adney opens the door, glaring at me. "Come on, let's go," she says in her gravelly voice.

I follow her to her office, towering over her short frame. We've never had any problems, Adney and I. Sometimes, it's almost like she completely understands me and what I go through, which I can appreciate.

Once the door's shut and she's behind her desk, while I'm in the chair opposite hers, Adney gets right down to business. "Why in the world do you have a problem with Robert Schaffer?" I start to tell her exactly why, but she cuts me off. "And why are you disrupting Mrs. Sanborne's class? What has that poor woman ever done to you?"

"For one, she's not very accommodating with her schedule," I retort, crossing my arms, ready to launch into a lengthy complaint.

Adney sends me an *are you serious* look, and I shut up. "Let's get one thing straight—the world does not revolve around you, Mr. Callahan. Just because you're missing out on the seventh-period conditioning class doesn't mean Sanborne needs to change her entire schedule to accommodate you. That's not how life works."

I sit there silently. There's no point in arguing. She'll have a comeback for every point I try to make.

And besides. She's kind of right.

"It's your senior year, kid. You should be riding high with the wins under your belt, and we have another home game this Friday. Life is good. Right?" She doesn't give me a chance to answer, just continues. Like my entire life centers on football and nothing else. "Yet you storm around campus like you're pissed off at the world. I saw you getting into it with

Cami Lockhart out in the parking lot at lunch. What's your problem? Why are you so angry?"

What sucks is I can't tell her the truth. That my best friend is talking shit on the girl I like, and now I'm starting to suspect Diego is fucking Cami in secret. That's messed up.

But I refuse to mention our fight. It didn't happen on campus, so Adney doesn't need to hear about it. Though I'm sure rumors are flying. Guess I'll have to play it off and leave her thinking I'm just…impulsive.

Hotheaded.

"Seriously, Jake." Adney's voice softens, and I glance up to find she's watching me with concern in her eyes. "Is there something bothering you? I don't believe your little outburst with Rob is the real problem."

I lift my chin, determined to keep quiet about everything that's happened. Like my major fallout with my friends. My ex-girlfriend who stole my phone for God knows what reason. Probably looking for evidence to hold against me somehow.

Then there's all the pressure from my dad, from the other coaches, from the team. Pressure from my friends to leave the girl I really want alone. People want to tell me what to do at all times, and it's fucking exhausting.

"I don't have any problems," I tell her, my voice low. My expression as neutral as possible.

She studies me for a long, too-quiet moment, her clutched hands on top of her desk, her gaze narrowed. Adney's the type to sit and watch you until you finally crack under the pressure. But she has no idea the kind of pressure I've been under lately. Hell, my entire life.

I refuse to crack.

"Fine. If Mrs. Sanborne sends you back in here, or any other teacher, you're getting Saturday school. For now, you're off the hook. Your friend Rob will be too. I don't want to hear another word about you two not getting along in Art 1, you hear me?" She stands.

That's my dismissal. I'm getting off easy.

Rising to my feet, I sling my backpack over my shoulder and salute her. "Loud and clear, Mrs. Adney."

"Get out of here," she says, and I leave her office, winding my way past the other administrative offices as I make my way out of the building. I open the door and I'm back out in the lobby, where I see Rob slumped in the very chair I vacated not even five minutes before.

"Jake!" Kelli waves me over, and I take the excuse slip from her extended hand, offering up a quick thanks as I shove the paper into my front pocket. I don't bother talking to Rob as I leave the building.

I don't bother talking to anyone.

* * *

I GO STRAIGHT to the locker room after I leave Adney's office, changing into my practice clothes before I jog out to my truck and leave my duffel bag and backpack in the backseat. I'm giving myself no reason to stick around once practice is over. Fuck that. I want to avoid any and all confrontations with Diego.

I contemplate waiting for Hannah once seventh period gets out, which is in—I check my phone—a little over fifteen minutes, but I know Diego and his crew—they're my crew too—would most likely spot us. And I don't want to risk it.

The conversation I need to have with Hannah has to play out in private.

Deciding I'll go to the field and wait for everyone, I head out there, jogging through the parking lot and the tennis courts, past the auto shop, where I wave at a bunch of dudes all standing around the open hood of a beat-up old truck. I jog by the weight room, where pretty much the entirety of my team is doing their strength and conditioning exercises or lifting weights.

When I finally make it to the field, I slow down, walking along the red clay track that surrounds it, my hands on my hips as I even out my breaths. There's someone standing in the middle of the field, and I squint into the sun, shading my eyes with my hand.

It's Tony.

I run toward him, coming to a stop directly in front of him, holding out my hand. "What's up?"

Tony clasps it, and we conduct a modified version of our elaborate handshake. "Nothing much. You're here early."

"So are you."

"I had a feeling you'd show up to the field first so you could avoid the locker room," Tony says.

My quiet friend knows me better than I thought. "You'd be right. It's not that I don't want to talk to Diego, but…"

"You don't want to talk to Diego. I get it." Tony nods, and I exhale loudly.

"This is all such bullshit," I mutter, resting my hands on my hips once more as I shake my head.

"How's the eye?"

"Hurts."

"And your ribs?"

"Just bruised." Nothing I haven't experienced before.

"Diego's lip is busted. Claims he has a cracked rib or two. He might try to pull out of this Friday's game as a sort of fuck-you," Tony explains. "This all comes from Caleb."

"How is not playing in this week's game fucking me over? It fucks us all over." Sometimes I don't understand Diego's logic.

"He's just butthurt that you would take some girl's side

over his. Despite the rumors that are floating around about him." Tony pauses. "And Cami."

We're quiet for a moment as I let his words sink in. "You think it's true?"

"Not quite sure. Caleb told me Diego and Jocelyn got into a big fight yesterday. She's still pissed at him."

"Cami gave my phone back to me at lunch," I tell him.

"I heard. I saw you two when I came back with Sophie."

"You guys hanging out?" Envy burns in my gut. I wish I could just take Hannah to lunch like no big deal.

"Yeah. We are." He sends me a look. "Don't tell me you're gonna give me shit for it."

I scoff. "Like I would. That would mean I'm a hypocrite."

"You going to apologize to Diego?"

"Fuck no. Caleb wants me to, but Diego's the one who started this shit by saying all that stuff about Hannah," I say, disgust filling me.

"He'll never admit he messed up," Tony says, and I know he's speaking the truth. "He's not real big on owning up to his mistakes. Look at his relationship with Jocelyn."

"You think she'll dump him?"

"Homecoming noms are happening soon," Tony says. "If Diego and Jocelyn are nominated? There's no way in hell she'll give up that shot at glory."

The bell rings, indicating school's out for the day, and I take a deep breath, exhaling slowly. I need to man up. Show my team and my coaches I know how to be a real leader and let all this trouble become a thing of the past.

I can hold a grudge like the best of them, but I refuse to let it fuck up our team. Can Diego make that same commitment?

We'll have to wait and see.

CHAPTER 22

JAKE

I'm in my room after getting out of the shower with a towel wrapped around my waist when there's a knock on the door. I barely finish asking who it is when the door swings open and my dad is standing in the doorway, his broad shoulders filling the space, a look of concern on his face.

"Can you talk for a minute?" he asks.

"Sure," I say warily, hitting the switch on the wall and turning on my walk-in closet light. "I need to change first." I gesture toward the open door.

"Go for it. I'll wait." Dad shuts my bedroom door and settles into my desk chair.

My mind is racing as I enter my closet and throw on some clothes. I don't even bother with underwear, just drop the damp towel on the floor and slip on some basketball shorts and a clean T-shirt real quick.

What does he want to talk about? I thought we kept it together pretty well at practice today. Diego complained he was injured and couldn't play, so Dad benched him, telling him he had to have a doctor's note if this continues. Diego sulked the entire time, sitting on the bench and yelling at everyone but me.

I caught his eye a couple of times, and I wouldn't look away. He was always the first to do it. I'm mad at him, but I'm also starting to realize I'm hurt. I thought he was loyal. Clearly, if he's actually messing around with Cami behind the scenes, then he's not.

Did Dad hear about our fight Friday night? How we all got drunk as fuck? He has to at least know about the fight. I wonder if Adney gave him a call and let him know what happened in art today. That would suck—that's Rob's grudge against me, not the other way around. And did my dad hear about my argument with Cami at lunch? God knows who else witnessed that.

There are so many things this little talk could be about, I can't figure out just one.

"What's up?" I ask casually as I exit my closet and make my way over to my bed. I sit on the edge of the mattress, opposite of where he's sitting, and wait for him to say something.

My heart feels like it's in my throat the longer he remains quiet. It's unnerving, and unlike with Adney earlier, now as I sit here in silence with my father, I'm ready to crack.

Ready to give.

Dad watches me, his gaze never wavering. "How are you?"

I blink at him, surprised by his simple question. "What?"

"I asked, how are you? Are you okay?"

My throat grows tight. When was the last time someone actually asked me that? A simple how are you. I can't remember. My family, we just go, go, go, and it's not like I blame my parents for overscheduling us. That's just how our lives are. How they've always been. Feels like we don't have much down time. And I try my best to act like I have my shit together, so everyone assumes I must. It's all fake, though. Times like this, I feel like I've lost complete control. I know my parents love me. I know that they're always watching out for my best interests, but…

The only one who seemed to care, who actually saw the cracks in my façade, was Hannah.

And like a giant asshole, I haven't reached out to her yet. What the hell am I waiting for? It's like I'm putting out all these little fires and saving her for last.

"You haven't been acting right for weeks, Jake," Dad says, and I blink at him in shock. "Hell, for *months.* Your mother and I are concerned, and at first, I tried to justify it. You're under an enormous amount of pressure, and trust me, I know what that's like. So tell me. How are you?"

"I'm…I'm tired," I admit, because it's the first word that comes to mind. "I feel like I haven't got a good night's sleep since school started." Since the start of summer, if I'm being truthful, but a lot of that is my own fault. I stay up late.

Dad ducks his head a little so he can meet my gaze. "You dealing with the team okay? You guys seem to be playing well together, though I thought I felt some tension between a few of you this afternoon. Despite that, I have a good feeling about this season."

"Yeah, we're good." I contemplate if I should tell him about the fight with Diego. "Uh, Diego and I had a little run in on Friday."

"Friday when? After the game?" When I nod, he asks, "What happened?"

I explain it all to him, deciding it's best if I'm upfront and truthful. I tell him how we all ended up at Diego's house after we got back from the game—I leave out all the drinking details—and how Diego said all those terrible things about Hannah. How I socked him in the face, and he punched me back, giving me the black eye.

Dad exhales loudly when I finish my story. "Your mother was dying to ask you about the black eye."

I did find it odd that no one called me out for it. "Why didn't she ask?"

"I told her not to. I wanted you to come to us and tell us what happened. It might've taken you a few days, but I'm glad you did it." He shakes his head. "I'm disappointed in Diego. I'm even more disappointed in you."

"Come on, Dad," I say, frustration fueling me. It's like he doesn't understand where I'm coming from. "He started it with all his shit talk about Hannah."

"This is the second fight you've gotten into since school started, and now you're fighting with one of your closest friends. I don't know what's going on with you, but you have to stop. Violence is not the answer to all your problems," Dad says.

"They all started it—" I clamp my lips shut at the look on Dad's face.

You need to learn how to control your temper. You know this." Dad shakes his head when I start to protest yet again, and I go quiet. "What Diego said wasn't right, but it wasn't right for you to solve the problem with your fist."

I stare down at my feet, absorbing his words. I know he's right, but it's still hard to hear. "I tried to keep my shit together today at practice."

"And I appreciate that. All of us coaches do." He hesitates for a moment before he continues. "I know you feel like all of this falls on you, but we're a team, Jake. We're all in this together, though you have a tendency to take on way too much of the responsibility when you shouldn't, whether we play well or terribly. I understand what that's like too."

I remain quiet, thinking of the things he's told me about his past, which isn't much. My grandfather was rich—he died when I was ten, leaving everything to Dad—and my grandmother died when Dad was a little kid. There was an evil stepmother involved at one point, but I don't know too much about that part of the story. When my dad and mom were first dating, I guess his stepmom didn't approve of their relationship and went a little crazy.

It's a story I've only ever got bits and pieces of, and I'd love to know more—all of us would. We've talked about it before, me, Autumn and Ava, but our parents are pretty tight-lipped with that info.

"Remember when you were in the sixth grade, and you went to counseling?" Dad asks, pushing me out of my thoughts.

I know where he's heading with this, without him actually having to say it. "No way," I tell him. "I don't want to talk to a therapist about my *feelings*. I've already done that, and I didn't like it."

"Your mother and I thought it helped you," he starts, but I shake my head.

"I thought it was complete bullshit." The therapist was older, practically a senior citizen. His name was Samuel. He actually let me call him by his first name, and at that age, I thought that was kind of cool. He always asked me how I was feeling. All of our conversations were about my feelings. If I complained about anything—school, my friends, other kids, my parents, my siblings, he always had to say, "But how does that make you feel?"

After a while, I hated it. I started making up crazy stories just to shock him—and entertain myself.

Once my parents decided we were leaving the big city and coming here, I of course stopped seeing Samuel. We moved, I seemed happier—and I was—and my parents forgot all about me needing a therapist.

And now here they are, thinking I need one again. They're worried about me, and I suppose I get it. This is the second fight I've gotten in in as many weeks. That sucks. It looks bad. But they shouldn't worry. I've got this.

Can't they see I've got this?

"What was bullshit were all the lies you used to tell that poor man." A mixture of anger and impatience appears on Dad's face, his mouth going tight. He rises to his feet and starts pacing. "Sometimes I wonder if you're too smart for your own good."

Something my father has told me before, actually.

"Tell that to my transcripts and overall grade point average," I say, making him pause in his pacing. "I'll be lucky to get into my first-choice college."

"You'll get in." His expression doesn't change. He doesn't even bat an eyelash. He believes in me that much. "Your skills on the football field will get you in alone. And your stats."

I bark out a laugh. "I'm not that good."

"You're fucking fantastic."

"I go to a school that sucks. We're a Division Four team Dad, that doesn't mean shit," I say.

"Two years ago you boys went far. The team almost cinched the state title," Dad points out.

"Thanks to Ash Davis," I mutter, wishing we could go to a Fresno State game and watch him play. I wouldn't mind talking to him either. Ask him how he deals with the pressure. "Now it's all on me."

"There you go again, taking on all the responsibility as usual." Dad points at me. "You have to stop doing that, Jake. It's not up to you, what happens out there on the field. There are so many other things coming into play, and you can't control it all."

What I can't control falls to shit. Lately, I feel like that's me. I can't control myself.

I'm falling to shit. Again and again.

"Listen." Dad approaches me, resting his hand on my

shoulder and giving it a firm squeeze. "You need to stop being so hard on yourself. I know it's not as easy as me telling you to stop, but work on it, okay?"

I drop my gaze to the floor and nod once, not wanting to look at him. I can't just shut my emotions on and off like everyone thinks I can. I may act like I feel nothing, but it's easier that way, to pretend. If I let down my guard, it's like I can feel *everything*.

And a lot of the time, that gets to be too much.

"You know, when you were younger, you used to take medication to control your behavior," he says, his voice quiet.

Of course I remember. When I was little, they thought I was hyperactive. I had a difficult time focusing at school. I got the typical ADD diagnosis and they gave me a prescription to calm me down. But I mellowed out too much, and always felt like I was in a fog, though it was hard for me to articulate that. Mom eventually figured it out on her own, and immediately took me off the pills. Instead, she tried to find holistic treatments for me and had me trying all sorts of weird juice concoctions and "smoothies" that sometimes tasted weird. Eventually, I seemed to calm down on my own, and they thought I grew out of it.

"Your mother and I have been talking and we think you should see a doctor," Dad says cautiously. "I'm wondering if there's more here going on than we know."

I shrug his hand off my shoulder, my emotions simmering just below the surface. Dad doesn't move and neither do I, and we're face to face. Practically *in* each other's faces. I stare into his eyes and realize his are bluer than mine. Sometimes mine can turn a little greenish, thanks to Mom's eye color. But otherwise, I'm his clone. His twin. I wish I were more like him.

But I'm not.

He's always so calm and I'm always pissed off. I tell myself to chill out. There's no reason to get mad. He's concerned about me, and so is Mom and maybe I should listen to them and do what they want.

Can't help but be offended, though.

"So you think I'm crazy," I say, my voice low.

"No," Dad says vehemently, shaking his head. "Definitely not. But you know your uncle has had similar issues in the past, Jake. And once he went on medication, he's been better. We just want—we want what's best for you. That's all."

I turn away from him, thrusting both hands into my hair, tugging on it so hard, my scalp aches. "Let me think about it." I drop my arms to my sides and briefly close my eyes.

"Your mother has already made you an appointment," Dad says quietly.

"What the fuck?" I whirl on him, letting the anger wash all over me, until I'm soaked in emotion. Reveling in the familiarity of it. "You didn't think to ask me first?"

"We're weeks out from the appointment, that's why your mom made the call today." He hesitates. "She's worried about you. We both are. And we both don't understand why you're so damn angry all the time. We just want to make sure you're all right."

"I don't want to go to a shrink."

"You don't have a choice. The appointment's been made. You can make this easy and go along with our choice, or you can make this difficult, be resistant, and we'll force you to go to the appointment anyway. We have your best interests at heart, Jacob. You *know* this."

I go to my window and stare at the mountains in the distance. The sun is setting, the waning light making me melancholy and I wonder if my parents are right.

I wonder if I'm fucking crazy after all.

CHAPTER 23

DREW

I walk into the master bedroom and quietly shut the door, then turn the lock. I don't want anyone barging in. Not Beck, who is like a freight train of emotion and noise. Not Ava, who's always needing her mother for something.

And definitely not Jake, who's pissed at me and most likely his mother too.

I need to talk to Fable alone.

I settle in on the edge of the mattress and wait for her. She was taking a shower earlier, and I thought that was good a time as any for me to talk to Jake and voice our concerns. Fable figured it would go over better if he only heard it from me, but that wasn't necessarily the case. What I said made him very angry.

Probably anything I would've said to him would make him angry. It was a no-win situation.

Minutes later the bathroom door swings open, steam billowing out, and I can't help but smile. My wife loves to take an extra-hot shower. Her skin is always rosy afterward, and I like to tease her that she should be careful or she might end up burning herself.

Unfortunately, I'm not in a teasing mood now. When she exits the bathroom, she stops short when she sees me, clad in a pair of panties and nothing else. All that pretty pink skin on display, but right now, I can't act on my normal impulses.

We have bigger concerns to concentrate on first.

"Drew," she says, her green eyes wide, her damp blonde hair twisted into a bun on top of her head. "I thought you'd still be with Jake."

All these years later, and my wife is still the finest woman on the planet. She's also one of the sweetest—besides our daughters. She's a good mother, a good wife, a good person. I am a lucky, lucky man.

I just wish I knew what was bothering our son.

"I talked to him," I start, but Fable silences me by holding up her index finger.

"Let me get some clothes on first," she murmurs as she dashes into our giant walk-in closet. Within seconds she walks back out, clad in one of my T-shirts that hits her about mid-thigh. She joins me on the edge of the bed, resting her head on my shoulder. "Tell me how it went."

I let her know it started out good and ended in semi-disaster. I tell her what he told me about his fight with his friend. My heart hurts for our son. I don't know why Jake behaves the way he does. All this anger bottled up inside of him can't be good.

"I worry that something else is going on," I tell her, and she gazes up at me with soulful eyes. "Maybe he's hurting because of someone else..."

"He's not you," she says softly. "We've been so involved in his life, we've been there every single step of the way. How can anyone else get in?"

"I wasn't there. For many years, I wasn't around much at

all." My tone is bitter, and I can taste it on my tongue. I regret missing so many moments when our babies were actual babies. I was more present for Beck from a young age than any of our other children.

"You're here now." She shifts so she's crawling onto my lap, straddling my hips. She wraps her arms around my neck, her hands on my hair as she gives it a little tug so I look up into her eyes. "And I was there the entire time, with our babies. Nursing them, holding them when they cried, taking care of their every need, and you were there too when you could be. For half the year, you were with us. After you left the NFL for good and we moved, you've been here. For a long time now, every single day, giving yourself to your kids, to the community. To the school. You help so many people, Drew, including your son."

"I feel like I don't help him enough." I slip my hands beneath the T-shirt and settle them on her waist. Her skin is warm and smooth, and she smells so damn good after getting out of the shower. Fresh and clean. "He won't talk to me."

"What teenager wants to talk to their parents? Did you want to talk to your dad when you were seventeen?" When I make a face, Fable continues. "Maybe if you stopped approaching him and let him come to you first, he might open up to you," she suggests with a faint smile.

I dip my head and kiss her, the need to connect with my wife almost overwhelming me. "If I tried that, he might never approach me again."

She laughs, running her hand slowly down my chest. My skin burns where she touches me, and I'm glad I locked that door. "I don't believe that."

I rest my hand against her cheek, cradling her face. "Did we do the right thing? Making that appointment for him? He says he doesn't want to talk to a therapist."

"Yes, we did the right thing. I'm wondering if his anger

issues have to do with his ADD diagnosis from when he was younger," she says.

I thought of that too. He had a difficult time focusing when he was little, and his attention span was short. As he got older, it was like he grew out of it. Until late middle school, when he would become angry over what we thought were small things. As the years went on, he seemed to have it under control.

Turns out, he was just good at hiding it. Until recently.

"He's going to be all right, Drew," Fable says, loving glowing in her eyes.

I kiss her. Drown in her. I want to believe her. I do.

But I can't help but worry.

CHAPTER 24

HANNAH

’m at school thirty minutes before the first bell rings and approaching the library when I hear someone call my name. Turning, I spot *him* standing there under a pine tree, a contrite expression on his ridiculously good looking face.

Jake.

Turning away, I pick up speed, buzzing toward the double doors of the library like my life depends on it. I hear him call my name again, but I don’t look back. Footsteps sound behind me, and I can tell they’re getting closer, but still I won’t look at him.

I refuse to.

Pushing through the doors, I barge into the library, breathing hard as I go left and slip inside the girls’ bathroom, thankful it’s empty. I brace my hands on the edge of the sink and stare at my reflection, my mind filled with all sorts of questions.

What does he want?

Why did he call my name?

Why did he *follow* me?

The bathroom suddenly door opens and he enters the room like he belongs in here.

"Girls only," I spit out, sounding like I'm eleven years old and afraid I'll get cooties. "You should leave."

"Can you just…hear me out for a minute?" He sounds exhausted. He looks even more so, and seeing him like this tempts me to give him a chance.

But no. I can't. He's an asshole.

"Why should I? Will you run off to your friends and tell them all the things I say and do? Make fun of me again with your girlfriend?" That's the part that hurts the most.

After he kissed me and told me he couldn't stop thinking about me.

I grip the edge of the cold sink, taking a deep breath. I wasn't good enough for him. He didn't like me like that after all. I must've been a terrible kisser. Would I have *kept* him if I'd let him have sex with me that night? Or if I would've given him a blowjob? Is that what keeps Jake Callahan coming around?

No way will I cheapen myself or lower my standards. I'm not that desperate.

"What are you talking about? I don't have a girlfriend," he tells me with all the seriousness in the world.

My heart aches. So does my head. I want to believe him.

But I've heard this before.

"What about Cami?"

He shakes his head. "I'm not with her. I never was."

I turn to face him, drinking him in. He's wearing jeans and a white Salty Crew T-shirt. His hair is getting long on top and it's curling a little, which is *ugh,* so adorable. His jaw is sharp enough to cut glass. His eyes are bluer than the ocean, and his mouth is filling my head with all sorts of thoughts.

None of them negative, which irritates me.

"You DM'd me Saturday night on Instagram and said it wasn't going to work. Then you sent me a photo of you and Cami together," I tell him, my entire body shaking with a mixture of angers and nerves.

His brows lower and he frowns. "What are you talking about? I never DM'd you. I didn't even have my phone Saturday night. I lost it at Diego's—*oh*."

I wait for him to say something else, my stomach churning as I watch anger wash over Jake's features. He pulls out his phone and taps at the screen, exhaling raggedly before his gaze meets mine. "Cami sent you those DMs."

My heart drops and hope rises. "Really?"

I want to believe him. But come on, how did Cami get his phone?

They were together, that's how.

"You heard about the fight Friday night?" When I nod, he goes on. "My phone fell out of my pocket in Diego's yard. I thought he still had it. But it turns out Cami swiped it. I did the Find my Phone app and it pinged at her house. She gave it to me yesterday at lunch after I kept badgering her about it."

That's why they were together at lunch yesterday. He was trying to get his phone back from her.

"Why didn't you message me last night?" I ask him.

"I don't know. Yesterday was…it was all fucked up, Hannah. Diego and I aren't talking. Caleb just wants us to forget it all happened. I think Cami is sneaking around with Diego behind Jocelyn's back. I got in that argument in art and had to go to Adney's office. Practice was rough. My dad's mad at me. My parents are concerned about me. The list goes on and on and on." He sounds weary, but still. I hate that in his list of grievances, he mentions Cami.

"Do you still have feelings for her?"

He frowns. "Who?"

I roll my eyes, frustrated. "Cami."

"Not at all," he says quickly.

I turn so my back's to him and I stare down at the sink, watching the faucet drip, drip, drip. Is he telling the truth? No matter where he goes, it feels like Cami is always there, lingering on the sidelines. His life is a mess. And if we were to get closer, my life would end up messy, too. Am I ready for that?

God, I'm really not sure.

"Go away, Jake. I don't think my heart can take another go-around with you," I murmur, keeping my head bent.

"Another go-around?" He becomes quiet, and I remain quiet too. But I can feel him getting closer. His warmth seeming to reach out and touch me.

I lift my head, my gaze going to the mirror to find he's standing directly behind me. "I'm not cut out for all this pretend stuff. I actually have feelings, unlike you, and you hurt them."

He presses his lips together and slowly shakes his head. "I'm sorry I hurt you."

We study each other in the mirror's reflection, neither of us moving. "Why are you here so early anyway?"

"Looking for you."

God, I really want to believe him. I do. "Well, you found me, and you apologized. I guess we're done."

"Hannah." He hesitates, looking to the side and I watch as he swallows. He has a great neck. He has a great everything physically. I hate myself for thinking like this.

He could work on his social skills, though. They're lacking.

Big time.

"What?" I ask when he still hasn't said anything.

His gaze meets mine in the mirror once more, and his

eyes are full of so much pain and confusion I can feel my heart cracking.

Stupid jerk heart.

"Can you turn around? Please?" he croaks.

Slowly I turn to face him, tilting my head back so I can look into his eyes. He's standing so close, my feet are nudged between his. My body starts to shake and I take a deep, trembling breath, desperate to calm myself.

"I'm sorry. So damn sorry," he whispers, his expression full of pain. "You're right. I'm a complete asshole. I suppose I don't deserve your forgiveness, but I'm hoping you'll give me another chance. Though honestly, I don't deserve you at all. You have to know though…"

He pauses and I stare at him, silently urging him on. But he doesn't say anything, and finally I can't take it anymore. "What do I have to know?"

"That I would never send messages like that to you. It was all Cami." He shakes his head, his expression full of disgust for a fleeting moment. I assume disgust for Cami. "You— mean a lot to me. I don't want to fuck this up."

"You've messed it up before," I say, my voice soft, my heart racing. Being this close to him is making me uneasy.

"If I could take it all back, I would."

Like I can't help myself, I reach out, touching the bruised skin beneath his eye. It looks so bad. Painful. I can't believe he got into another fight. "Does it hurt?"

He winces when I touch him in a particular spot, and I drop my hand. "Like a bitch."

"Did you deserve it?"

"Diego was talking mad shit about you. So was Cami. I had to do something. So I…I hit him."

I hate that he's fighting with his best friend, and I'm the root of this problem. Will he resent me for causing this rift?

This isn't good. Being with Jake isn't smart. I don't know if I'm willing to take that chance.

"Maybe Cami was right. Maybe this won't work between us." I gently shove at his chest to try to get by him, but that's like trying to push a brick wall. Pointless. Anger and sadness rushes over my body, threatening to choke me and I shake my head, trying my best to hold back the tears. "Please just— get out of my way," I whisper.

He grabs hold of my hands, interlacing our fingers together, his touch almost too intimate. Panic ripples through me. "Please listen to me."

I want to wrench my hands out of his grip, but he slowly smooths his thumbs back and forth across my hands, and it's like I'm a snake falling under the charmer's spell. I go completely still as he stares at me, his expression full of pain and want and I don't know what else.

"What else is there to say?" I ask, my voice pleading.

"Just...give me another chance." His fingers tighten around mine. "Please, Hannah. I got overwhelmed yesterday trying to handle all this shit, and I'm sorry we didn't get a chance to talk. I'm so fucking sorry Cami sent you that DM. Just—hear me out. Let me show you what I want."

I'm incredulous. "What do you want? Because it certainly doesn't feel like I'm a priority to you."

"I'm a dick," he spits out. "I should've come to you first. But you gotta understand, there's a lot on my plate. I'm under a lot of pressure. But just know that I'm sorry. I regret what I did to you."

"You hurt me," I confess, my voice trembling and I jerk my hands out of his hold. "Maybe we're better off as friends."

I don't mean a word of what just came out of my mouth.

"That's all you want from me? *Friendship?*" He raises his brows.

"Yes, is that so hard to believe? You're the one who kissed

me first, like you had to prove to me that there's something more between us when we both know that's an absolute lie." I'm the one lying now. I'm lying through my freaking teeth.

"A lie, huh?" He grabs me by the shoulders, making me cry out, but not because his touch is rough or he's hurting me. No, his hands are excruciatingly gentle, and the look on his face…*God.* He pulls me in close, his head drops, and then his mouth is on mine. A slow and soft, drugging kiss that makes my bones weak and my head spin. When his tongue traces my upper lip, I open to him without thought, my tongue meeting his. And when his arm slips around my waist and he tugs me even closer, I go without protest.

"Does that feel like a lie?" he whispers harshly against my lips, his big hand sliding down over my butt and hauling me in so our hips align. I can feel him, every inch of him, and when his lips capture mine once more, I rub against him slowly. Like a cat.

He moans and somehow hauls me in closer, one hand splayed across my butt. The kiss turns deeper. Our tongues tangle, our breaths mingle, a little whimper sounds low in my throat and his hand shifts upward. Along my hip, over my waist—

A loud, thudding knock suddenly sounds, causing me to spring away from him. We're both breathing hard, staring at each other, his mouth damp, his lips parted, his eyes hooded.

What did I just do? What did we just do?

"Hey, open the door! Come on!"

We both glance at the door before we look at each other.

"I locked it," he tells me, his voice gruff. He clears his throat, then reaches down and readjusts himself.

Holy crap, I think I gave Jake Callahan a boner at school. I don't know what to say, how to react, what to do.

But it's not like I can do anything at all because that girl is still pounding on the bathroom door.

Huffing, I stomp over to the door and turn the deadbolt before throwing it open. A brunette is standing there, her mouth hanging open. She's vaguely familiar, but I can't remember her name. And I'm sure she's gaping at me because Jake is looming directly behind me.

"This is the girls' room," she says slowly, like Jake's an idiot for being here.

Sounds like something I'd say.

Glancing over my shoulder, I send Jake a withering stare before I slither past her, making my escape. Leaving him to deal with the confused girl who's still standing in the middle of the doorway. He calls my name, but I ignore him.

This time, he doesn't chase after me.

* * *

"Rumor has it you and Jake Callahan had sex in the girls' bathroom at the library before school started this morning."

This is how Sophie greets me at lunch.

My jaw drops open so far, I'm afraid it'll hit the picnic table. "Wh-what did you just say?" I ask once air has returned to my lungs.

She settles onto the bench across from me and leans across the table, putting her face in mine, her voice going extra low. "People are saying that you and Jake were caught in the girls' bathroom in the library before school. And that you two were having—sex."

I slowly shake my head. "It's not true."

"Of course it's not true," Sophie says, like the loyal friend she is. She sits up straight, her posture perfect, as usual. "I just wanted you to know what they're saying."

A couple of sophomore girls walk by our table, their hands covering their mouths as they whisper to each other, both of them glancing in my direction before they run away giggling. I stare after them in utter disbelief.

I'm sure they were talking about me. And Jake.

Having *sex.*

On campus!

Please. Like I'd ever do that. After over three years at this school, you'd think people would know me better by now.

"I've never been gossip material my entire high school life," I say quietly.

"Welcome then," Sophie says cheerily. "It's an interesting place to be."

It's like this for the entirety of lunch. I can hear their whispers, see their gazes lock on me briefly before they look away with laughter or sneers or more gossip. I hear Jake's name mentioned numerous times, though never mine. Considering he's nowhere to be found in the quad, I guess it's safe to talk freely about him.

I can't help but wonder where he is. Off with Cami maybe?

But no, there *she* is, sitting with her cheer team friends at a table across the way from us, her expression sulky as she looks around like a lost little puppy. I wonder if she's heard the rumor yet.

She has to have. I bet she's not happy about it either.

I'm also sure the one who started the rumor was the girl who found us in the bathroom in the first place. I don't even know her name. I think she's a junior and it starts with K? Kaylee or Kylee, something like that? I'm not sure, but clearly she has a big mouth.

Did she notice Jake was…hard? I mean, he did some rearranging, but I didn't allow myself to look at his crotch again before I made my escape, so I have no idea if he was standing in the middle of the girls' bathroom with a tent in his shorts.

Someday, I'll find this funny. Maybe even kind of hot? But for right now, I am completely mortified.

My phone buzzes near the end of lunch and I check it to see I have a Snap notification.

From Jake.

I thrust my phone screen toward Sophie, who's chatting nonstop with Marty. I appreciate that he hasn't mentioned that nasty rumor once this entire lunch period.

"Open it," Sophie says, her expression eager. Like she's secretly enjoying this. And maybe she is. I suppose I can't blame her. This is about the most exciting thing that's happened to us our entire high school lives.

"I'll wait a few minutes," I tell her coolly, though inside my stomach is tumbling over itself. I should've never eaten that turkey sandwich. Now I feel like puking it back up.

Oh my God, I can't believe I didn't realize this sooner, but…

"Where's Tony?" I ask.

"They had a meeting at lunch today," she answers, and when I frown, she continues, "The football team. Lots of prepping is going on for this week's game."

I thought our most important game will be during homecoming week, when we play our biggest rival. I'm surprised they're giving this week's game so much attention, but what do I know about football?

"Plus Tony mentioned there might be scouts coming to this week's game. From colleges," she further explains.

Ah. Okay, that makes sense.

"So that's where Jake is too, in case you were wondering," Sophie finishes with a smile. "Now open his Snap."

"Fine." With shaky fingers, I open it to find a selfie of him staring off to the side, looking very, very serious. And very, very handsome, despite the black eye.

The Snap reads:

Do you forgive me yet?

Without thought I screenshot that sucker, not even caring if he got a notification just now telling him I did. I then take a quick selfie of me scowling directly into the camera, and type the words:

Not quite.

And then I tap the blue and white arrow, sending it to him.

"Did you just screenshot his Snap?" Sophie asks, surprise written all over her face. We don't normally do that type of stuff. If we want to keep a good photo of someone and not let them know, we take a photo of the photo on the other person's phone. It's convoluted and completely over the top but...hey, no judgement. It works.

I nod, pushing the phone away from me. "He looked really good."

"He got a notification."

"I know." I shrug.

Sophie's eyes widen. "So he knows you did that."

"I don't really care." In fact, I open up my photos and study the screenshot of Jake, marveling at his handsomeness. I sort of hate how good-looking he is. And then again, I sort of love it.

Those lips have been on mine. His tongue has been in my mouth. And he wants a second chance with *me.*

What is this life?

Sophie studies me for a while, her delicate brows wrinkled, a little frown curling her mouth. "Are you *sure* you didn't have sex in the bathroom with Jake?"

"I didn't," I say, rolling my eyes. I know she's joking, and I know I'm acting different too. It's all so confusing, I don't know what to think, or how to act. "I'm just...I don't care what he thinks anymore. I'm still sort of mad at him, and I told him that. And he deserves to suffer a little bit, don't you think?"

She blinks at me, surprise written all over her face. "Uh, what happened to my best friend? When did she become such a rebel?"

"What are you talking about?"

"If this rumor thing would've happened a year ago, you would've run home and cried buckets," she observes.

I raise a brow. "Buckets?"

Sophie nods. "You would've wanted to go lock yourself away in your room and die a slow, torturous death. Or you might've wanted to fling yourself into the lake and drown. Now, though? It's like you don't even care." She hesitates. "It's kind of weird."

"The rumor isn't true, so why does it matter? I mean, really, do people think Jake would have sex with *me* in the library bathroom?" I rest my hand against my chest. Even with everything that's happened between me and Jake, I have to say the idea of it is pretty farfetched.

Sophie waves her hand around the quad. "Clearly, yes. They all seem to believe the rumor."

"They just like the idea of someone having sex on campus and getting away with it," I say dismissively.

"Okay, whatever." Sophie shakes her head, but there's a smile teasing the corner of her lips. Like she doesn't mind this new Hannah she's witnessing.

You know what? I don't mind her either. Actually, I kind of like her.

A lot.

Though I'm not liking myself after a few minutes. I keep my attention focused on my phone like I'm desperate, waiting for Jake to Snap me back, but he never does. He also never opened my Snap to him, so that makes me feel a little better. Yet it also makes me feel a little worse.

Is he ignoring me? Has he already found someone else to distract him? Pretty much any girl at this school would want a chance at Jake Callahan. They'd line up for him, every single girl clamoring, *pick me, pick me!* He could have his choice.

Am I really delusional enough to believe he actually chose me?

By the time I'm walking to the art room for my last class of the day, I'm a nervous wreck. Jake still hasn't opened my snap, and the class I'm about to go to is the one he's in. Will he talk to me? Start another argument? Try to kiss me in front of everyone?

I don't know what to expect.

When the bell rings, he's still not in his seat, and Rob Schaffer is clearly thrilled.

"Looks like I scared Callahan away," he crows, a giant smile on his smug face as he crosses his arms in front of his chest.

I'm so tempted to say something, but I keep my mouth shut. Ever since that incident at Cami's party after the sixth grade, when everyone had to hold him down before they made me kiss him, Rob and I haven't really gotten along. Like why would I want to be nice to a guy who treats me so terribly? He makes fun of me, I know he does, though most of the time it's behind my back. Pretty sure he thinks I'm pathetic.

Well, guess what? I think he is too. More than that, he's a complete jerk.

Better to just leave him alone.

I'm sorting through the seemingly thousands of colored pencils Mrs. Sanborne has, tossing out broken ones and putting the ones that need to be sharpened aside, when my phone buzzes. I check to see Jake has finally replied to my Snap. Like the eager beaver I am, I open it immediately.

It's another selfie and he's looking straight at the camera this time. His full lips are pursed, his eyebrows are lifted and his eyes are so blue, so mesmerizing, I find it hard to look away. He's gorgeous despite the black eye. It actually makes him look even…sexier. The messages says:

Looks like I need to work on making you like me again.

Without hesitation I screenshot the photo, take a quick selfie of me with one lifted eyebrow, and answer him.

You're going to have to work real hard.

He responds almost immediately, his lips quirked up on one side, almost like he's smiling.

That's what she said.

I can't help the laugh that escapes me, my fingers going to my mouth as if I can silence myself. He must watch *The Office.* I mean, who doesn't? I'm dreading the day when Netflix doesn't stream it any longer.

Snapping another selfie, I send him a message along with it.

Did Jake Callahan just make a joke?

Seconds later, another selfie, but only from his forehead up. Just seeing his thick, dark hair makes me want to run my fingers through it.

Oh my God, Hannah, you need to stop!

I can be funny. And why are you taking screenshots of all my selfies?

I take our messages right to text.

Me: **Because I like having evidence of your groveling.**

Jake: **I think you just want to keep photos of me. Which means you care.**

Me: **I don't care.**

Jake: **I think you might. Just a little.**

Me: **I shouldn't. Was it really Cami who sent those messages?**

Jake: **Why would I lie to you? It was definitely Cami. Ask Tony. He drove me home Friday night when I realized I lost my phone.**

I tape my finger against my lips, wondering what I should say to him next.

Me: **Why would she do that?**

Jake: **Because she's a total bitch.**

Jake: **I'd rather not talk about her. I'd rather talk about me and you.**

Then he sends six heart eyes emojis.

Me: **What else is there to discuss?**

Jake: **I miss you.**

My heart kicks into high gear, but I tell myself to calm down. Being sweet and sending emojis doesn't mean he can completely worm his way into my heart. I'm not that easy.

Not yet, anyway.

Why aren't you in class? I finally ask.

Jake: **Scouts are coming to this week's game. My dad's putting me through some extra drills. I already got it excused.**

Me: **Are you excused for the rest of the week?**

Jake: **Yeah. They want us in top shape so we perform well in front of the scouts.**

I bite my lip, sad that he won't be in class for the rest of the week. I'll definitely miss him.

Me: **Think you're going to win?**

Jake: **We are DEFINITELY going to win, Hannah. Just you watch.**

I can't help but smile. I like his confidence.

I bet you will, I finally respond.

Jake: **Do you miss seeing me in Sanborne's class?**

Me: **No.**

Jake: **Come on...**

Me: **NO.**

Jake: **I think you're lying.**

Me: **We need to change the subject.**

I chew on my lower lip, wondering what I can tell him that'll switch up our conversation.

Ooh, I know.

Me: **You know who doesn't miss you at all? Rob. He says he scared you off.**

Jake: **That motherfucker. I hate him.**

Me: **He hates you too.**

Jake: **The feeling is mutual.**

Me: **At least you don't have to deal with him since you're not here.**

Jake: **True. Hey. Can I ask you a question?**

Nerves swoop in my stomach.

Me: **What?**

Jake: **Just promise me you'll give it some thought. You don't have to answer right away.**

Me: **What is it?**

Jake: **Promise me first. Okay?**

Me: **Fine, okay, I promise.**

Jake: **Will you wear my jersey Friday?**

I press my lips together and glance around, making sure Mrs. Sanborne isn't watching me. She's too busy wandering around the tables and helping everyone come up with a concept for their colored pencil sketch, and I'm sure she thinks I'm a lot further in my sorting project than I am, but screw it. I can work fast under pressure.

And I need to answer Jake.

Me: **Are you sure you want me to wear it?**

His response is quick, like he's just sitting on his phone and not conditioning, like he's supposed to.

Jake: **I definitely want you to. Just think about it first, before you give me an answer.**

Me: **Okay.**

Jake: **I also want to talk to you after practice, if you're not busy.**

I should tell him I'm busy. Real busy. I do have a paper I need to work on for world religions. But it's not due until Friday night at midnight. I'll be at the game Friday, though.

Right? Yes, I know I will, whether I'm wearing a certain someone's jersey or not.

And hey, it's only Tuesday. I have plenty of time to work on that paper.

Jake sends me another text.

Hannah? Can we talk later?

Maybe I can stay in the library and work on the paper, and then meet with him after football practice? If we stay on campus, nothing too crazy can happen. It's a public place. He won't try to kiss me in front of people, right? Only in secret places. Like at my apartment in the middle of the night, or the bathroom in the library.

Or my ego has totally inflated, thinking Jake will try to kiss me again. I mean, really, who do I think I am?

Sure, I finally say to him. **After practice?**

Yeah. See you then.

HANNAH

By the time five o'clock rolls around, I'm a bundle of nervous energy. Football practice doesn't end until five-thirty, and I do my best to linger in the library, but eventually I can't take it any longer. By five-fifteen, I gather up all my stuff, shove it in my backpack, and get the heck out of there.

Sitting on a bench across from the library, I send a couple of texts to Sophie, knowing she's on a quick break between her dance classes. Since I never get to see her right after school, I text her all the details about the conversation I had with Jake, and how I'm meeting with him after practice.

My phone immediately rings. It's Sophie.

"So you're really going to talk to him?" is how she greets me.

"Yes," I say with a sigh. "In fifteen minutes. I'm so nervous."

"What are you guys going to talk about?"

"I don't know. He wants another chance with me. I believe him when he says Cami sent those texts and the photo from his phone." My voice goes low as I look around, making sure no one is nearby. "Is this a dream, Sophie? Tell me, because it feels super real."

"It's not a dream, Hannah. This is your life, and Jake seems really into you. Just—watch out. He seems to be carrying a lot of extra baggage right now," she says, my ever practical friend.

"You're right. The stuff with Diego, and Cami of course." And who knows what else?

"I keep hearing rumors Diego and Cami are having some sort of secret affair," she says, her voice hushed.

"Do you really think Diego would do that?"

"I don't know. From what I've heard, he cheats on Jocelyn. A lot."

I really don't want to think about the drama right now. "Jake asked me to wear his jersey this Friday," I admit.

"Already? Tony hasn't asked me yet." She sounds disappointed.

"He will," I say confidently. At least Tony doesn't confuse Sophie with a bunch of off-and-on behavior. He's pretty straightforward.

"Are you going to wear it?" Sophie asks.

"I don't know." I pause. "Should I?"

I want to, but then again, I don't. It's a claim of sorts, when a girl wears a boy's jersey. A way for the boys to mark their girls as theirs—or potentially theirs. Like we're a piece of property. The feminist in me says it's an old-fashioned, downright misogynistic ritual that should be abolished.

The other part of me thinks it's awesome and I'm dying to walk around campus with Jake's number on my chest.

"You should. And I'll wear Tony's if he asks me."

"Like I said, he's going to ask you," I remind her.

"I hope so," she says, her voice, drifting.

"Stop doubting him. You two are totally going to be *the*

couple of the senior class," I say, and I mean it. They're a cute couple.

"Oh my God, Hannah. What if you end up going out with Jake? Like boyfriend and girlfriend? And Tony and I actually end up together too? That means we can double date!" she squeals in my ear, making me wince.

"Don't get ahead of yourself. You and Tony might be a couple, but Jake and I have a long way to go," I say, ever full of skepticism.

"Tony and I aren't official either," she says with a little sniff. "We're just talking. That's it."

"Talking and going to lunch and dinner and whatever else you two do, uh huh," I tease her.

"Please. He hasn't even made a move on me. Not like that. At least we're not having sex in the bathroom," she tosses back at me.

We both start laughing.

"You have to keep me posted," she says after our laughter dies. "Tell me what happens. FaceTime me later tonight, okay? I want to hear every groveling, begging word Jake says to you."

"He's not going to beg," I say assuredly. "Come on, this is Jake Callahan we're talking about."

"And he seems pretty into you," she points out. "From what you're telling me, he feels like crap for what Cami did to you. And what he did to you too."

"He wasn't that bad…"

"He was terrible. He completely forgot you! Don't let him off the hook so easy," she reminds me.

"Okay, fine," I say with a sigh.

We chat a few more minutes and then Sophie has to go. I check the time on my phone when the call ends.

Oh crap. It's almost five thirty. I gotta go too.

I'm approaching the school parking lot when I spot him

in the distance, flanked by his friends. They're all talking and laughing, and Jake actually has a faint smile on his face, which is the first smile I've seen from him in a while. He's also wearing a navy blue baseball hat backwards, covering up his glorious hair, and he's got on white practice shorts. A navy T-shirt stretches across his chest, his biceps straining against the sleeves, and I wonder if these boys wear their shirts a size too small to show off their muscles.

I wouldn't put it past them.

It's nice, being able to stand there unnoticed and watch Jake in his element, hanging out with his friends. Spying on him like this, does it make me some sort of weird stalker?

God, I hope not.

As they draw closer, I can make out their voices, hear them cursing and laughing and generally talking shit. Caleb won't shut up, and when he throws his head back and laughs, I can't help but think to myself that he's handsome. The longish golden brown hair and the sparkling hazel eyes, the tanned skin and lean muscles. He has a nice smile, and an infectious laugh.

But Caleb is a complete player. Not someone a girl can be serious with, because he's not serious whatsoever. He breaks hearts wherever he goes.

And then there's Tony. Quiet, dependable, sad little rich boy Tony. Diego's nowhere to be seen. Clearly, the fight between Jake and Diego is still going on.

Caleb approaches his car first, saying goodbye to his friends as he branches off from them. Tony walks with Jake all the way to his truck, and I watch as Jake glances around, his dark brows furrowed, his mouth curved downward into a frown.

He's looking for me. I know it.

And he's afraid I've ditched him.

Tony is facing him, continuously talking as Jake pulls his

phone out of his pocket. He taps at his screen a few times before holding his phone up to his ear.

My phone rings in my hand, showing an unknown number is calling. I answer it.

"How did you get my number?" I keep my gaze glued on him to see his reaction.

The devilish smirk on his face is too adorable. And the tiniest bit annoying. "I have my ways."

"Seriously, how did you get it?"

He ignores my question. "Are you bailing on me?"

"No."

"Then where are you?" He glances around the parking lot once again, Tony doing so as well, though I'm guessing he has no clue who he's looking for.

"I can see you," I tell him, unable to hide the smile in my voice.

"Are you spying on me right now?"

"Maybe."

He starts walking, leaving Tony behind, who calls out a goodbye to Jake before he heads for his car. Once he's out of sight, I take a few steps to the right, putting myself directly in Jake's line of vision.

"There you are," he says.

The pleasure in his deep voice is undeniable, and my toes curl in my Birks.

He draws closer, ending the call and shoving his phone into his pocket, his expression serious as he approaches. I freeze in place, immobilized by the look on his face, the anticipation of this moment rendering me speechless. I had all sorts of things I wanted to say to him prepped in my brain, but when the time comes, I'm without words.

No surprise.

Jake stops directly in front of me and I tip my head back to meet his gaze. Those pretty blue eyes meet mine, and right now, I feel like we're the only two people in the world. Which of course is totally false, considering lots of people are going to be milling around soon, waiting for their parents to pick them up or for the sports bus to take them home.

"Hey." He lifts his chin at me in that typical boy way.

"Hi," I squeak, then clear my throat, feeling silly.

His lips curve upward. "You still mad at me?"

"Definitely." I nod. I can't help the smile that spreads across my face.

"Can I entice you by taking you to Starbucks to earn some points?"

I study him for a moment, just letting myself drink him in. If I were smart, I'd tell him to go to hell. Actually, if I were smart, I would've *already* told him that.

But for some reason, I'm willing to give him another chance. Not that I'm going to tell him that right away.

"Yes," I finally say. "You can."

"Let's go then." He gently takes my arm and turns me so we're walking toward his truck. "Before everyone else shows up out here."

"Are you embarrassed to be seen with me?" My tone is light, but I sort of mean it. Does he want to hide me away? That's how I felt before everything blew up.

I won't be his secret side piece. Not again.

Jake comes to a complete stop, turning me so I'm facing him. "Do you think I'm embarrassed by you?"

Shrugging, I drop my head, staring at my shoes. "I don't know."

He slips his fingers beneath my chin, tipping my face up so I have no choice but to look at him. "I'm not. If you want to stay here with me staring at you like this while everyone stands around and watches us, I will. If you want me to wait with you in the middle of this walkway with you tomorrow morning when the first bell rings and every single person who goes to this school has to pass by us, I will. I'll do whatever it takes to prove to you that I want to be seen with you, Hannah."

His thumb streaks across my chin, making me tingle, and I smile up at him, though it's tremulous at best. "Taking me to Starbucks is a good start."

A growl escapes him and he drops his hand from my face, grabbing my hand as he practically drags me to his truck, his stride is so long. I take two steps for his every one so I can keep up. "You're going to make me work for this, aren't you?"

"You deserve it. It's the least you can do," I tell him.

He glances over his shoulder. "I look forward to proving to you that you matter to me."

I can't help the butterflies that suddenly break free in my stomach.

Lord help me, I'm in big, big trouble.

* * *

Because he has something to prove, he insists on us going into Starbucks and ordering our drinks versus using the drive thru. He gets a venti ice water and a protein pack to eat, and I get my favorite iced caramel macchiato with extra caramel drizzle. The place is crowded, and there are people in here who we go to school with. Jake ignores every single one of them and so do I, but he has to know they're talking about us.

Our being together at Starbucks isn't dismantling the sex-in-the-bathroom rumor whatsoever.

We find a small table with two chairs tucked away in the corner, and the barista is calling Jake's name within minutes of us sitting down. He leaves to go pick up our drinks, and I watch as pretty much every head in the room swivels to look in my direction, all of them turning away quickly when they realize I'm facing them. Witnessing them obviously check me out.

At least a lot of them have the decency to look embarrassed when they get caught.

Jake returns with our drinks, and he settles in, tearing into the protein pack and eating the cheese and salami while guzzling down his water. I sip my drink and watch in fascination as he devours the food. He eventually holds the plastic container toward me with the last piece of cheese and salami in it. "You sure you don't want something to eat?"

I shake my head, still too nervous. My stomach is tumbling over itself like damp clothes inside a dryer. "I'm fine. Please, eat it."

He shoves the cheese and meat into his mouth, then glances over his shoulder to stare longingly at the case that holds the cold snacks and waters and juices. "I should've bought two."

"You can go buy another. I don't mind," I tell him.

"Nah, I'll eat at home later. Unless you want to grab something to eat with me?" he asks hopefully.

"I have to get home soon," I tell him truthfully. "I'm making dinner."

"Your mom has to work tonight?"

I nod, taking another sip of my macchiato.

"Want me to come by later?" He lifts a brow, his expression downright hopeful.

Another moment where I should deliver a firm *hell no*.

Instead, I shrug. "I don't know. Should you?"

"You want me there?"

I shrug again. "I don't know if it's a good idea."

He winces, resting his hand on his chest, directly over his heart. "Ouch. You wound me."

"I'm worried you'll hang out with me all week and then ghost me," I say wryly, describing exactly what he did before.

His expression turns contrite and he dips his head like he can't look me in the eyes. "I probably don't deserve a second chance."

"No, you probably don't," I agree with him cheerily.

He scoots his chair in closer, his knees knocking against mine beneath the table. "Then why are you giving me another chance?"

"I haven't confirmed that I am yet."

"Can I confess something to you?" His gaze meets mine once more.

I study his face, how open his expression is. He usually has a wall up, but now I'm the one with the wall. It's only made of wood, though. He'd be able to knock it down with a couple of firm kicks, I'm sure. "Sure."

"You're the first girl I've spent time with who wants nothing from me."

"You've told me that before."

"Well, you deserve to hear it again. I had a shit weekend, and I made it worse because I didn't reach out to you. I should've." He hesitates. "Part of the reason I had such a terrible weekend was because you weren't at the game Friday."

My mouth drops open at his confession. "R-really?" I'm stunned. I didn't think he noticed.

I didn't think he cared.

He nods. "I get why, but I was still—upset, I guess. And then I got in that stupid fight, and I lost my phone, and I didn't know what to do. I didn't have your number, nothing."

"I'm sorry I wasn't there." I feel terrible. I didn't know it mattered that much.

"It's all good," he says with a shrug, but I can tell he's trying to play it off.

"How did you get my number earlier?"

His cheeks turn ruddy and he ducks his head. "I asked Tony to get it from Sophie."

That little sneak. She never told me. "Tricky."

"Not really. I can't believe I didn't ask for it sooner."

"Can I ask you a question?"

"Whatever you want to know, I'll tell you. I'm an open book." He leans back in his chair, spreading his arms wide, and my mouth goes dry at how attractive he looks. God, he's killing me right now.

"What did Diego say about me that made you punch him?"

He winces, his arms dropping by his sides. "You don't want to know."

"Yes, actually I do."

Sighing, he leans forward, practically putting his face in mine. "Trust me, Hannah. You don't."

"Jake, it'll get out eventually. Don't you think it's better if I hear it from you?"

He runs his fingers through his thick, dark hair, messing it up. Looking adorable. "He called you a loser. So did Cami. Then he made some—sexual comments about us, about you, and then he said it was cool if I was slumming with you."

Ouch. "That's so…harsh."

"I told you." He shakes his head. "I'm sorry."

"You don't have to apologize." I reach for his hand, sliding my fingers over his. "You weren't the one who said it."

He turns his hand up, interlocking our fingers, his expression pleased. "I hit him in his big fucking mouth. Just cold-cocked him out of nowhere."

"I'm not one to promote violence, but thank you. For defending me." I squeeze his hand and he smiles.

"I will always defend you," he says softly, his eyes glowing with sincerity. "Fuck that guy. He won't ever get away with saying shit like that about you."

His words make me want to swoon. Ridiculous, right? They're fighting over me, yet there's a tiny part of me that finds it romantic.

"If we actually try this, will your other friends say stuff like that?" I ask.

"They better not," he says swiftly, sounding angry.

"It's just that your friend group is so…"

"Clique-ish?" he finishes for me.

"Yes."

He smiles ruefully. "We're definitely clique-ish, but I can get them to turn around."

"You'll have to get them to turn around to accept me? Really? I mean, I get it. There are social tiers at this school, and I'm in the bottom one." I'm not even halfway done with my drink, but I suddenly don't want to finish it. This conversation is making my stomach upset.

"You're not bottom-tier." He brings our linked hands up to his mouth, dropping a kiss on my knuckles, right in front of everyone. My skin tingles from where his lips touched me, and I instantly want more. More kissing. More touching. More Jake.

I can feel everyone watching us. Staring. I'm sure more things will be said at school tomorrow. Maybe they'll say we had sex in the middle of Starbucks. "I don't want to talk about my friends anymore," he murmurs.

"I don't either." At least we can agree on that.

"Let's get out of here," he suggests, and I shake my head.

"Can I drink the rest of my macchiato first?"

We talk for a little while longer, and I eventually finish my drink as we chat. I bring him up to speed over what happened in art today, and he tells me how hard they're conditioning for the game and the scouts this Friday. He doesn't bring up me wearing his jersey, and neither do I.

I don't want that pressure yet.

"I should get home," I tell him after I check my phone to see it's past six-thirty. I send Mom a quick text letting her know I'll be there soon and that I'm still fixing dinner. "I need to feed my mom before she goes to work."

"What's for dinner?"

"I was thinking tacos."

"Can you cook pretty well?" He rises to his feet and gathers our empty cups, taking them to the garbage. I follow after him as we exit the coffee shop.

"I'm okay. I can get by."

"I can't cook for shit."

"Do you have a personal chef at home?" I'm teasing, but sort of not. I mean, the Callahans are mega rich. The might have housekeepers and chefs and maybe even a butler. Who knows?

"Yeah. She's real good. I love everything she makes." He grins, and it's a dazzling sight. He doesn't let those smiles out into the wild too often, so when you spot one, it's a sight to see. "She's my mom."

I laugh too, feeling a little giddy. When Jake's in a good mood, everything's lighter. "I actually thought you might have a cook. Someone you hire out."

"We have a housekeeper who comes in once a week, but my parents expect us to clean our rooms and do our own laundry, especially Mom. My dad's family was wealthy, but my mom's was pretty broke. She grew up with a single mother who had a lot of problems." Jake hits the keyless remote on the truck as we both head toward the passenger side door. "Mom says we're spoiled but not *too* spoiled, whatever that means."

His mom sounds like a good person. I've heard positive things about Fable Callahan. I've always liked her name too. So unique.

Once we're in the truck, I decide to question him further.

We opened up to each other before, but there is still plenty I don't know about Jake. "Do you get along with your family? Your brothers and sisters?" I'm not even exactly sure how many he has.

"Yeah, I guess." He shrugs. "For the most part. Autumn, me and Ava are all close in age, so there was lots of fighting sometimes, especially between Autumn and Ava. Our little brother Beck, we all love him because he's much younger than us, so there's almost like this…separation, you know?"

I nod, though I don't suppose I really get it. "There's a big age gap between my brother and I. We were never that close. And once he graduated and joined the Navy, I never see him. He never comes home." Makes me think Mom's relationship with him has never been that great, which is sad.

"That's too bad." He hesitates for a moment. "My family drives me crazy sometimes, but I'm glad I have them. We take care of each other, you know?"

No. I don't know. My mom and I take care of each other, but it's like Joe isn't even a part of our life. It's kind of sad.

Instead of being brutally honest and telling him how I feel, I offer up a smile and say, "Yeah."

He doesn't need to hear about my brother and his neglectful behavior. That's a story for another time.

Jake starts the truck's engine. "Ready to go home? Or can I keep you for a little while longer?"

My melancholy thoughts disappear just like that.

"I need to go home," I say, though I sort of wish he could keep me, and that this day wasn't ending. It definitely started out different than I thought it would. I can't forget that Jake kissed me in the bathroom.

My lips are tingling just thinking about it.

He drives me to my apartment complex, and I'm about to hop out of his truck when he touches my arm, stopping me from opening the passenger side door. I turn to find him watching me, his expression open. Almost…

Vulnerable.

"Are we good?" His voice is hushed, and I'm tempted to tell him yes. Don't worry about it. We're so good, it goes beyond good. But I just can't. Not yet.

"We're getting closer," I tell him truthfully, smiling faintly at him before I withdraw from his touch, exit the truck, and head up the stairs toward my front door.

I don't look back, not once, and I know he remains there until I'm safely inside.

Only then do I hear him gun the engine and pull out of the parking lot.

CHAPTER 26

JAKE

I'm in my bedroom after just getting home from dropping off Hannah when I get an Instagram notification on my phone.

elibennettqbnumber1 mentioned you in their story

Fuck me standing. Here we go again.

Reminding myself to stay calm, I open up the app and find the story Eli tagged me in. Eli's standing in the middle of his school's football field, wearing a pair of black gym shorts and nothing else, his face sweaty as he squints toward the waning sun. In the distance, I can see other members of his team approaching, all of them walking in a line, reminding me of a gang coming to back their leader.

This dude is the biggest show boater I have ever seen, swear to God.

"We just had the best practice of our fuckin' lives today." He points at the camera, and I wonder what pussy ass he forced to film him. Probably some freshman who's honored to have Eli shout at him.

"Only a couple more weeks until the big game, where

we're going to beat the Badgers' asses on their own damn turf on homecoming!"

The rest of his team is now standing behind him, a wall of black, purple and gold. They're all yelling, their fists in the air and adding a lot of *fuck yeahs* as background noise.

They're a bunch of morons.

"So watch out, Jake motherfuckin' Callahan. We're training hard in preparation of destroying you, and your team." He jabs his finger at the camera again. "I can't wait to beat your smug ass and watch your dad come to me after the game and congratulate us on a solid win." More yelling from the rest of the guys, and Eli nods and laughs. "Just knowing he's going to do that will burn your ass, won't it?" He leans closer to the camera, a giant shit-eating grin on his face.

God, I hate this guy so much.

"If you only knew what's really going on, you'd die, bro. Just fuckin' die!" He tips his head back and literally howls at the sky like he's a coyote. They all start howling, a couple of them beat their chests with their fists, and I wonder if they're high.

I also wonder where the hell their coaches are. Our coaches would have our asses if we did something like this days before the game, on social media for the entire world to see. We shit talk the Mustangs all the time, but we don't do it on camera.

Where I come from, we call that evidence. And we want no evidence of us saying something that might come back and bite us in the butt later.

"Life's a mystery, and right now I'm having the time of my life with someone from *your* life." He puts his hands together like he's praying, bowing toward the camera with a smirk. "She's a tasty little piece, I'll give her that. Sassy as fuck and not willing to give an inch, despite how many inches I want to give her."

They all start laughing again, including Eli. Anger simmers low in my belly, and I can only assume he's talking about Cami. Like I give a shit if he's fucking around with Cami. Doesn't he realize I'm over her? I figured he was over her too.

"Oh, wait a minute! I see you got yourself a pretty little redhead now, fucking her in the library. Pretty balls-out for you, Callahan," Eli taunts. "I was told you're more of a boring missionary man, but maybe you're becoming more adventurous now that you're the big senior on campus. Untouchable. Well, guess what, asshole? My boys are gonna be touching *you* all fucking night in a couple of weeks, and that pretty little redhead isn't going to be able to nurse you back to health either. You'll be too fucked up! By us!"

I exit out of the story and toss my phone across the room, breathing deep as I start pacing. That asshole makes me fucking insane with the things he says. And I've got to endure it for the next couple of weeks. Bringing Hannah into his rant is taking it way too far. And who else is he talking about?

It has to be Cami. I can't think of anyone else I know or have been associated with who'd stoop so low as to fuck around with Eli the asshole Bennett

My phone starts ringing from where it's lying on the floor, and I go and scoop it up to find Tony's name flashing on the screen. I answer immediately.

"You see Eli's story?" he asks.

"Yeah." I exhale raggedly. "He fucking sucks. They all do."

"How the hell did he find out about the bathroom rumor so quickly?" He sounds truly perplexed.

"Come on, bro. Word travels fast. You know this." Our schools keep tabs on each other, each campus having spies who spill to the others.

"Right. You're right. Why does he keep doing this shit? Acting like he's gonna win?" Tony asks, practically growling. "We're still weeks out. Why is he trying to start shit now?"

"I don't know, because he's a complete narcissist who wants all the attention on him at all times?" Frustration makes me want to punch a wall—preferably with a photo of Eli's smug face pinned on it.

"Wonder if he knows about the scouts coming to our game and wants to get inside your head," Tony says.

Tony's so damn smart.

"Probably," I mutter. "Who do you think he's talking about?"

"What do you mean?" He sounds confused.

"The person in my life who's a tasty little piece. Sassy as fuck," I explain. "You think he means Cami?"

"Pretty sure Cami isn't fucking around with Eli," Tony says. "I thought she was sneaking around with Diego."

My stomach turns. I'm still mad at Diego for…everything. And I need to learn how to forgive him for the betterment of the team.

"Supposedly," I say, pausing for a moment "Then I have no idea who Eli's talking about."

"He's just saying that shit to get in your head and piss you off, man. You *know* how he is. And look, it's working." He chuckles. "For all we know, he's probably talking about your mom. He might have a crush on her. Back in the day, we all did."

My fingers grip my phone so tight, they start to ache. "If he says one word about my mom, I'll murder the son of a bitch."

Tony chuckles. "He's such a dumbass, he probably *is* talking about her."

We chat for a while longer, Tony trying to soothe my

ruffled feathers, telling me I shouldn't worry. He also mentions I need to talk to Diego soon, and I know he's right. Our team needs to come together right now, not be torn apart over something stupid.

Hannah's not stupid, though. Far from it. I care about her. I wish I could go over to her place tonight, but I'm not going to push my luck. I need to take it slow with her.

After I end the call with Tony, I hear Mom yelling from downstairs, though I can't make out what she's saying. I'm sure dinner is ready.

I need to get my shit together before I make an appearance at the family dinner table.

Completely distracted by Eli's "come at me bro" video and my conversation with Tony, I exit my room with my head down and my thoughts elsewhere. I'm headed for the stairs when Ava pops out of her bedroom as if she were lying in wait, stopping directly in front of me and blocking my way.

"What do you want?" I can tell by the look on her face she's bursting at the seams to tell me something.

"I heard a rumor about you going around school today," she says, her brows shooting up into her hairline.

"It's not true," I say immediately, annoyed she'd even question me.

"You didn't have sex with Hannah Walsh then?" She crosses her arms, even taps her foot.

"Of course not. Like I'd have sex in the school library." I shake my head, actually appreciating the distraction. The idea isn't a bad one—sex in the library bathroom. It was too damn easy to lock that door, and it took a while for someone to eventually want in. They open the library at least forty-five minutes before school starts. Plenty of time to meet up and fuck around…

"Oh." She blinks at me, her eyes wide and full of surprise. "I figured you'd say you would never have sex with Hannah."

"What's wrong with Hannah?" I feel immediately defensive, and I mentally tell myself to remain calm. I've tried my best to stay even-keeled today, and I think I've done a pretty good job, save for watching that dumbass video Eli made.

The one thing that helped more than anything else? Having Hannah to focus on. And the upcoming game with the scouts in attendance, though that's making me extra nervous.

Plus, it's nice that I don't have to go to art class all week, so I won't have to deal with Rob. I'll miss seeing Hannah in that class, though.

Eli Bennett is another matter altogether. The way he's taunting my ass on social media on a daily basis is annoying as fuck. He's like a mosquito that buzzes around your head, gets real close to your ear. The whining gets so bad, you swat at it, thinking you hit it. Killed it.

But then he comes right back, whining and buzzing. Never leaving you alone.

"Absolutely nothing is wrong with Hannah," Ava says, kicking me out of my thoughts, and I can tell she's being honest with me. "I just figured you didn't like her, what with the way she rejected you so thoroughly when you asked her to wear your jersey."

I'm annoyed she would bring that up, only because she knows. "Who told you about that?"

Ava shrugs. "Your charming ex-girlfriend was bragging about it before the game the day she wore your jersey. I still can't believe you let her do that."

"Don't worry, it's never going to happen again," I reassure her. "Hey, have you heard any rumors about Cami and Diego hooking up?"

Ava presses her lips together, a dead giveaway she knows something. "Maybe."

I told her all about the fight over the weekend, and she never mentioned she knew anything. "What have you heard?"

Sighing, she leans against the wall, crossing her arms. "I heard Cami telling Baylee that she was going to meet with Diego later tonight."

"Where?"

"I don't know." She shrugs. "I just heard her say that they needed to talk, and Diego was pissed about everything going on, especially with you. I guess he's blaming you for not playing when scouts are coming to the game this Friday?"

"He's the one who's acting like a baby," I say through tight lips.

"Don't be mad at me. I'm just repeating what I heard." She pushes away from the wall. "Honestly, if he's going to do you like that, I would punch him in the face too."

"I didn't hit him because of Cami. I hit him because he was talking shit about Hannah," I remind her. "And by the way, I asked Hannah to wear my jersey this Friday."

"Again?" She tilts her head.

I nod. "I like her."

"Really?" She looks skeptical.

"Yeah. Really. Is it so wrong, me and Hannah potentially being together?" I wait for her reaction. Ava and I are only a year apart in school, and we've always had a close relationship. Good close and bad close, if I'm being real. I value her opinion, not that I would ever say that out loud.

"No, not at all. She's just…not your usual type, you know? She doesn't run in your social circle," Ava says.

"Don't forget we run in the same social circle," I remind her.

"Oh, trust me. I know. And you tend to keep yourself

firmly planted in that circle." She contemplates me with that assessing gaze of hers. "Why Hannah?"

"I don't know." I'm being defensive again. I need to stop. "I like that she actually listens to me. She's sweet. Funny."

Her body drives me wild. So does her mouth.

Can't say that out loud though.

"I think Hannah is really nice," Ava says, just before she makes a little face. "I'm just happy you're over Cami for good."

"You like Hannah?" I like saying her name. It feels good to talk about her with Ava. I don't always get along with my sister, but I always listen to her feedback. She's family, and we stick together, even when we're irritated with each other.

Right now, I'm feeling nothing but love for Ava. We haven't argued in a while, and it's been nice. Though I haven't seen much of her lately. I'm always busy, and so is she. I have no idea who she's been hanging out with, beyond her usual friend group.

Meaning guys. A guy. Does she have one in her life? If she doesn't bring them up, that usually means no.

Ava nods. "Definitely. I'm in leadership with her, you know."

Oh, that's right. Why do I always forget Ava's in that class? She's actively involved in all sorts of school things, it's hard to keep track. "Do you guys ever talk?"

"Not really. I'm on the dance-planning committee and she paints signs."

"She's an artist."

"Really?" A smile teases the corners of Ava's mouth. "And you've suddenly found yourself appreciating fine art?"

"Shut up," I mutter as I walk around her and start heading down the stairs. "Dinner's almost ready."

The moment I say it, Mom yells irritably from the kitchen, "Kids! *Dinner!*"

My sister is about to go down the stairs when an idea hits me and I reach out, grabbing her arm to stop her. "Eli Bennett tagged me in yet another one of his videos."

Ava yanks her arm out of my grip. "So?" she asks warily.

"I don't know why he has such beef with me."

"You're both the quarterbacks for each other's biggest rival, duh." She rolls her eyes. "Just—ignore him. He's harmless."

"Harmless my ass. He's coming for me. He wants blood."

"You're being so dramatic right now. He's not *coming* for you," she says, rolling her eyes. "Why do you guys act like this game is such a do-or-die moment? It's not even for another couple of weeks."

"Did you watch today's video? Or any of the other videos he's made where he's tagged me? That asshole threatens me practically on the fucking daily," I say, irritation making my blood burn. "He's saying all kinds of shit to get under my skin."

"And wow, would you look at that? It's working," Ava says. I can tell she doesn't want to have this conversation. She sounds just like Tony. What is it about Eli that burrows so deep into my soul? All I have to do is think about his name and I'm instantly pissed.

It sucks.

"Don't let that guy bother you. He truly is all bark and no bite." Mom yells yet again and Ava sends me a look. "We better go."

Ava follows me down the stairs and I think about what she said. I bet Eli is lying about everything. Who the hell could he be fucking around with that's close to me? Even if he is back to messing around with Cami, it's not like I'd care. I'm not with her. I don't *want* to be with her.

He might've mentioned Hannah, but I'm pretty positive

he hasn't come into contact with her ever. Though I need to ask her.

Tonight.

We enter the kitchen to find Dad and Beck already sitting at the table, Mom grabbing a giant bowl from the counter and bringing it over. We're eating at a later time than usual tonight, because Mom wanted to wait for them to return from Beck's football practice. I grab myself something to drink before I settle at the table with the rest of the family.

We talk about our day, the three of us giving noncommittal answers, even Beck, who's usually always a chatterbox. But we're all starving and we're all equally shoving food into our mouths. Dad is keeping the conversation flowing with Mom, and I know he does that to make up for our lack of communication.

What are they going to do when we're all gone? Thank God they have each other.

"Jake has a new love interest," Ava says when we're almost finished eating.

I shoot her a glare, but she just sends an angelic smile at me in return, like she doesn't have a care in the world.

"Is this true?" Mom turns to look at me with wide eyes. "And when you say new, do you mean *brand* new?"

Even Mom knows I keep up the back-and-forth thing with Cami. And she's never approved of her, even the first time around.

"Totally brand new," Ava reaffirms, her smile growing as my scowl deepens. "And she's such a *nice* girl. I'm sure you both would like her."

"What do you mean, a nice girl?" Dad asks, his voice gruff, his gaze skeptical.

"You know what I mean, Daddy. It's not some mean girl who's hot for Jake because he's the most popular, richest boy in school," Ava explains. "She's quiet. Artsy. Oh, and she's in leadership with me. She makes all the signs you see hanging around school and at the games."

"Who is this mystery girl, Jacob?" Mom asks.

If I could smother my sister without actually killing her, I so would. Right now I miss Autumn, who would tell Ava to shut the hell up and next thing you know, they'd start arguing. More yelling would ensue, Mom would beg them to stop, Dad would raise his voice, and yet again, I'd avert another interrogation.

"Yeah, who is she?" Dad asks. Beck doesn't say a word. Just keeps eating his food, his big green eyes unblinking as he watches us.

"Her name is Hannah," I say reluctantly. "She's a senior."

"Is she new this year?" Mom asks with a little frown. I'm sure she's skipping over every kid's name in the senior class. Considering we're a class of around seventy-five, Mom feels like she knows just about everyone.

Ava's watching me, giggling. I send her a death stare. It doesn't seem to make a difference. She loves watching me squirm.

"I've gone to school with her since we moved here," I tell Mom.

"Oh." Mom sits up straighter. "Well, you've never mentioned her before."

"We don't really run in the same—social circles."

"Ah." Understanding lights Mom's eyes, and she sends Dad a pointed look before she focuses her attention on me. "Is she pretty?"

"I think she is."

"Is she going to the game Friday night?" Dad asks.

"She'll be there. I'm not gonna introduce her to you guys, though." Not yet. I don't need to put her through the *hey meet my parents*, drill. It's too early. She's not even ready to completely forgive me yet. She hasn't committed to wearing my jersey either.

This might all end up being a big nothing. Thanks to Ava, Mom will keep asking me questions about Hannah too.

"Aw, I'm offended." Mom mock pouts.

"So rude, Jake," Ava teases. I send her another death glare. It doesn't faze her one bit. I know she's enjoying herself right now.

"I'm just glad you're not back together with Cami." I'm about to say something, but Mom holds up her hand, stopping me. "I know you two were serious and you were so in love, but she drove you crazy, Jake, and you know it. All that torturous back and forth."

I was just as guilty, not that Mom would ever see that. I'm her child, so I'm a perfect angel.

Ha.

"He did that to himself," Ava adds.

Thanks, sis.

"You had a good practice today," Dad says, thankfully changing the subject. "You all did. Very focused, and it's only Tuesday."

"Yeah, we're trying to stay on top of it. We don't want to lose focus, what with the scouts coming," I say with all the seriousness I can muster. "We have to win that game."

"I believe you'll win," Mom says, smiling at me. She always believes we're going to win, even when we know we're going to lose. "Just make sure you look extra good out there. Work on those throws."

"Hell yeah I will," I say with an enthusiastic nod.

"You should see our halftime routine," Ava adds. "And we've already been working on the homecoming routine too. Wait until you see it. We're going to make the Mustangs cheer team look like total ass."

"Ava," Mom chastises.

"What? Jake says hell and it's no big deal, but I say ass and I get called out for it? How is that fair?" Now it's Ava's turn to glare at me.

"You both need to stop cussing, especially in front of Beck," Mom says primly.

"What's the big deal, Mom? I say ass at school all the time," Beck says with a little shrug, making all of us at the table start to laugh.

Except for Mom, who's scowling at her precious baby.

Just another fun night with the Callahans.

CHAPTER 27

HANNAH

Mom's been gone for work for almost an hour when there's a knock.

I glance up from my laptop screen, staring at the door, Maxine hopping off the couch the moment she hears the knock and running to my bedroom. Instinct tells me I know who's here. Jake never mentioned he was coming over tonight, but we were chatting for a while over Snap until he mysteriously went quiet about twenty minutes ago.

Just enough time for him to drive to my apartment.

Setting my laptop aside, I climb off the couch and go to the door, peering through the peephole. Yep, there he is, standing on my doorstep, and without hesitation I unlock and open the door. "What are you doing here?"

"Glad to see you too." He pulls me in for a quick hug before he enters the apartment. My body still tingles from his too-brief touch.

I shut and lock the door, then lean against it, watching him. "I didn't know you were coming over."

He turns to face me. "Surprise."

We stare at each other in silence, the air growing heavy between us. I took a shower earlier, and I'm wearing a pair of pink cotton pajama shorts with white polka dots and a white tank top with no bra.

Oops.

His gaze roams over me hungrily, settling on my chest for a few minutes too long, and I feel my nipples tighten under his watch. My lips fall open and I try to say something, but my throat is dry.

And the way Jake's watching me is making me lose all train of thought.

"I was gonna ask if you wanted to go for a drive," he says, then clears his throat.

"Clearly I'm not dressed for it." I wave a hand at myself.

"Yeah," he says roughly, rubbing his hand along his jaw.

My bare toes curl into the carpet and I push away from the door. "Want to watch a movie?"

"Only if you'll sit with me."

"Of course," I say, flashing a smile from over my shoulder as I walk past him. I grab my laptop from where I left it on the couch and set it on the coffee table before I settle in. Jake joins me, sitting right next to me before he grabs the blanket behind us and drapes it over our bodies. "What do you want to watch?"

"I don't care." He extends his arm across the back of the couch, toying with the ends of my hair with his fingers, leaning his head close to mine. "You smell good."

"I just took a shower," I tell him, my entire body on high alert as I keep my gaze trained on the TV. I take the remote from where it's lying next to me on the couch and turn the TV on. It's already queued up to Netflix and I start scrolling through our options. "Maybe something scary?"

"Whatever you want," he says, his tone easy, like he doesn't have a care in the world.

I glance over at him to find he's already watching me. We look at each other quietly for at least thirty seconds before I finally say, "What?"

"I missed doing this," he admits. "I missed you."

His words make my heart swell with happiness. "It's only been a few days."

"A few days too long for me." His arm slides from the couch to land around my shoulders. I'm sure that was his plan all along. "And I like it when you sit close to me."

"Clearly." I can't stop the smile from forming on my lips. I am completely falling under his spell. He makes it so easy.

Or maybe that's just us. I can't deny we're drawn to each other. Sitting like this with him, no one else around, the apartment quiet, the only sound the refrigerator humming in the distance, I could get lost in him.

I think of the last night he was here, and how willing I was to take it further.

Despite everything that's happened between us, I'm still willing.

He tips his head down, his lips drawing close, and I dodge away from him, refocusing my attention on the TV screen. "Let's watch this." I hit the remote, choosing one of the newer scary movies Netflix's added, and I set the remote down, snuggling in close to Jake's side.

He's solid and warm, and it feels so good to be sitting this close to him. I lean my head against his chest and he squeezes my shoulders. Closing my eyes, I inhale deeply, letting his spicy masculine scent wash over me.

"You okay with this?" he asks, and I love that he's checking first.

"Yeah," I answer.

That's all we say. What else *is* there to say? We're supposed to be watching the movie, but I can't concentrate.

All I can think about is him. How I'm practically lying on top of him.

I'm going to let him make the first move, I think, as he tugs the blanket over our laps, his legs brushing against mine. He has on shorts too, and I can feel his hot skin, the wiry hair on his legs. I try not to react to his closeness, instead keeping my focus on the movie as it starts. But it's so difficult.

His heart beats steadily beneath my ear, and I rest my arm on the blanket that's lying over his stomach. His fingers press into the bare skin of my upper arm, drifting up and down, up and down, lulling me under his trance. My eyelids grow heavy until I finally close them, savoring the sensation of being held by Jake.

We sit like this for at least the first thirty minutes of the movie, though I don't fall asleep. I'm ultra-aware of every sound he makes, every little movement. His other hand sneaks under the blanket, and the next thing I know, he's grabbing my legs, draping them across his thighs, his fingers tickling as he skims over my knees. My thighs. I lift my head away from his chest, sending him a questioning look, and he studies me, pressing his full lips together before he dips his head and settles them on mine.

That's it. There's the first move. I forget all about the movie. This is what I've been waiting for since the moment he walked into the apartment. Totally unlike me, but then again, being with Jake is totally unlike me, so I'm throwing all preconceived notions away and running on pure instinct.

I curve my fingers around his nape, into his soft hair, holding him to me. He growls against my lips and I open my mouth, his tongue sweeping inside, searching, tangling with mine. His hand ends up between us, his fingers skimming over the bare skin of my chest, above my tank top. He dares to go lower, lower, and when they brush against my breast, my nipple, I jump, startled. His hand immediately falls away and disappointment floods me.

He breaks the kiss, pressing his forehead against mine as he looks into my eyes. "Too much?"

Slowly I shake my head. "You just—surprised me."

Jake pulls away, his expression a little worried, his eyes serious. "I don't want you to think I came over here just to—"

I press my fingers against his lips, silencing him. My gaze never leaving his, I whisper, "I want it too."

He grabs my wrist and brings my hand to his mouth, dropping the softest kiss to my knuckles. I'm breathless as he kisses each finger with a soft, barely-there press of his lips. He lets go of my hand and I wrap my arm around his neck, sinking my fingers into his silky-soft hair that curls around my fingers almost lovingly. A gasp escapes me when he kisses me again, his big hand returning to my chest, his thumb brushing back and forth across my nipple, making it pebble. I lean into his touch, wanting more, wishing he would pull the fabric down and expose me completely, but he takes his time, driving me slowly out of my mind.

The kiss becomes reckless, as reckless as his hands. He's touching me everywhere and all I can seem to reach is his hair, his strong neck. His thick shoulders, his broad chest. His skin is so hot, and I tug on his shirt, gathering the bottom of it in my hands and pulling it up, up, up. He breaks away from me, his lips swollen and damp as he makes quick work of getting rid of his T-shirt, tossing it on the floor.

I gape at him, drinking in all those muscles on display. Lord help me, he has a six-pack. He is in top physical shape, a perfect male specimen, and I'm pale-skinned and dotted with freckles. My butt's probably a little too big and there's a dimple square in the middle of the back of my left thigh.

I hate that dimple with all I've got.

He doesn't seem to care. He kisses me, pressing me into the couch cushions, and somehow, someway, I end up on my back again, just like last time. He's hovering above me, his hands on my waist, his fingers slipping beneath the thin cotton of my shirt. I'm trembling from his touch, his fingertips imprinting on my skin as he slides those hands up. Across my stomach, over my ribs, until he's cupping my bare breasts underneath my shirt.

Like I have no control over myself, I arch into his hands, my eyes sliding closed when he crushes his mouth on mine. He presses his leg between my thighs, rubbing directly on the spot where I ache the most, and I grind against him, sparks lighting me up deep inside every time I do it.

So of course, I keep doing it.

The tank is discarded. I don't even know what happened to it. Jake kisses my throat, my collarbone, my chest.

"You've got a freckle right." He pauses, his mouth brushing the underside of my right breast. "Here."

I nearly jump out of my skin. He keeps kissing me there, his lips and tongue teasing, and I'm lost. His knee is pressed tight against my center, and a thousand different sensations rush over me, making my head spin.

Making me whimper.

It's like I was just flung over the edge of the cliff and I'm freefalling. Listen, I've tried to masturbate before, but I couldn't ever find what I was supposed to be looking for, which made me feel dumb. So I gave up.

Looks like Jake and I figured it out together real quick.

When I can finally breathe again, and my heart has calmed somewhat, I open my eyes to find Jake smiling down at me, his expression full of satisfaction.

"I made you come," he whispers.

I cover my face, embarrassed. "Stop."

"Hey." He peels my hands off my face, then kisses me

stupid. When he breaks away, he's still got that satisfied look on his face. "It's okay. I wanted that to happen."

I wave a hand at him. "What about you?"

"We'll worry about me later." He climbs off the couch. "I'll be right back."

I watch as he heads into the bathroom and shuts the door before I sit up and search for my tank. I put it back on, then run my hands through my hair. The movie's ending credits are rolling, and I want to laugh. We completely lost track of time. Well, at least I did. I was too wrapped up in the sensation of being in Jake's arms, feeling his hands and mouth all over my body.

And I want to experience that again. Again and again.

"I should go," he tells me once he exits the bathroom. I hand him his shirt and he slips it back on. "I need to get home."

"Okay." I rise to my feet and he wraps his arm around my waist, pulling me into him. I brace my hands against his chest. "I'm glad you came over."

He smiles, dipping down to kiss me lightly. "I bet you are."

I swat his chest. "You're making fun of me."

"You're cute when you're embarrassed." His hand slides down until it's cupping my butt, and he hauls me in close so I can feel him, the hard press of his erection. "Just wait until next time."

With that, he lets me go and heads for the door, unlocking and opening it before he pauses and turns to face me again. "See you tomorrow?"

Nodding, I touch my lips. They're swollen. And my jaw actually hurts from all the kissing. But it's not a bad pain. Not at all. "Drive safe."

"Lock the door when I leave."

"I will," I say with a giggle. Who am I?

"Good night, Banana."

I lock the door. I turn off the TV and fold the blanket, draping it over the couch. I shut off the lamp and pretty much float all the way back to my bedroom.

And when I fall asleep, my head is filled with thoughts of Jake.

CHAPTER 28

HANNAH

It's two weeks later and I'm sitting in my world religions class during sixth period when a crackle sounds over the speaker, followed by the voice of Mrs. Adney with an announcement.

"Good afternoon, students. Homecoming nominations are here, and we're excited to let you know who they are. Starting with the freshman class, prince nominations are…"

Sophie leans over and taps me on the arm with her pen. "I think you'll get nominated."

I send her an incredulous look. "Um, no. I'm a nobody."

"Not anymore," she says with a little smile. "Everyone knows who you are now."

"What, because of Jake?"

Sophie laughs. "Duh."

It's been quite the two weeks. Everyone knows Jake and I are together because we just…are. So are Sophie and Tony. We both wore their jerseys the past couple of Fridays at school, and at both games we had so much fun. After they won the game when the scouts were watching, we ran down to the field with the signs we made for them, and took photos with our new boys. They couldn't linger for long since the coaches wanted them both to speak with the scouts, but it was long enough for Jake to give me a sweaty hug and kiss me in front of everyone.

When we broke apart and he jogged off the field, I caught Cami glaring at me with barely contained disgust.

Or maybe that was for Jocelyn, who was also on the field hanging all over a pissed-off Diego. He hardly played the game due to his rib injury—an injury he received because of the fight he got into with Jake.

After that game, we all went to Tony's for his traditional home game afterparty. It was a lot quieter than the first party we went to. No opposing team showed up. Only a few girls from the cheer team appeared. Cami was scarce, which made me happy.

The next week was an away game, and Sophie and I rode together to watch it. Again it was a lot of fun, but away games are never as exciting, only because we're not at home. Thankfully, our team won, and this week is a bye week, so there's no game. Next week is homecoming, and it's a biggie because they're playing the Mustangs.

Jake and I have been getting closer and closer, and not just sexually, because that is definitely happening too. But we spend as much time together as we can, and we're having so much fun. Talking for hours. Watching movies at my place. And then forgetting all about the movie as get lost in each other.

"…and Ava Callahan is our final junior homecoming princess nominee," Mrs. Adney announces.

I smile, my gaze meeting Sophie's. "Jake's sister."

"That's so great," Sophie says with an enthusiastic nod. I can practically smell the nervousness radiating from her, she's so hyped up.

"Okay, and now for our senior nominees. For homecoming king, it's Caleb Burke, Tony Sorrento, Jacob Callahan, Diego Garcia, Michael Burnett and Robert Schaffer."

What? I mouth to Sophie who's shaking her head in amazement. Who in the world nominated Rob the jerk? Though really, he hasn't been that bad lately, thank goodness. Even he and Jake are somewhat getting along.

"And now for our homecoming queen nominations. They are as follows: Cami Lockhart."

Of course.

"...Sophie Whitmore."

I literally squeal at hearing my friend's name. She just sits there in shock, blinking at everyone as she absorbs it.

"Bridget Peterson, Jocelyn Douglas, Paige Rodriguez and..."

I hold my breath. I told myself I wasn't going to get my hopes up, but here I am with secretly crossed fingers, praying I'll hear my name.

"Hannah Walsh."

It's Sophie's turn to squeal for me. She's so excited, she's bouncing up and down in her seat, making her entire desk rattle and shake as it skids across the floor. The entire class applauds, because half of the queen nominations are in the class, and I can't help myself. I glance back at Cami, who's staring at me with lowered brows and a disgusted look on her face.

"Is this some kind of joke?" she asks out loud.

She would say something like that, I swear.

Thankfully, the announcement happens during the last fifteen minutes of class, and our attention is ruined for the rest of the period. Mrs. Madsen offers all of us her congrats and basically gives up on her lecture. I'm grateful—like I can concentrate right now after hearing my name called.

Sophie and I scoot our desks closer together and chat as we wait for the bell to ring, my friend going over all the many things we'll need to do in a short amount of time in preparation of homecoming week.

"Oh God, now I'll need to find a dress," I say with a moan, shaking my head. "Like I can afford that."

"Don't worry about it. We'll find you something," Sophie says with confidence, her eyes sparkling. "I can't believe we both got nominated! I want you to win."

"Nooo." I shake my head, speaking straight from my heart. "I want you to win. You and Tony."

"Whoever wins, it doesn't matter. It's just cool we were nominated! And really, we're so lucky. Not only did we get nominated, but so did our boyfriends!" Sophie claps her hands like she's just watched the best live performance of her life. "This is so freaking exciting."

"Yeah." I'm excited too. Really I am. I secretly wanted this.

But I'm realizing the homecoming nomination puts such a spotlight on me. On Jake. On *us*. And while Jake is comfortable in the spotlight and will take all of this in stride like it's no big deal, I'm not used to this kind of attention.

At all.

Sophie chatters nonstop, and I just nod and agree with her every once in a while. Once the bell rings, we exit the classroom together, Sophie still talking, me still nodding and listening. But I'm distracted. Girls walk past, girls I've never spoken to before in my life, and they're offering both of us their congratulations. I smile and thank all of them, not as enthusiastically as Sophie, but I'm doing my best.

Marty finds us at standing at Sophie's locker, and he looks as shocked as I feel. "You hang out for a couple of weeks with football players and now you two are on the homecoming court?" He shakes his head. "Talk about fast movers."

"We're not on the court yet," I point out. The seniors have the biggest number of nominees. At the coronation ceremony on Wednesday night of homecoming week, all the princes and princesses are crowned, and the top three senior boys and senior girls are selected to go on to the court. Then the homecoming king and queen are crowned during half-time on Friday night.

"True." Marty's eyes go wide. "What if you don't get selected and your boys do? What are you going to do then?"

Sophie swats him on the arm. "Don't be so negative! Let us enjoy this moment while we can."

"Sorry, sorry," Marty says irritably.

My heart sinks. I don't think he's pleased with our sudden popularity. We haven't been hanging out with him as much as usual since we're spending our extra time with the new boys in our lives, and I hope he isn't mad at us.

I tell myself I need to invite Marty over once home-coming is over and we can hang out like we used to. Watch a movie or scroll through Tik Tok for hours.

"I've got to go to class," I tell my friends with a weak smile. "I'll see you guys later?"

They both say goodbye and I leave them to chat about homecoming stuff.

I need the break. It's all making my head spin.

By the time I spot the open doorway of the art building, I see Jake is there too, waiting for me. He pushes away from the wall and approaches me, pulling me into his arms for a long, delicious hug.

"Congratulations," he murmurs against my temple before he kisses it.

"Congrats to you too," I tell him, pressing my face against his chest for as long as I can before I reluctantly pull away from him.

"You excited?"

I give him a weird smile. I can tell it's weird—I can *feel* it. "I don't know. Should I be?"

He starts to laugh. "Usually girls are. It means they get to wear a fancy dress and possibly a crown. It's bragging rights, you know? Your photo in the yearbook. You get to ride in a classic car in the parade."

"I suppose." I shrug. "I'm not used to all the attention, you know?"

"I know." He touches my hair, tucks a few strands behind my ear, his gaze full of yearning. I feel that same yearning for him right now, but we're not about making public spectacles of ourselves. We keep our private moments—private. "You're gonna look pretty up on the stage standing beside me."

"We're running together then?"

"Um, yeah." He shakes his head, chuckling. "Who else would I run with? Cami?"

I give him a light sock on the chest, making him laugh harder.

Since we've been spending so much time together, I've never seen Jake so happy. It's like he's always in a good mood. Always smiling. The quarterback for our rival team keeps posting these vaguely threatening videos on Instagram or Snapchat, calling out Jake, practically begging him to throw up and fight him, yet they don't seem to faze Jake.

Well, they might be fazing him a little bit, but he seems to get over it quickly, especially when we're together and I can reassure him that nothing's going to happen.

At least, I hope nothing happens.

"Are *you* excited?" I ask.

He shrugs. "Not really. I was nominated my freshman year and…I lost."

I frown. "To who?" What's funny is I don't remember. Heck, I didn't go to the coronation nights. Not back then. I didn't care, and I didn't have many friends.

"Caleb."

Figures. Pretty much every girl I've gone to school with

has suffered through a crush on Caleb at one point or another. Fresh-out-of-middle-school Caleb was definitely the most popular boy out of all the various Caleb versions.

"My sophomore year I was nominated and won," he continues. "And when you win in the first three years, you can't be nominated again until you're a senior. So I didn't have to deal with it at all last year."

"Who did you win with your sophomore year?" Honestly, I can't remember. I only started paying closer attention to our popularity contests last year. Wincing, I brace myself to hear him say Cami.

"Jocelyn." He shakes his head. "Diego was so pissed."

"I bet." I smile, but it fades quickly when I ask, "How are you and Diego doing?"

I know for the last week they've come to an unspoken truce. Jake is still mad at him. I would guess Diego is still angry with Jake as well.

But they've come together for the team. Diego seemingly recovered quickly from his rib injury, and is off the bench and back on the field. Thankfully he should be good for next week's game. We've been waiting for this game for what feels like a long time. I'll be sort of glad when it's all over. Not that I'd ever admit that out loud.

"We don't really talk that much anymore." Jake's expression turns grim and he stares off into the distance, lost in thought. He does that a lot where Diego is concerned.

What's strange is nothing came of the Cami and Diego rumors. Jocelyn and Diego are still together. Cami is single but flirting heavily. Constantly posting selfies on her Snapchat stories with suggestive clothing and provocative poses. I can't help but think she looks kind of desperate.

Or maybe that's me hating on her because I can.

"Maybe you should try to talk to him about everything," I suggest, but Jake's already shaking his head.

"He has to apologize to me first. What he said was pretty low. If I let him get away with it, he'll do it again. I know how he is." He sends me a pointed look. "And you don't want to see what would happen if he said something about you again. Especially now."

Now that Jake and I are closer. Now that I know what Jake looks like mostly naked. We can never manage to get all our clothes off when we're alone, but I sort of know why. What if someone walked in while we're in the middle of… whatever? I doubt it would ever happen, but I don't know that for sure.

And neither does Jake. So we don't take any chances.

Sometimes I can't help but wonder if we've moved too fast. We got together and got naked with each other pretty quickly. Within a week of us making it somewhat official, I knew Jake's O face and he saw mine.

But then I reassure myself that we're teenagers. This is normal. Whenever Jake and I are alone together, the chemistry is almost unbearable. I get all anxious and shaky the minute he puts his hands on me. Oh, and needy.

So, so needy.

"Well holy shit, look who's here. It's Mr. Homecoming," Jake says in greeting when he spots Rob.

I turn to find Rob walking toward us, a smile on his usually scowling face. "Ya damn right I got nominated. It's gonna suck when you lose, Callahan," he says smugly.

Jake laughs. For some weird reason, these two have come to terms with each other, and I'm not even sure how it happened. They give each other endless shit every day in class, slinging insults good naturedly at each other and confusing both the freshmen girls at their table and Mrs. Sanborne.

All I can do is laugh.

"You really think you've got this in the bag?" Jake asks Rob.

Rob stops in front of us, his gaze going from Jake to me and back to Jake again. "For sure. You can't get *all* the glory at school."

"Who are you running with?" I ask, curious.

I don't think Rob's talking crap on me anymore. Did Jake say something to him to make him stop? Or is it because of Jake and the status our relationship brings me? That's completely ridiculous, but if that's what it takes to get Rob to shut his mouth, whatever works.

"Bridget." His cheeks get red and I immediately suspect he's interested in her. They could make a good couple. Running together for homecoming court is a great way to spend a lot of time together. Though I don't think I've ever seen them even breathe the same air before, but what do I know?

We all walk into class, Jake and Rob settling in at their table with the freshmen twins—that's what Jake calls them— and I go talk to Mrs. Sanborne, who's standing beside her desk, and ask her if there's anything special she needs me to work on.

"First, let me say congratulations," she says with a big smile. "A homecoming nomination is kind of a big deal."

"Thanks. I guess so." I shrug, at a loss for words. "It just feels weird."

"Why?" Mrs. Sanborne tilts her head, contemplating me.

"I don't know. Jake and I have been going out for only a couple of weeks, and I'm automatically nominated for home-coming? It's like being with him gives me instant star status at school, and it's just…weird. I'm not used to the attention," I explain.

"Your friend Sophie was nominated too," she says gently, and I know what she's thinking. Both of us have fast tracked to the highest popularity tier, when we were just a couple of nobodies only a few weeks ago.

"Yeah, and she's just like me," I say. "We're both not that popular." At least we weren't.

"Maybe your class is tired of seeing the same girls get nominated," Mrs. Sanborne suggests, which I can see.

"Cami was nominated yet again," I say, then clamp my hand over my mouth.

Guess I gave away my feelings about Cami.

"And she's one of those girls who's always nominated for everything. I understand. She might get sick of being nominated too."

Doubtful.

"I was certainly never that girl in high school. I never got the cute quarterback as my boyfriend either." She smiles, and I can feel myself blush. I really hate my fair skin sometimes.

"There's more to Jake than being cute," I admit, feeling foolish. She's a grown woman and I'm a little girl in my first relationship. Starry-eyed and full of lust. It's such a great feeling, but I'm sure I look foolish to Mrs. Sanborne.

"I'm sure there is. You're a girl who won't settle for all flash and little substance." She gently pats my cheek, smiling. "Enjoy it, Hannah. Try not to waste your time overthinking everything and questioning everyone's intentions. Someday you'll realize you blink and it's all over. Enjoy these moments. Have fun with your cute boyfriend. He seems happier lately, and I think he owes that to you."

I think about her little speech for the rest of seventh period, mulling over what she said. I do want to savor these moments, but I'm also that girl who overthinks everything. I can't help myself.

And for some reason, I've got this…weird feeling about homecoming. Almost a foreboding sensation, like something bad could possibly happen.

Though maybe something good will come out of it too. Sophie and I could end up having the time of our lives. I can say with the utmost sincerity that I won't mind losing to her. She's my best friend. I'd love to see her wearing that crown.

I'll be mad if we lose to Cami, though. I really, *really* hope my fellow students have better sense than to give her so many votes that she'll win. Pretty much everyone I know thinks Cami is awful. The rest of the nominees are nice girls. Bridget is a cheerleader. So is Paige. Jocelyn is one half of the most notorious couple at school. But Cami is the cheer captain.

Meaning she has a shot.

And if she and Jake both win?

I'll never live the humiliation down.

CHAPTER 29

JAKE

*W*e're out on the field running drills like we do. Once we're finished, Dad wants me to work on throwing to Diego.

I feel like he did this on purpose. That he's been doing it on purpose since he found out Diego and I still aren't really talking. He hasn't said it outright, but he wants us to work out our shit.

Not really sure if that's possible.

Deciding I'll be the bigger person and break the ice, I call out to Diego as I toss him the ball, "Congrats on the home-coming nom."

He catches the ball with ease, then tosses it back at me. "Thanks. Same to you."

"Jocelyn excited?"

"Yeah." He smiles as he walks toward me, his steps slow, and I can tell he's semi-reluctant. Both in the smile and the conversation. But hey, I can pretend to get along with him, so he can too. "She said she doesn't want a repeat of sophomore year."

"When we won together and left you in the dust?" I laugh,

though he doesn't, and I immediately let it fade. "That won't happen," I say assuredly.

"You think you're going to win with your new girl?" He doesn't say this in a rude way. More like he's just being very matter of fact.

"Not particularly. People don't know Hannah that well." I do. I know her very, very well.

But I feel like she was nominated because we're together. Same with Sophie. And if that makes me seem like a jerk for thinking that, then I guess I'm a jerk. But come on. People are sheep, and if they see us with our new girlfriends, then they're going to nominate those girlfriends believing they're worthy. It's fucked up, but that's high school for you.

"Maybe Tony and his new girl will win. Don't know what to think about Rob's nomination." He laughs and so do I, because Rob's nomination is truly a surprise. He's a dark horse coming out of nowhere. "That guy has always been kind of a jerk."

"We're getting along okay." Diego knew about my little tiff with Rob in art class.

Diego's eyebrows shoot up. "That's surprising."

"You just have to know how to deal with a guy like that," I say, grateful that my parents drove home that mantra. Everyone's different, Mom said to me more than once. What matters is how *you* handle them. If you understand what makes them tick and don't hold their faults against them, you'll be better off.

Sometimes, Mom gives the absolute best advice.

"Kind of like how you have to know how to deal with me?" He sends me a sheepish glance, and I know what he's talking about. The shitty words tossed so casually at each other. The blows that were thrown pretty easily too. It's like we had all this built-up resentment toward each other and it exploded that night.

But I still need the apology.

"What you said was really fucked up," I tell him, deciding to just be one-hundred percent truthful. "You pissed me off."

"I'm sorry." His expression is so damn serious, I know he's truly remorseful. I can tell. "I was mad that night. Frustrated. Jocelyn and I were fighting, and I took all my anger out on your girlfriend."

Relief hits me—he finally apologized. Diego is not one to say sorry easily. He'd rather have someone hold a grudge against him for life than admit he said or did anything wrong. It makes him a very frustrating person to deal with sometimes, but we've got history. We've been friends since we were twelve.

And I'm not ready to lose our friendship yet.

"I'm sorry I hit you. That I started the fight," I say. "I didn't need to take it there."

"You were mad and I deserved it." He shrugs.

"Hey you two! Work on your throws, Callahan! Now!" This comes from my father, who's waving his clipboard around like he wants to smack my and Diego's asses with it.

"Yes, sir!" Diego yells just as he starts to go in a full-out run. "Throw it, asshole!" he yells at me.

Without hesitation, I send the ball flying into the air, watching it spiral. Diego keeps running, gets almost to the twenty-yard line when he finally looks back, holds his hands up into the air, and the ball lands perfectly into his palms. He grips the ball, tucks it against his chest and barrels into the end zone. I go running after him, slapping the back of his practice helmet before I knock my helmet against his in a move we've been pulling together since our youth football days.

"Fucking magical, bro," I tell him, and he's grinning.

"We pull that shit next week at the game and we've got this," Diego says.

He's right. We have to leave the past behind us. Forget all the ugly shit we said. Forget Cami—I'm pretty sure he's not messing around with her now, though I think he did before. Who knows?

Really, who cares? It's none of my business.

Practice is good. We're playing with ease, everything coming together perfectly. It helps that we don't have a game this week and we can focus all of our attention on the homecoming game. I can hear music coming from the old baseball field where the cheer team practices. They're practicing their halftime routine, working extra hard, and Ava keeps promising me it's going to be a good one. Just like we have beef with the football team, our cheer teams have beef as well, and they're always trying to outperform each other.

It's kind of funny, how every team at our school takes the rivalry with the Mustangs so seriously.

Once practice is over, we're all in the locker room talking shit like we do, when Caleb gets a notification on his phone. "Oh shit, it's Bennett. He tagged me in his story on Insta," he says, grinning at us before he opens his phone. "This ought to be good."

I check my phone to see Eli didn't tag me. "Did he tag you?" I ask Diego, and he looks at his phone before shaking his head.

"He's never tagged me before," Caleb says as he waits for Eli's story to start. "Wonder what he's up to."

The story opens with a few cheerleaders shaking their purple metallic poms at the camera, and that's all you can see. They rattle and rustle, then fall away to reveal Eli standing there out on their football field, shirtless and clad in only a pair of purple gym shorts. He's wearing sunglasses and a gold chain with a #1 charm hanging from it.

The egotistical bastard.

"Congrats on the homecoming nom, Caleb," Eli says as he

rests his hands on his hips. "Gonna suck real bad when you lose out to your bestest homies Callahan and Garcia during that coronation ceremony next Wednesday night."

Caleb scowls. "How does he find out this info so fast?"

"If you weren't such a fuckboy who's already smashed every single girl in the junior and senior class, then maybe you'd get a few more votes." Eli grins.

"Fucker," Caleb mutters.

Diego sends me a look, but I keep my expression neutral. Eli's not wrong when it comes to Caleb. He's the biggest player I know. He's never had a serious relationship for the entirety of high school. He doesn't want to limit the girls he talks to, so he doesn't ever have just one special girl.

And it's backfired on him. Slowly but surely, girls at our school have lost interest in him. They don't take him seriously because he doesn't take them seriously either.

"Damn, how can I forget about Sorrento?" Eli shakes his head. "There's the one who might win with his new charity case of a girlfriend. They'd look cute out on the field when they get crowned, am I right? Callahan will be crying to his daddy that he didn't win, and Diego will be relieved considering he's still fucking around with Cami, but whatever! You're all gonna be so damn distracted, you won't be able to focus. And that's when we'll steal the win right from under your noses."

"Dude, Tony is going to want to kick Eli's ass after he sees this," Caleb breathes.

Diego says nothing. He doesn't need to. His infuriated expression says it all.

And here I thought he wasn't messing around with Cami still. Maybe I was wrong.

"So have fun with your kiddie games during homecoming. We'll be over here practicing football, getting ready to kick your asses." Eli leans in closer to the camera, lifting his sunglasses and winking. "Congrats, assholes!"

His story is over.

"Are we really going to let him get away with this?" Caleb asks us, his gaze going from me to Diego. "And where's Tony? He's gonna fuckin' freak when he sees that video."

"He's outside on the phone." He'll sneak out when he can and chat with Sophie, even for a few stolen minutes. Those two are totally into each other, maybe just as much as I'm into Hannah.

Diego remains quiet, his expression dark. Like I can't help myself, I have to say something. "So. Is it true?"

He meets my gaze, his lips tight. "What do *you* think? You're going to believe Bennett over me?"

"I've never heard you confirm whether the rumors are true or not," I say simply. Caleb sends me a look, one that says *what the hell are you doing?* But I ignore him. "Is Eli right? Have you and Cami hooked up?"

Diego looks away, his hands on his hips, frustration written all over him. He inhales deeply, his nostrils flaring. "Yeah. It happened. But it's not *still* happening. Eli's talking mad shit as usual, trying to stir us up. Pit us against each other."

Finally Diego tells us the truth. I'm relieved, though still kind of pissed he messed around with Cami, of all people. "All that talk about Cami, how you were so positive she wasn't fucking around with Eli. It's because she was fucking around with *you*."

"Are you really going to be mad at me about this right now?" His gaze meets mine and I glare at him in return. "If you are, it's making me wonder if you still have feelings for her," Diego taunts, a vicious smile on his face. "Does Hannah know that you have a thing for your ex?"

I'm poised and ready to lunge. "Fuck y—"

"Hey, hey." Caleb steps in between us, his arms spread and his hands on our chests, like he's trying to keep us apart. "I thought you two were getting along."

"We are," I say easily, trying to tamp down the anger that's simmering just beneath the surface. "You're right. It's all good."

I'm lying through my teeth.

"He's doing this on purpose," Caleb says, his hands dropping away from our chests. "Eli's trying to tear us apart, and you know what's worse? You're both letting him do it. You're letting him get in your heads and it fucking sucks. Both of you need to calm your tits and get your shit together."

For once, Caleb's the logical one. He's right. I know he is. Eli Bennett's greatest talent is stirring the pot. He's a decent football player, but he's an even better talker. Girls fall at his feet, and he leaves them all in the dust. People want to be his friend. He doesn't give a shit about school, yet he's somehow able to convince his teachers to change his grades even when he doesn't put in the work. He's got a slick tongue.

And he knows how to twist his words to make us not trust each other.

Doesn't help, though, how easily Diego attacked me just now.

"Let's forget this," I tell Diego, and he slowly nods, his jaw still tight. "We need to work together and not let Eli fuck with our heads."

"Sounds good," Diego says through tight lips. He glances over at Caleb. "I'll talk to you later."

He grabs his stuff and exits the locker room, leaving me and Caleb alone. No one else on the team has necessarily checked their social media yet, but it's coming. They're all going to see that video Eli posted and ask questions.

"We need to call a team meeting," I tell Caleb. "Maybe this weekend?"

"You know what we need to do?" Caleb starts tapping away at his phone screen, grinning at me as he shows me what he brought up. The Mustangs football schedule. "We need to go to their game Friday night and stir it up."

I squint at the screen, reading that they have a home game Friday. "Let's rally the troops and go."

"It's only fair," Caleb says with a little shrug. "Maybe if we scream loud enough we can get in their heads and fuck with their game."

"Just showing up all together will piss them off," I say. "Good idea, Caleb. Will you send out a text tonight?"

We have a group chat that the varsity team communicates on that our coaches aren't a part of, and we prefer it that way, so we can put together plans like this.

"Sure thing," Caleb says with a nod, right before his expression turns serious. "You're not…still into Cami, are you?"

"Hell no," I say vehemently. "Diego's just trying to get under my skin."

"Yeah. You seem pretty into that Hannah chick."

I feel immediately defensive. Caleb hasn't said many nice things about her either, though he's been pretty quiet since we've become serious. "Is he seeing Cami?"

Caleb stares at me for a long, quiet moment before he looks away, his expression conflicted. "I'm supposed to keep my mouth shut."

Right. That's confirmation Diego is still getting with Cami on the low. Meaning Diego lied to my face just now.

How can I trust him if he can't tell me the truth? I thought we were friends. Best friends. Why is he so hell bent on destroying his relationship with Jocelyn? His friendship with me? All for Cami?

She's not worth it.

CHAPTER 30

HANNAH

I'm in the kitchen, leaning against the counter, watching Mom buzz around as she gets ready to leave. I'm anxious for her to go, and I don't usually feel that way. But Jake is coming over later, and he says he has a surprise for me. I have no idea what it could be.

But I can't wait to see what it is.

"You're going shopping with Sophie on Saturday, right?" Mom asks as she pours the freshly brewed coffee into the travel mug she takes to work.

"Yeah, we're going to Macy's and a few other dress shops in the mall down in Fresno." I really hope I can find something. I've been given a pretty small budget when I know girls go all out for homecoming. Three hundred–dollar dresses and expensive shoes. Getting their hair and makeup professionally done. I'm banking on finding twenty-dollar heels at Target and a dress under one hundred dollars somewhere. "I hope I find something."

"You will. I'm sure whatever you find, it'll be beautiful. I might even have a few extra dollars to spend if it's a dress you really love." She adds some creamer before twisting the lid back onto the tumbler.

"Don't get my hopes up," I tell her, though it's too late. My hopes are definitely up.

"I'm off Saturday." She drops this information casually, surprising me. "Do you want me to go with you?"

Oh gosh, not really. Sophie and I have been planning this shopping excursion since we found out we got nominated.

"Um, it was just going to be Sophie and me, but…" My voice drifts and Mom laughs.

"I get it. You're a senior and you don't want your mom tagging along." She smiles at me. "I'll probably hang out with Rick anyway. But if you need my opinion, don't hold back on sending me photos over text!"

"Of course I will." I smile at her, thankful she's being so understanding. Throughout my high school years, she's allowed my independence to the point I've often wondered if she even cares where I'm at. But now I'm so used to her not being around that much, it almost feels suffocating when she's here more than usual.

"Is Marty going with you guys?" she asks.

A sigh escapes me. Marty's been distant since we started dating Tony and Jake. And now with the homecoming stuff, he's staying away even more. I miss him. "I'm not sure. We invited him to go."

"I hope he does. I'm sure he feels a little abandoned by you girls, now that you have boyfriends." She sends me a pointed look. "Speaking of your boyfriend, when do I get to meet him?"

Not really looking forward to that either. I've never brought a boyfriend to meet my mom before, and I'm worried how she might react to Jake. Not that she's going to make a fool of herself or anything, but she might stare at him a little too long because he's so attractive. Or worse, she'll say something embarrassing. Plus, he has money and she might zero in on that. I told her his dad is Drew Callahan and she knew exactly who I was talking about. The entire town knows who the Callahans are.

"At the coronation ceremony next week?" I suggest. There will be so many people around, surely that could work out.

"Sounds good. I can't wait to meet him."

"Yeah." I hesitate, wondering if now is the right time to bring this up. "Um, I was thinking about it, and I still want to try to find a job. You know, since money is always so tight."

If I had my own job, I could pay for my dress and accessories myself. Or save my money and eventually get a car. Save for college. Save for whatever I need or want.

"Right now, school is your job," Mom says firmly.

"I can work a couple of nights and weekends," I start, but she shuts me down with a look.

"I don't want to argue with you about this. I need to go." She comes to me and wraps her arm around my shoulders, pulling me in so she can drop a kiss on my forehead. "Have a good night. Love you, sweetheart."

"Yeah, yeah. Love you too," I say morosely, watching as she takes her coffee, picks up her purse from where she left it on the couch, and walks toward the door.

I don't know why she doesn't want me to have a job. I know it'll be hard with us having to share a car, but we can figure it out. We live pretty close to the main part of town. I can walk or ride a bike to my new job if I have to. Yeah, I don't have a bike either, but I'm sure I could find one used somewhere for a pretty cheap price. I have a little money still saved from the summer. I just want to be able to buy things on my own, without having to ask her for money. I want to save some for when I graduate high school and eventually live on my own. There are so many things I need...

Meaning I need money to get them.

Mom leaves the apartment and I go to the door, twisting the deadbolt and sliding the chain lock into place. Maxine comes wandering out of my bedroom, blinking up at me with a drowsy face and emitting a pitiful meow.

"You sleep way too much," I tell her as I scoop her up and cuddle her close. She's purring as usual and I press my face into her soft fur, thinking about Jake. He always shows up around nine-thirty, so I have about forty-five minutes until he arrives. I already took a shower. The house is in pretty good shape, cleanliness wise, though I don't think he really notices or cares.

I light a Bath and Body Works candle Sophie gave me for my birthday that I only burn on special occasions. I'm wearing my favorite black leggings that make my butt look good and a thin charcoal-gray hoodie I won last year at a rally when one of the baseball players threw it right at me in the bleachers, bopping me in the face with it. That kind of sucked when everyone laughed at me, but the free shirt was worth it.

Earlier I blew my hair dry and straightened it right after I got out of the shower, and now I'm back in the bathroom, applying mascara carefully so my eyelashes look extra good.

Like he cares. Like he even notices?

But I care. And after I'm done with the mascara, I grab a tinted lip balm and carefully smooth it over my lips, staring at my reflection in the mirror that hangs above the sink. I hate my freckles, I always have. If I could scrub them away, I so would. I stay out of the sun since that just makes them multiply. Which means I'm pale as a ghost and I hate that too, but I sunburn easily and I can't get tan to save my life, so…

Yeah. I'm sort of a mess.

Throwing the lip balm back in the drawer, I slam it shut and exit the bathroom, then pick up a little around the living room. I snag the blanket from underneath Maxine and she complains to me with an irritated meow as I fold it and toss it over the back of the couch. I turn on both lamps in the room, decide that's too bright and turn off one. I also turn off the kitchen light, because that is waaaay too much light and I like it better when it's darker in my house. That way he can't see how shabby and old our furniture is.

I glance at my phone to see I've only wasted twelve minutes.

Great.

Scrolling Instagram and checking out everyone's stories on both IG and Snap doesn't waste enough time either. I'm nervous. Fidgety. Feels like a bazillion butterflies just set loose in my stomach, it's so fluttery and jumpy. I smooth my hands over my hair again and again. Chew the lip balm off my lips so that I have to go back into the bathroom and reapply another coat. Once I'm done, I go back out into the living room, plopping my butt on the couch.

I think of all the things Jake and I have done on this couch, and my skin catches fire as the memories flood me. Not because I'm embarrassed, but more because I wish he was here right now. With me. I'm fascinated with his hands. They're large and his fingers are long, and when they touch me...

A shiver slips over my skin and I sigh, remembering how he touched me the last time he was here. His fingers between my legs, playing me just right. His mouth on mine. His mouth...everywhere. We've taken it further and further, and while we haven't had actual sex yet, we've done a lot of other things and I'm always left feeling like I want more.

More, more, more.

It's heady stuff, being in a relationship with the hottest boy at school. The same boy who started coming over to my house just to hang out and make sure I was safe. He may come across like a boy with a chip on his shoulder and pissed off at the world, but he's really not. He's sweet. Thoughtful. And he actually cares about me.

It's freaking surreal.

To curb my restlessness, I decide to throw myself into cleaning the kitchen and wiping down the counters. When the knock finally comes, I check the time.

9:42 p.m.

He's a little later than usual.

Smoothing my hand over my hair, I slowly go to the door and undo the locks before I open it. He's standing before me in his usual late-night attire of a T-shirt and sweats, and his dark hair is damp and curling, like he just got out of the shower.

My imagination goes wild, and I sort of wish we could take a shower together.

He tilts his head to the side. "Let's go."

I frown, fighting the panic that wants to rise. We never leave my apartment during the week, so he's throwing me. "Where?"

"It's a surprise." His smile is mischievous and I'm immediately intrigued.

"Am I dressed okay?" I glance down at myself, then look up to catch him thoroughly examining me before his gaze finally meets mine.

My skin goes warm at the way he looks at me. Ooh, this boy I swear. He's going to destroy me by the time this is over.

Seriously I shouldn't think like that. What if…what if this is never over? What if it's just me and Jake, going through life together? My ever-practical self likes getting lost in this idea…

"You're always dressed okay." He hesitates and his gaze grows heated. "More than okay. Grab your keys and let's go."

Maxine takes that moment to show up at my feet, ready to dart out, and Jake grabs her before she can make her escape. "Nice try," he tells her as he cuddles her close to his chest. "I'm faster than you."

I watch as he brings Maxine in and deposits her on the couch, then leans over it and starts scratching her on the head. Swear to God, Maxine has a big crush on my boyfriend. Not that I can blame her.

"Let me get my stuff," I tell him as I make my way to my bedroom. I blow out the candle before I grab the small purse that hangs from a hook on the back of my door and place my wallet and phone inside before I start for the bathroom so I can get my tinted lip balm. Not paying attention to where I'm going causes me to bump right into Jake as he magically appears in my bedroom doorway.

He grabs me before I fall. He is so warm he could probably set me on fire and I slip my hands up his chest, curling my arms around his neck. His strong hands grip my waist, holding me in place, and I tip my head back.

"You okay?" The amused concern in his deep voice makes me feel a little embarrassed, but I tell myself to get over it. "Hannah?"

Curling my hands so they're cupping his nape, I smile up at him, hoping he'll kiss me. "I'm fine. Perfect. Thank you for saving me."

"Anytime." He lowers his head and kisses me soft and slow, his tongue slipping inside, his hands sliding over my butt. He pulls me in close, our hips aligned, and I know if we keep this up, we won't leave the apartment.

And I really want to see my surprise.

"We should go," I murmur against his perfect lips.

He kisses me once. Twice. Stares down at me with that certain look on his face, the one that tells me he's completely into me. If I could snap a photo of it so I could keep it forever, I so would. "We could stay here."

"No." I shake my head. "I want to see my surprise."

He reaches out, my breath lodging in my throat when he tucks my hair behind my ear, his fingers lingering. "We could mess around on your bed."

We keep it on the couch because I know the moment we end up in my bed, it's going to happen. We'll have sex. Am I ready for that?

Sometimes I think yes, sign me up. Other times, I'm scared.

Tonight? I'm a little scared. And I want to see what he has planned.

"Let's save that for another night." I grab his hand and lead him toward the door. "Come on. Let's go."

We leave my apartment and walk down the stairs, Jake going to the passenger side of his truck to open the door for me like a gentleman. I get into the truck, settling into the passenger seat, and he shuts the door, jogs around the front of the vehicle, and climbs inside.

"Where are we going?" I ask once he's pulled out of the parking lot.

"You'll see," he says mysteriously, turning right once we hit the intersection and then making a right onto the highway after we stop at that light.

The windows are rolled down, the cool mountain air blowing on my face as we drive into the night. I close my eyes and breathe deep, letting the anticipation wash over me. I wonder what he has planned.

A weird thought hits me, all of my old insecurities filling me with anxiety. Could he be taking me somewhere only to humiliate me in front of his friends? You know, like you see in those crazy teen movies on the Lifetime channel. He'll take me to some isolated barn in the middle of nowhere, and his friends will all be waiting for us—including Cami. They'll tie me up against a tree and mock me, Cami hanging all over Jake while he just smirks and encourages everyone to call me names and throw things at me. Like rotten food or whatever.

I open my eyes, sneaking a glance at Jake, who's reaching for a knob on his car radio to turn up the volume. He has his phone connected and a Spotify playlist he created is on, playing some rap song I vaguely recognize.

What in the world is wrong with me? Jake and I have been together for the past couple of weeks. We're solid. So why did my imagination just go into full overdrive? No way would he do something like that. That's the kind of situation is saved for fiction only. Jake isn't out to get me.

"This isn't some sort of set up, is it?" I ask, my voice barely above a whisper.

"What?" He turns down the volume, glancing over at me quickly. "I didn't hear what you said."

"I asked if this was some sort of set up. Where you're taking me." I gesture toward the desolate dark road he just turned onto. "Are you kidnapping me?"

His lips curve into the barest smile and my heart flutters. "You want to be kidnapped?" He keeps his gaze straight ahead.

Yes, yes, yes, I think but I don't want him to think I'm some sort of weirdo. Though he already knows I'm kind of weird. "I just had a crazy thought, that's all. My imagination can run away from me sometimes."

"What was your crazy thought?"

"You don't want to know."

"Oh yes I do," he says eagerly. "Come on. Tell me."

"I had this sudden image of you taking me to an abandoned barn where all your friends and *Cami.*" I pause, and he grimaces. That grimace is terribly reassuring. "They're waiting for us so they can tie me to a tree before they all start throwing rotten eggs at my hair," I explain to him, as serious as I can be.

He chuckles, and I feel the sound right down to my soul. "You really think I'd do that to you?"

"Of course not. That's just…" My voice drifts and I bite my lower lip. I'm sure all the lip balm is gone again. "My past insecurities coming to light via my overactive imagination."

"Hannah." I really like it when he says my name, but right now he sounds extremely serious. "Even before we started seeing each other, I would've never done something like that to you."

"I know, I know." When he glances over at me, I smile, but he just frowns in return.

"You don't sound too sure about that."

"It still feels so unreal to me sometimes," I confess. "That we're together. That you actually like me."

We're both quiet, the silence becoming heavier the longer neither of us speak, until finally Jake says something. "I more than like you, Hannah."

My heart starts to race. It's too early for proclamations of love and all that, but we've spent so much time together this last month and I know what he means. I feel so close to him. I care about him. And I know…

I know I could fall in love with him.

"And to think it all started with that innocent little moment during lunch in the quad," I muse.

"What moment during lunch?" He's frowning as he drives.

"Are you actually forgetting the first time you asked me to wear your jersey?" My voice pitches higher and I'm sure he can tell I'm annoyed.

"I'm just playin' ya." He smiles again and I want to sock him in the arm, but I restrain myself. All I can do is laugh. "You're getting all worked up."

"You have that effect on me," I say teasingly, reaching out

to poke him in the side. He flinches away from my touch, laughing.

"Aw, lighten up, Banana." He reaches out and settles his hand on my knee, giving it a quick squeeze before leaving his hand there. Just like that, the tension looms between us, the air shimmering with promise. "I swear I'm not going to take you to some fucked-up barn in the middle of a field with Cami waiting to greet you with a knife in her hand."

"A *knife*?" Ooh, his imagination is worse than mine. "That sounds downright frightening."

"Trust me, she's pretty damn scary," he says. "Did I tell you Diego confessed to me that he's definitely been sneaking around with Cami?"

I gape at him like an idiot for a few seconds too long before I finally find my voice to speak. "Are you serious?"

He nods. "We talked at practice today. We were actually getting along, and practice was going good. But then Bennett tagged Caleb in one of his videos and we watched it together and…"

He's quiet for a while and so am I. Sophie already talked to me about it. Eli said some pretty crappy things about her and Tony, which hurt her feelings, but I tried to lighten the moment by saying she's hit peak high social status, what with Eli Bennett mentioning her in his daily *come at me, bro* stories.

That's what Jake calls them, and I think it's fitting. With the provoking things he says in his little mini rants every day, it seems Eli is hungry for a fight, which I don't get.

"What happened?" I ask when Jake still hasn't said anything.

"Eli mentioned that Diego is still getting with Cami in that video, and I called Diego out on it. I asked him if it's true and he said it was, but not anymore. We started to argue, but

Caleb told us that's exactly what Eli wants: us divided, so it's easier to beat us next week."

"Caleb's probably right," I tell him.

"Yeah. I agreed. So did Diego. But after he left the locker room, I asked Caleb if Diego was actually seeing Cami now, and he sort of confirmed it without coming right out and saying it, if you know what I mean," Jake explains, slowly shaking his head. "My best friend is acting like a total piece of shit right now, and I hate it."

My heart hurts for him. And for Jocelyn too. "Does his girlfriend know?"

"I think so. Maybe? Maybe not? I don't know. Lately they haven't been arguing from what I've seen, but that doesn't mean much. Diego and I haven't really been talking until today, and it went downhill pretty fast thanks to Eli Bennett." Jake slammed his palm against the steering wheel. "I hate that guy."

"Which one?"

He sighs. "I don't hate Diego, he's my friend. I can't give up on him. I'm just…disappointed in him and what he's doing. I don't know why he feels the need to cheat on his girl. She's stuck by him for a long time, but over the last year, he hasn't been faithful."

That's terrible. If I were closer to Jocelyn, I'd tell her, but we're not really friends. She's nice to me and I'm friendly to her, but that's about as far as we take it.

"Maybe I should talk to Cami, though I'm sure she won't tell me shit about her and Diego," he says out of nowhere, and I have an immediate response.

"No way." I'm not a controlling girlfriend by any means, but the very last thing I want is for my new boyfriend to talk to his conniving bitch of an ex about their mutual friend's relationship problems.

And why would he anyway? Not like she'd tell him she's hooking up with Diego.

"You don't like that idea?" He's smiling again, and I know he's teasing me. His mood has completely shifted, and I'm relieved.

"We used to be friends," I admit. "Cami and I."

"Really?" He sounds surprised.

"Back in elementary school. Like fourth or fifth grade? I even went to a few slumber parties at her house. Her birthday parties. We were all friends then." Until middle school and she became the diva of the sixth grade. Oh, I went to her swim party that summer between sixth and seventh grade, but it turned into a total fiasco with the kissing-Robbie-Schaffer incident. I was pretty much banned from her invite list from then on.

"Were you close?"

"Sort of." I shrug. "Not close enough that she'd keep me as a friend beyond the age of twelve."

We're quiet for a moment and I realize we're on the east side of the lake, going a way I've never really been before.

"She sucks," Jake finally mutters, his annoyance making me laugh. I can't help it, and he smiles too. "She's so selfish. She wants things to go her way all the time, and it doesn't matter what anyone else wants."

"She's kind of a nightmare," I agree, not wanting to say too much more. She's not worth my words, or my worry.

"Maybe Cami and Diego should actually get together. They'd probably make a perfect couple," he says.

I know what he means. And that's not necessarily a compliment.

"And uh, just to warn you, but Cami's waiting for you right over there," he says seriously, gesturing toward the lake. "You know. By that old barn and clutching a carton of rotten eggs."

I can't contain the smile that spreads across my face. "Good to know. Glad I brought my secret weapon then," I say lightly, playing along.

"Oh yeah? What's that?"

"My lip balm." I grab my bag and open it, pulling the balm out. "I could probably take her eye out with it if I throw it hard enough."

"I don't know. I think her spidery eyelash extensions will protect her from moving projectiles," he says, making me laugh.

A few minutes later he pulls into the parking lot of one of the local resorts that sits right on the lake. The resort has a restaurant, a little grocery store, a bunch of vacation cabins that people rent throughout the summer, plus a boating dock. Since it's mid-September, the cabins are mostly empty, though I spot lights on in a few of them. It's late enough that both the store and restaurant are closed, so the parking lot is pretty much empty.

The parking lot also has a great view of the lake.

Jake backs the truck into a spot, puts it in park and shuts off the engine. "You ready to see this?"

Apprehension fills me. "Definitely."

"Wait here and let me set everything up first, okay?" We turn to face each other and he reaches out, cupping my cheek. His thumb smooths over my skin, pressing gently against the corner of my mouth, sending a rush of tingles all over my body. He must see some apprehension in my gaze because he says, "Hey. Trust me."

Without a word I slowly nod and he climbs out of the truck, slamming the door behind him.

Trust me.

A few weeks ago, I would've thought absolutely not. But now…

Now, I'm putting all of my trust in him.

I hope it's not a mistake.

CHAPTER 31

HANNAH

*W*ithin minutes of him leaving the truck, he's back at my door, opening it for me. "You ready?"

I hop out, watching as he slams the door. "Where are we going?" I ask.

"You'll see," he says mysteriously.

I follow after him, curiosity filling me. I could hear him moving stuff around, the truck shaking with the movement, but I have no idea what he was setting up. The tailgate is down and when we stop at the very back of his truck, I see that he's laid out a thick sleeping bag and a couple of blankets. There's a pile of pillows closer to the cab end of the truck, and a small ice chest sits to the side.

"What is this?" I ask, happy nerves waging a war in my stomach.

"I thought we could look at the stars," he says with a one-shouldered shrug. Before he can explain further, I'm tackle-hugging him, kissing his neck as I hang all over him. "I take it that you're cool with this?"

"Yes, yes. I love it." I rise up on tiptoe and press my mouth to his, keeping it short and sweet before I smile up at him. "This is very romantic, Jake."

"I know." His cheeks actually turn ruddy and my heart feels like it's soaring. He releases his hold on me and I immediately miss him. "I planned on taking you somewhere more remote, but then you mentioned abandoned barns and people throwing rotten eggs at you and I figured you might get scared if I took you to the middle of nowhere."

I laugh and he chuckles too.

"So that's why we're here." He points at the Pines Resort behind us. "So you'd feel safe. But we still have a great view of the sky."

"Aw." I don't know what else to say. I'm touched. Surprised.

"Or we could we make out in my truck and then head back home. Keep it simple. Whatever you want to do," he says, suddenly looking awkward.

I'm rooted to the spot, unable to move, my voice escaping me. Jake doesn't make many romantic gestures, but this is a big one and I'm a little overwhelmed. Plus, I'm not saying much, so he must take that as a bad sign, because all of a sudden, he starts to reach for the tailgate, as if he's going to close it and our little romantic star gazing moment is over before it even began. "Are you okay? Maybe this was a bad idea after all."

"No, no." I reach for him, touching his arm, halting his movements. "I love this idea. Let's stay here."

Slowly he pulls me back into his arms, holding me close as he drops a kiss to the tip of my nose. "Want me to help you into the back of my truck?"

"Please," I whisper, just before he picks me up and deposits me into the bed of his truck as I squeal.

He climbs in behind me with a wicked grin and heads for

the small ice chest, lifting the top. "You want something to drink?"

"Sure. What do you have?"

"I have Coke, Diet Coke, water, beer," he rattles off.

I wrinkle my nose. "We probably shouldn't drink beer."

"I'll have a Coke." He pulls the familiar red can out of the ice chest, then points at me. "You want one?"

"I'd rather have water." A soda this late at night is never good for me. The caffeine will make me jittery.

I'm jittery enough, being here tonight with Jake, all alone with the lake and the stars.

He hands me a cold bottle of water and then shuts the ice chest lid, moving around with his can clutched in one hand until he's leaning against the pillows that are propped up behind the truck's cab, his long legs stretched out in front of him. He pats the empty space beside him. "Come on, Banana. Join me."

I scoot over to where he is and plop my butt next to him, surprised by how cushy the pillows are. Twisting open the cap, I take a sip of water, staring out at the water.

"You okay?" he asks. "Are you comfortable?"

Nodding, I shoot him a quick smile before I tilt my head back to look at the sky. "It's dark tonight."

"No moon," he says, his gaze following mine. "It's the best time to see the stars."

"I've never been here before," I tell him, taking another drink.

"What? Are you serious? So you've never eaten at the restaurant?" He sounds incredulous.

"Nope. We don't come to the lake much. I mean, why should we? We live here." I don't say what I really want to, which is this is where the rich kids hang out during the summer, and I'm never a part of that group. Or there are the kids who work up here at the resorts that line the lake. Lots of tourists visit the lake throughout the summer, and the resorts like to hire plenty of teens and people in their early twenties to work a variety of jobs and shifts. I've heard it can be a lot of fun.

But I didn't have a car to get me up here this past summer. Maybe by next summer I will, though…

Huh. I doubt it.

"When I was a little kid, my parents would bring us here for vacation. We came a couple of summers in a row," he tells me, his voice soft, his head angled back so he can stare at the sky while I openly stare at him. I could look at his pretty face all night long. "We loved it here. They would rent a pontoon boat and we would spend all day on the lake, getting sunburned and eating barbecued hamburgers. Mom would slather us with sunscreen and get so annoyed when we still got burned."

"Sounds fun," I say when he goes quiet.

"Yeah, it was." Jake turns to look at me, and I startle a bit when I realize how close we're sitting. Kissing close. But I don't try to kiss him. I like hearing him talk, opening up to me. "I loved staying in the cabins. We slept in bunkbeds, and I would fight my sisters for the top bunk. I'd always win too."

"I'm sure you would," I say with a little smile.

He returns his attention to the velvety sky. "We'd have a fire every night, and we'd play with kids whose families were staying here too. It was great. My parents took us everywhere, but this was my absolute favorite place. Same with my sisters. Pretty sure that's why my parents decided we should move up here," he explains.

"Where did you live before?" I ask softly.

"Bay Area. Near San Jose." He sends me a questioning look. "My dad played for the Niners."

"Right. Mr. Retired NFL Quarterback," I say, and he

confirms my answer with a nod. "It's kind of wild that he would move his family to our little town."

"My parents didn't like living in the busy city. They both grew up in areas that weren't so congested. They wanted us to live somewhere where the schools weren't overcrowded and the real estate was reasonable." He chuckles, shaking his head. "Though my dad is richer than God."

A pang of envy makes my chest tight and I try to ignore it. He didn't choose to be born into his wealthy family. He just lucked out.

Can't help but feel a little jealous over it, though. I mean, what's it like, to never worry about money? To do whatever you want and not have those types of restrictions on your life.

I have no clue.

"I sounded like a complete ass just now," he says.

Our gazes meet once more and I can't help but smile. "You kind of did," I admit. "But you're just stating a truth, so…"

"Yeah, but I know your family must struggle a little." He clears his throat, dropping his head so he's studying the now mostly empty Coke can in his hand. He brings a knee up, then puts the can to his lips, draining it before he reaches over and opens the ice chest, lodging the empty can inside. He then pulls a bottle of water out. "I shouldn't make assumptions."

"Your assumptions are pretty on target," I tell him. It's funny how we've been hanging out for over a month and we've never really talked about our families. "It's just my mom and me."

"What happened to your dad?"

I shrug. "They split when I was so young, I barely remember him." They weren't married. It's always embarrassing to admit that, but it's such a common thing, I should get over myself. "And he never came back around, never fought for custody, and never gave us money either. It's like once I was born, he lost all interest in my mom and my brother. And me, of course."

Jake remains quiet and I can feel him watching me, though I'm not looking in his direction. I wonder what he thinks of my family story. When you think about it, we are polar opposites. Our lives couldn't be more different. We didn't have the same friend group, nothing.

Yet somehow when we're together, we make complete sense.

"Totally different than your family, huh?" I say, trying to lighten the moment as I reach out to pull one of the thin fleece blankets over my legs. The fabric is so soft, I want to wrap myself in the blanket like a burrito.

"I'm sorry your dad is such a jerk, Hannah," he says softly.

I shrug. "It's not your fault."

We're quiet for a moment, and I can hear the night seemingly come alive. Crickets chirping. Frogs croaking. The lonely hoot of an owl. The eerie howl of a coyote in the distance. A breeze slips through the trees, making their branches sway and the leaves rustle and a shiver slips over me.

"You know what I like about you?" He doesn't give me a chance to respond, he just keeps on talking. "You don't want anything from me. And *everybody* wants something from me. To be the best football player, to win the game for the team, the school, the community. Girls don't listen to what I have to say or actually care about me. They just want to be seen with me, so everyone thinks we're together and people will talk about us. That's it. That's all I'm good for."

His eyes meet mine in the mostly dark night, but I can see how they sparkle. The determined set of his jaw, the straight line of his lips. He is deathly serious.

And my heart is breaking for him right now.

"You really believe that?" I ask softly.

"I know it's true," he says vehemently. "I know for a fact that's how people view me. Except for…"

His voice drifts off and he clamps his lips shut.

"Except for what? Who?" I ask when he remains quiet.

"You."

CHAPTER 32

JAKE

I am being totally open with Hannah. More open than I've ever been with a girl before. I can hear my mother's words ringing in my head about me being sensitive and how girls like it. No girl I've ever been with ever liked it. None of them cared.

None of them really cared about me or who I am or what I think about.

Hannah just wants to spend time with me. She asks for nothing. She listens. She acts like she cares, and I believe she actually does. When we originally met, I treated her like shit and she still helped me when I was hurt. No other girl would've done that for me. Not even Cami.

Especially not Cami.

My confession pleases Hannah. I see it in the way she watches me, how she's gone completely still. This moment between us feels big. Like we're about to take our relationship to another level. It's been fun so far, but I wanted her to know how I really feel.

How much she means to me.

Reaching out, I slide my hand into her silky hair, cradling

the side of her head. Her breath catches, those full lips pressing together before they part once more. I dip my head, my mouth hovering above hers for long seconds that feel like minutes.

Hours.

Anticipation ripples through me just before my mouth is on hers. And the simple kiss rocks me. When our lips first touch, I'm rocked.

Every single time.

I tilt my head to the side and kiss her again. And again. Those sexy-as-fuck lips are so fucking soft. Sweet.

So sweet.

She's shaking. I can feel her body tremble, and I know she senses how serious this moment is too. I take the kiss deeper, and without hesitation she opens to me.

Always so responsive.

I slide my tongue into her mouth, touching hers. My entire body prickles with awareness at first contact, starting at the top of my head and sweeping over me, all the way to my fucking toes. I circle my tongue around hers, tasting her, coaxing her.

I want her to feel as greedy for me as I do for her.

It's always like this between us. We keep kissing, on and on, like we don't want to come up for air. Any time one of us tries to break the kiss, the other starts it all over again. I keep tugging her close. Closer. She comes eagerly, until she's practically in my lap, her arms curling around my neck, her hands in my hair. Her knees are on either side of my hips, and it would be so easy to slip my hand between her legs. I've done it before, many times. But never like this. Practically in public.

Fuck it. I reach for her, my hand cupping between her legs, her heat radiating against my palm. I bet she's already wet for me.

"Jake," she whispers against my lips, her lower body slowly thrusting against my hand. "What are you doing to me?"

She's not talking about me touching her. It's what she's feeling in the moment, and I feel the same way. How quick this is happening. How strong my feelings are for her.

I want her. Always.

I think I'm falling for her.

Taking a deep breath, I remove my hand from between her thighs as I break away from her lips, running my fingers through her hair instead. It's silky-soft, and she closes her eyes, a little sound of pleasure coming from her swollen lips. "That feels so good."

Her voice, that noise she just made, goes straight to my dick.

Typical. I'm dying to fuck her, but I refuse to push it. Push her. I'm pretty sure she's a virgin, though we haven't had that talk yet, but it's cool. We can mess around. We're having a good time doing it. I'm learning everything that makes her feel good, and I've become pretty familiar with her body in a short amount of time.

As in, I know how to make her come. And I love watching her fall apart.

"Before you came into my life, no one ever touched me, I swear," she continues, her eyes opening to meet mine.

"Yeah?" I can't stop touching her. Like right now, I play with her hair, watching her. The way her lids are at half-mast over her eyes. Her lush lips are still parted, little puffs of air escaping. She tilts her head to the side, a wistful sigh emanating from her, and I lean in and kissing her once more.

"Yeah," she murmurs when I pull away from her lips and start kissing her neck. "Now I feel like I can't get enough of you, Jake."

I feel exactly the same way.

Glancing around, I check to see if there's anybody nearby, but we are the only ones in the parking lot. No one has passed by on the road since we've arrived.

We're pretty much all alone.

Without hesitation, I slip my hand beneath her T-shirt, touching her stomach. She becomes tense, though her voice tight as she says, "Maybe we shouldn't do this here."

"No one else is around." My hand wanders up, over her lacy bra, slipping beneath the thin fabric to cup her, my thumb playing with her already-hard nipple. A gasp escapes her when I give it a slight pinch. "No one will see us."

She thrusts her chest into my palm, a sure sign she likes what I'm doing. "What if we get caught by like…the cops or something. That would be so embarrassing."

"Come here." I grab the blankets and pull them over us, making a kind of tent over me as I readjust her so she's lying on her back. "No one can see you."

She giggles as she stares up at me. "But everyone can see you."

"You're just paranoid." I shift down, carefully pushing her T-shirt up before I drop a kiss on her flat stomach, feeling her skin quiver beneath my lips. "Let me help you forget."

There's no more protesting. Her hands go to my hair, guiding me where she wants me the most. I rain kisses on her stomach, her ribs. Along the bottom edge of her bra. I reach behind her and unhook it, and she sheds the scrap of fabric quickly, leaving herself bare. I help her get rid of the T-shirt and then I'm kissing her there. All over her soft, lush skin. The underside of her left breast, then her right. The valley in between them. Her nipples are so hard, I can see them thanks to the lone streetlight that's illuminating the back of my truck, rosy little points aiming straight at the sky.

I pull one into my mouth and suck. Nibble it. Her fingers

tighten in my hair to the point that it almost hurts, but I keep sucking. Licking. Biting.

My girl really gets off on her tits being sucked.

I go on like this for long, torturous minutes, my dick resting heavily against her hip. Everything inside of me aches, is wound up tight, and I feel like I could break at any moment.

And she hasn't even really touched me yet.

She kicks off her shoes and so do I, her legs winding around mine.

We dispose of her leggings next. Then my shirt. My sweats. Until she's only wearing a skimpy pair of panties and my erection is straining the front of my boxer briefs. She reaches between us, touching me lightly, and my cock jumps, eager for more attention.

"I want to kiss it," she whispers, and I groan against her neck at the images her words bring up in my mind. I want her to do a lot more than kiss it, that's for fuckin' sure.

She hasn't given me a blowjob yet, and I haven't asked for one either. Just hand jobs. I've taught her how I like to be touched and she's a fast learner. As in, she can make me come pretty fast too.

"Hannah." My voice is a warning and she shoves at my shoulders so I have no choice but to lift away from her.

"Please. I want to know what you taste like." Her eyes are wide and unblinking, and I have to confess, I never thought sweet, shy but feisty Hannah would be so bold sexually.

But she's pretty fucking bold.

"You're going to kill me," I say with another groan as she shoves me again. I go easily, flopping onto my back, grateful I brought all the blankets and sleeping bags, plus the pillows from our outdoor furniture. If Mom knew I brought these, she'd probably ground me for life.

Her outdoor furniture is beyond expensive.

Hannah hovers above me, tugging my underwear down, my erection springing free, and she keeps tugging until I'm kicking them off my feet. She stares at my cock, her eyes wide, her lips parted before she lifts her gaze and looks at me.

"You act like you've never touched it before," I tell her, trying to make a joke, but I'm dying to feel her mouth on my dick, so my voice comes out strained.

She doesn't say a word. Just shoots me a quick look before she curls her fingers firmly around the base of my erection, then dips her head to wrap her lips around just the tip. I close my eyes at the sensation, her tongue darting out for a lick, teasing my hard flesh. I rest my hand at the base of her neck, my fingers tangling in her hair as she licks and teases, her lips wrapping around me once more, testing as she takes it farther into her mouth.

If a cop came by right about now, I wouldn't even give a shit. I'd just give him a look that says *can you blame me* and not stop Hannah. Why would I stop her?

It all feels too fucking good.

She takes me deep. Deeper. She strokes me too, her fingers gripping me tight like I taught her, though it's never tight enough. I'm leaking all sorts of precome, getting closer and closer to my breaking point. It's been a while since I've had a blowjob. Since I've been with another girl. None of them matter anymore, though.

None of them make me feel what Hannah does.

"You like that?" she asks minutes later, when my entire body is shaking and my teeth are clenched. I stare at her glistening mouth, her eyes wide as she studies me, naked save for a pair of panties and her tits on full display, and I nod at her furiously.

"I don't know if you want me to, uh, come in your

mouth," I admit, and she smiles just before she lowers her head once more.

"I want you to," she says, right before she pretty much swallows me whole.

My hips lift as if I have no control over them, and I tell her to grip me tighter. She does as I ask, her lips suctioning around me, her tongue licking, and that's all it takes.

I'm coming into her mouth with a low grunt. She takes the first hit, then pulls away, her hand shifting up and down my shaft, milking me as I spill all over her fingers. One last shot leaves me, marking her chest, and I flop back onto the blankets, groaning as the shudders still wrack my body.

Once I've settled down, she leans over me, her face in mine as she grins. "I made you come."

Laughing, I pull her in, kissing her deeply. Those four words have become our running joke now. "I'm about to make you come next."

"Promises, promises," she says teasingly.

I help clean up the mess I made, and then we're kissing again. The night air washes over my body, cooling my skin, but I still feel hot inside.

I'm burning up. For Hannah.

Before long, I'm slipping off her panties, my hand sliding between her legs. She's hot and wet, drenched for me, and I slip one finger inside her. Then two. Stretching her. Wishing I could fuck her.

But I don't think she's ready yet. And I'm not going to push.

I haven't gone down on her yet either, and I'm dying for a taste. I work my way down her curvy body, mapping her pale skin with my lips and tongue, until my hands are spreading her thighs apart and I'm face to Hannah's pussy for the very first time.

Hesitating, I take her in for a moment. She has reddish

pubic hair and she's so pink and wet. Leaning in, I lick her, making her jolt.

She tastes delicious. A little salty. Musky. I lick again. And again. Searching her folds with my tongue, finding her clit, sucking it between my lips. A whimper sounds from above me, and she's lifting her hips, pushing her pussy into my face, and I slip my hands beneath her, gripping her ass, holding her to me as I feast on her.

"Oh God," I hear her gasp, and I'm thinking she's already close.

I tease her clit with the tip of my tongue. "Right there?" I murmur against her trembling flesh. "Is that good?"

I lick her again, and she grips my hair, guiding me to the right. I suck her clit again and again, my fingers thrusting inside her, and within minutes she falls completely apart, her entire body shaking, whimpering as the tremors take over her body.

Once she's calmed down, I gather her in my arms, pulling the blankets up over us, both of us staring up at the sky silently. She strokes my chest. I kiss her forehead.

"I guess we should go star gazing more often," she eventually murmurs, making me laugh.

Making my heart want to fly straight out of my chest.

I'm in love with this girl.

I know it.

CHAPTER 33

HANNAH

It's coronation night. All the homecoming princes and princesses from the lower grades have been crowned. Jake's sister won for her class, along with Wyatt, who's a junior on the football team. I know it made Jake happy to see them both win. I saw the pride on his face when they announced his sister's name while we were waiting backstage, and he hugged her tight when she came back there, nearly sending her crown toppling from her head. He gave Wyatt a high five and a clap on the back, and it was like he couldn't stop smiling.

I don't think I've ever seen him this happy around other people, and I like it.

He looks amazing in his navy suit, crisp white shirt and light blue tie. I can't stop staring at him, and every time he catches me, I can only smile at him helplessly.

Now all the senior couples are standing together on the stage, side by side. Rob and Bridget. Diego and Jocelyn. Caleb and Paige. Me and Jake. Tony and Sophie. And Mike—he's one of our star basketball players for the varsity team—and Cami.

I already feel like a princess. A nervous, shaking princess, in my beautiful sparkly, dark blue, fitted strapless dress I found when I went shopping with Sophie and Marty. We found it at the mall, and it was actually on clearance. I don't know how I got so lucky that it was the only one left, and that it was my actual size. Like it was meant to be just for me. It fit perfectly, no alterations needed, and after I bought it for only twenty-five dollars, I practically wanted to cry.

Sophie looks gorgeous too. Her dress is short—every dress is short on my beautiful, tall friend—and it's white, with iridescent sequins all over it in a halter style. She can't stop smiling and Tony can't stop smiling at her, and I'm feeling all the love tonight. Despite the sour look on Cami's face. Despite the uncomfortable tension that's radiating from Diego and Jocelyn's direction, I am on top of the world at this very moment. And if they don't call my name, I'll be disappointed, I can admit that, but overall I know I'll be okay.

I'm having my moment, and I'm soaking it up for as long as I have it.

Our student body president Gannon is the coronation host tonight, and he's just been given the envelope with the homecoming court's names inside. I squeeze Jake's arm and he smiles down at me in this reassuring way that eases my nerves. Somewhat.

"All right, and now here are the remaining nominees for our senior homecoming court. King nominees are—Diego Garcia."

Everyone applauds as Diego smiles, standing up straighter. Jocelyn looks like she wants to be sick.

"—Tony Sorrento."

Sophie squeals and so do I, then immediately clamp my lips shut.

"—and Jake Callahan."

Oh my God. Another squeal escapes me. I'm in shock, but then again, not really. Of course my boyfriend would make the homecoming court. I lean my head against his arm, smiling up at him. He's beaming out at the crowd, and I'm so proud of him. He looks so handsome in his suit. So freaking grown up.

"Now for our remaining queen nominees. They are..." Gannon pauses, and I feel like I'm being strangled, I can hardly breathe.

"—Sophie Whitmore."

More squealing from both of us. I am giddy with excitement.

"—Hannah Walsh."

I'm stunned. *Floored.* What the ever-loving fuck just happened? Gannon called my name. Me! My knees are so watery, I'm afraid I might faint.

No one really knows Sophie and I at this school. Not really. And they definitely never pay any attention to us. Is the entire student body sick of the same girls getting nominated for everything or what?

"And Cami Lockhart! Congrats, ladies and gents! We can't wait to see who'll be crowned Friday night!" Everyone in the crowd applauds and Gannon calls for the other class winners to join us on the stage.

I'm clutching Jake's arm so tightly, I might be cutting off his circulation as we shuffle to the right, making room for the others who are back on the stage. I'm grinning from ear to ear, and my face is starting to hurt from smiling too much, but I don't care. Sophie leans forward, catching my eye, and we start laughing. I can't believe I get to participate in the homecoming parade Friday morning. The rally before lunch. The court procession Friday night. That I could possibly be crowned the homecoming queen.

Shit, this means I have to get another dress!

"Shit, Jocelyn didn't get nominated," Jake whispers near my ear as Gannon wraps up the ceremony with a quick thanks and good night.

I glance up at Jake with worried eyes before I look over at Diego. Jocelyn's already off the stage, along with the rest of the senior nominees who aren't on the final court. Now it's Diego and Cami who are standing together. She has her arm hooked through his, and their body language is telling. They're not smiling—even their bodies are angled away from each other. Clearly they're uncomfortable with the results.

Or they're faking being uncomfortable, considering they're still messing around.

The lights come up and the audience starts to clear out. Remaining on the stage, Sophie and I seek each other out, and I wrap her up in a big hug, hopping up and down with her as we squeal and yell our congrats to each other. Once that's over with, Rob approaches me, and with a solemn face and Bridget still hanging on his arm, he says, "Congrats, Hannah."

"Thank you, Robbie," I say, shocked he would be so kind.

He shrugs. "Tell your jerk boyfriend I hope he loses."

Bridget smacks his arm, but I start laughing. "Go tell him yourself."

Grinning, he leaves in search of Jake, taking Bridget's hand in his. Looks like there was a homecoming romantic match made. So sweet.

I eventually find Jake and he hugs me, murmuring against my hair, "You look beautiful. I want you to meet my parents."

It's like I can't help it. My entire body goes tense and I pull away from him, frowning. "Right now?"

"Yes, babe, right now," he whispers, taking my hand and leading me off the stage, where I see Jake's parents talking to Ava and Wyatt, the junior winners. My palms are sweating and my heart is racing, yet the fact that Jake just called me babe keeps running through my mind. And I liked it. I always thought that kind of thing was cheesy, but not when it's your boyfriend saying it.

I am such a sucker for this boy.

"Honey, congrats," Jake's mom says, opening her arms to him. He goes easily, giving his petite mother a tight hug before he pulls away and then she's facing me. "You must be Hannah. I'm Fable."

"Hi," I say, about to offer my hand to shake, but she pulls me into her arms, giving me a warm hug. "It's so nice to meet you," I say into her hair.

"You look so pretty. I hope you two win Friday night," Fable says as she pulls away from me, keeping her hands on my shoulders. "I love your dress."

"Thank you." She accepts me so easily. She's smiling at me like I make her happy and maybe I do, if she thinks I'm the reason her son is so happy.

And I'd like to think I am.

"Dad, you know Hannah?" Jake asks.

Drew Callahan turns to smile at me and he pulls me in for a more restrained hug. He smells good. "I've seen you at the games. It's nice to officially meet you."

"Nice to meet you too." He makes me even more nervous. Maybe it's that star presence he's got. This man is a celebrity, and you can feel it shimmering off of him. A famous football player, a former sports announcer, Drew Callahan has been in commercials, on billboards, in magazines and on TV. He's the real deal, and he's my boyfriend's dad.

It's kind of wild.

We make small talk, me and Ava complimenting each other on our dresses, me complaining that I have to buy another one and she laughs, saying she'll end up getting another one too.

"I have a really pretty dress that was too long on me and I

didn't end up wearing it for winter formal last year," she says. "I still have it. Maybe would you want to borrow it?"

"Oh my gosh, really?" I smile at her, my stress easing at her offer. "I would love to try it on and see if it fits."

"We look about the same size." She grabs my hands, holding them out at my sides. "You should come over tomorrow and you can try it on."

My heart skips a beat. I would love to go to their house, but I want Jake to be the one who invites me…

"That's a good idea," Jake chimes in, smiling at me when he catches my gaze. "You should come over. Maybe for dinner?"

"Let's all go out to dinner now," Fable suggests. "Beck's at his friend's house and we'll pick him up on the way home, so I don't have to worry about him only wanting to eat chicken nuggets and getting bored."

Drew laughs, slipping his arm around his wife's shoulders. "Sounds good to me. Would you like to go with us, Hannah?"

I'm thrilled that they invited me. "Um, I would love to." I look around, trying to spot my mom, but I don't see her. "I think my mom's here, though. I haven't seen her yet."

"She can come too," Fable suggests. "Maybe you should go find her."

"I'll be right back," I tell Jake before I start wandering around the theater where the ceremony was held.

The crowd is thinning, though there are still plenty of people there. I spot Sophie's family and go over to say hello, hugging everyone including my friend yet again. Marty is standing with them, looking miserable, and I give him an extra-long hug too.

"I was waiting to congratulate you, but now I'm out." Marty nods toward the swarm that is most of his family. "I don't want to hang out with Diego. Look at how miserable he is."

Wincing, I glance over at where Marty's indicating. Diego is surrounded by his family, and he does look pretty miserable. Jocelyn is nowhere to be seen. This might be the moment that breaks them up for good.

"There you are!"

I turn to find my mother standing in front of me, a giant smile on her face. She pulls me in for a long hug, and when she finally releases me I swear there are tears in her eyes. "I am so proud of you!"

"I did nothing, Mom," I start but she hushes me.

"Just let me have my moment." She releases me and grabs hold of Marty, pulling him in for a long hug as well. "It's been too long since I've seen you."

"My best friends found boyfriends," Marty says, his tone a little snide and making me feel bad. "But it's good to see you."

We make idle chitchat for a while and once Marty leaves, I mention the Callahans invited us to dinner, but my mom shakes her head.

"I'm so tired." She smiles, and I see it. Her face is pale, and there are dark smudges beneath her eyes. "I think I'll just go home. But you go on and have dinner with them. I'll meet them another time. I love you."

"Thank you, Mom." I hug her again, giving her a quick kiss on the cheek. "I'm so glad you came."

"I would do anything for you, sweetie. You know this."

We chat for a few minutes before Mom leaves. I'm headed back to where the Callahans are still gathered when I hear a familiar voice say, "You're going to lose."

Stopping in my tracks, I glance to my right to find Cami standing there with a look of disgust on her pretty face. She looks freaking amazing in a tight black dress that emphasizes her perfect curves and long, long legs. "Congratulations to you too," I say sarcastically.

She rolls her eyes and takes a few steps toward me, close enough I can smell her cloying perfume and see the streaks of highlight on her cheekbones. She wears too much makeup. "I don't even understand how you or your skinny friend got on the homecoming court, but with you two as my competition, I'm pretty confident I've got this one cinched."

"Don't you think people have figured out what a bitch you are and that maybe you won't win after all?" Ooh, I'm not sure where that came from, but I'm so tired of dealing with this girl's endless bullying. She's treated me terribly for years.

I'm over it.

"More like they're going to figure out what a phony you are. It's all a façade." She waves her hand, as if she's drawing an outline of me. "Beneath the cute dress and the pretty smile is a complete loser who no one likes."

It's just the same old sad song coming from her. Everyone who's not a part of her inner circle is a loser. It's lame.

She's lame.

"Whatever, Cami," I tell her, sounding weary, because I *am* weary. So tired of her repeated insults and her queen bee attitude.

Before she can form another repetitive sentence, I leave her where she stands, not once looking back. I lift my head, smiling at everyone I walk past, and when I come to a stop by Jake's side, I wrap my arm around his, holding on to him like he's my lifeline.

"Did you find her?" he asks, and when I send him a confused look, he says, "Your mom?"

"Oh, yes. I did." Seeing Cami the snake made me momentarily forget who Jake was asking about. "She had to bow out of going to dinner with us though. She's tired from working so much lately, and wanted me to apologize to everyone for her," I explain.

"That's too bad. I wanted to meet her." Jake slips his arm around my shoulders and tugs me in close, dropping a kiss on my forehead.

"Shall we leave and go to dinner?" Fable asks everyone.

"I'm starving," Ava says.

"Where's Wyatt?" I ask, looking around.

"He had to go. Couldn't make it to dinner with us," Ava says, pointing at Jake. "Big bro here scared him away."

"Wyatt doesn't need to be given any false hope," Jake says firmly. "He doesn't have a chance with my sister."

"You're going to make your future daughter's boyfriends very scared someday," his mom teases, and I'm immediately hit with the image of Jake and I with our own home and our own babies.

Okay, I'm totally rushing this, but when his mom says something like that, can you blame me? Not that I think Jake and I are going to end up married or anything but…

You never know.

CHAPTER 34

FABLE

"She seems like a nice girl," I say to my husband as we drive home.

We're alone. Just the two of us, which is becoming a more and more common thing. We need to pick Beck up from our neighbor's house, where he's hanging out with his best friend. They live right up the road from us, so we have the luxury of talking freely without any big ears listening to us.

My children have some of the biggest ears ever, especially Ava and Beck.

"She does. She's making our son happy, that much is clear," Drew says, keeping his gaze on the road ahead.

We went to dinner with Jake and Hannah and Ava, and we had a great time talking and laughing, and getting to know Hannah. Jake couldn't take his eyes off of his new girl-friend, which made my heart happy. He seems kinder. Gentler. Not as angry. The tender look he has in his gaze when he smiles at Hannah reminded me of the way my Drew looks at me.

Still. To this day.

Jake reluctantly went to the appointment with the therapist, and afterward, when we talked to him about it, the three of us decided together he should keep seeing her, starting every other week for now. No recommendations of medication yet, but just knowing that he's going to see someone regularly makes us feel better.

We did the right thing, making that appointment. Our son will realize that someday. His anger issues can't be ignored any longer. Not by us, and not by him either.

"You think she makes him happy?" When Drew glances over at me, I continue. "Hannah and Jake."

"Definitely. Doesn't mean he can stop going to therapy though," Drew says, shaking his head. "You know he'll try to get out of it."

"I'm not so sure about that," I say, gazing out the window. I think of my brother. Owen dealt with so many emotions over the years, most of them anger, especially toward our mother. I always thought it was because of what she did to him, to us, but as we got older, Owen went to therapy on a regular basis. He also got on medication.

I believe our son has the same issues as my brother.

"Ava left pretty quickly," Drew says, knocking me from my thoughts.

"Yes, she did," I murmur.

"Where did she say she was going again?" Drew asks, his brows lowered.

He doesn't like how his baby girl is always gone, always busy. It was hard enough, dealing with Autumn growing up on him. With Ava, he seems to be suffering just as mightily. "She said she was going over to Ellie's house for a little while, and that she'd be home by midnight."

"That's late for a school night," he says with a scowl.

"She's celebrating." I rest my hand on his thigh, giving it a squeeze. "Let her enjoy her moment. She's princess of the junior class! I'm proud of her. Did you see how shocked she looked when they called her name?"

"Did you see how surprised Jake's girlfriend looked when they called her name? I thought she might faint."

"It was cute." Jake didn't look surprised at all when they announced his nomination. This is what happens when your son is the most popular boy at school. Things aren't as special to him anymore—with the exception of one thing.

"Do you think they're having sex yet?"

Drew whips his head in my direction, his blue eyes wide. "Are you meaning Jake and Hannah?"

I nod, waiting for my husband's answer.

"Yeah, probably," he says, his voice more on the terse side as he returns his attention to the road. "Did you see the way he looks at her?"

"That's what I was thinking," I say with a sigh. "I hope they're being smart and using protection."

"I'm sure he is. I remember Ash telling Jake he was sorry for stealing from his box of condoms back in the day," Drew says sarcastically.

"What? What do you mean?"

"Oh, remember when Ash Davis was staying with us? Well, I overheard him tell Jake one day that he was really sorry for stealing his condoms and Jake told him it was no big deal." My husband sends me a pointed look. "Our son was a sophomore at that time. Fifteen."

"Probably with Cami," I practically spit out.

"Bet you were thrilled to see she was nominated."

"Ha. I don't like that girl. I hope Hannah or her best friend, that pretty tall girl, beats her."

"Yeah. We'll see."

We shall see. Good overrides bad almost every single time, and I have high hopes that Jake and Hannah will be the homecoming king and queen this year. Talk about a picture-perfect moment.

Jake will go on and take his team in to win the game against the Mustangs. He'll be homecoming king and his sister is the princess. It'll be a perfect night.

Just perfect.

CHAPTER 35

JAKE

Thursday night, I get home late after the team dinner. The cheer team was there, along with band, and we all celebrated together. Dad gave an uplifting, pump-you-up speech. The band brought dessert—cupcakes. The cheer team boosted morale just by being there. The majority of those girls are dating or wanting to date someone on the team.

Cami sat right by Diego the entire night, not giving a shit about what people might say. I guess that means he and Jocelyn are finished. And that makes me a little sad, even though their relationship was a nightmare there at the end. But it's the end of an era.

We invited Hannah to come over for dinner, forgetting we already had plans. Ava left the team dinner pretty fast after it ended, picked up my girlfriend and brought her over. I'll take her back home later.

Maybe we'll get a little alone time. We'll see.

"Hey," I say as I enter the kitchen to find Mom in there, helping Beck with his homework. He has a vocabulary test every Friday, and they're going over the list of words and how to use them. I remember doing the same thing with Mom when I was Beck's age. "Where's Ava and Hannah?"

"Up in Ava's room trying on dresses." I'm about to leave and go in search of her when Mom stops me. "Stay here for a minute. Let them bond for a little bit."

Rolling my eyes, I humor her and go to the fridge to grab myself a blue Gatorade.

"Mom, I think I've got this," Beck says, sounding confident.

"Are you sure, honey?" I shut the refrigerator door just in time to see Mom ruffle Beck's hair so badly, he ducks away from her touch. The hurt look on Mom's face says it all.

Her baby isn't such a baby anymore.

"Yeah. I'm gonna go play *Madden* with my friends online." Beck jumps off the stool. "Night, Jakey!"

"Night, bud," I say with a wince as my brother runs out of the kitchen.

"How was the dinner?" Mom asks once Beck's gone.

"Good. Inspiring."

"And practice?"

"We're as ready as we're ever going to be," I tell her. She doesn't ask, but I know what she's referring to. Things are still tense between Diego and me, but we're doing pretty well about leaving it off the field. What worries me is that Tony twisted his ankle a couple of days ago, so he's been taking it easy, but he claims he's ready for tomorrow.

We'll see. At least the defensive line is healthy and tough as fucking nails, and I know they plan on doing whatever they can to take Eli down.

And speaking of Eli, he hasn't made one of his videos in the last two days. It's some kind of miracle and a relief that I don't have to hear and see him run his mouth. I figured with the game getting this close, he'd be posting stories three times a day just to try to distract us—specifically me.

But no. He's remained disturbingly quiet.

"I have faith in you guys. You want the win," Mom says with all the confidence in us that she normally has.

"They want it too. Nothing would make them happier than to make us lose our homecoming game." That whole ceremony thing during halftime is a big distraction too, and everyone knows it, including the Mustangs. I remember participating in the homecoming halftime ceremony my sophomore year, but it was no big deal then. I was on the JV team and my game was finished. I had all the time in the world.

I won't tomorrow night. I'll be sweaty and tired in my uniform, missing the halftime speech from our coaches in the locker room while I have to stand there out on the field and see if I get crowned or not.

It's kind of a bunch of bullshit, not that I would ever say anything to Hannah. She's so excited about this, and so is Sophie. Tony and I, we're already over it. We care more about the game and beating the Mustangs' asses.

Mom and I make small talk, and a few minutes later Dad's walking into the kitchen, sweeping Mom into his arms and kissing her thoroughly. I look away, only slightly uncomfortable. We're used to our parents hugging and kissing on each other all the time.

I think it's why I always want to hug and kiss on Hannah. It's like I can't stop touching her when she's with me. In fact...

"I'm going to check on Ava and Hannah," I tell my parents, not even waiting for their answer.

I run up the stairs, taking two at a time and stumbling at one point, nearly falling. I can only imagine what would happen if I somehow injured myself and couldn't play the game. My dad would have my ass. Everyone would. They'd be so disappointed.

I'd be disappointed too.

Slowly—carefully—I approach Ava's bedroom, surprised to see the door is open. I can hear Ava and Hannah chatting animatedly inside, both of them laughing, and I pause for a moment, thankful my sister isn't some snobby bitch. She's always been pretty easygoing, more easygoing than our older sister, though I would never call Autumn unkind or arrogant. I have a feeling she'll like Hannah once she meets her.

I'm even more grateful that Ava and Hannah get along. Maybe they could actually be friends. That would be kind of awesome.

"Jake, what are you doing?" Ava suddenly calls.

I move so I'm standing in the open doorway, smiling at them. "How did you know I was in the hall?"

"She could smell you." Ava gestures at Hannah, whose cheeks turn pink. "Creepy, I know."

I enter Ava's bedroom and pull Hannah into my arms, dropping a kiss on her upturned lips. "A little creepy," I agree.

"Hey, I recognize your cologne," Hannah says, smiling up at me.

"Did you find a dress?" I ask Hannah before I glance over at my sister.

"Yes." Ava grabs the dress, which is covered with black plastic. "Remember, don't show it to him. You want it to be a surprise."

Hannah nods as she takes the dress from Ava's hands, slinging it over her arm. "Could you drive me home, Jake? I have homework I need to finish."

Frowning, I grab hold of Hannah's elbow and steer her out of my sister's room as Ava calls goodbye to the both of us. "Want to see my room real quick?"

"Definitely."

When we get to my room, I give her a quick tour, which is probably three times as big as her bedroom, but I don't mention that fact.

"This is where the magic happens?" she says when she approaches the bed.

I laugh and grab her by the waist, pulling her close to me so her back is to my front. She's still clutching the dress in her arms. "No, the magic always seems to happen back at your place," I murmur just before I kiss the side of her neck.

She squirms away from me, laughing. "That tickles."

"You like it." I pause for a moment, not letting her go. "You really have homework?"

"Oh yeah. A lot of it. Might take me all night."

"That sucks. Tomorrow's a big day." All the homecoming festivities are happening from the time school starts and straight through lunch tomorrow. "What shitty teacher is making you do homework?"

Hannah withdraws out of my arms and turns to face me, her expression mysterious. "No one," she whispers, her eyes wide and full of mischief. "I wanted to get out of here so I could spend a little time with you alone at my apartment."

"Oh. Well, shit." Anticipation thrums through my veins at the promise in her words. "Let's get out of here then."

* * *

THE MOMENT we enter Hannah's apartment, she heads straight to her bedroom, where she hangs the dress Ava let her borrow on the back of her door. I follow after her, pulling Hannah into my arms and kissing her thoroughly.

"I missed you," I whisper against her lips once we both come up for air.

She smiles. "We've been together for the last hour."

"Not like this." I slip my fingers beneath her shirt, touching the bare skin of her waist. "We haven't been alone like this for a few days."

"It's been really busy this week," she says, sucking in a

sharp breath when I slide my hand down and across her perfect ass, giving it a squeeze.

"Yeah. Hold on. I'll be right back." I go back out into the living room to make sure the door is locked. I spot Maxine sitting on the couch, sleeping, and I give her a quick scratch before I head back to Hannah's bedroom and shut the door. "Your mom is working?"

She nods, her eyes big as she studies me. "Should we do this?"

"What do you mean?"

Hannah's quiet for a moment before she says, "You know what I mean."

I do. I know exactly what she's referring to. I have two condoms in my wallet. I put them in there this morning for some reason, feeling like it was going to happen soon.

Like right now.

"We should," I say. "But only if you want to."

She toes off her shoes and I follow her lead, kicking off my Nike slides, though I leave my socks on. "I want to do this."

Just like that, my dick is hard. She barely has to touch me and I get hard, so there's that.

"I do too," I tell her just before I lunge toward her.

We tumble to the bed, our mouths fused, our bodies entwined. We're lying side by side, our legs tangled up, our hands wandering, our kisses spiraling out of control. Our teeth clack together as our tongues seek each other's, and I flip her over so she's lying on her back and I can take control of this situation.

She lets me take control, and I like that. There's never a struggle, and it never feels awkward between us. It just... happens.

Naturally.

We help each other shed our clothes, until we're

completely naked. She runs her hands over my shoulders, my chest, my stomach, her fingers seeking my cock. When she grabs hold of me, I groan, a shudder moving through me as she strokes and strokes, taking me right to the brink. I bat her hand away and she laughs, trying to grab me again.

But I won't let her.

It's my turn to drive her out of her mind. I kiss her breasts. Suck her nipples. Lick her stomach. I kiss the inside of her thighs, put my mouth on her molten-hot pussy and suck and lick. Just when she's right at the edge, I back off, rising up on my knees with a smile.

"You're a jerk," she pouts, and I smile, my heart tight, my emotions threatening to overwhelm me.

God, what I feel for this girl…I can't find the words.

Well, I can. In fact, I decide to tell her how I feel at this very moment.

"I love you," I tell her, shocked that the words slipped out of my mouth so easily.

She blinks up at me, her big blue eyes wide. "Really?"

I nod, for some reason unable to speak. Too overwhelmed with emotion, I guess. This is what she does to me. She makes me want. She makes me feel. She eases my mood, she makes me smile, she makes me laugh. Since she entered my life and rejected me without hesitation, I've been intrigued. I still am.

The need to know everything about her consumes me. She consumes me. And I like it.

Bending over her, I kiss her for long, tongue-filled minutes, trying to communicate with my actions how much I care about her. "I've fallen in love with you," I whisper against her lips. "I love you, Hannah. So fucking much."

"I love you too." She wraps her arms around my neck, her hands in my hair, her gaze locked on mine as we stare at each other. "I do."

"Yeah?" I smile at her and she smiles in return.

"Yeah. Did you bring a condom?" she asks hopefully.

Chuckling, I crawl off her bed and grab my shorts from where I discarded them on the floor, opening my wallet and pulling out the two condoms I stashed in there this morning. "I've got two," I say, waving them at her.

"I think we'll only need one. We have to go to bed early. We have a big day tomorrow," she says primly, and I start laughing all over again.

This girl. She's the only one who can make me forget my troubles. Who can lift my mood. Who can make me laugh during sex and make me fall in love with her.

How'd I get so lucky?

CHAPTER 36

HANNAH

*H*ow did I get so lucky? My boyfriend is currently standing naked in my bedroom, two condoms dangling from his fingers, while I lay naked in the middle of my bed, hot and anxious for him to join me.

We're going to have sex right here, right now. And I'm so ready. I love him. He loves me. We're in love. And this is the perfect time to have sex, right? During homecoming week, the night before the big game, both of us showing our love for each other in the purest, most primitive, natural way.

"What are you waiting for?" I ask, and he joins me in bed, pulling the comforter over us, and depositing the condoms on my rickety bedside table, along with his phone.

He pulls me into him and kisses me, his tongue doing a thorough search of my mouth. I can taste myself on his lips, on his tongue, and it turns me on, which might be weird, but I'm running with it. Jake doesn't judge me or have certain expectations when it comes to me, to us, to sex.

That's one of my favorite qualities about him. We accept each other. Once we got past the bullshit, it became easy between us, and I love that.

I love him.

"You look so pretty right now," he whispers once he breaks the kiss, his gaze following the same path that his fingers take as he drifts them across my body. I smile up at him, my heart growing light at the tender glow in his beautiful blue eyes. "I can't believe you're mine."

"Oh my God, stop. You're going to make me cry," I tell him, my voice thick with emotion as I close my eyes, fighting the tears that threaten to spill.

"Hell no, don't cry." He kisses me again, and I laugh against his lips, a few tears falling anyway. He brushes them from my cheeks with gentle fingers before he kisses them away, kissing me all over my face. His soft lips blaze a path across my chin, my jaw, my nose, my cheekbones, my forehead. Just before he returns to my mouth, his tongue thrusting, his hands starting to wander.

"I don't want to hurt you," he says minutes later, his fingers between my legs, testing me. I'm wet. I can actually hear how wet I am, and I spread my thighs wider, closing my eyes when he hits a particularly sensitive spot.

I'm a little bit scared, not gonna lie. Having sex could shift our relationship. It changes things. This is a serious moment. A big one. Jake Callahan will be the boy who takes my virginity, and I will never, ever forget him.

"You won't hurt me," I whisper, gasping when he brushes my clit with his thumb. We've messed around so much the past few weeks, we know each other's sensitive spots. It's been the best time of my life, these nights with Jake. And the days too. At school, hanging out with his friends and mine. Watching him play football.

It's straight out of one of my favorite teen movies. The ones with the happy endings.

"I probably will," he says, sounding miserable, which is the cutest thing. "It's your first time."

"Then make it count," I tell him, and when he looks at me, I smile tremulously, trying to be brave. "I won't break, Jake. Just—let's do it. Please."

He grabs a condom and tears open the wrapper, rolling the latex on. Watching him fills me with need, especially when he gives his erection a quick tug after putting the condom on. I wonder if he'll let me watch him jerk off one day.

I'll have to ask him. But not tonight.

We get into position, Jake shifting me around easily on the mattress, until his erection is poised at my entry. I spread my legs as wide as possible, ready to feel him enter me, and then he's right there, the tip of him brushing against my folds, teasing me. It feels so good, I can't help but whimper, and then he starts to press inside.

He's thick, filling me. Pushing deeper. Deeper. There's a pinch. A sudden sense of being extremely uncomfortable, like he's about to push through a too-tight hole. But he has infinite patience as he keeps going, slowly sliding deeper, until he's fully inside me.

Once he stops moving, my eyelids flutter open to find him hanging above me, his eyes tightly closed, the muscles in his neck standing out in stark relief. Sweat drips from his head and I reach up, touching his cheek gently. He opens his eyes, gazing at me with so many emotions swirling in his eyes. Love. Lust. Raw need. Hope. Worry.

"It doesn't hurt," I tell him, and his brows wrinkle as if he's confused.

"Are you sure?"

I nod as I move my hips, testing myself. Testing him. So far, so good. "It feels—nice."

"Nice?" Jake shakes his head. "You want it to feel better than nice."

Before I can say anything, he starts moving, drawing

almost all the way out of me before he pushes inside. Again and again he does this, starting out slow at first. Slow and easy. I adjust to his movements, picking up his rhythm, until we're moving together. Faster and faster. Harder and harder. At one point, I can only cling to him, letting him take me, watching him with utter fascination. He's beautiful. What we're doing right now, it's beautiful, because we love each other and this moment, this night, means everything to me. To him.

Glancing down, I can see him entering me, pulling out, entering me again. My body starts to tingle the longer I watch us. It's like having my own personal porn channel, which makes me giggle.

Jake pauses, breathing heavily, his chest heaving as his gaze meets mine. "What's so funny?"

"I'm, um, watching you—you know—down there." I start giggling again, a little embarrassed, which is ridiculous. Sex is weird. And wonderful. "And I thought, wow, it's like watching my own personal porn channel."

He looks down too, his gaze glued to the spot where our bodies are joined, and he flexes his hips as he pushes in, then slowly withdraws. "That's fucking hot," he murmurs, his head bent, his hair tickling my skin.

"I know," I murmur back, a whimper leaving me when he starts moving faster. We're both watching, and I can feel it building. The tingling. My muscles growing tight, my inner walls clenching, my breaths quick. I'm ready to fall over that ledge.

Jake kisses me. "I love you," he whispers against my lips, and that sends me over the edge. I'm falling. Coming. My entire body shivering and tingling as I clutch him tight. The last shudders ripple through me just as Jake starts coming with a grunt, thrusting one last time, holding himself pressed deep inside me as he shakes, my name falling from his lips with a groan before he collapses on top of me.

"Well, that happened fast," I tell him minutes later, when we're wrapped around each other and staring at the ceiling.

"It was kind of hard for me to control myself," he admits, and I kiss his chest, thankful for his honesty. "You're lucky I wasn't a two-pump chump."

I start laughing. "That would've sucked."

"I wanted to make it good for you." His voice is very serious.

"You did." I tip my head back and we kiss, our lips clinging. "It was so good."

His phone dings with a notification and he reaches for it automatically, like he can't help himself. The after-sex glow is leaving me mellow and happy, so I don't protest. I'd probably do the same thing.

"Fuck," he mutters, tapping the screen so Instagram opens. "Eli finally posted to his story and tagged me in it."

Dread makes my heart drop, along with a healthy dose of irritation. I am so over Eli Bennett and his ridiculous stories. He's a complete dick, and I hate what he says about my boyfriend and me.

Jake leans back and holds the phone so both of us can see it. The story starts and it's from one of their school rallies. Every member of their football team is being announced, and the story stops on Eli right after he's introduced, pausing on him mid strut into the gymnasium, his arms above his head and a giant grin on his face. "Eye of the Tiger" starts playing.

"This guy's ego is out of control," Jake mutters with disgust.

"Stop watching it then. Who cares what he has to say?" If I could snatch that phone out of his hand and turn it off, I so would.

"I have to watch it," he says, never tearing his gaze from the phone.

I roll my eyes but say nothing. Now the video switches to a close-up of Eli's jersey. A purple number one in the middle of his chest. He's such an arrogant ass.

"See this, Callahan?" A finger appears, and I assume it's Eli's. "Number one, baby. I'm number one in the mountain area, and don't you ever fuckin' forget it. Last three games, we've won. Four and one, and we're about to make it five and one as of tomorrow night. Homecoming's gonna suck for you, bro. Sorry 'bout it." He starts laughing, and Jake makes a disgusted noise.

The camera pulls back and now Eli's filling the screen, the arrogance in his expression impossible to ignore.

"You and your pretty redhead? Ain't. Gonna. Win." Eli claps between each word. "My money's on Cami and your best friend. They're the real couple right now, though rumor has it someone else is knocked up with a little baby Diego." Eli taps his finger against his bottom lip, before a devious smile spreads across his face. "You never heard that from me, though."

Oh crap. Is he talking about *Jocelyn?*

"Such a shame you won't get that crown, Callahan, and you won't get the win on the field either, so it's going to be a double loss tomorrow night. Your girlie will console you, though. You two seem really into each other. I wish you the best," Eli continues.

"He doesn't mean it," I start, but Jake hushes me.

Huh. That was kind of annoying. I mean hello, we just had sex and said we loved each other. Now he's shushing me so he can listen to Eli go on and on.

"...there won't be much celebrating happening tomorrow, I'm guessing. Will you two show up to the homecoming dance Saturday night? I'm hoping to go with my favorite princess, but we'll see. She's worried about causing trouble, but I told her you won't even notice, will you, *bro?*"

The story ends.

"Fuck." Jake sits up, pushing the comforter off and climbing out of bed. "Shit, fuck." He runs his hand through his hair as he bends over and starts grabbing his clothing and jerking everything on.

I sit up too, clutching the comforter to my chest as I watch him get dressed. "What's wrong?"

"It's bothered me for weeks. He keeps mentioning some mystery girl, and at first I thought he was talking about Cami. But that theory went to shit when we figured out she's messing around with Diego." He pulls on his shorts, forgetting his underwear, and then tugs on his T-shirt. "He just gave me all the clues. I think I figured it out."

"Who's he talking about?" I don't think I picked up one clue from all that shit talking Eli just did. It all sounds like a bunch of garbage if you ask me.

"Coming to our dance with his favorite *princess?* Heavy emphasis on the word *bro?*" Jake shakes his head, his eyes glazed, his mouth hanging open slightly for a moment. I think he might be in shock. "He's talking about my sister. Ava."

"*What?*" No freaking way. She wouldn't see Eli behind her family's back.

Would she?

"Yeah. Yeah, I think that's it. He's with Ava. He's messing around with *Ava.* Or at least, that's what he claims. It can't be true. No way. Fuck that. She wouldn't do that to me. To our school, to our family." He sits on the edge of the bed and slips on his socks—I don't even remember him taking them off—and then scoots his feet into his slides. "I gotta go."

"Jake—" I start, but he rises to his feet, turning to face me. "Please don't go. Not now. Calm down first. You can't go blazing into your sister's room in the middle of the night and demand that she tells you what's going on."

"Why the hell not? He's the fucker who's been taunting my ass for *months*. And if he's actually been secretly fucking around with my sister this entire time? Shit." Jake shakes his head. "I'll feel like a complete dumbass."

"Maybe they really like each other," I suggest, but Jake scoffs.

"Please. He's using her."

"People could say the same thing about you with me."

"This is different. *We're* different." He sends me a pained look. "You don't believe that, do you? You're everything to me."

My heart constricts at his words, and the raw emotion behind them. "Of course not," I say automatically.

"Good, good." He glances around as he shoves his hand into his pocket, jangling his keys, completely distracted. "I should go."

"No." He's standing close enough that I can reach out and grab his hand. "Stay here with me. Just for a little while longer."

I can see his internal struggle. He wants to stay with me. He also wants to go home so he can confront Ava. I know he needs to talk to her, but he will say something he regrets if he goes to her in anger.

"Please," I murmur when he still hasn't said anything.

With a big sigh he collapses on the bed with me, pulling me in close. I rest my head against his chest, his heart hammering beneath my ear. We lay there in silence for a few minutes, my mind racing, going over everything Jake just said.

"Shit's always happening," he mutters, his fingers tangling in the ends of my hair. "I wish I could just sit here in your room for the next week and spend time with you. No one else."

"I wish we could too." I drape my arm across his middle and tilt my head back to find he's already watching me. "But that's not very realistic."

"Maybe we could get out of here after football season," he says. "Go away for the weekend."

In my dreams.

"I don't know if my mom would agree to that," I say as I settle my head on his chest once more.

He chuckles, the sound reverberating against my ear. "My parents probably won't go for it either."

We talk like this, about nothing and everything, for almost an hour. About football and family and hopes and dreams. We don't mention Eli or Ava at all. Eventually, his heart calms down—and hopefully his anger does too.

"It's late. I should go," he finally says as he slowly climbs out of my bed. "You understand, right Banana? I love you."

I scramble out of bed when he swiftly exits my bedroom, grateful I had him grab an old T-shirt for me halfway through our conversation so I'm not completely naked. I walk out into the living room to find him already at the door and undoing the lock.

"Maybe you should talk to Ava tomorrow, Jake. In the morning. Sleep on this first," I suggest. He turns to face me for a second, his jaw going tight. And then he tears his gaze from mine, like he can't look at me. Because he can't make that promise, I can tell.

"I'll be calm," he tells me, his voice tense, though his gaze is soft as he studies me. "I'll listen to what she has to say."

"Promise me you will. *Promise.*" I send him a pleading look and he nods. "And text me later. Okay? Let me know how it goes."

"I will. I promise," he says before he kisses me, his lips

lingering on mine. I can taste the regret there. Not regret over what happened between us, but what's happening now thanks to Eli. "Tonight was—perfect."

"Until now," I murmur, and the relief that hits me when he smiles and chuckles almost knocks me over.

"Yeah. Until now. But we'll be better tomorrow." He kisses me again. "I love you."

I don't think I'll ever get tired of hearing him say those three words. "I love you too. Drive safe, okay?"

"I will." He hugs me one last time. "Bye."

My heart races as I remain standing in front of the door and watch him drive out of our parking lot. Worry lingers long after he's gone, making me wish I'd left with him. So many emotions are swirling within me, I don't know what to do, or how to think. All I can focus on is Eli Bennett. I hate what he's done to Jake.

To us.

CHAPTER 37

JAKE

*A*ll I wanted to do was floor it all the way home so I could talk to Ava that much sooner, but I restrained myself. I drove the speed limit. Pulled into our driveway slowly. Parked my truck, locked it. Slipped inside the house as quietly as possible so as not to disturb anyone. Like my parents.

Like my sister.

I creep up the stairs like I'm breaking into my own house, hesitating in front of Ava's closed door. I carefully lean my head against the wood, can hear voices coming from within the room, and I'm positive she's watching something on her laptop. That's her usual evening routine when she's home, which isn't often anymore. Hell, I'm not home much myself.

I don't think she's talking to someone. I don't hear her.

Shit. What if she is? What if she's talking to Eli?

Frustration rips through me and I tell myself to keep it together. It was tough, but I kept my anger in check the entire drive home. I focused instead on Hannah. What happened between us tonight. That's what should make this night memorable. The fact that we finally had sex, that we confessed we're in love with each other. That's a big fucking deal.

But finding out my little sister is messing around with an asshole who's been tormenting me for months—no, *years*—that's a pretty big fucking deal too.

I decide to hell with it and knock quickly before I open the door and stride inside her room like I own the place. Ava's in bed, leaning against a pile of pillows under her fluffy white comforter, her laptop resting on the bed to her right. She blinks rapidly when she spots me, leaning over to tap the spacebar to pause whatever she's watching. The look she gives me is the typical *what the hell do you want* expression she usually reserves only for me.

"You're out late," she says.

"We need to talk," I tell her through clenched teeth as I stop at the foot of her bed.

She sits up straighter, tilting her head to the side. "Nice of you to just barge right on in uninvited."

"I figured you'd tell me to go away if I asked through the door," I say honestly.

"You'd be right. I would've," she answers just as honestly in return.

We're quiet for a moment, staring each other down. Does she know I know? She doesn't look scared or worried. She appears completely unaffected. Irritation is written all over her face though, so I'm pretty positive she thinks I'm just being an annoying big brother.

"Ava," I finally say when I can't take the silence any longer.

"Jake," she returns, mimicking my tone.

"Tell me the truth." I pause for only a moment before I continue. "Are you seeing someone in secret?"

More rapid blinking. Her cheeks turn the faintest shade of pink and she drops her gaze. Like she can't look at me. "No. Don't you think you'd know if I was seeing someone?"

"So you're not…dating anyone." I rest my hands on my hips, staring her down even though she's not looking at me.

"No, I'm not."

"Not even someone at say…a different school."

Her gaze meets mine once more, her expression completely neutral. "No."

Damn. I gotta give it to her. I figured she'd crack immediately, but so far she's holding strong. I almost want to believe her.

Almost.

"What are you trying to say huh, Jake? What are you getting at?" she asks when I stay silent for a little too long. She sounds put out. Irritated. Like this conversation is a minor annoyance, when it's anything but.

Because if she really is seeing Eli, this is huge. I will look like the biggest idiot alive if Eli is fucking around with my sister behind my back. It's humiliating, knowing that he could've said stuff to Ava, and maybe they both laughed about me. How stupid I am, that I didn't even know. That I didn't even *see.*

Too wrapped up in my own bullshit to notice what's playing out right in front of my fucking face.

"You're a liar," I finally say, my voice deathly quiet.

She lifts her chin, defiant as usual. She was the youngest child for many years until Beck came along. The spoiled princess. Autumn and I gave her endless crap when we were little, especially Autumn. Sister jealousy is a real and sometimes messy thing.

But they love each other just as fiercely as they fight. Autumn will protect Ava to the bitter end, especially against me. If she knew I was having this confrontation with Ava right now, she'd probably be pissed. Defensive of Ava.

Well, Autumn isn't around to protect Ava. It's just me and her.

"What are you talking about?" Ava asks. "If you're just going to antagonize me all night, you should leave. I need to go to sleep. We have a big day tomorrow."

She sounds like Hannah. I remember how I promised her I'd be calm when I spoke to Ava. And that I'd let Hannah know what was going on.

I can't worry about Hannah right now.

"You're with Eli, aren't you." It's not a question. I know she's with him.

A sigh escapes her and she throws her hands up into the air before they flop against the comforter. "You saw his Instagram story."

She doesn't bother denying it. "You're damn right I did. And he dropped enough clues for me to finally figure this shit out," I say vehemently.

"I keep telling him to delete it," she says her voice bitter as she shakes her head. "He finally did."

Icy cold shock washes over me at her words, at her confirmation that she talks to him. Holy shit. "You spoke to him. Tonight."

Ava hangs her head, plucking at the comforter fabric. The air shifts in the room, and it's like I can feel how uncomfortable she is. "Yeah."

"Because you two are together."

More silence. And it's downright deafening because the longer she remains quiet, the more I know—I fucking *know*—she's with that guy.

"Do you know what this is going to do to my reputation at school?" I tell her, my voice rising. She puts her finger to her lips, reminding me I need to keep quiet, and I lower my tone, but only because I don't want my parents to find out about this. Not yet. "Everyone at school is going to laugh at me, knowing you were seeing Eli behind my back. Playing me for a fool like that. Jesus, Eli must *love* this."

"Jake, my relationship with Eli has nothing to do with you," she starts, but I interrupt her by laughing my ass off. In fact, I keep laughing for so long, she crosses her arms and glares at me for a few minutes until she finally asks, "Are you finished now?"

"No," I say, my laughter dying. "I'm not even close to being finished with you. And you know this has everything to do with me, Ava. He's my biggest rival. Eli and I have hated each other for years."

"It's pointless, your rivalry. I keep telling him that, but he won't listen to me. He's just as stubborn as you," she says morosely.

"Do not compare me to that asshole." I jab my finger in her direction.

She rolls her eyes. "You sound just like him. I swear to God, you two are so similar sometimes, it's scary. That's why you hate each other. You're in constant competition with yourselves and with each other."

"That doesn't make any sense."

"It makes perfect sense, Jake! You two are cut from the same cloth, just like Dad, just like Ash Davis, just like Diego and Caleb and Tony and all the boys on Eli's team too. You're all highly competitive, overrun-with-testosterone guys who are out for each other's blood, and it's ridiculous. It's just a football game," Ava says.

Her words shake me to my core. "*Just* a football game? Are you listening to yourself right now? I know you don't give a shit about sports, but this game is everything to me. This entire season is do or die. We have to win. We've never lost to the Mustangs and I refuse to be the first team to lose to them in our game history. I fucking refuse, Ava."

"Eli is dying to be the first quarterback to get the win against our team," she admits softly.

"Interesting how you call it *our* team," I tell her.

"Because it is. I go to that school just like you do. I'm a cheerleader there. It's our team," she retorts.

"You're a traitor," I say, my voice low, my blood pressure boiling. My accusation makes her flinch.

"You're being unreasonable," she says.

"How long has this been going on?"

"It doesn't matter—"

"How long?"

"Jake, seriously. What does it ma—"

"Ava! How. Long?"

She looks away again, her lips forming a pout that reminds me of when she was little. She used to pout like that a lot. Dad always gave into that face. I'm not about to fall for that shit though. "Since…the summer."

I'm shook all over again. "Are you serious right now? When exactly did you two start—seeing each other?"

"At the football camp at Heron Lake in June." Her gaze meets mine once more, and I see the regret there that she's hurt me. That it's come to this. I see the worry and the sadness, it's all there, pouring out of her green gaze. Eyes like Mom. She's blonde like Mom too. I can see why Eli was drawn to her.

But he's just using her. I know he is. He's going to leave her behind, she's going to cry and it's going to be hard to comfort her because I won't be able to stop thinking that she should've known better.

"I didn't mean for this to happen. You have to know this, Jake. I don't want to hurt you, and neither does Eli. Not like this. What we're doing shouldn't matter to you. Like I said earlier before you interrupted me, our relationship has nothing to do with you. Eli cares about me, and I…"

She swallows hard, and I swear to God, her eyes glisten with tears.

"I care about him too," she admits in a choked whisper. "A lot."

"He's using you," I say calmly.

"No, he's not," she says. "Don't you get it? This has nothing to do with you, Jake. The world doesn't revolve around you and football and all that other bullshit. This is about me and Eli. We're in love."

I laugh again, one short bark before I clamp my lips shut. "That fucker doesn't know how to love."

"What do you know about him? Huh?" When I say nothing, her expression turns triumphant. "Nothing, that's what I thought."

"I know he's using you to get to me. He doesn't give a shit about you," I spit out.

That was the wrong thing to say. Ava's face turns beet red and she hops out of bed, pointing at the door. "Get out."

Now I'm the one blinking at her. "What?"

"Get. Out," she bites out. "I'm not going to let you tell me what Eli feels or how he's using me. You have no clue what you're talking about. Leave my room. Now."

I stare at her for a moment. She stares back. I exhale loudly and she doesn't move a muscle. She's still as a statue. Her face is stony. Like a mask.

Like I don't know my sister at all.

* * *

I TAKE A LONG SHOWER, trying to wash my anger away but it doesn't help. My sister is with Eli Bennett. She's been with Eli for months. She claims they're in love.

I can hardly wrap my mind around it.

Once I'm out of the shower, I wipe the condensation away from the mirror, staring at my reflection. Funny, how everything can look normal, yet you've had your world rocked in the most unexpected way.

Only when I'm in bed do I finally text Hannah, feeling like a complete jerk. I shouldn't have put her off. She's the most important person to me, yet tonight, the first time we have actual sex, it's almost as if I treat her like an afterthought.

I don't deserve this girl.

I'm home. Safe. ILY

That's all I say, because what else can I say? Sorry I'm an asshole? Sorry I took your virginity then ran out on you?

Hannah immediately responds.

I love you too. How did it go with Ava?

I don't even hesitate when I type out and send her my answer.

It's all true. She's been with Eli for MONTHS. Since the summer. She admitted everything to me.

Consumed with frustration, I call the first person I can think of. The person I know will understand where I'm coming from.

"You okay?" This is how Tony greets me. It's not normal for me to call him at one in the morning, so of course, he assumes I'm in some sort of trouble.

"I found out something."

"What?"

"Eli's been with Ava."

There's silence, and I can only assume Tony is processing what I just told him. "Like they're actually together? Boyfriend and girlfriend?"

"Yeah," I rasp out. "She admitted it."

"So that's who he's been talking about," he says. "The princess."

"You saw his story?" I ask.

"I did. He's a prick, Jake. Don't let him get in your head.

We'll take him down," Tony says with all the assuredness I need to hear.

"My sister will hate me," I tell him, tamping down the anguish that threatens. I feel so conflicted. I want to pound Eli's smug face in, but I know that'll hurt Ava, especially if she's telling the truth when she says she loves him.

Did she ever care about hurting me?

"It is what it is," Tony says, sounding resolute. "This information will only push you to take them down even harder tomorrow night."

"True." I pause before I say, "Thanks, man."

"For what?"

"For answering my call. For not overreacting when I told you what I found out." A few weeks ago it would've been Diego I called first, and he would've demanded we go to Eli's house and call him out. Or fuck up his car. Do something destructive, it wouldn't matter what. He would've encouraged me to send a message, and I would've happily agreed.

"We don't need to do anything except play tomorrow's game and win. There's no need for anything else," Tony says.

I blow out a harsh breath. "You're right."

"You gonna be okay?"

"I'll be fine," I say, even though it feels like I'm lying through my teeth.

"Call me if you need anything else," he says. "I'll answer no matter what time it is."

"I know. Thanks." I end the call before I get emotional, which is lame. But damn, this shit is overwhelming.

It's messing with my head.

There's a text notification from Hannah.

What are you going to do?

I respond immediately.

Destroy him.

CHAPTER 38

HANNAH

"You look beautiful," Sophie says to me, her tone reverent as I stand before her in the dress I borrowed from Jake's sister for the halftime ceremony. "I love your dress."

"Thank you," I say just before I hug her. "I love yours too."

It's Friday night, and we're in the classroom building that's closest to the football field, getting ready for the half-time coronation. Cami is somewhere in here too, along with the other girls who won homecoming princess for their class. Like Ava.

But Ava's keeping her distance from me, and I hate that. I'm sure it all has to do with what happened between her and Jake last night, and their argument about her relationship with Eli.

Earlier this morning, Jake told me about the conversation he had with his sister, but didn't offer up too many details, and I didn't ask. We've had so much going on today with all the homecoming festivities like the parade and the rally. It's been too difficult for us to have a serious discussion in private. So I let it go for now.

And while Jake has been pretty much his normal self when I've been with him today, I know it bothers him, that Ava and Eli are together.

Worse? He finds out about their relationship right before tonight's big game.

I suppose I can't blame him for being upset. Though he probably shouldn't take it so personal. We can't help who we fall in love with, right? Because that's what Ava told him, that she's in love with Eli Bennett, and he feels the same.

Mind blowing.

"I'm so nervous." Sophie shakes her hands out, then does a weird little hop step that makes her skirt flare out. "Worse than I get when I'm about to go onstage and perform at a dance comp."

I drink her in, admiring her gorgeous dress yet again. It's a simple A-line style, strapless, ice-blue satin fabric. There's a slit in the skirt that rises pretty high, but Sophie can carry it off with her long legs. If I were wearing it, I'd probably flash my underwear all night.

"You'll be fine." I reach out and press my hand to hers. "I hope you win."

"No, I hope you win," she tells me.

"Neither of you bitches are going to win," says a familiar voice from behind us.

We both turn to find Cami watching us, her hair pulled back into a high ponytail that's so tight, I swear her eyes look tugged back at the corners as if they're permanently narrowed. She's wearing a long yellow dress, with delicate flowers appliqued to the bodice and waist, with a gauzy pale yellow skirt. The straps are made out of glittering stones, and she's rocking a serious spray tan that's a tad too dark. If I didn't dislike her so much, I'd tell her that her dress is beautiful, because it is.

But I keep my mouth shut and glare at her instead.

"Butt out," Sophie says to Cami, surprising me.

Cami sneers. "You two are pitiful."

"Seriously, Cami, leave us alone," Sophie says, her voice firm. "If you can't be nice, then we don't want you around."

Cami glares at us, and I swear she's sputtering as she tries to come up with something to say. In the end, she stomps her foot like a spoiled child and huffs off, gathering her skirt in her hands as she runs away.

Sophie and I turn to look at each other once she's gone. "You're so brave," I tell my friend.

"I'm over her antics," Sophie says with a little wave of her hand. "Mean girl vibes have no place here tonight."

"No kidding."

"Five minutes!" someone suddenly yells. "We'll be headed out to the field in five minutes, so hurry up, everyone!"

I glance at myself in the full-length mirror someone brought just for tonight. The dress I borrowed from Ava is long and white and lacy. The skirt and bodice are made of tulle and it's sleeveless, with a deep V in the front, though it doesn't necessarily reveal too much. The dress almost looks like it should be completely see-through, but there's a nude lining underneath, covering everything. It's the most sophisticated dress I've ever worn in my life.

I'm sure it cost a fortune. I'm so grateful to Ava for letting me borrow it.

Within minutes we're lined up at the doors, Mrs. Adney leading us out to the campus golf carts that will take us to the field where the ceremony is being held. We load into the golf carts, each class couple sitting together and me and Sophie on the back of one, while Cami rides alone in another with a sulk on her face.

As we draw closer to the field, I can see the scoreboard. There's less than a minute on the clock and the first half is over.

And we're…

Losing.

By a single touchdown.

Worry gnaws at my gut. Jake is going to be distracted. Upset. I *hate* that we're losing. Yes, we still have the entire second half to turn it around, but Jake is going to blame himself, and I don't know if I'm going to be able to console him.

"They're losing," Sophie says as she leans in close to me.

"Yeah." I send her a tight smile. "This sucks."

"God, I know! But we can't focus on that. We just have to smile and look pretty, right?" Sophie puts on a dazzling smile and does this weird jazz hands thing, making me laugh. "It isn't the end of the world if we lose to them, though I'm sure the boys will be totally disappointed."

I don't bother telling her most everyone at school will be disappointed. And most likely the community too. This is such a huge game. Homecoming against our biggest rival, and Jake is carrying all the responsibility on his shoulders, even though he's not the sole reason why they win or lose.

Doesn't matter. He still feels responsible.

Once the buzzer sounds and the second quarter is over, the team jogs off the field, with the exception of the boys who are participating in the ceremony. Jake, Diego and Tony head toward us, with Wyatt, the junior homecoming prince, just ahead of them.

There's lots of chaos as everyone gets ready. Adney is trying her best to coordinate us properly as they announce the winners by class, leading up to the seniors. Jake approaches me with a strained smile on his face, his eyes widening when he takes me in.

"Damn, girl, you look fucking gorgeous," he breathes as he stops to stand beside me.

My cheeks go hot and I smile up at him as we hook our arms together. "Thank you."

"I'm afraid to touch you." He's a mess. They're wearing their white uniforms tonight, and his is already dirty, like he's been through a lot. There's a streak of blood across the front of his jersey, and his dark hair is curling at the ends and damp with sweat. There's black smudges beneath his eyes and even though he's all sweaty and banged up, he looks...

Hot.

"Oh, you can touch me," I say with a little smile, my voice flirtatious.

He smiles but it fades fast as we wait our turn. "They're winning."

"I saw."

"Eli is being extra dickish tonight."

"Are you surprised?" I ask him.

"Not really." He glances down at me, his hot gaze trailing over me, making me shiver. "I have to win this game."

"You will," I tell him, trying my best to be positive. That's what he needs to hear. I'm not about to bring him down right now.

"I wish I felt as positive as you sound," he says with a wistful sigh.

"Just focus on winning," I say, keeping my voice low so hopefully no one can hear me. "Don't let Eli get into your head. Or anyone else. Just focus on the game, on each play, and make it happen."

"Okay coach," he says, and his good-natured tone makes me relax. "I appreciate the pep talk."

"Any time," I tell him breezily.

Each class prince and princess are announced before they stand in a line against the backdrop that people from my leadership class set up hurriedly once the quarter was finished. Once Wyatt and Ava are presented as the junior class prince and princess, it's time for the seniors to come out.

Tony and Sophie walk out first.

Then Diego and Cami.

And finally, me and Jake.

I'm a bundle of nervous energy as our student body president talks about homecoming traditions, how important they are, and then reminds students about the dance tomorrow night. They draw the moment out for what feels like forever, and I'm trembling like a leaf.

"It's okay," Jake says to me. "You're my queen no matter what."

I glance up at him with a giant smile, my nerves momentarily forgotten. "That's the cheesiest thing you've ever said to me."

"First, our homecoming king is…Anthony Sorrento!"

The stands roar with approval and my heart dips for only the briefest moment before it soars back up. Tony won. I bet this means that…

"And tonight's homecoming queen is…"

There's a drumroll from the band up in the stands and the wait is excruciating.

"Sophie Whitmore!"

More cheering. Diego looks relieved. So does Jake. Sophie is laugh-crying as Mrs. Adney sets the sparkling crown on her head. I'm clapping so hard my palms hurt, and there are tears in my eyes. Tears of happiness for my friend.

I'm not sure how this happened, but we've gone from the loner crowd to Sophie winning homecoming queen in a matter of weeks. Is that because of who she's dating?

Probably.

Does that make the majority of our student body shallow?

Sure does.

But who cares? This is a moment Sophie will never, ever

forget. And neither will I. Our photos from tonight, from the entire week, will be in the yearbook, captured forever.

"I have to go," Jake tells me once the ceremony is over and we're supposed to head back to the building so we can change into our regular clothes.

Sophie and Tony are still taking photos for the yearbook staff and various family members, and I'm pretty sure there's a photographer from the local newspaper snapping a few pictures too. Diego is already gone, headed for the locker room.

"Good luck," I tell Jake, right before he wraps me up in his arms and hugs me tight. I press my face against his chest, grimacing when I feel his protective gear beneath his jersey shift beneath my cheek.

"You are so beautiful," he whispers as he reluctantly pulls away, his hands cupping my face. I smile up at him and he dips his head, kissing me softly. "I love you."

"I love you too." I rise up on my tiptoes and give him one last kiss. "You're going to win."

"I hope you're right."

"I know I am," I say with as much confidence as I can muster.

As I watch my boyfriend jog across the field toward the locker room, my heart pangs. I hope I'm right. I hope they win tonight.

If they don't, there will be hell to pay.

And Jake won't have any problem collecting.

CHAPTER 39

JAKE

It's midway through the fourth quarter and we're finally leading on the board—by one touchdown. My nerves are shot to hell. I'm so tense, I feel like a gentle breeze could wash over me and I'd break apart. I've been clenching my jaw the entirety of the game, and it aches like a bitch.

I'm a damn mess. We all are, especially the seniors. This game is everything to us. Last homecoming, last chance to play our rivals, last chance to beat them. We aren't going down without a fight, and we're trying our damnedest to win.

No way will I go down in school history as the first quarterback to lose to the motherfuckin' Mustangs.

From the start of the game, Dad and I couldn't talk to each other without getting heated, so we're keeping our distance. And it's okay. I get it. He's tense too. He might want this just as bad as I do.

Okay. Probably not. But pretty close.

The ceremony during halftime was a big distraction I wish we could've avoided, but seeing Hannah looking gorgeous in that dress was worth it. My girl is beautiful. I am lucky she's mine, and I don't tell her that enough. Once this game is over and I can breathe normally again, I'll tell her. I'll let her know on the daily that she makes me feel like the luckiest man on the planet.

I'm just glad I didn't win. Tony's our homecoming king and I felt total relief when I heard his name called. I didn't need that win, though I know Hannah was excited for it. I wanted the win for her, never for me. She was so happy for her best friend though, and extremely glad Cami didn't win. I can't blame her.

"Hey."

I glance to my right to find Diego standing beside me, his helmet dangling from his fingers, his hair a wild mess around his head, his gaze focused on the field, just like mine. Swallowing hard, I try to keep my voice easy. "What's up?"

"You're not still mad at me, are you?" When I glance over at him, I find he's already looking at me. "I hate that our friendship blew up over girls. It was always bros before hos, right?"

He starts out well and screws it up by calling Hannah—and Cami and Jocelyn—hos. Typical Diego. "I'm not mad at you."

It's the truth. Anger is a draining emotion. It's exhausting, being so pissed off all the time, and I'm trying my best to control it. The therapist mentioned in our first session that I might have oppositional defiant disorder, which can be linked to ADD. And while I was resistant to her suggestion, I did a little research that night after I got home.

And I think that might be what I have. It makes sense. I had ADD when I was a kid, but I seemed to "calm down," as my parents put it, and they eventually took me off the meds. I never liked the foggy feeling those pills gave me anyway.

I don't know what that diagnosis would mean for me and

how I'd have to deal with it, but at least I'd know what's causing me to feel this way all the time.

"It's no excuse, but I've been dealing with some shit, and it got to me. I'm sorry for everything I've said. I'm sorry for how I fucked everything up. I complained about you to Caleb and I know he feels bad for treating you like shit too." Diego looks well and truly miserable. "I went over to my cousin's house last night and apologized for everything I said about him over the years. I'm on the make amends tour right now."

He smiles, but it doesn't quite reach his eyes. He just looks flat out sad.

"It's cool," I tell him, reaching out to give his shoulder a gentle shake. "There's been a lot of shit thrown at us lately."

"I'll say," he mutters under his breath.

We watch the game for a while, my fists curling as the Mustangs get closer and closer to the end zone. Defense has held them from scoring so far. They've got one more chance, and then we're up. And that clock just keeps winding down.

"We got this," Diego tells me, and when I glance over at him, I see he's holding his hand up for a high five. Something we haven't given each other in a while.

Smiling grimly, I slap my palm against his. "Yeah, we do."

It's our turn to get back out there. I hear Dad yell words of encouragement. I glance up at the stands to see Hannah's red hair and I wave at her, pleased as shit when she spots me and waves back.

"Good luck," I hear Eli yell at me from the visitor side-lines and I glare at him.

"Fuck off," I mutter under my breath, making him laugh.

I seriously hate that guy. What does Ava see in him?

Their defensive line is good, I can't deny it. They're able to hold us from scoring pretty well and this time is no exception. They take out my receivers time and again, and I keep having to throw the ball long and out of bounds, praying no one shoots out of nowhere and grabs it for an interception.

But then.

The timing is suddenly perfect. I'm ready to throw the ball, my gaze searching, searching. It feels like I'm moving in slow motion, but it takes all of five seconds.

Tony is covered by two.

Diego is completely alone. Uncovered. Open. Our gazes meet.

Lock.

He throws his hands up.

He's far—almost too far, but I throw the ball. It spirals through the air in a perfect arc. Diego is running, his hands up, glancing over his shoulder at the last second…

The ball lands in his gloved hands.

He runs. Fast as a motherfucker. The ball is tucked under his arm and he's pumping those legs. I'm yelling.

Diego! Run!

Guys from the sideline are yelling. The cheer team is hopping up and down, their metallic poms sparkling from the stadium lights, and the people in the stands are roaring their approval.

Diego crosses into the endzone before doing a little dance. The announcer yells, "Touchdown!"

And the crowd goes wild.

We have less than two minutes on the clock, and now we're up by two touchdowns.

I run to Diego on the field and stop right in front of him, grabbing the back of his helmet and knocking our protected heads together. "Fuck yeah, brother! That was *amazing!*"

"Thanks to you," he tells me with a giant grin, and he looks so happy. Happier than I've seen him in a long time. "I can't believe that throw!"

"I can't believe that catch," I say as we jog back to the sideline together. Everyone congratulates us, slapping our backs, including my dad, who's smiling from ear to ear.

"That play was perfection," he says and I can't help but stand up straighter at his compliment.

That's all I've ever seemed to want in life. To make my dad proud.

We get the extra point and now we've got a fourteen point lead on the Mustangs. With a little over a minute and a half to go in the fourth quarter. We're going to win this. Diego's touchdown just clenched it. I don't want to be a cocky asshole, but as I watch the game wind down, I rest my hands on my hips and grin like a damn fool.

This win feels better than any other I've ever experienced.

The buzzer sounds, and the game is over. We all rush the field, screaming and yelling, the coaches right there with us, the cheer team coming out onto the field too. The announcer sounds like he's screaming into the mic, congratulating us on an epic win for homecoming night. It feels good.

So damn satisfying.

There are local TV news stations at the game, and next thing I know, I've got a mic in my face, and I'm talking to a reporter about highlights from the game. Once we're done, she's headed toward my dad, and I watch him speak to her, that pleased expression on his face making me feel pleased too.

"I'm so proud of you," Mom says before she wraps me up in a hug. I cling to her for a moment, pressing a kiss to her cheek before I pull away and smile down at her. "You glad the game's over?"

Laughing, I say, "Definitely."

I'm receiving plenty of congratulations and high fives, and I'm reveling in the moment, but where's Hannah? I look for her everywhere, but I don't see her smiling face or her noticeable red hair. Where is she?

This is a moment I never want to forget, and I want her with me.

I catch a glimpse of my sister running over to the other side of the field, freezing when I see Eli wrap Ava up in a tight hug, his hand sliding from her lower back to her butt for the briefest second. I look away with disgust, hating how seeing her with him makes me feel.

Like she's a traitor. Like she doesn't care about me or our family. I know that's not true, but of all the guys who live on this mountain, she chooses *that* one?

It sucks.

But I can't worry about Ava and Eli now. I'll talk to her later.

I need to find Hannah.

All at once, the crowd seems to part, and it's just like a scene in a movie. One minute, I can't find my girl anywhere and the next minute...

She's standing only a few feet away from me, as if a beam of light is shining down upon her, making her sparkle. She's smiling at me, and I wish I had my phone or a camera so I can catch this moment forever. The look in her eyes is nearly my undoing. Her gaze is full of love and pride and happiness.

All for me.

Someone's talking to me, but I don't hear them anymore. Leaving them, I head for her, my steps quickening, my heart racing and then she's in my arms and I'm holding her close, twirling her around, making her laugh.

"You won," she whispers before breaking into a huge smile.

"We won," I whisper back, dipping my head and kissing her right there. In front of everyone.

There are tongues involved. I don't even care. She tries to pull away, but I keep her close. Almost immediately she gives into the kiss as she slips her arm around my neck, her fingers sliding into the hair at my nape. A collective *aww* seems to rise from the crowd and that's my cue to end this, though I'm not embarrassed.

Hell no. I'm kissing the girl I love and I want everyone to know it.

Once the crowd has mostly dispersed and we're done talking to everyone or taking yet another photo together or with a group of people, I take a quick shower. When I finish, I grab my gear and go with Tony to meet Hannah at my truck, where she's waiting with Sophie. We're all supposed to go to Tony's house. Of course, he's having a party after the game, and he has even more reason to celebrate tonight. The big win, plus he was crowned homecoming king.

It's an important night for him. For all of us.

"Remember the first time we talked at Tony's house?" Hannah asks after I start the truck.

I glance over at her, remembering how confused I felt when I first saw her there. How much she affected me, and how I didn't like it.

Yet deep down, I did.

"Yeah. We played doctor," I tease her.

She smirks. "You wish we played that kind of doctor."

"You took care of me when no one else would," I murmur, reaching out to take her hand so I can interlace our fingers together. "And you put Dora bandages on my face."

"They were the only ones I could find." She squeezes my hand.

"I love you," I tell her, unable to hold it back any longer.

Her smile is soft. As soft as the glow in her eyes. "I love you too."

"I couldn't have done this without you."

She scoffs. "I doubt that."

"No, it's true. I won that game for myself, for the team, for the town. But I also won it for you. You're everything to me, Hannah." Leaning over the console, I cup her face with my free hand, tilt her head up and press my mouth to hers.

Her lips are soft and accepting. She opens up to me, and I deepen the kiss, my tongue doing a slow, thorough sweep of her mouth. A sigh escapes her. And then a whimper. I break the kiss before I do something reckless, like try and strip her right here in my truck, in the school parking lot. Pressing my forehead to hers, I breathe deep, inhaling her sweetness.

"You make me want to lose control," I whisper. "And fuck, you smell so good."

She pulls away from me, gesturing toward the steering wheel. "Come on, let's go."

I frown at her. "What's the hurry?"

"Let's go to Tony's. Maybe we can find a secret room in that giant house of his. Just the two of us," Hannah says, her voice full of promise.

Hope sparks within me. "Yeah?"

She laughs. Reaches across the console to rest her hand on my thigh for a too brief moment. "Oh yeah. I will always want to find a secret room to hide away with you, Jacob Callahan."

I smile the entire way to Tony's, the wind in my hair, my girl by my side, the music playing loud on my stereo as we talk and laugh. This is by far the best night of my life.

Hannah and I will have even more good nights together.

I just know it.

* * *

Want more Jake and Hannah? Check out this bonus scene!

* * *

Ava and Eli's story is next in Addicted To Him, the third book in The Callahans series! Keep reading for a sneak peek!

ADDICTED TO HIM

CHAPTER ONE

Ava

Summer

First of all, I didn't want to go to the football camp in the middle of nowhere.

It's bad enough that we live in a small town, full of small-minded people. I would give anything to move back to the Bay Area. To live in suburbia with people who think more like me. Who want to live more like me.

But I'm here. Stuck. I've been here for a long time, and I've come to terms with it.

Sort of.

The clock is ticking, and I'm getting closer and closer to graduation. AKA, getting out of here. I've got two years of high school left. I'm going to work my hardest to obtain an internship the summer before I start college at a non-profit that helps women and children, somewhere, preferably, out of the country, and then I'll leave. I don't care where I go. I just want out.

Back to why I'm here. We're in the Sequoia National Forest, at a facility that hosts a giant football camp every summer. High school teams from all over the area come to this elite camp, and, this June, Dad and the rest of the coaches brought our varsity football team.

Dad also brought us—Mom, Jake, me and Beck—because he thought it would be like a vacation. That's exactly how he sold it to us. Mom was all for it. So was my older brother, Jake—but, of course he was, he benefits from this the most.

Our little brother, Beck, is thrilled at the idea of swimming in the lake for the next four days. Or going fishing. Or boating. Or playing in the dirt. Or eating ice cream.

Me? I just finished my sophomore year, and all I want to do is hang out at my pool or at the lake with my friends.

Instead, I'm stuck at this camp, at another lake, in another forest, surrounded by boys I don't care about, and without decent cell phone service or Wi-Fi, supposedly to bond with nature and hang out with my family, minus my big sister.

So jealous of Autumn right now, who's spending the summer on the beach in Santa Barbara—where she goes to college—with her boyfriend, Asher Davis. I'm jealous of the beach time and the Ash time. Her boyfriend is so freaking gorgeous, and so madly in love with her. If only I could find someone like that.

If only.

We arrived at the camp about an hour ago, and we're staying in a large cabin that sits right by the lake. The temperature is much cooler, since we're at a higher elevation, and while I see why Dad wanted us to all go with him, I'm kind of bored.

And we only just got here.

"I'm going for a walk," I call out to my parents, as I open the front door of the cabin.

"Stay close," Mom yells from the bedroom they're staying in. Dad's in there with her, and I'm pretty sure they're unpacking all their stuff and getting settled. "There are bears out there."

"There's bears at home," I call back.

"They're meaner up here!" Mom starts to laugh, and I can't help it, so do I.

"See ya," I say, as I open the door.

"Dinner is in less than an hour." Mom approaches the door of their bedroom, her gaze meeting mine.

I check the time on my phone, frowning. "But it's only five o'clock!"

We always eat late at our house. Everyone's so busy, so it's hard to get us all around the table at the same time.

"We have to be at the dining room by five forty-five," Mom explains, exiting the bedroom to smile at me, clutching a sweatshirt in her hands. "If you want, just meet us there. You remember where it is?"

"Right next to the office where we checked in." I open the door, leaning on it. "I probably won't be gone long. I'll just meet you back here."

No way am I going to the dining hall alone, surrounded by about a bazillion teenage boys. I mean, that's every sixteen-year-old girl's dream, I suppose, but not mine. The last thing I want to do is gain their attention, especially since I'm probably one of the few girls here their age.

How embarrassing.

"Have fun." She offers me a little wave, before she turns and goes back into her bedroom. "Bye, honey!"

"Bye." I shut the door behind me and stay on the wrap-around porch, breathing in the pine scented air. The lake isn't too far. I can walk along it for a while, most likely with no one else around. All the guys are off participating in football things. Jake's not in the cabin. He took off with his friends, Diego and Caleb. I don't even think he's staying with us at our cabin.

At least he has something to do.

I skip down the stairs and head along the dirt path that takes me to the lake. A breeze washes over me, making the water ripple, and I can hear the pine trees sway in the wind. Birds are chirping, wild flowers are still in bloom and scattered everywhere. All I can see is blue sky, blue water, green grass and towering trees. No humans in sight.

It's actually kind of nice. Peaceful.

Pulling my phone out of my shorts pocket, I take a few photos of the scenery, wishing I could post them on my Instagram story because this place is gorgeous. But there's no service out here. The lack of bars on my phone screen confirms that fact. I literally have no internet, and I'm a teenage girl.

I'm totally thinking like a spoiled brat, but this feels like a death sentence.

I walk around the lake for a while, but eventually get bored. Pretty sure this is going to be my weekend mood.

Good times.

I'm about to head back to the cabin when I hear something.

Like footsteps.

Pausing, I turn around, but see nothing.

I keep going, following the dirt trail that leads directly to our cabin. That's when I hear a voice.

"Hey! You play football or what?"

Stopping, yet again, I glance over my shoulder, squinting, since the sun is shining directly in my eyes.

There's a boy about twenty feet away. He's tall. Lean.

Vaguely familiar.

"No, I don't play football." I turn to face him fully, holding my hand over my forehead, so I can shade my eyes. He's still standing there, watching me, and I see recognition dawn on his face.

"I know you." He points at me.

"I know you too." Tilting my head, I try to place his face. He has sunglasses on, so I can't see his eyes, which would probably help me recognize him. I know, for sure, he doesn't go to my high school. Maybe our rival high school? Yeah, I think that's it. He's…

Oh. Shit. I know exactly who he is.

"You're Ava Callahan." He saunters up the walkway, pushing his sunglasses up, so they rest on top of his head. His eyes are hazel. He has a bit of a baby face. Sparkling eyes and full lips.

He's super cute.

And my brother's worst enemy.

"You're Eli Bennett," I tell him, turning up my nose because *hello*, I can't talk to the enemy. Jake will flip.

His smile is dangerous. As in, seeing it makes my belly flutter. "My reputation precedes me."

"More like my brother hates you," I remind him.

He laughs, completely unfazed. "It's just a fun rivalry."

"If you say so." I cross my arms, studying him. He's a good football player. Not as good as Jake, though. They're both quarterbacks, just like my dad. Just like Autumn's boyfriend, Ash. In my life, I'm constantly surrounded by cocky, arrogant QBs—though Dad isn't cocky or arrogant. Maybe he was when he was younger.

I can tell the boy standing in front of me certainly is.

"Why are you here?" he asks.

"I came with my dad." I wave my hand toward the cabin behind me. "My whole family is here."

"I thought I saw some of the guys from your team around." He shakes his head, scratching his jaw. It's razor sharp and very attractive. "Huh. This changes everything."

"So, your team is here, too?" Oh man. Jake is gonna be so pissed.

"Yeah. This is the best camp around. Is your dad speaking?"

"I think so." I take a step back when he takes a step forward, uncomfortable with his nearness.

More like, uncomfortable with my reaction to him standing so close to me.

"Your dad is an inspiration. I wish he coached us at our school, but then I wouldn't be the QB." He shrugs, a smirk on his face. "Gotta give the position to daddy's boy."

Oh. Those are fighting words. "Pretty sure my brother earned his position."

"If you say so." He throws his words back at me.

Ew. I kind of hate this guy.

"I have to go." I turn and start toward the steps that lead up to the cabin, my heart hammering. He says nothing, but I can feel his gaze on me. Assessing me. Sizing me up.

I'm tempted to look back, and I tell myself not to. Don't do it. Don't give him the satisfaction of knowing that you're curious.

But it's like I can't help myself. I stomp up the stairs noisily, glancing over my shoulder at the last second to find him standing in the spot where I left him, his gaze on me, a smile curling his full lips.

"See ya around, Ava Callahan," he says.

I offer a halfhearted wave like a complete dork and bolt into the cabin, slamming the door before I lean against it and release the breath I didn't know I was holding.

Well.

That was interesting.

* * *

Read Addicted To Him, available now and FREE in Kindle Unlimited!

… [1]

ACKNOWLEDGMENTS

As always, a huge thank you to my readers for taking the time out of your day to read this book. I appreciate you more than you'll ever know. It gives me so much joy to hear from you, whether on social media or via email. You are all just the best!

Thank you to the reviewers, book bloggers and readers who gave shout outs everywhere about this book. The support has blown me away, and I know you all about died when you saw the cover, am I right?

Thank you to my beta readers, specifically Sarah P, Brittany E (I love our Before the 90 Days conversations!), Brittany U, Sarah S, Jan C and Malia K. Your input is valuable (and sometimes a little scary, I cannot lie) and I hope I made this story better because of your suggestions.

Also, to Nina and again to Brittany, for encouraging me as I write this series, and a special mention to Brittany for loving Eli Bennett from the Friends series. This is why he's in this book, and gets his own book with Ava. I always had such secret love for him, and it was so much fun writing him. He's so awful! But deep down, he's not. He's a sweetheart. And you'll get to see how much of a sweetheart he is in his book, Addicted to Him…

It would mean everything to me if you could take a few moments and leave an honest review for **Falling For Her.** Thank you.

ALSO BY MONICA MURPHY

BILLIONAIRE BACHELORS CLUB (REISSUES)

Crave & Torn

Savor & Intoxicated

NEW YOUNG ADULT SERIES

The Liar's Club

KINGS OF CAMPUS

End Game

LANCASTER PREP

Things I Wanted To Say

A Million Kisses in Your Lifetime

Birthday Kisses

Promises We Meant to Keep

I'll Always Be With You

You Said I Was Your Favorite

New Year's Day

Lonely For You Only (a Lancaster novel)

LANCASTER PREP: NEXT GENERATION

All My Kisses for You

THE PLAYERS

Playing Hard to Get

Playing by The Rules

Playing to Win

WEDDED BLISS (LANCASTER)

The Reluctant Bride

The Ruthless Groom

The Reckless Union

The Arranged Marriage boxset

COLLEGE YEARS

The Freshman

The Sophomore

The Junior

The Senior

DATING SERIES

Save The Date

Fake Date

Holidate

Hate to Date You

Rate A Date

Wedding Date

Blind Date

THE CALLAHANS

Close to Me

Falling For Her

Addicted To Him

Meant To Be

Fighting For You

Making Her Mine

A Callahan Wedding

FOREVER YOURS SERIES

You Promised Me Forever

Thinking About You

Nothing Without You

DAMAGED HEARTS SERIES

Her Defiant Heart

His Wasted Heart

Damaged Hearts

FRIENDS SERIES

Just Friends

More Than Friends

Forever

THE NEVER DUET

Never Tear Us Apart

Never Let You Go

THE RULES SERIES

Fair Game

In The Dark

Slow Play

Safe Bet

THE FOWLER SISTERS SERIES

Owning Violet

Stealing Rose

Taming Lily

REVERIE SERIES

His Reverie

Her Destiny

BILLIONAIRE BACHELORS CLUB SERIES

Crave

Torn

Savor

Intoxicated

ONE WEEK GIRLFRIEND SERIES

One Week Girlfriend

Second Chance Boyfriend

Three Broken Promises

Drew + Fable Forever

Four Years Later

Five Days Until You

A Drew + Fable Christmas

STANDALONE YA TITLES

Daring The Bad Boy

Saving It

Pretty Dead Girls

ABOUT THE AUTHOR

Monica Murphy is a New York Times, USA Today and international bestselling author. Her books have been translated in almost a dozen languages and have sold millions of copies worldwide. Both a traditionally published and independently published author, she writes young adult and new adult romance, as well as contemporary romance.

facebook.com/MonicaMurphyAuthor

instagram.com/monicamurphyauthor

bookbub.com/profile/monica-murphy

goodreads.com/monicamurphyauthor

amazon.com/Monica-Murphy/e/B00AVPYIGG

pinterest.com/msmonicamurphy

tiktok.com/@monicamurphyauthor